Harlequin Mar~~~~~
Collection

Love and marriage don't necessarily go together. Or at least the relationship doesn't always start out that way!

The contract of matrimony is more business than personal with the couples in these two stories. Yet as our temporary wives and necessary husbands spend time with each other, the honeymoon soon becomes very real as they discover they want their marriage of convenience to become a marriage of love—forever!

So put aside your traditional perceptions of white dresses, overflowing bouquets and quaint steepled churches and enjoy the journey as our heroes and heroines go from wedded *business* to wedded *bliss* on a roller-coaster ride to their happy beginning.

If you enjoy these two classic stories, be sure to check out more books featuring marriages of convenience from the Harlequin Special Edition line.

A *New York Times* bestselling author, **Christine Rimmer** has written over ninety contemporary romances for Harlequin. Christine has won the RT Reviewers' Choice Award and has been nominated six times for the RITA® Award. She lives in Oregon with her family. Visit Christine at christinerimmer.com.

Look for more books from Christine Rimmer in Harlequin Special Edition—the ultimate destination for life, love and family! There are six new Harlequin Special Edition titles available every month. Check one out today!

New York Times Bestselling Authors

Christine Rimmer
and
Allison Leigh

THE MARRIAGE AGENDA

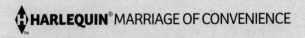

HARLEQUIN® MARRIAGE OF CONVENIENCE

ISBN-13: 978-0-373-60114-1

The Marriage Agenda

Copyright © 2015 by Harlequin Books S.A.

The publisher acknowledges the copyright holders of the individual works as follows:

The Marriage Conspiracy
Copyright © 2001 by Christine Rimmer

The Billionaire's Baby Plan
Copyright © 2010 by Harlequin Books S.A.
Allison Leigh is acknowledged as the author of this work

Recycling programs
for this product may
not exist in your area.

Printed in U.S.A.

www.Harlequin.com

CONTENTS

THE MARRIAGE
CONSPIRACY

Christine Rimmer

For those who sought friendship
and found lasting love.

Chapter 1

It was hot, without a hint of a breeze. Mid-October and it felt like the dog days of August. The wedding guests wandered beneath the sweet gums and pecan trees that shaded Camilla Tilly's backyard, faces shining with sweat, sipping cold drinks in which the ice melted too soon.

Joleen Tilly, Camilla's oldest daughter and sister to the bride, stood at the cake table from which she'd just shooed away three frosting-licking children. Joleen felt as if *she* was melting in her ankle-length rose-colored satin and lace bridesmaid's gown.

And she couldn't help suspecting that the cake was melting, too. The icing looked thinner, didn't it, in a couple of places? The cake had five layers, each bordered with icing swags and accented with buttercream roses. Hadn't the top four layers slid sideways the tiniest bit, wasn't the whole thing leaning to the right, just a little?

Joleen shook her head—at the cake, at her own discomfort, at the whole situation. She had tried to convince her sister to rent a hall, but DeDe dug in her heels and announced that she'd always dreamed of getting married in Mama's backyard. There was no budging DeDe once she dug in her heels.

So here they all were. Melting.

And way behind schedule. The ceremony was supposed to have started an hour ago. But Dekker Smith, the closest thing the Tilly sisters had to a big brother and the one who had promised to give DeDe away, had yet to arrive.

As Joleen stewed about the missing Dekker, about the cake, about the sweltering heat, her uncle Hubert Tilly wandered over, beer in hand. He stood beside her, leaned her way and spoke out of the corner of his mouth. "It's about time we got this thing started, don't you think?"

"Yes. And we will, Uncle Hubert. Real soon."

"Good." Her uncle lifted his beer to her in a toast. "Here's to you, Joly. We all know it's bound to be your turn next." He threw back his big head and drank.

Joleen, who sometimes got a little tired of hearing how it would be "her turn next," smiled resolutely and watched uncle Hubert's Adam's apple bounce up and down as he drained the can.

"Well, what do you know?" Uncle Hubert said when he was through guzzling. "It's empty." The can made groaning, cracking sounds as he crushed it in his beefy fist. "Better get another..." He headed off toward the coolers lined up against the garden shed. Joleen watched him go, hoping he wouldn't get too drunk before the day was over.

She turned her attention to the cake again and decided that it should not sit out here in this heat for one minute longer. Her mother's Colonial Revival house had been built in 1923. But thirty years ago, when her father bought it, one of the first things he'd done to it was to put in central heat and air.

She grabbed herself a couple of big, strong cousins— a Tilly, from her father's side and a DuFrayne, from her mother's. "Pick up that cake table," she told them. "And do it carefully."

The cousins lifted the table.

"Okay, good. This way…" Joleen backed toward the kitchen door slowly, patting the air with outstretched hands and speaking to her cousins in soothing tones. "Watch it…careful…that's right…." She opened the door for them and ushered them into the coolness of her mother's kitchen. "Watch that step. Easy. Good."

Once she'd closed the door behind them, she led them to the little section of wall on the far side of the breakfast nook. "Right here, out of the way. Just set it down easy." The cousins put the table down.

Joleen let out a long, relieved sigh. "Perfect. Thank you, boys."

"No problem," said Burly, the DuFrayne cousin. His full name was Wilbur, but everyone had always called him Burly. "When's this thing getting started, anyway?"

"Soon, real soon," Joleen promised, thinking about Dekker again with a tightening in her tummy that was a little bit from irritation and a lot from worry.

Dekker had called yesterday afternoon and left a message on the machine at Joleen's house. He said he wouldn't make it for the rehearsal, after all, but that he'd be there in plenty of time for the wedding. Joleen wished she'd been home when he called. She would have gotten some specifics out of him—like a flight number and an arrival time, for starters.

And maybe even an idea of what the heck this particular trip was about, anyway. Dekker had told her nothing so far. The last time she'd actually spoken to him, early last Wednesday morning, he would only say that he was leaving for Los Angeles right away. He'd promised he'd be back in time for the rehearsal—which, as it turned out, he was not.

Joleen assumed it must be a business trip. A lot of his clients insisted on strict confidentiality, so that would account for his being so hush-hush about the whole thing. And sometimes, she knew, his job could be dangerous. Was this one of those times?

Joleen pushed that scary thought right out of her mind.

She'd tried more than once to reach him on his cell. And each time she did, she got a recorded voice telling her that the "customer" wasn't available and offering her the chance to leave her name and number. She *had* left her name and number. But she'd never heard back.

"Joly, you are lookin' strained," said the Tilly cousin, whose name was Bud. "You okay?"

"Well, of course I am." She arranged her face into what she hoped resembled a confident smile. "Help yourselves to a beer. There's plenty. Outside in the coolers. And right there in the fridge, too."

Bud and Burly turned for the refrigerator. Joleen went out the kitchen door again, into the blistering backyard.

Her aunt LeeAnne DuFrayne, Burly's mama, was standing under one of the two patio ceiling fans, holding the front of her dress out at the neck so that the fan's breeze could cool her a little. As Joleen went by, Aunt LeeAnne let go of her dress and caught Joleen's arm.

"You have done a beautiful job here, hon."

"You're a sweetheart to say so, Aunt LeeAnne. Too bad it's so darn hot."

"You can't control the weather, hon."

"I know, I know."

"The backyard looks festive. And Mesta Park is such a lovely area. I always admire it so every time I visit."

Mesta Park lay in the heart of Oklahoma City, a charming old neighborhood with lots of classic prairie-style houses and graceful mature trees. Joleen's mother had owned the house on Northwest Seventeenth Street since she herself had been a young bride.

Aunt LeeAnne patted Joleen's arm. "I do think we ought to start the ceremony soon, though, don't you?"

"Soon," Joleen repeated. What else could she say?

Aunt LeeAnne stopped patting. She gripped Joleen's arm and whispered in her ear, "I see that you invited the Atwoods."

Joleen made a noise in the affirmative and flicked a quick glance toward the well-dressed couple standing by themselves near the punch table. Bobby Atwood, the couple's only son, had died just six weeks ago, in a power-skiing accident on Lake Thunderbird. Pictures of the funeral service had dominated the local news. Atwood, after all, was an important name in the state of Oklahoma.

In spite of what had happened between herself and Bobby, the sight of his grieving parents at graveside had proved too much for Joleen. She hadn't been able to stop herself from reaching out to them.

"You have a good heart, Joly," whispered Aunt Lee-Anne. "There aren't many who would be so forgiving."

"Well, it seemed like a nice gesture, to ask them if they'd like to come."

Aunt LeeAnne made a small, sympathetic noise and patted Joleen's arm some more.

Joleen added, "And I do want Sam to know his father's parents."

Sam. Just the thought of her little boy lightened Joleen's mood. She looked for him, caught sight of him with her younger sister, thirteen-year-old Niki, about twenty feet away, near the tall white picket fence that surrounded her mother's backyard on three sides. Niki, in a rose-red dress identical to Joleen's, had agreed to watch Sam so that Joleen could handle all the details of running the wedding.

Sam had his daddy's hair, thick and straight and sandy colored. As Joleen watched, he threw back that sandy head and let out his almost-a-baby laugh. At the sound of that laugh, Joleen's heart seemed to get bigger inside her chest.

Then she noticed that Bobby's father was staring right at her.

Robert Atwood quickly looked away. But not before she saw a lot more than she wanted to see in his cold, gray glance. Her little boy's grandfather did not approve of her. And he was looking down his snooty nose at the members of her family.

The Atwoods moved in the best circles. They hung out with the governor and his pretty wife, attended all the most important political and social events in the city. Robert Atwood's expression made it painfully clear that he found this small-scale backyard wedding to be tacky and totally beneath him.

And now he was staring at Sam. So was his wife, Antonia. The woman wore a look of longing so powerful it sent a chill down Joleen's spine in spite of the heat.

I probably should have listened to Dekker, Joleen thought. Dekker—who'd better show up soon or they were going ahead without him—had warned her to stay away from Robert Atwood and his wife.

"Unless you're after a little of the Atwood money," he'd said. "Sam *is* entitled to some of that."

"It is not the money, Dekker. Honestly. We're gettin' by all right."

"Okay. Then forget the Atwoods. They have too much money and too much power and, given the kind of son they raised, I'd say they're way too likely to abuse both."

She had punched him playfully on the arm. "You are so cynical it scares me sometimes."

"You ought to be scared of the Atwoods, of the trouble they'll probably cause you if you tell them about Sam. I mean it. Take my advice and stay away from them."

But she hadn't taken her friend's advice. Robert Atwood sold real estate on a grand scale. He dealt in shopping centers and medical complexes and skyscrapers with a thousand and one offices in them. She had called him at Atwood and Son Property Development.

At first, Bobby's father had refused to see her or to believe that his precious son could have fathered a child he didn't even know about. In the end, though, the hope that there might be something of Bobby left on the earth must have been too powerful to deny. He had called Joleen and asked if he and his wife might meet Sam. And as soon as they set eyes on her baby boy, they knew who his father had to be.

"Joly, hon…"

Joleen looked into her aunt's flushed face and smiled. "Hmm?"

"I just have to say this. I have got a powerful feeling that we will be watching you take your walk down the aisle very soon now." Aunt LeeAnne beamed up at her.

Joleen kept her smile. But it did get old sometimes.

Here's to you, Joly. We all know it's bound to be your turn next….

I just know you are going to meet someone so special….

I see a man in your future, hon. The right man this time….

Those she loved would not stop telling her that true love and happily-ever-after were coming her way.

Joleen fully understood why they did it. None of them could quite believe that she, the levelheaded one, the both-feet-firmly-on-the-ground one, had gone and fallen for a rich boy's honeyed lies.

They felt sorry for her. They wanted the best for her.

And to them the best meant a good man to stand at her side, a husband to help her raise her child.

"I don't think so, Aunt LeeAnne."

"Well, you just think what you want. I am right about this and you will see that I am."

Oh, please, Joleen thought. As if she even had *time* for love and romance at this point in her life. She had a toddler to raise and a business to run—not to mention a recently delinquent thirteen-year-old sister and a stunningly beautiful fifty-year-old widowed mother who somehow managed to fall in and out of love on what seemed like a weekly basis. DeDe might be off her hands after today, but Niki and her mother still counted on Joleen to be there whenever they needed her.

And really, Joleen didn't mind being the one they counted on. She was happy. She honestly was. With her precious little son and her beloved if somewhat trouble-some mama and sisters, with the beauty salon she and her mother operated together and with lots of loving family and good friends—including Dekker, who in the past few years had become her closest friend.

Dekker, who was now so late she doubted he would make it at all.

Nope. It would not be Joleen's turn next. Not for a decade or so, at least. Maybe more than a decade. Maybe never. In any case, not "next."

But she didn't tell her aunt LeeAnne that. Instead, she hooked her arm around her aunt's round shoulders and gave a loving squeeze. "Whatever you say."

By three-thirty, Joleen decided they had waited long enough. She left the drooping guests behind beneath the pecan trees, entered the house and climbed the stairs to her mother's big bedroom on the second floor, which today was serving as the bride's dressing room.

DeDe, who looked absolutely breathtaking in floor-length white satin, came at her the minute Joleen appeared in the doorway. "Where is he? Is he here yet?"

Joleen shook her head.

"Oh, no." DeDe stopped in midstride and caught her full lower lip between her small white teeth. "How's Wayne holdin' up?"

Wayne Thornton was DeDe's groom. "Wayne is great. He's down in the kitchen right now, hanging out with Bud and Burly."

"He's not mad?"

"Wayne? Are you kidding?" Wayne Thornton was a veterinarian. He was also about the calmest, most easygoing person Joleen had ever had the pleasure to meet.

"I promise you, Wayne is fine. Waiting patiently, swapping jokes with Bud and Burly."

"I want to see him."

"Well, all right, I'll just—"

"Wait. Stop right there."

Joleen did as her sister commanded.

"What do you think you're doing?" DeDe accused. "You know I can't see him. It would be bad luck."

Joleen lifted a shoulder in the tiniest of shrugs. Of course, she knew that. But if she'd been the one to say it, her sister would have insisted that Joleen run downstairs that instant and come right back up with Wayne. Like Niki, DeDe had had some troubled times in the past. She'd settled down a lot in the last couple of years, but she hadn't gotten rid of her stubborn streak, of a certain contrariness to her nature. Joleen never locked horns with her if she could avoid it. Locking horns with DeDe almost never paid off.

DeDe sighed. "I'm goin' nuts." She whirled in a rustle of satin, flounced to their mother's big four-poster bed, turned and plunked herself down on the edge of it. "Where *is* Dekker?"

Joleen approached and sat beside her sister. She took DeDe's hand. "Honey…"

DeDe yanked her hand away. "Don't say it. He promised he would be here and we are gonna wait for him."

"Honey, we *have* waited. For over an hour. You have to think of your guests. They are dyin' out there."

"Well, I can't help it. It wouldn't be right to start without Dekker. You know that it wouldn't."

Joleen had no quick comeback for that.

The problem was, in her heart, Joleen *agreed* with DeDe. It *wouldn't* be right to start without Dekker.

Dekker Smith might not be blood to them, but he truly was family. His mama, Lorraine, had been *their* mama's best friend. Lorraine was gone now, and Dekker hadn't lived next door since he graduated high school, but he looked out for them all, especially in the past ten years, since Joleen's father had died.

Dekker spent his holidays with them. He had been the one who taught both Joleen and DeDe how to drive. He could always be counted upon to show up with his toolbox when something needed fixing—not to mention to stand up for any female named Tilly any time things got rough. Two years ago, when DeDe had her little run-in with the law, Dekker had gone with Joleen to the police station to bail her out and he'd made sure she got the best lawyer around. Same thing with Niki, when she'd been in trouble last year. Dekker was right there, to help out.

He was family in the deepest way, and of course DeDe wanted him there to see her married.

But they couldn't wait all day to start the wedding march. "DeDe, I think we are just going to have to go ahead."

"But we *can't* go ahead," DeDe cried.

"Yes, we can. And you know that Dekker will understand. You know that he—"

"*I* won't understand. Don't you get it? I want Dekker to give me away."

"Well, I know you do, but he is not here."

DeDe glared. "Oh, you, Joly. Always so *logical.* I cannot stand to hear logic at a time like this."

"Well, I am so sorry to be reasonable when you would rather not, but—"

DeDe cut her off by bursting into tears.

Joleen closed her eyes and silently counted to ten.

When she opened them again, she saw her mother, Camilla, hovering in the doorway to the hall. "What is it, baby? What has happened here?"

"Joly says we have to go ahead." DeDe sobbed. "She says we can't wait for Dekker."

"Oh, now, honey…"

"I want him here, Mama. I want him to give me away."

"Yes, and we all understand that."

"It won't seem right if he isn't here."

"Oh, I know, I know…"

DeDe let out a frustrated wail. The cry brought Camilla out of the doorway. She rushed across the room, slender arms outstretched. Joleen slid to the side and got out of the way. DeDe stood. Camilla gathered her close.

"Aw, baby," Camilla cooed. "Now, you know you are going to ruin your face, carrying on like this. Now, you just settle down…."

But DeDe was not settling down.

And Camilla had started crying, too. Tears filled her huge brown eyes and spilled down her cheeks. Sobs constricted her long white throat. Joleen backed away a few more steps, as her middle sister and her mother held on to each other and wailed.

"Honey, honey," Camilla cried. "Don't you worry. It's okay. We will wait. We will wait until Dekker gets here. We'll wait forever, if we have to. Till the end of time, I swear it to you…."

There was a gasp from the doorway. Joleen looked over.

Niki. She had Sam perched on her hip—and her hazel eyes were already brimming. Sam had a teething biscuit stuck in his mouth. He sucked it steadily, not much disturbed by all the excitement on the other side of the room.

But then, why should he be disturbed? His grandmother and his aunts never hid their emotions. He was used to lots of crying and carrying on.

"Mama?" Niki gulped back a sob. "DeDe? What is going on?"

Her mother and middle sister only cried all the harder. Niki's face started to crumple.

Joleen reached Niki's side in three quick steps. "Before you start," she warned, "give me my baby."

"Here." Niki held Sam out. He reached for Joleen automatically, gurgling, "Mama!" And then his biscuit-gooey little hands encircled her neck, his soft weight was on her arm and his sweet, slightly dusty smell filled her senses.

With a hard sob, Niki flew across the room. Camilla and DeDe enfolded her into their embrace. The three hugged and bawled, their arms around each other, a sniffling, tear-streaked huddle of satin and lace.

Joleen stood a few feet from the door, resolutely calm as always, holding her baby and watching her mother and sisters wail and moan, wondering how in the world she would manage to calm them all now.

"What is this, a wedding—or a wake?"

Joleen turned toward the sound of that deep, wry voice. It was Dekker, in the doorway. He had made it, after all.

Chapter 2

Relief washed through Joleen—and a sweet rush of affection, as well. She should probably be good and angry with him for being so late, but how could she be angry when she was so glad to see him? And he looked so handsome in the nice lightweight suit they had picked out together just for this occasion.

He also looked…easy within himself and relaxed. Something good must have happened out there in Los Angeles.

"You're late," she muttered.

He shrugged. "Air travel is not what it used to be. I sat at O'Hare for ten hours."

"Your cell phone—"

"Needs recharging. Sorry. I tried to call you."

"At my house?"

"Right. From a pay phone, this morning around eight."

"I left at seven-thirty."

"And I also called here. Twice. Got a busy signal both times."

She wasn't surprised. The house had been full of people all day and the phone had been in constant use.

"Dek!" Sam shouted. He let go of Joleen's neck and reached for the man in the doorway.

"Whoa, big guy." Dekker stepped up and took him.

About then, DeDe stopped sobbing long enough to glance across the room. "Dekker! You made it!"

The three Tilly women broke from their huddle and rushed for the door. Joleen got out of their way again. They surrounded Dekker and Sam, all of them talking at once.

"Where *were* you?"

"We've been waiting for *hours*…."

"We were so afraid you wouldn't make it."

"Is everything all right?"

"Is everything—"

He chuckled. "Everything's fine. There was just a little matter of a long delay between flights. But I am here now." He had Sam on one arm. He wrapped the other around DeDe, who looked up at him through shining eyes. "And I am ready to give away this gorgeous bride."

Twenty minutes later, down in the backyard beneath the pecan trees, the wedding march began. A blessed breeze had actually come up, so it wasn't quite as stifling as it had been for most of the day. The ceremony went off without a hitch. And when Wayne Thornton kissed his bride, everyone could see that this was a true, love match.

Joleen had had her reservations, when DeDe and

Wayne first announced that they would marry. After all, DeDe *was* only twenty. It seemed young to Joleen.

But looking at the two of them as they repeated their vows, Joleen let go of her doubts. Wayne was a good, steady man. And DeDe adored him almost as much as he worshipped her. In the end, Joleen supposed, the two had as good a chance as any couple at lasting a lifetime side by side.

She was pouring more ginger ale into the punch bowl, feeling kind of misty-eyed and contented for the first time that day, when Dekker appeared at her side.

"What the hell are the Atwoods doing here?" He spoke low, for her ears alone.

She gave him her most determined smile and whispered back, "I invited them."

"Damn it, Jo. I hope you know what you're doing."

"Me, too—and would you go in and get me some more of this ginger ale?"

Midnight-blue eyes regarded her steadily. "I wish you had listened to me."

"I did listen—then I did what I thought was right." She waved the empty bottle at him. "Ginger ale? Please?"

Shaking his head, he turned for the back door.

The afternoon wore on.

Camilla, on something of an emotional roller coaster this special day when her middle baby was getting married, had a little too much sparkling wine and flirted blatantly with anyone willing to flirt back.

"You probably ought to say something to her, hon," advised Aunt LeeAnne as Joleen was putting the finishing touches on the buffet.

Joleen shook her head and took the lid off a chafing dish. "My mother is a flirt. Always has been, always will be. I have enough to worry about without trying to fight a person's nature."

"When your father was still with us—"

"I know. All her flirting was for him then. She never looked at another man. But he's been gone for so long now. And she is still very much alive. She will never stop lookin' for the kind of love she had once."

"So sad…" Aunt LeeAnne looked mournful.

Camilla's musical laughter rang out as she pulled one of the groom's uncles from a chair and made him dance with her.

"I don't know," said Joleen. "Seems to me that she's having a pretty good time."

Aunt LeeAnne picked up a toothpick and speared a meatball from the chafing dish. "Mmm. Delicious. What is that spice?"

"Cumin?"

"Could be—or maybe curry?"

"No. I don't think there's any curry in those meatballs."

Aunt LeeAnne helped herself to a second meatball, then shrugged. "Well, I suppose you're right about Camilla…."

Uncle Hubert Tilly staggered by, yet another beer clutched in his fist.

Aunt LeeAnne clucked her tongue. "Now, there is someone to worry about. He has been drinkin' all afternoon, and in this heat…" Aunt LeeAnne frowned. "He looks peaked, don't you think?"

"True," said Joleen. "He does not look well."

"Someone really should talk to him…." Aunt LeeAnne gazed at Joleen hopefully. Joleen refused to take the hint, so her aunt added with clear reluctance, "Someone of his own generation, I suppose."

"Be my guest."

So Aunt LeeAnne DuFrayne trotted off to try to convince Uncle Hubert Tilly that he'd had enough beer.

Uncle Hubert didn't take the news well. "What?" he shouted, leaning against the trunk of the sweet gum in the southwest corner of the yard. "I've had enough? What're you talkin' about, LeeAnne? There ain' no such thing as enough."

Aunt LeeAnne tried to whisper something into his ear. He shrugged her off and stumbled away. Aunt LeeAnne pinched up her mouth for a minute, then shook her head and returned to the buffet table.

"Well, I guess you are right, Joly. There is no savin' that man from himself."

"You tried your best." Joleen handed her aunt a plate. "Taste those buffalo wings. And the pasta primavera is pretty good, too."

Aunt LeeAnne took the plate and began to load it with food.

Out of the corner of her eye, Joleen could see Robert Atwood, standing at the edge of the patio, Antonia, as always, close at his side. Robert wore a look of aloof disdain on his distinguished face as he watched Uncle Hubert's unsteady progress toward the coolers lined up by the garden shed.

"Joly, is that pickled okra I see?"

Joleen turned her widest smile on another of her father's brothers. "You bet it is, Uncle Stan. Help yourself."

"I surely will."

With the buffet all ready to go, Joleen went to check on the punch table again. The bowl needed filling. She took care of that. Then she went back inside to look for those little frilly toothpicks that everyone kept using up the minute she set them out.

She got stalled in the kitchen for several minutes. Burly had a traveling-salesman joke she just had to hear. Once he'd told it and she had finished laughing, she found the toothpicks and headed for the back door once more.

Outside again, she discovered that her mother was dancing with yet another of the guests from Wayne's family. And Aunt LeeAnne whispered in her ear that Uncle Hubert had gone behind the garden shed to be sick.

Joleen suppressed a sigh. "I'll go see to him."

"I think that would be best. I'd do it, of course, but you saw what happened the last time I tried to give the poor man a hand."

When Joleen got to the other side of the shed, she spotted two little DuFraynes and a small niece of Wayne's peeking around the far end. Uncle Hubert sagged pitifully against the shed wall, his head stuck in among the dark pink blooms of a tall crape myrtle bush.

She dealt with the children first. "You kids go on now."

The three stared for a moment, then began giggling.

"I mean it. Do not make me get your mamas."

The giggling stopped. Three sets of wide eyes regarded her. Joleen put on a no-nonsense glare and made a sharp shooing gesture with the back of her hand.

The three vanished around the end of the shed, giggles erupting again as soon as they were out of sight. The giggles faded away.

Uncle Hubert groaned. And then his thick shoulders

shook. Joleen swallowed and pressed her lips together as she heard splattering sounds behind the bush.

She waited until that attack of sickness had passed. Then she dared to move a few steps closer. "Uncle Hubert…"

Her uncle groaned. "Joly?"

"That's right."

"Go 'way." He spoke into the crape myrtle bush.

Joleen edged a little closer. "Uncle Hubert, I want you to come in the house with me now."

"I'm fine." He groaned again. "Go 'way."

"No. No, you listen. It's too hot out here. You can lie down inside."

"No." He made a strangled sound. His shoulders shook again, but this time nothing seemed to be coming up.

Joleen waited, to make sure he was finished. Then, with slow care, she moved right up next to him. "Come on, now…" She laid a hand on his arm. "You just come on."

"No!" He jerked away, half stumbling, almost falling, bouncing with a muffled gonging sound against the metal wall of the garden shed. "Leave," he growled. "Go…"

Joleen stepped back again, unwilling to give up but unsure how to convince him that he should come with her.

A hand clasped her shoulder.

Dekker. She knew it before she even turned to see him standing right behind her. She felt easier instantly. Between them they would manage. They always did.

"Need help?"

She nodded.

He raised a dark brow. "You want him in the house?"

She nodded again.

He stepped around her. "Hubert…"

"Ugh. Wha? Oh. Dek."

"Right. Come on, man. Let's go…"

"Ugh…"

"Yeah. You need to stretch out."

"Uh-uh…"

Dekker took Uncle Hubert's arm and wrapped it across his broad shoulder. Uncle Hubert moaned. He kept saying no and shaking his head. But he didn't pull away. Slowly Dekker turned him around and got him moving.

Joleen went on ahead, warning the other guests out of the way, opening the back door, leading the way through the kitchen and into the hall. Uncle Hubert would probably be most comfortable upstairs in one of the bedrooms, but she didn't know how far he'd be willing to let Dekker drag him. So she settled for the living room.

"Here," she said, "on the couch." She tossed away her mother's favorite decorative pillows as she spoke, then spread an old afghan across the cushions. It would provide some protection if Uncle Hubert's poor stomach decided to rebel again.

Dekker eased the other man down. Uncle Hubert fell onto his back with a long, low groan.

"Let's get his shoes off," said Dekker, already kneeling at Uncle Hubert's feet. Before he had the second shoe off, Uncle Hubert was snoring. Dekker set the shoes, side by side, beneath the coffee table. "They'll be right here whenever he needs them."

Joleen stood over her uncle, shaking her head. "It

seems like we ought to *do* something, doesn't it? We shouldn't let him go on hurting himself this way."

Uncle Hubert had lost his wife, Thelma, six months ago. The heavy beer drinking had started not long after that.

"Give him time," Dekker said. "He'll work it out."

"I hope he works it out soon. A man's liver can only take so much."

"He will," Dekker said. "He'll get through it."

They were good words to hear, especially from Dekker, who had never been the most optimistic guy on the block. "You sound so certain."

He winked at her. "I oughtta know, don't you think?"

They shared a long look, one full of words they didn't really need to say out loud.

Three years ago, Dekker's wife, Stacey, had died. His mama, Lorraine, had passed away not long after. Dekker had done quite a bit of drinking himself in the months following those two sad events.

Dekker said, "Maybe you ought to start whipping up a few casseroles."

It was a joke between them now, how Joleen had kept after him, dropping in at his place several times a week, pouring his booze down the drain and urging him to "talk out his pain."

He wouldn't talk. But she wouldn't give up on him, either. She brought him casseroles to make sure he ate right and kept dragging him out to go bowling and to the movies. Good, nourishing food and a few social activities *had* made a difference.

It had also brought them closer. She was, after all, five years younger than Dekker. Five years, while they were growing up, had seemed like a lifetime. Almost as if they were of different generations.

But it didn't seem that way anymore. Now they were equals.

They were best friends.

She said, "You still have not bothered to tell me why you thought you had to fly off to Los Angeles out of nowhere like that."

"Later," he said. "There's a lot to tell and now is not the time."

"Were you…in danger?"

"No."

"Was it something for a client?"

"Jo. Please. Not now."

On the couch, Hubert stiffened, snorted and then went on snoring even louder than before.

Dekker said, "I think we've done all we can for him at the moment."

"Guess so. Might as well get back to the party. We're probably out of frilly toothpicks again."

Dekker grinned. "DeDe grabbed me a few minutes ago. Something about cutting the cake?"

"No. It's too early. They're still attacking the buffet table. But it is a little cooler now. Safe to get everything set up."

"Safe?"

"That's right. We can chance taking the cake back outside."

"This sounds ominous."

"A wedding can be a scary time."

"Tell me about it."

She took his big, blunt-fingered hand. "Come on." They left Uncle Hubert snoring on the couch and went out to the kitchen, where they enlisted Burly to help Dekker carry the cake back out to the patio.

Once the cake was in position for cutting, Joleen went looking for Niki and Sam. She found them on the front porch, building a castle out of Duplo blocks.

"Mama. Look." Sam beamed her his biggest, proudest smile.

"Wonderful job, baby." She asked Niki, "Did he eat anything yet?"

Niki nodded. "He had some corn. And that fruit dish—the one with the coconut? Oh, and he ate about five of those little meatballs."

"Milk?"

"Yeah—and what's with those Atwood people?"

What do you mean? Joleen wanted to demand. *What did they do?*

She held the questions back. Sam might be only eighteen months old, but you could never be sure of how much he understood. And she didn't want Niki stirred up, either. She gestured with a toss of her head. Niki got up and followed her down to the other end of the long porch.

"What do you mean about the Atwoods?" Joleen kept her voice low and her tone even.

Niki shrugged. "I don't know. They sure stare a lot."

"Have they…bothered you?"

"I don't know, Joly. Like I said, they just stare."

"They haven't spoken to you at all?"

"Well, yeah. Twice. They tried to talk to Sam, but you know how he is sometimes. He got shy, buried his head against my shoulder. Both times they gave up and walked away."

So. They had tried to get to know their grandson a little and gotten nowhere. Joleen found herself feeling sorry for them again.

"No real problems, though?"

"Uh-uh. Just general creepiness."

Joleen reached out, brushed a palm along her sister's arm. "You've been great, taking care of Sam all day."

"Yeah. Call me Wonder Girl." Niki was good with Sam. She took her babysitting duties seriously. In fact, Niki was doing a lot better lately all the way around. She'd given them a real scare last year. But Joleen had begun to believe those problems were behind her now.

"Want a little break?"

"Sure— Can I get out of this dress?"

Joleen hid a smile. Rose-colored satin was hardly her little sister's style. Niki liked black. Black hip-riding skinny jeans, equally skinny little black T-shirts, black Doc Martens. Sometimes, for variety, she'd wear navy blue or deep purple, but never anything bright. Certainly nothing rosy red.

"Go ahead and change," said Joleen.

Niki beamed. "Thanks."

They rejoined Sam at the other end of the porch. "Hey, big guy," Joleen said. "I need some help."

Sam loved to "help." He considered "helping" to be anything that involved a lot of busyness on his part. Pulling his mother around by her thumb could be "helping," or carrying items from one place to another.

Sam set down the red plastic block in his fist and leaned forward, going to his hands and knees. "I hep." He rocked back to the balls of his feet and pushed himself to an upright position.

Joleen held out her arms.

He said something she couldn't really make out, but she knew he meant he wanted to walk.

So she took his hand and walked him down the front steps and around to the backyard. When she spotted the Atwoods alone at a table on the far side of the patio, she led him over there.

Okay, they were snobs. And they made her a little nervous.

But it had to be awkward for them at this party. They didn't really know a soul. Joleen had introduced them to her mother and a few of the guests when they first arrived. But they'd been on their own since then.

All right, maybe Robert Atwood had given her cold looks. Maybe he didn't approve of her. So what?

She was going to get along with them if she could possibly manage it. They were Sammy's grandparents and she would show them respect, give them a little of the slack they didn't appear to be giving her.

And besides, who was to say she hadn't read them all wrong? Maybe staring and glaring was just Robert Atwood's way of coping with feeling like an outsider.

When she reached their table, Joleen scooped Sam up into her arms. "Well, how are you two holdin' up?"

"We are fine," said Robert.

"Yes," Antonia agreed in that wispy little voice of hers, staring at Sam with misty eyes. "Just fine. Very nice."

Joleen felt a tug of sympathy for the woman. A few weeks ago, when the Atwoods had finally agreed to come to her house and meet Sam, Antonia had shown her one of Bobby's baby pictures. The resemblance to Sam was extraordinary.

What must it be like, to see their lost child every time they looked at Sam?

All the tender goodwill Joleen had felt toward them when she saw the newspaper photos of them at Bobby's funeral came flooding back, filling her with new determination to do all in her power to see that they came to know their only grandson, that they found their rightful place in his life.

"Mind if Sam and I sit down a minute?"

"Please," said Antonia, heartbreakingly eager, grabbing the chair on her right side and pulling it out.

Joleen put Sam in it. He sat back and laid his baby hands on the molded plastic arms. "I sit," he declared with great pride.

Antonia made a small, adoring sound low in her throat.

Joleen took the other free chair at the table. As she scooped her satin skirt smooth beneath her, Robert Atwood spoke again.

"Ahem. Joleen. We really must be leaving soon."

Protestations would have felt a little too phony, so Joleen replied, "Well, I am pleased that you could come and I hope you had a good time."

Robert nodded, his face a cool mask. Antonia seemed too absorbed in watching Sam to make conversation.

Robert said, "I would like a few words with you, before we leave. In private."

That got Antonia's attention. A look of alarm crossed her delicate face. She actually stopped staring at Sam. "Robert, I don't think it's really the time to—"

"I do," her husband interrupted, his voice flat. Final.

Antonia blinked. And said nothing more.

Joleen felt suspicious all over again—not to mention

apprehensive. What was the man up to? She honestly wanted to meet these two halfway. But they—Robert, especially—made that so difficult.

She tried to keep her voice light. "Well, if you need to talk to me about something important, today is not the day, I'm afraid. I think I told you, this party is my doing. I'm the one who has to keep things moving along. There's still the cake to cut. And the toasts to be made. Then there will be—"

"I think you could spare us a few minutes, don't you? In the next hour or so?"

"No, I don't think that I—"

"Joleen. It is only a few minutes. I know you can manage it."

Joleen stared into those hard gray eyes. She found herself thinking of Bobby, understanding him a little better, maybe. Even forgiving him some for being so much less than the man she had dreamed him to be. Joleen doubted that Robert Atwood knew how to show love, how to teach a child the true meaning of right and wrong. He would communicate his will—and his sense that he and his were special, above the rules that regular folks had to live by. And his son would grow up as Bobby had. Charming and so handsome. Well dressed, well educated and well mannered. At first glance, a real "catch." A man among men.

But inside, just emptiness. A lack where substance mattered the most.

"Joleen," Bobby had said when she'd told him she was pregnant. "I have zero interest in being a father." The statement had been cool and matter-of-fact, the same kind of tone he might have used to tell her that he didn't feel up to eating Chinese that night. "If you are having a baby, I'm afraid you will be having it on your own."

She'd been so shocked and hurt, she'd reacted on pure pride. "Fine," she had cried. "Get out of my life. I don't want to see you. Ever again."

And Bobby had given her exactly what she'd asked for. He'd walked out of her life—and his unborn child's—and never looked back.

She thought again of Dekker's warnings.

Forget the Atwoods. They have too much money and too much power and given the kind of son they raised, I'd say they're way too likely to abuse both....

She rose from her chair. "Come on, Sam. We've got to get busy here."

Robert Atwood just wouldn't give it up. "A few minutes. Please."

Sam slid off the chair and grabbed her thumb. "We go. I hep." He granted Antonia a shy little smile.

"Joleen," Robert said, making a command out of the sound of her name.

Lord, give me strength, Joleen prayed to her maker. She reminded herself of her original goal here: to develop a reasonably friendly relationship with Sam's daddy's parents. "All right. Let me get through the cutting of the cake. And the toasts. Then we can talk."

"Thank you."

"But only for a few minutes."

"I do understand."

Joleen kept Sam with her, while DeDe and Wayne cut the cake and after, as the guests took turns proposing toasts to the happy couple. Then she handed Sam back to her sister, who was now clad comfortably in her favorite black jeans.

By then it was a little past seven, and growing dark. The breeze had kept up, and the temperature had dropped about ten degrees. It was the next thing to pleasant now, in the backyard. Joleen went around the side of the house and plugged in the paper lanterns that she and a couple of cousins had spent the day before stringing from tree to tree.

There were "oohs" and "aahs" and a smattering of applause as the glow of the lanterns lit up the deepening night. Joleen felt a glow of her own inside. She had done a good job for her sister. In spite of more than one near disaster, it was stacking up to be a fine wedding, after all.

Camilla had a decent stereo system in the house. And yesterday, after the lantern stringing, Joleen and her cousins had wired up extra speakers and set them out on the patio. So they had good, clear music for dancing. DeDe and Wayne were already swaying beneath the lanterns, held close in each other's arms. So were Aunt LeeAnne and her husband, Uncle Foley, and a number of other couples as well—including Joleen's mother. Camilla moved gracefully in the embrace of yet another middle-aged admirer.

"You did good, Jo." Dekker had come up beside her.

"Thanks."

"Welcome." He was staring out at the backyard, his eyes on the dancers.

Joleen thought of Los Angeles again, wondered what had happened there. She was just about to make another effort at prying some information out of him when she remembered the Atwoods.

She supposed she'd better go looking for them.

Dekker sensed her shift in mood. "What's the matter?"

"Oh, nothin'. Much. I have to say goodbye to the Atwoods."

His brows had drawn together. "I don't like the way you said that. What's going on?"

Teasingly, she bumped his arm with her elbow. "You are such a suspicious man."

"When it comes to Robert Atwood, you bet I am. I don't trust him."

"I noticed. He wants a few minutes with me before they leave, that's all."

"A few minutes for what?"

"I don't know yet. But I'm sure he's plannin' to tell me. When he gets me alone."

"I don't like it."

"Dekker. Chill."

"'When he gets you alone.' What does that mean?"

"It means I am giving him five minutes. In Daddy's study."

"Why? I can tell by the way you're hugging yourself and sighing that you don't want to do that."

"I want to make it work with them."

"People do not always get what they want."

"Dekker—"

He cut her off. "It's pride, Joleen. You know it is. You're ashamed that you had such bad judgment about Bobby. You want them to be different from him. But Jo, they *raised* him. You have to face that."

"I was a fool with Bobby. This is different."

"No. No, I don't think it is."

"You think I'm still a fool?"

He made a sound low in his throat. "Damn it, Jo…"

She stood on tiptoe and whispered to him. "It is only five minutes. Then they will leave and we can enjoy the rest of the party."

"You are too damn trusting."

She planted a quick kiss on his square jaw. "Gotta go."

He was silent as she walked away from him, but she could feel his disapproval, like a chill wind on the warm night. She shrugged it off.

Dekker had seen way too much in his life. He'd been a detective with the OCPD before Stacey died. He'd quit the department during the tough time that followed. But before that he'd seen too many examples of the terrible things people can do to each other. Now he worked on his own as a private investigator, which gave him an ongoing opportunity to witness more of man's inhumanity to man. Sometimes he saw trouble coming whether it was on the way or not.

Joleen put on a confident smile. She *was* going to do her best to make things work with the Atwoods. It was her duty, as the mother of their grandchild.

She could stand up just fine under Robert Atwood's cold looks and demanding ways. What could he really *do* to her, after all? She held all the power, when it came to their relationship with Sam.

She would not abuse that power. But she wouldn't let Robert Atwood walk all over her, either.

Joleen found the Atwoods waiting by the back door. They followed her into the kitchen and on to the central hall, where Uncle Hubert's snoring could be clearly heard through the open door to the living room.

Joleen held up a hand. "Just one minute."

The Atwoods stopped where they were, at the foot of the stairs. Joleen moved to the living room doorway. Uncle Herbert lay just as she and Dekker had left him two hours before, faceup on the couch, his stocking feet dangling a few inches from the floor. Gently she closed the door.

"This way." She led Sam's grandparents across the hall to the room her father had used as his study. She reached in and flicked the wall switch. Four tulip-shaped lamps in the small chandelier overhead bloomed into light.

The room was as it had always been. Samuel Tilly's scarred oak desk with its gray swivel chair waited in front of the window. His old medical books and journals filled the tall bookcases on the inner wall. There was a worn couch and two comfy, faded easy chairs.

"Have a seat." Joleen closed the door.

The Atwoods did not sit.

They stood in the center of the room, between the couch and her father's desk. Robert looked more severe than ever. And Antonia, hovering in his shadow as always, looked nothing short of bleak—too pale, her thin brows drawn together. She had clasped her hands in front of her. The knuckles were dead white.

Joleen said, "Antonia? Are you all right?"

"Oh, yes. Fine. Just fine…"

"But you don't look—"

Robert interrupted, "My wife says she is fine."

"Well, I know, but—"

"Please. I have something of real importance to propose to you now. I'll need your undivided attention."

Joleen did not get it. Antonia looked positively stricken, and all her husband could think about was what he wanted to say? A sarcastic remark rose to her lips. She bit it back. "All right. What is it, Mr. Atwood?"

Robert cleared his throat. "Joleen, after the spectacle I have witnessed today, I find I cannot keep quiet any longer. I have come to a difficult but important decision. It is painfully obvious to me that my grandson cannot get the kind of upbringing he deserves while he is in your care. Antonia and I are prepared to take him off your hands. I'm willing to offer you five hundred thousand dollars to sign over custody of young Samuel to me."

Chapter 3

Joleen forgot all about Antonia's distress. She could feel her blood pressure rising. So much for trying to make it work with the Atwoods.

She spoke through gritted teeth. "I'm sorry. I'm sure I could not have heard you right. You did not just offer to *buy* my baby from me—did you?"

Antonia squeaked. There was no other word for it, for that small, desperate, anguished sound. She squeaked and then she just stood there, wringing her hands.

Robert, however, had no trouble forming words. "Buy your baby? What an absurd suggestion. Of course, I'm not offering to *buy* Samuel. What I *am* offering you is a chance. A chance to do the right thing. For your child. And for yourself, as well."

"The right thing?" Joleen echoed in sheer disbelief. "To sell you my baby is the *right thing?*"

Robert waved a hand, a gesture clearly intended to erase her question as if it had never been. "I know that you have never attended college—except for a year, wasn't it, at some local trade school?"

"Who told you that?"

"I have my sources. Now you will be able to finish your education. You'll be able to do more with your life than run a beauty shop."

"I happen to like running a beauty shop."

He looked vaguely outraged, as if she had just told an insulting and rude lie. "Please."

"It's true. I love the work that I do."

He refused to believe such a thing. "I am offering you a *future,* Joleen. You are a young, healthy woman. You will have other children. My son only had one. Antonia and I want a chance to bring that one child up properly."

"Meaning *I* won't bring Sam up properly."

"My dear Joleen, you are twisting what I've said."

"I am not twisting anything. I am laying it right on the line. You don't think I will bring my son up right, so you want to *buy* him from me."

"You are overdramatizing."

Joleen, who, since the loss of her kind and steady father a decade before, had always been the calmest person in her family, found it took all of her will not to start shrieking— not to grab the brass paperweight on her father's desk and toss it right in Robert Atwood's smug face.

"My offer is a good one," Robert Atwood said.

Joleen gaped at him. "I beg your pardon. It is never a good offer when you try to buy someone's child."

"Joleen—"

"And what is the matter with you, anyway? Your 'offer' is bad enough all by itself. But couldn't you have waited a day or two? Did you have to come at me on my sister's wedding day?"

"Please…" croaked Antonia. She looked as if she might cry.

Robert put his arm around her—to steady her or to silence her, Joleen wasn't sure which. He held his proud white head high. "Once we'd made the decision, the sooner the better was the way it seemed to me. Might as well make our position clear. Might as well get you thinking along the right track."

A number of furious epithets rose to Joleen's lips. She did not utter a one of them—but she would, if this man went on saying these awful things much longer.

This conversation can only go downhill, she thought. Better to end it now.

"Mr. Atwood, I'm afraid if you stay very much longer, I will say some things that I'll be sorry for. I would like you to leave now."

Antonia made another of those squeaky little noises. Robert squeezed her shoulder and said to Joleen, "I want you to think about what I've said."

I am not going to start yelling at this man, she told herself silently. She said, "I do not have to think about it. The answer is no. You cannot have my child. Not at any price."

Robert Atwood stood even taller, if that was possible. "My dear, I would advise you not to speak without thinking."

"Stop calling me that. I am not your dear."

"Joleen, I am trying to make certain that you understand your position here."

Joleen blinked. This had to be a nightmare, didn't it? It could not be real. "My position?"

"Yes. You are an unwed mother."

Unwed mother. The old-fashioned phrase hurt. It made her sound cheap—and irresponsible, too. Not to mention a little bit stupid. Someone who hadn't had sense enough to get a ring on her finger before she let a man into her bed.

Maybe, she admitted to herself, it hurt because it was all too true. She had not been smart when it came to Bobby Atwood. Which seemed funny, at that moment. Funny in a sharp and painful way. A tight laugh escaped her.

"Don't try to make light of this, Joleen."

The urge to laugh vanished as quickly as it had come. "I promise you, Mr. Atwood. I am not makin' light. Not in the least."

"Good. For child care, you rely on your family members, and they are not the kind of people who should be caring for my grandson."

Joleen thought of that paperweight again—of how good it would feel to grab it and let it fly. "You better watch yourself, insultin' my family."

Robert Atwood shrugged. "I am merely stating facts. Your mother, from what I understand, and from what I witnessed today, is sexually promiscuous. Your younger sister has been in serious trouble at school and was arrested last year in a shoplifting incident. Your other sister has had some problems with the law, as well. None of those three—your mother or those sisters of yours, are the kind I would trust around my grandson. If it comes down to it, I will have little trouble convincing a judge that females like that aren't fit caregivers for Samuel, that he would be much better off with Antonia and me."

Joleen couldn't help it. She raised her voice. "'Females like that'?" she cried. "Just who do you think you are, to call my family *females like that?*"

"You are shouting," said Robert Atwood.

"You're darn right I am. I was warned about you and I should have listened. But I didn't, and look what has happened."

"Joleen—"

"That is all. That is it. You won't get my baby, don't think that you will. And I want you out of my mother's house."

Right then the door to the front hall swung inward. It was Dekker, all six foot three and 220, or so, very muscular pounds of him. "Joleen. Everything okay?"

The sight of her dear friend calmed her—at least a little. She said quietly, "Everything's fine. The Atwoods were just leaving."

"You'll be hearing from my attorney," Robert Atwood said.

"Fine. Just go. Now."

Apparently, he'd said all he came to say. At last. With great dignity he guided his wife toward the door.

Which Dekker was blocking. "What's this about a lawyer?" he demanded.

Robert Atwood spoke to Joleen. "Tell this thug to step out of my way."

Joleen longed to tell Dekker just the opposite—to ask him if he would please break both of the Atwoods in two. But, no. It wouldn't be right to kill the Atwoods. Not on DeDe's wedding day, anyway.

"It's okay, Dekker. Let them go."

Dekker, who had a fair idea of what had been going on in Samuel's study, stepped aside reluctantly. The Atwoods left the room. He followed them, just to make certain they got the hell out.

Once they went through the front door, he shut it firmly behind them. Then he returned to Joleen.

She was standing by her father's desk, a pretty woman in a long dress that was not quite pink and not quite red. Her heart-shaped face was flushed, her full mouth tight. A frown had etched itself between those big brown Du-Frayne eyes.

Dekker quietly closed the door.

Her mouth loosened enough to quiver a little. "Please don't say 'I told you so.'"

Just to make sure he had it figured out, he said, "They want to take Sam away from you."

He hoped that maybe she would tell him it wasn't so. But she didn't. She picked up a brass paperweight of a Yankee soldier on a rearing horse from the edge of Samuel's desk. "I thought about smashing Robert Atwood in the face with this."

Dekker shook his head. "Bad idea. And, anyway, violence is not your style."

"Right now I feel like it could be. I feel like I could do murder and never think twice."

"You couldn't."

She clutched the brass figure against her body and looked at him with fury in her eyes. "He called my mother *promiscuous,* Dekker. He said Mama and DeDe and Niki weren't fit to take care of Sam. He raised a shallow, sweet-talkin' lowlife like Bobby—God forgive me for speakin' ill of the dead—and he has the nerve to come in my mother's house and say that my people are not good enough to do right by my child, that *I* am not good enough, that—"

In two long strides, he was at her side.

She looked at him with a kind of bewildered surprise—that he had moved so fast, or maybe that, in moving, he had distracted her from her rage. "What?"

"Better give me that."

She only gripped the paperweight tighter. "He offered me *money,* Dekker. Money for my baby. Five hundred thousand dollars to let them have Sam."

Dekker swore. "I'm sorry, Jo. You shouldn't have had to listen to garbage like that." He put his hand over hers. "Come on. Put this thing down...."

She allowed him to pry her fingers open. He set the paperweight back in its place on the desk. Then he took her by the shoulders.

"What else?" he asked, when she finally met his eyes.

She swallowed, shook her head as if to clear it of so much hot, hurtful rage. "When I...when I told him no, that I wouldn't take his money and he could not have my child, he started talkin' lawsuits, how he would not have any trouble convincing a judge that Sam would be better off living with him and Antonia."

Predictable, thought Dekker. He said, "Anything more?"

Those big eyes narrowed. "He knew. About how Niki got picked up for shoplifting last year. And he seemed to know about DeDe, about her little joyride in that stolen car."

In fact, it was one of Niki's friends from the bad-news crowd she'd been hanging around who'd actually tried to walk out of the department store with a cashmere sweater under her coat. But Niki *had* been there. She had known of the attempted theft and done nothing to stop it. And before that, there had been a series of incidents at school, bad grades and detentions, minor vandalism of school property and truancies, too.

As for DeDe, between the ages of fifteen and eighteen, she had been a true wild child. She went out with bad boys, she drank, she experimented with drugs. She'd ended up before a judge after the incident with the car, when she'd hitched a ride with a boy she hardly knew. The boy had shared his bottle of tequila with her and taken her down I-35 at a hundred miles an hour.

She'd gotten off easy, because it was her first arrest and because she hadn't known that the car was stolen and because, by some miracle, the judge had believed her when she swore she hadn't known. But she'd come very close to doing some time. After that, she'd cleaned up her act.

The problem with Niki and DeDe, the way Dekker saw it, was losing their father—and not getting enough attention and supervision from their mother. Camilla loved her girls with all her heart, but she'd been sunk in desperate grief for the first year or two after Samuel's death. And since then she was often distracted by all the boyfriends. She also worked long hours at the salon that she and Joleen now operated together.

Joleen had done her best to pick up the slack, to be there for her sisters, to offer attention and to provide discipline. She'd taken a lot of flack from both DeDe and Niki for her pains. They'd acted out their resentments on her; they'd fought her every time she tried to rein them in.

But recently things had started looking up. Niki had left the bad crowd behind. She took school seriously, was getting As and Bs rather than Ds and Fs. And DeDe had really settled down, as well. Joleen had dared to let herself think that the worst part of raising her own sisters was behind her.

Not that the reform of the Tilly girls would matter one damn bit to a self-righteous bastard like Robert Atwood.

"Oh, I cannot believe this is happening." Joleen pulled away from Dekker's grip and sank to one of the faded easy chairs. For a moment, she stared down at her lap, slim shoulders drooping. Then she pulled herself up straight again. "When I asked him *how* he knew those things about my sisters and my mother, he said he had his *sources*. Dekker, that man has had someone snooping around in our lives." She said it as if it were some sort of surprise. "Why, I would not put it past him to have hired someone, some private detective..."

"You mean someone like me?"

She let out a small, guilty-sounding groan. "Oh, Dekker, no. I didn't mean it that way...."

"It's okay. *I* did. I'm damn good at what I do. When I dig up the dirt on someone for a client, I get it all. I'm sure whoever Robert Atwood hired has done the same."

She put up a hand to swipe a shiny golden-brown curl back from her forehead. "Dekker, it won't work, will it? He couldn't get Sam by claiming that my mother and sisters are unfit. Could he?"

Dekker wished he didn't have to answer that one.

Joleen picked up his reluctance. "You think it *could* work, don't you?" Her shoulders drooped again. "Oh, God..."

He dropped to a crouch at her feet. "Look. I'm only saying it *might* work. Your sisters and your mother all pitch in, to take care of Sam when you can't."

"So? Good child care costs plenty. If I had to hire someone, I couldn't come close to affording the kind of care I can get from my family for free." She leaned toward him in the chair, intent on convincing him of how right she was—though somewhere in the back of her mind, she had to realize she was preaching to the choir. "They are good with him, Dekker, you know that they are. And as for Niki and DeDe, it's been a long time since there's been any trouble from either of them. And Mama—well, all right. She likes men and she loves to go out. Is that a crime? I don't know all her secrets, but I know she is not having *affairs* with all of them. She is no bed hopper. She loves the romance of it, that's all. She loves getting flowers and going dancing. But then, after way too little time with each guy, she can't pretend anymore. She admits to herself that the latest man is not my father. So she moves on to the next one—and what in the world does that have to do with how she is with Sam?"

"It's got nothing to do with how she is with Sam. The truth is, Camilla is a fine grandma. You know it and I know it. But I'm trying to get you to see that it's not the truth that matters here."

She blinked. "Not the truth?"

"No, Jo," he said patiently. "It's the way things look. The way Robert Atwood and the lawyers he gets will *make* things look. It's appearances. A war of words and insinuations. Atwood's lawyers will take what your sisters have actually done and make it look a hundred times worse. They'll leave out any extenuating circumstances, minimize things like recent good behavior. It will be their job to make it appear that DeDe and Nicole are a pair of hardened criminals. And they'll make your mama look like some kind of—"

Joleen put up a hand. "Don't say it, okay? She's not. You know she's not."

"That's right. I know. But my opinion doesn't count for squat here. You have to come to grips with that."

She just didn't want to get it. So she launched into a renewed defense of Camilla and the girls. "They're great with Sam, Dekker. All three of them. He is nuts about them, and they take wonderful care of him. They—"

"Joleen. Listen. The point is not what good care they take of Sam. The point is, what is a judge going to think?" He caught her hands, chafed them between his own. "If the Atwoods hired me to work up a negative report on Camilla and your sisters, I could get enough together to make them look pretty bad."

She swallowed again and tugged her hands free of his. "Oh, I hate this."

Should he have left it at that? Maybe. But he had to be sure she understood the true dimensions of the problem.

"Jo."

She made a small, unwilling noise in her throat.

He laid it on her. "There's also the little problem of Robert Atwood's influence in this town. He has power, Joleen. Lots of it. You have to face that. He's contributed to a hell of a lot of big-time political causes and campaigns, and he has supported the careers of a number of local judges."

"What are you tellin' me? That some judge is going to give my little boy to the Atwoods as payback on some political favor?"

"It could be a factor."

"Well, that's just plain wrong."

"It doesn't *matter* that it's wrong."

"But—"

"I keep trying to make you see. Right and wrong are not the issues here. It's money, Joleen. Money and power.

You can't underestimate what big bucks and heavy-duty influence can do."

She swiped that cute brown curl off her forehead again. "Oh, why didn't I listen to you? I never should have called him. I never should have—"

"But you did. And even though I thought it was a bad idea, I do know that you did it for the right reasons. For Sam's sake. And to give the Atwoods a chance to know their grandson."

"It was also pride, Dekker," she said in a small voice. "I've got…a problem with pride. I want to do right. I want to do right so bad, I get pigheaded about it. And I, well, it's exactly what you said earlier. I'm ashamed. I was supposed to be the one with both of my feet on the ground in this family. But look at me…"

He couldn't help reaching out and running a finger along her soft cheek. "You look just fine."

She caught his hand, squeezed it, let it go. "You know what I mean. I ended up with a baby and no husband, got myself 'in trouble,' made the oldest mistake in the book. So when I called Robert Atwood, I was hopin'…to make up for that, somehow. To be bigger than the mess I got myself into. To get past my own bad judgment in falling for Bobby by reachin' out to his folks in their hour of need. It was pride, Dekker. You were right. Just plain old pigheaded pride."

"And now it's over and done with. You need to let it go and move on."

"How can I let it go when I am so *furious* at myself?"

"Look at it this way. It's very likely, even if you hadn't told them they had a grandson, that the Atwoods would have found out about Sam eventually. We may not travel in their circles. But word does get around."

"You really think so?"

"Yeah." He rose to stand above her. "Now. Are you finished giving yourself hell?"

She blew out a long breath. "Oh, I guess."

"Then we can start thinking about what to *do,* about how to fight what they're going to be throwing at you. The main attack is going to be on the fitness of your child care, the way it looks now."

She stared up at him. "What are you telling me?"

"I think you know."

For an endless few moments, neither of them spoke. Noises from outside the study rose up to fill the quiet—a woman's laughter beyond the high leaded-glass window that looked out on the side of the house, the music on Camilla's stereo, something slow and bluesy and sweet.

"All right," Joleen said at last. "I'll find someone else to watch Sam when I'm working. It will be tight, but I'll manage it."

"Good."

"And then somehow I will have to tell my mama and my sisters why they are suddenly not to be trusted with the little boy they all adore."

"You don't have to tell them anything tonight. You've got a little time to think it over. You'll come up with a good approach."

"It doesn't matter what approach I take, there will be hurt feelings. There will be cryin' and carryin' on—and then I've got to get a good lawyer, right?"

"Yes. But don't worry there. I'll find you the right man."

"And then I have to *pay* the lawyer. Oh, what a mess. There is no way around it. This is going to cost a bundle."

Dekker knew that Joleen made an okay living, working with her mother. She supported herself and Sam and she did a decent job of it. He also knew that there wasn't much left over once all the bills were paid. Quality child care and a good lawyer would stretch her budget way past the breaking point.

But it was okay. Money, after what had happened in Los Angeles, would be the least of their problems. Dekker wanted to tell her as much. However, that would only get her started asking questions about L.A.

Right now, they had a limited amount of time before someone would be knocking on the study door, demanding that Joleen get out there and deal with some other minor crisis. When he told her about L.A., he didn't want to be interrupted.

"Don't look so miserable," he said. "We're just getting it all out there, so we can see what we have to deal with."

"I know." But she didn't know. He could see by her worried frown that the money problem was really bothering her.

He strove to ease her fears without saying too much. "The money issue can be handled."

"I don't see how." She looked down at her lap and shook her head.

"Jo, I'll help out. The bills will get paid."

"Oh, no." She glanced up then, her frown deeper than before. "You work hard for your money. And we both know you don't have much more of it than I do."

Joleen was right—or she would have been right, as of a few days ago. Before the trip to Southern California, Dekker would have had to rob a bank to be of much use to her financially. He'd gone into something of a downward spiral, right after his wife, Stacey, died. He'd quit his job and sold his house. He had not worked for several months while grief and guilt did their best to eat him alive. With Joleen's help, he'd pulled himself out of it. But by that time he didn't have a whole hell of a lot left.

For almost two years now he had operated a one-man detective agency in a one-room office over a coin laundry downtown. It paid the rent and put food on the table, but that was about it.

Or it had been. Until he'd flown to L.A. and learned that he had money to burn. He was a rich man now, and he had every intention of spending whatever it took to help Joleen fight the SOB who thought he could take her child away.

"I have a few extra resources," he said. "I mean it. Don't worry about money."

"Dekker. You are not listening."

"No. *You're* the one who's not listening."

"I couldn't take money from you."

"Sure you could—for Sam's sake."

"No. It wouldn't be right. I couldn't live with myself if I—"

Someone knocked on the door. "Joly?" It was DeDe's voice. "Joly, are you in there?"

Joleen glanced toward the sound and sighed.

Dekker said softly, "It's all right. We'll talk more. Later. After the party's over and everyone's gone home."

"You know that's going to be good and late."

"It's okay. I'll be available."

"Thank you," she said. Even if he hadn't been a brand-new multimillionaire, the look she gave him then would have made him feel like one.

"Joly?" DeDe knocked again.

Joleen pushed herself from the chair and smoothed out her skirt. "Come on in."

The door swung inward and DeDe demanded, "What are you doing in here? I have been looking all over for you."

"Well, you have found me."

DeDe glanced from her sister to Dekker, then back to Joleen again. "What's going on?"

Dekker laughed. "None of your business. What do you need?"

DeDe wrinkled her nose. "Oh, it's Uncle Stan. He wants some *special* coffee." In the Tilly and DuFrayne families, *special* coffee was coffee dosed with Irish Cream and Grand Marnier.

"And?" Joleen prompted.

"I can't find the Bailey's."

"Did you look in the—"

DeDe groaned. "I looked *everywhere*. Would you just come and find it?"

"Sure."

"And it's almost eight. I think I should throw the bouquet pretty soon."

"Good idea."

"I want you to stand about ten feet, in a direct line, behind me when I do it. Understand?"

"DeDe." Joleen looked weary. "The whole idea with the bouquet is that everyone is supposed to get a fair chance at it."

"Too bad. It's my wedding. And my big sister is catchin' my bouquet."

Chapter 4

Joleen did catch the bouquet.

It wasn't as if she had a choice in the matter. DeDe, after all, had made up her mind that Joleen would be getting it. And there was just no sense fighting DeDe once she'd made up her mind.

Cousin Callie Tilly, one of Uncle Stan's daughters, who worked at a bank and had just hit the big three-oh with no prospective husband in sight, was a little put out at the way DeDe went and tossed those flowers at the exact spot where Joleen stood. Callie grumbled that she was older than Joleen and she needed that bouquet more.

But her own father told her to quit whining and have herself a little *special* coffee. Which cousin Callie did. And then one of Wayne's friends, a handsome cowboy in dress jeans and fancy tooled boots, asked Callie if she would care to dance. Her attitude improved considerably after that.

Joleen put Sam to bed upstairs in her old room at a little after nine o'clock. When she went back outside, she did some dancing herself. She danced with Uncle Stan and Bud and Burly. And with another friend of Wayne's, a tall, broad-shouldered fellow who ran an oyster bar in Tulsa. He told her she had beautiful eyes and that she knew how to follow. He claimed there were way too many women who tried to lead when they danced. Joleen smiled sweetly up at him and wondered if he was casting some kind of aspersion on modern women as a whole.

Then she decided she was just too suspicious. A guy called her a good dancer and she started thinking of ways to take it as an offense.

But then again, after what had happened with Bobby Atwood two years ago and with Bobby's father just this evening, well, was it any wonder she had trouble trusting men?

After the oyster bar owner from Tulsa, she danced with Dekker. Thank God for Dekker. Now there was a man that a woman could trust. She was so very fortunate to have a friend like him, who came straight to her aid anytime things got tough.

Of course, she would never take the money he insisted he would give her. But it meant the world, that he would offer—and that he always came through for her and her mama and her sisters, too.

Anytime any one of them needed him, he was there.

And did she ever need him now. She needed his clear mind and his steely nerves—not to mention all he knew from being first a cop and now a private investigator. Dekker saw all the angles. Yes, he was way too cynical—but right now she needed someone who looked at the world through wide-open eyes. Someone to show her how to fight Bobby's father at his own game.

Joleen closed her eyes and laid her head on Dekker's broad shoulder.

"It's going to be all right, Jo," he whispered against her hair.

Something in his tone alerted her. She lifted her head and looked up at him. "You've thought of what to do. I can hear it in your voice."

"Could be."

She couldn't read his expression. "What *are* you thinking?"

"Later." He guided her head back to rest on his shoulder. "After everyone's gone home. We'll talk about it then. About *all* of it…."

At eleven DeDe and Wayne took off for Wayne's house. They'd spend their wedding night there and then leave in the morning for a twelve-day honeymoon at a two-hundred-year-old inn on the Mississippi shore.

Wayne's new peacock-green SUV had been properly adorned for the occasion, with Just Married scrawled in shaving cream across the rear window, Here Comes the Bride on the windshield and tin cans hooked to the rear bumper by lengths of thick string.

Joleen had the bird seed ready, wrapped in little rose-colored satin squares and tied with white bows. She passed it around and DeDe and Wayne ducked through a rain of it as they raced for the car. Then everyone stood on the sidewalk beneath the Victorian-style lamps that lined all the streets of Mesta Park, waving and calling out last-minute advice.

"Good luck!"

"Don't do anything we wouldn't do!"

"But if you do, take pictures!"

Wayne revved the engine and pulled away from the curb. The handsome SUV rolled off into the night, tin cans rattling behind.

Most of the guests took their leave then, turning for their own cars, waving goodbye and making happy noises about what a great time they'd had. A few stayed on—Callie and her cowboy, one of Camilla's admirers, Aunt LeeAnne and Uncle Foley—to enjoy another dance or two out in the lantern-lit backyard. It was after one when Camilla, Joleen and Dekker showed the last of them to the door.

"'Bye, now. Drive with care…." Camilla shut the door, turned off the porch light and then stretched like a sleek and very contented cat. "Oh, it has been a long and lovely day." Her smooth brows drew together. "Now, where did Niki get off to?"

Joleen said, "She went up to bed about half an hour ago."

"Our little Sammy all snuggled in?"

"I put him down in my room."

"Well." Camilla gave her oldest daughter a lazy smile. "I believe I am ready for bed myself. You and Sammy stayin'?"

"I think so. I'd just as soon not wake him. And tomorrow I'd only be headin' back over here to start cleaning up."

"Good. You'll lock the doors when you're through down here, then?"

"I will. Right now, though, Dekker and I are goin' out in back for a while, to enjoy the peace and quiet."

"Don't you start in cleaning up tonight," Camilla warned. "I mean it. It's late. You've worked hard enough. We'll take care of everything tomorrow."

"I won't lift a finger, I promise."

Camilla was not convinced. She shook her head and clucked her tongue. "I know how you are. The only child of mine who will work instead of playin' if given the choice. You have to learn to slow down a little, baby. Smell the flowers now and then."

"Mama, I'm not cleaning up a thing tonight. We're just going to sit outside and talk some, that's all."

"What do you two talk about? Always with your heads together. Thick as thieves, I swear."

"Nothing important, Mama." Well, all right. That was a flat-out lie. But the truth, right then, would not have served. When the time came, Joleen would tell her mother whatever she thought her mother had to know.

Camilla was already on her way up the stairs. She paused on the third step and cast a glance toward the door to the living room. Uncle Hubert was still in there, snoring away. They could hear the low rumblings even through the closed door. "Put a blanket over Hubert?"

"I will. Right away. 'Night, Mama."

"'Night..." Camilla went on up.

Joleen got a chenille throw from the closet under the stairs. She and Dekker spread it over Uncle Hubert, who just went on snoring, gone to the world.

"You want a beer or something?" she asked Dekker before they went outside.

"I wouldn't mind some ice water."

That sounded good to her, too, so she fixed them two tall glasses and led him out into the night.

Camilla had a matching pair of chaise lounges with nice, thick, floral-patterned cushions. For the wedding party, Joleen had put them near the fence, under the sweet gum in the corner of the yard. A low patio table sat between the lounges, just perfect for setting their glasses on.

"You think it's too dark out here?" Joleen asked. They'd unplugged the lanterns a little while before.

"I like the dark."

So they went over and stretched out on the lounges and stared up through the leaves of the sweet gum at the stars. They hadn't had a single frost yet, so cicadas serenaded them from the trees, making it seem as though it was still summer. Now and then, from the wires overhead, night birds trilled out their high, lonesome songs. The moon had gone down some time before, but as her eyes adjusted, Joleen found she could see well enough, after all. There were no clouds, and the stars were like diamonds sewn into the midnight fabric of the sky.

Joleen set her glass down and leaned back, aware of a jittery feeling in her stomach. Anticipation. She just knew that her friend had come up with a way out of this tight spot she had got herself into.

He had said as much, hadn't he?

Everything will be all right, Jo. Dekker was not the kind to give her empty words. If he said things would be all right, it was because he honestly thought they would be.

She waited, her jitters increasing, wishing she could see inside his mind, that she could know what he was thinking, what kind of plan he had thought up—and at the same time reticent, not wanting to push him, feeling it was only right he should say what he had to say in his own time. And in his own way.

He sipped his ice water, set it down next to hers. And then, finally, he spoke. "I want to tell you about Los Angeles first."

Oh, not now, she thought. She did want to hear about whatever had gone on out there, but right now, as far as she was concerned, everything took a backseat to the problem of Robert Atwood and the threat he posed to Sam.

Be patient, she silently reminded herself as she sucked in a slow breath and let it out with care. "All right. Tell me about Los Angeles."

It was a moment before he said anything. Cicada songs swelled, then faded off when he spoke.

"Do you remember, about a week and a half ago, that couple who showed up at your mama's front door—Jonas Bravo and his wife, Emma?"

Joleen remembered. Jonas Bravo and his wife had told a strange story about a baby, a baby that had been Jonas Bravo's younger brother. They'd claimed that the baby had been kidnapped thirty years ago. And that they were looking for a Lorraine Smith, who was supposed to know something about the kidnapping. Joleen had told them that the Lorraine Smith who used to live next door wasn't going to be able to help them, since she was no longer alive. Then Camilla had mentioned that Lorraine had a son. As soon as they heard that, they'd asked to speak with Dekker. Camilla had suggested they try him at work.

Joleen sought her friend's eyes through the darkness. "I thought you said it was nothing. That they were mistaken—that it must have been some other Lorraine Smith they were looking for."

"I lied."

She considered that admission for a moment, then asked, "Well, and why did you go and do that?"

"Because I didn't want to deal with what they'd told

me. I didn't want to think about it and I didn't want to talk about it, either."

"You mean you were lyin' to *yourself?*"

"That's right."

The little hairs on the back of Joleen's neck were standing at attention. "You're saying that your mama did know something about a kidnapped baby?"

He made a low noise, a noise that meant yes.

"So when Jonas Bravo and his wife showed up at your office…"

"They told me about the baby, Jonas's younger brother. And I told them I didn't know anything about any baby, and neither had my mother. I asked them to leave. And they did."

"Okay. But I don't see what—"

"I left out a few details, when I told you about it—like the fact that Jonas said he believed *I* was the baby."

Joleen's mouth felt dry. She picked up her ice water and knocked back a big gulp. "Wait a minute. Jonas Bravo said that *you* were the kidnapped baby?"

"Right."

"The kidnapped baby who was Jonas's brother?"

Dekker was nodding at her. "Jonas said he believed that I had been kidnapped by 'our' uncle, Blake Bravo, for revenge against Blake's own brother, Jonas's father."

"Revenge? Why?"

"That's a whole other story. Evidently, Blake was a real shady character, had been disinherited. He blamed his brother for it. So he came up with this scheme to kidnap his younger nephew and hold the baby for ransom. He had an accomplice, according to Jonas."

"Not…Lorraine?"

"Yes. Lorraine."

Joleen had that feeling again, the one she'd had in her father's study when Robert Atwood had told her he would take her child from her: that feeling of stark unreality—the absolute certainty this couldn't be real. "This is crazy. Lorraine was your *mother*. We all know that."

"Not according to Jonas Bravo. He told me that the woman I'd always believed to be my mother had helped Blake Bravo kidnap me. That Blake had demanded—and got—two million dollars worth of diamonds as a ransom."

"Two *million?* Whoa. The Bravos must have had plenty of money."

"They did. And they *still* do. Jonas manages the Bravo holdings. He's an excellent businessman. They call him the Bravo Billionaire."

Joleen took another swallow of ice water. "They?"

"The newspapers, the scandal sheets. Bravo is an important name in Los Angeles." Dekker was watching her. He waited till she set her glass down again before he said, "So Blake got the diamonds—but he never returned the baby he had kidnapped. He and Lorraine disappeared, along with that baby, never to be seen or heard from again."

"The baby that was…you?" It all seemed so incredible.

"Right. That's what Jonas claimed."

"And you denied it."

"Yes. I said it wasn't true and I asked him and Emma to leave. But I couldn't stop thinking about the things that he'd said. I remembered my mother's diary."

This was more news to Joleen. "Lorraine left a diary?"

"Yes. She asked me not to read it until she was gone. I

put it away. And I *never* read it. I guess I just didn't want to deal with what I would find in there. But after Jonas and his wife paid me that visit, I couldn't stop thinking about it. I dug it out of her things."

"And?"

"It contained her confession. She verified everything Jonas had told me. That she helped kidnap me as a baby and that she—well, she decided she wanted to keep me. She couldn't have kids of her own. She wrote that, from the moment she lifted me out of my crib, the night that they took me from the Bravo mansion, she knew she would never give me up. In the end, after several months of moving around, living under various aliases, Blake set her up with a new identity. And a house."

"The house…next door?"

"You got it."

"So that means Jonas Bravo…"

"*Is* my brother."

"And you took off for L.A. on Wednesday because—"

"As soon as I read what Lorraine wrote, I felt I had to go looking for him, to tell him what I'd found."

"Oh, Dekker." She reached across the distance between them and brushed his arm with her fingertips. "I'll bet you couldn't get there fast enough."

His white teeth flashed in the darkness as he gave her a smile. "I knew you'd understand."

"I do. I just…well, I can hardly believe it. You have a *brother*…." Which was wonderful, really. Finding out he had more family, to Joleen's mind, would be nothing but good for Dekker.

The part about Lorraine, though. That was just terrible. And so hard to accept.

Lorraine Smith had been a quiet woman, and a little

bit shy, a person who tended to fade into the background in a crowd. Joleen had always thought of her as gentle. And good at heart.

Incredible, Joleen thought. Impossible.

Lorraine was not Dekker's mama, after all. Lorraine was a kidnapper, and Dekker was the baby that she stole.

She said, "I do wish you'd explained all this earlier. I got pretty worried. I thought all kinds of things, that you might be in danger..."

"I wasn't in danger. I just couldn't talk about it. Not then, when I first found out."

"I am not blaming you, Dekker. You did what you had to do. And that was to contact your brother and to share with him what you found."

"Which brings us around to the situation with Robert Atwood."

The quick shift in subject surprised her. For a few minutes there, with all this shocking news Dekker was laying on her, she'd actually forgotten Bobby's father and the threat he presented to Sam. "Wait a minute. What does your being Jonas Bravo's brother have to do with Robert Atwood?"

"Remember earlier I told you that money would be no problem?"

"Oh, Dekker, don't start with that again. I appreciate your offerin' to help out that way. It means so much that you would, but I told you, I cannot allow you to—"

"Jo, I'm a rich man now."

Her mouth was open, since he'd cut her off in the middle of a sentence. She shut it, then opened it again to say, "Huh?"

"The Bravos never gave up on the idea that I might be alive somewhere. Arrangements were made for me, a huge trust set aside, just in case I might someday show up again."

His words made her head spin. "Arrangements…a huge trust?"

"Right. What I'm trying to say is, I have millions, Joleen."

There was that word again. Millions. Millions in diamonds. And also… "Millions of *dollars?*"

"What else?"

"Well, I don't know. I can't…Dekker, are you serious? You are a *millionaire?*"

"I am serious, Jo. I am a millionaire." He was grinning again.

"Well. I can't…I don't…"

He chuckled. "You are sputtering."

"It's just…so much to take in all at once. Oh, what a crazy day it has been."

"It's not over yet."

She peered at him suspiciously. "There's more?"

"You bet. There's my solution to your problem."

That made her smile. "I knew it."

"Knew what?"

"That you had come up with a way to get me out of this mess."

"And I have. It came to me a few hours ago, while we were dancing. Like a bolt right out of the blue. You're going to think it's insane at first. But give me a chance, let me convince you."

"Dekker. What? Convince me of what?"

"I want you to marry me, Jo."

Chapter 5

Joleen discovered that she understood the true meaning of the words, *struck speechless*.

Dekker chuckled again.

And Joleen found she could talk, after all. "It's a joke, right? You are makin' a joke."

"It's no joke, Jo."

"Well, but you are grinnin'. And what was that sound I just heard coming out of your mouth? If that wasn't a laugh, I will eat that bouquet my sister made me catch tonight."

"Sorry." He took pains to arrange his expression into more serious lines. "I couldn't help it. You should have seen the look on your face. Like that time when you were…oh, about eight, I think. And that kid from up the block poured crushed ice down your pants."

Joleen was thinking that sometimes she wished she

hadn't known Dekker all her life. He remembered too many things she would just as soon forget.

He asked, "What was that kid's name?"

"Foster Stutterheim. I hated him."

"I think he had a thing for you."

"Well, and didn't he have a fine way of showing it?"

"He got your attention. You have to admit that."

"That's right, he did. I never spoke to him again."

"You were always way too hard on your admirers."

She thought of her one big mistake. "Not always."

Dekker's eyes gleamed at her. "Well, okay. There *was* Bobby Atwood."

"And I was *not* hard on him, and look where it got me."

He made a low noise in his throat. "Don't."

"What?"

"Don't start beating yourself up again."

"I won't."

"Good. We're dealing in solutions here."

"Right—and I still don't believe what you said a minute ago. Maybe you didn't say it. Maybe I just imagined it."

"I said it. And I want you to consider it."

"But Dekker, *why?* I mean, what good would our getting married do?"

"A lot. Remember, this is about appearances. About how things *look.* And it always looks better if a woman is not raising her child on her own. It looks better if she's married—and don't start making faces. I didn't say it was fair. I didn't say it was right. I didn't even say it was *true* that a married woman will necessarily be a better parent than an unmarried one. I'm just saying that people—and judges *are* people—tend to think of a two-parent home as the best thing for a kid."

"Well, I understand that, but—"

"Wait. I said I wanted a chance to convince you, remember?"

She nodded.

"Then will you let me finish doing that?"

"Sorry."

He continued, "I'm a rich man now. And if we're married, you're not going to be giving me any of that 'I can't take your money' talk. My money will be your money. One of Robert Atwood's arguments will be that he can provide for his grandson better than you can. If you're married to me, that argument is shot down."

"But, Dekker—"

He stopped her with a look. "I also want you to consider what's been bothering you the most. Which is how you're going to afford both good child care *and* the legal battle that's coming up. If you marry me, the cost of all that will be no problem. You can hire the best damn lawyers, and you'll be able to pay for top quality child care. Hell, if you want to stop working altogether, be there full-time for Sam, you could do that, too."

"Oh, I don't think so. You know me. I *like* to work."

"Does that mean I've convinced you?"

She wasn't ready to admit *that* yet. "I only said I like to work."

"So fine. Work. And put Sam in the best day care center in the city."

She had to admit that his arguments made sense.

But there were a few issues he hadn't covered—awkward, uncomfortable issues. Issues she felt a little bit embarrassed to bring up, even with her very best friend.

But still, they were issues that needed discussing before they did anything so wild and strange as to marry each other in order to keep Robert Atwood from taking her child.

"Say it," he said after a few very long minutes in which neither of them had made a sound. "Whatever it is, we can't deal with it if you won't get it out there."

She scrunched up her nose at him. "Well, I know that."

"Okay, then. Talk."

"It's just..."

"What?"

She stared at him, struck by the tone of his voice. He sounded...so excited about this. In the soft glow of starlight he looked eager and intent, his eyes focused hard on her, watching her so closely.

Such earnestness surprised her.

Most of the time it was hard to know what Dekker Smith was feeling. It wasn't that he *hid* his emotions, exactly. Just that he guarded them. He kept them in check. He could be warm and funny and gentle and kind. But most of the time he made it seem as though nothing was life-or-death to him. As if he could turn and walk away from anything, that there was nothing—and no one—he really *needed* to get by.

Of course, she had learned a few years ago how deep his feelings actually went. It had almost killed him when Stacey died.

But still, he didn't make a habit of letting what was going on inside him show.

Not so right now.

Now he did seem eager. And earnest. And excited.

Three words that, until that moment, she would never have used to describe Dekker Smith.

"Jo." His voice was gruff. "What *is* it? Damn it, talk to me."

She made herself say it. "It's just that, while I do love you and I know that you love me, it is not a man-and-woman kind of love. I guess I'm saying, what *about* love, Dekker? And, well, what about sex?"

He sent her a look of great patience. "Let's tackle one insurmountable obstacle at a time, all right?"

"Please don't make light. I think this is important."

"I didn't say it wasn't."

"But you—"

"I only meant that we'll work it out. Day by day, as we go along."

"Well, Dekker, I'm sorry. But I just can't."

"You can't take it day by day?"

"No, I mean I wouldn't feel right unless we came to some kind of understanding about what we're going to do when it comes to…the things that men and women do—and why are you looking at me like you find me *amusing?*"

"Because I do find you amusing—in a good way."

"Oh. In a good way, huh?"

"Yeah."

"That's supposed to make it all right that you are laughin' at me?"

"I am not laughing at you."

She made a humphing sound. "Well, I don't care. Whatever you're doing, it's not going to stop me from talkin' about this. Sex is a problem, and we have to face it."

"I disagree. Sex is *not* a problem. Not right now, anyway, not unless you insist on *making* it a problem."

"But…well, I mean, that's just not *us,* it's not what we are together. We are deep and true friends. But we are not lovers."

"Right. So?"

"Well, even if we didn't sleep together, if I was married to you, I would be *true* to you. And I would really hate it if you were not true to me. Marriage, even a marriage for practical reasons, is still a sacred trust, Dekker. A trust that should be respected and…" She could see that he was only waiting for his turn to talk. Fine. "What?" she demanded. "Say it. Go ahead."

"I would be true to you."

"You would?"

"Yes."

"But what if you—"

"Don't start in with the thousand and one possible reasons I might have for wanting to sleep around. I don't need to hear them. I said, I'll be true to you, even though we're not lovers."

"But what happens when—"

He cut her off, his voice low. "Fact is, it's just not that important to me."

She felt her cheeks warming. "It's not?"

"Right. It's not."

Maybe she had misunderstood him. "You mean, uh, you're telling me that *sex* is not that important to you?"

"Sex. Love—what you call man-and-woman love, anyway. When it comes to that, well, I'm pretty much dead meat."

Dead meat. How sad. Joleen had known that what had happened with Stacey had scarred her friend in a deep way. But she'd been telling herself he was slowly getting over the pain of that time.

Not so, evidently.

He went on. "I'd rather be with you than with a lover anyday. And I never planned to marry again—at least not until I thought of marrying you tonight. I've got to tell you, Jo. I like this idea. A marriage to you sounds damn good to me. Hell. To be legally a part of the family—of *your* family, and Sam's—sounds pretty terrific, as a matter of fact. Until you brought it up, I didn't even think of the sex issue. It didn't seem important. I guess I had some idea that, since Bobby Atwood did a number on you, you felt more or less the same way I do about love and romance and everything that goes with it."

Joleen found herself wondering, *did* she feel the same way—emotional dead meat when it came to man-woman love?

Well…

Not really.

"Oh, Dekker…"

He was sitting very still. "I'm listening."

She strove for just the right words. "I, well, I can see how you would think I don't want anything to do with love. The family drives me crazy, always after me to find someone, always telling me my turn for true love is comin' right up. Lately it seems like every wedding I go to, I'm the one who gets the bride's bouquet tossed in her face."

"They do it because they want the best for you," he reminded her gently.

"I know they do. I know all their hearts are in the right places. But still, it aggravates me no end. It's like the old saying goes. Once burned, twice shy. Bobby did

burn me. Bad. I just don't want a thing to do with it—
with love and romance—not right now."

"But?"

"Well, to you, Dekker, at this moment, because of the
seriousness of what we are considering, I am willin' to
admit something."

"Do it."

"Even on the day that Bobby turned his back on me,
even then, when I had to face the fact that I'd made a
worse mistake in judgment than my mama and my sisters ever made. Even then, I knew deep in my heart that
someday—maybe not for years and years—but *someday*
I would try again."

He looked at her levelly. "Years and years, Jo. Do
you hear yourself? You are talking about a *long* time."

"Maybe so. But still. Someday, I can't help but hope,
I will find love—and I mean the real and lastin' kind."

"Too bad you need a husband right now. A husband
with a fat wallet, a husband you can count on."

"Well, okay. You may be right, but—"

"Let me put it this way." He leaned closer. They'd
been talking quietly, but right then, he lowered his voice
even more, as if they were a pair of conspirators, as if he
were about to suggest the most dangerous conspiracy of
all. "You could marry me now. We could deal with the
Atwoods together, present a united front. And eventually, once the Atwoods are no longer a threat to you and
Sam, if you feel you've got to have more than I can give
you, well then, we'll end it."

She hated to say the ugly word, but it did require saying. "Divorce, you mean?"

He nodded.

She found herself leaning toward him as he leaned

toward her. "So. We could marry…" She was whispering, too, keeping her voice way down low so that only he could hear, though it was nearing two in the morning and they were alone in her mother's dark backyard. "We could marry and live together and be just what we are—friends, and that's all. But we'd also stay true, to each other. Respect our vows. And then, if the time comes when one of us wants more than the other can give, we would get ourselves a divorce."

He nodded again. "That's exactly right."

She thought of the family. "What would we tell everyone? Would we try to make them think that all of a sudden the two of us discovered we were in love?"

"However you want to handle it. Maybe calling it love would be the best way to go. You've got some pretty big talkers in your family."

He had a point there. She said, "Aunt LeeAnne comes immediately to mind."

"That she does. And it's possible, if we let it be known that this marriage is really for Sam's sake, the Atwoods might get hold of that information. They could twist it to make it look as if there's no real commitment between us, as if it's only a marriage on paper, entered into so that you wouldn't lose Sam to them."

"Well. And that would be the truth, more or less, wouldn't it?"

His gaze did not waver. "There is, always has been and always will be, commitment between us."

Oh, he was so right. They did share a very deep commitment. She swallowed, gave a nod.

He said, "Let me put it this way. If you think the Atwoods have a right to that particular truth, then we probably don't need to be having this conversation."

She took his meaning. "Because we might as well not be married at all, if Robert Atwood is going to be able to call our marriage a sham. That's what you're saying, right?"

He nodded.

"Okay." She flopped back against the cushion and stared up through the trees at the starry night sky. "So we'd need to make everyone think it's a real marriage, in every way. We'd need to—"

He chuckled again. "Jo. Settle down."

"Well, I want to get this all straight in my mind. I want to know exactly how we would manage everything."

"And I'm trying to tell you that we don't need to 'make' them think anything. We'll just say we love each other and we've decided to get married. I don't see why we have to go into any big explanations about what *kind* of love it is."

Easy for him to say. She sat up a little straighter. "Maybe *you* won't. You're the man. The women in my family will not be askin' you why, all of a sudden, you're getting hitched to your best friend."

"You can handle them."

"How?"

"Let them ask. Answer with care."

She knew he had the right idea. But she did hate evading and telling lies. If she and Dekker did this, she would have to lie at least a little and evade a whole lot.

She told him, "The family *will* have to know that the Atwoods are after Sam. Eventually, when we get to court, I don't see any way we could hide it. And then there's the babysitting issue. I'm going to have to tell my mama and my sisters why they suddenly can't watch my child."

"Our getting married will make that easier."

"How?"

"We'll tell them about the money I've got now, money that means you can start paying for day care, so you won't have to take advantage of them so much anymore."

For the first time since they'd started this particular discussion, Joleen felt a smile curving her lips. "Hey. When you say it that way, it doesn't sound bad at all."

"And it's the truth, too."

"Just not the *whole* truth."

"Truth enough."

Was it? Well, all right. Maybe it was.

He picked up his empty water glass. "I think I wouldn't mind a beer, after all."

"Help yourself." She gestured toward the coolers still lined up by the garden shed.

He rose from the chaise and went to get himself a cold one. Joleen let her head drop back to the cushion again.

Strange. The more Dekker had talked, the more he had laid out all the reasons they ought to get married, the more his crazy idea seemed like the best way to handle her problem.

He was right about a lot of things.

Like when he said that neither of them was in the market for a grand passion right now—and that maybe neither of them would *ever* be. In that case the marriage could turn out to be just right for both of them, and in a forever way, too.

But however long it lasted, she felt certain they could make a go of it, make it work. Make a *good* marriage. Maybe there wouldn't be passion or even sex. But she had lived without sex and passion for a good part of her life. Going without those things hadn't killed her yet. And Dekker had just told her—and really seemed to mean it—that he could do without them, too.

Oh, and they did have so much that they shared. Yes, sometimes he was closemouthed, even with her. But she *never* kept secrets from him. She loved nothing so much as talking things over with him. And the thought of having him at her side, as her husband, when she faced the Atwoods, created the sweetest, most wonderful feeling of relief in her troubled heart.

He came back to her, stretched his big body out in the chaise next to hers again. She heard the popping sound as he opened his beer. She turned her head to him as he drank and watched him with fondness, waiting for him to look at her.

When he did meet her eyes, she spoke softly. "Thank you. For bein' my true friend."

He set the can on the low table between them. "Are you going to marry me?"

"Yes, Dekker. I am."

Chapter 6

They broke the news to the family the next day, at dinner. Uncle Stan and his wife, Aunt Catherine, were there. So were Bud and Burly. And Aunt LeeAnne and Uncle Foley. They'd all come by in the afternoon to help with the after-wedding cleanup.

Uncle Hubert was there, too. He had never left. He hadn't been much use as a worker, since he was nursing a sick hangover from his excesses the day before, but he came to the table when Camilla called him, so he heard the announcement right along with everyone else.

Niki cried. And so did Aunt LeeAnne.

"Oh, what did I tell you, hon?" Aunt LeeAnne sobbed. "I said you'd be next and wasn't I right?"

Joleen handed her aunt a tissue, gave her a hug, and agreed that yes, she had been right.

Uncle Hubert said, "This calls for a little drink, to celebrate."

Aunt LeeAnne sniffed. "The last thing anyone needs right now, Hubert, is a little drink."

Hubert, sober right then and at least somewhat abashed after his behavior at the wedding, had the grace not to argue with her. "Pass those little red pepper things," he mumbled.

They were having take-out. Camilla had ordered five giant-size deep-dish meat-lover's-style pizzas to feed the hungry cleanup crew.

Niki grabbed a tissue of her own and blew her nose. Then she reached for another big slice. "Oh, I can't believe it," she sniffled and swiped at her still-leaking eyes. "Dekker and Joly…married. Dekker will be like my brother for real…."

There were more hugs, from Aunt Catherine and Uncle Stan. And lots of good wishes and hearty congratulations from Bud and Burly and Uncle Foley, too.

Camilla did not cry. She didn't say much, either, a fact that Joleen hardly noticed, since everyone else seemed to be talking nonstop.

After they'd finished off the pizzas, Joleen said she and Sam had to get on home. Tomorrow, after all, would be a workday. She had laundry to take care of and she needed to fit in a trip to the store. Her refrigerator was empty. In the past few days DeDe's wedding had put her own life completely on hold.

Dekker said he had to get going, too. He walked her to her hatchback economy car before climbing into his battered metal-flake blue Plymouth Road Runner, which he'd had since time began and which bore the dubious distinction of being a year older than he was.

Joleen strapped Sam into his car seat in back and then went around to slide behind the wheel.

Dekker shut her door and leaned in her window. "I thought it went pretty well."

"I thought so, too. But there's a lot more left to tell."

They hadn't even mentioned the change in Dekker's fortunes. That would take some explaining and seemed better accomplished one-on-one. Joleen would tell her mother and Niki the story privately. And she'd tell DeDe, too, as soon as her middle sister returned from her wedding trip.

And then there was the news about the Atwoods. They'd have to get into that unpleasant subject with the family at some point.

And the new babysitting arrangements would have to be handled, as well. As a rule DeDe watched Sam in the mornings, Joleen or her mother took over for a couple of hours after lunch. Then when Niki got home from school, she would be on duty until six or so, when Joleen got through at the salon. Dotty Hendershot, the sweet older lady who lived next door to Camilla, in the house where Dekker had grown up, would pick up the slack.

All that would change now. But further discussion last night had brought them to the conclusion that they didn't have to deal with the child-care issue right away. The wedding would be simple and soon—by the end of the week, they were thinking. And Dekker had proposed a honeymoon, one with Sam included. Dekker said he could afford it, and they both agreed it would be good to have a little time away together, just the three of them, at the start of their new life as a family.

So they would take two weeks for a wedding trip— destination to be decided in the next few days. And when they came home, Joleen would begin looking for the right day care for Sam. By the time the Atwoods geared up to drag her before a judge, she and Dekker would have all the bases covered.

Dekker touched the side of her face. "What is that frown for?"

"Just thinking about how much has to be done."

"Worrying, you mean."

"Maybe…"

"You worry too much, Jo. We'll get to it. To all of it. Little by little."

She produced a smile for him. "I know."

"One thing you do need to deal with right away. Your blood test. I'm going to get mine taken care of tomorrow."

"I've got no appointments between one and three. I'll see if I can fit it in then."

"Good. And what do you think of a week in L.A. and then maybe Maui for the other week?"

"L.A.? Would we visit your brother?"

"If that's okay with you. I have a standing invitation."

"We'd stay at his house?"

"That's right."

"But wouldn't that be inconvenient for him, on such short notice?"

Dekker laughed. "We could stay at Jonas's house for a month and never even set eyes on him, if he didn't want to see us. Angel's Crest is enormous."

"Angel's Crest?"

"The Bravo mansion."

"His house has a *name?*"

"That's right. Angel's Crest is on a hill, in Bel Air. It's an incredible place. Ocean and city views from just about every room in the house. It's been in the Bravo family for three generations, I think Jonas said."

"This is sounding very interesting."

"And did I mention Mandy? I want Sam to meet her."

"Who?"

"Amanda is two. She's Jonas's adopted sister."

"Wait a minute. Your, uh, *real* mother adopted a baby girl, before she died?"

"That's right. And now Jonas and Emma are raising her."

"So Sam will have an aunt who is two?"

"I hadn't thought of it that way, but yes. He will."

"Well, what can I say? Sam just *has* to meet his Aunt Mandy."

"Are you telling me yes to a week in L.A.?"

"I sure am."

"And then Hawaii?"

"Why not?"

"Or maybe I'll just wait. Keep it open-ended. We can decide what we want to do next after we get to L.A."

"That's fine."

"Okay, then." He stepped back from her door, touched his temple in a goodbye salute and headed for his own car.

Joleen returned to her mother's at eight-thirty the next morning. Camilla had agreed to watch Sam for a couple of hours. Joleen planned to run a few errands without the distractions a toddler presented before she opened the salon at nine-thirty. When she came to work herself, Camilla would take Sam to Dotty next door.

Camilla was never an early riser by choice. Usually, Joleen had to shake her awake and stick a cup of coffee under her nose any time she had babysitting duty before ten or so.

But that morning Joleen walked into the kitchen with Sam in her arms and found Camilla sitting in the breakfast nook, her coffee already in front of her, wide-awake and fully dressed.

Joleen started at the sight. "Mama. You're up."

"Yes, I am, baby," said Camilla in a determined tone.

Sam put both hands on Joleen's shoulder and gave a push. "Dow, Mama. Pway."

Joleen bent to let him to the floor. He toddled off toward the living room where Camilla kept a big bin of toys just for him.

"Has Niki already left for school?"

Camilla nodded, picked up her coffee and took a delicate sip.

"Uncle Hubert and everyone finally go home?"

"Yes, they did."

Joleen wondered why it felt as if something wasn't right. "Everything okay, Mama?"

Camilla answered by lifting a shoulder in a shrug.

"Well," Joleen said brightly. "Since you are up and about, I might as well get goin'. When's your first appointment?"

"I have got a facial and cosmetic consultation at eleven." Camilla didn't do hair anymore. She specialized in facial care—everything from herbal masks to makeovers. A couple of years ago she'd brought in a pricey new line of products, which she used and promoted exclusively. The line was a big success, mostly because Camilla had the knack for exploiting and enhancing the natural beauty of each of her clients.

"Okay, then." Joleen started for the front door. "I'll see you at eleven."

"Baby." Her mother's voice was flat.

Joleen turned. "What *is* the matter, Mama?"

"Have some coffee."

"I really want to get—"

"I know you do. You *always* do. But whatever it is can wait. We need to talk."

"Mama, can't we talk a little later? I've got to be at the shop in an hour and before that I want to—"

"Don't argue with me, now. Get yourself some coffee and sit down here with me."

"Mama, I have got to get goin'."

Her mother just looked at her.

"Oh, all right." Joleen got a mug from the cupboard, filled it and took the chair across from her mother. "Now, what is it that just cannot wait?"

Camilla had stopped looking at Joleen. Now she stared into her coffee cup, her mouth drawn down at the corners, as if there might be something in there that shouldn't be.

Joleen, who needed to get to the cleaners and make a quick stop at WalMart before she headed over to one of the major beauty supply houses to pick up a few popular products they had run low on, couldn't keep herself from making a small, impatient sound in her throat.

Camilla heaved a deep sigh and shook her head at her coffee cup. "I find I don't quite know how to say this."

That suits me just fine, Joleen thought. "It's okay. We can talk later." She started to stand. "Tonight, after—"

"No, you don't." Camilla's hand closed over her arm. "You are not escapin' me."

Joleen stared at her mother's hand, which was soft and slim, the smooth square-filed nails polished a shimmery bronze. It did not look like the hand of a fifty-year-old woman, not by a long shot. Joleen wished her own hands looked half that good. But Joleen still did hair. And she had no shampoo girl, so she spent a lot of her working life knuckle-deep in lather. Very hard on the hands.

Camilla said. "I have been awake half the night worryin' over you."

"Why?"

"Sit back down."

Joleen dropped into the chair again. "All right, Mama. I'm sitting. Talk."

"I am just going to ask you directly."

"I sure wish you would."

Camilla let go of Joleen's arm and threw up both hands. "What on God's green earth has possessed you to think a marriage between you and Dekker is a good idea?"

Joleen felt pure indignation. She decided to let it show. "Mama! I *love* Dekker. And he loves me."

Camilla smacked one slim, soft hand on the table and waved the other one in the air. "Yes, and I love your uncle Foley. But I never would marry him."

"Uncle Foley is your *brother,* Mama."

"Exactly. And that's how I love him. Like a brother. The same way that you love Dekker Smith."

Oh, this was getting sticky already. As Joleen had known it would, as she'd tried to get Dekker to understand it would.

Half-truths and evasions, she though glumly. Comin' right up...

"Well?" said her mother on a hard huff of breath.

"I love him," Joleen said again, and she stared her mother straight in the eye.

Her mother stared right back. "You don't love him

the way a woman loves a man," she accused. "And he doesn't have that soul feelin' for you, either."

"You do not know that," Joleen said. "You do not know what we feel."

"Oh, yes I do. I know my baby. And I know Lorraine's boy. I also know that you both deserve better than to marry a person who does not set your heart on fire. You both deserve it all. Passion and excitement. And magic. I want those things for you—and I want them for Dekker, too."

Joleen wrapped her hands around her cup. The warmth felt comforting against her palms. She said honestly, "Both Dekker and I had those things once, Mama. They didn't last."

"Bobby Atwood and Stacey?" Her mother made a low, scoffing sound.

Joleen's indignation level rose again. "Yes. Bobby Atwood. And Stacey. You know how Dekker was about Stacey."

"There *were* terrible problems in that marriage, baby."

"I know that. I am not saying they didn't have problems. I am only saying he loved her. In a passionate way. A *soul* way. And Bobby, well, it shames me to have to admit it now, but I was long gone in love with that man."

"Oh, that is *so* not true."

"Mama—"

"You *thought* you were long gone in love with that man. You *wanted* to be. You were waiting for your knight in shinin' armor to thunder in on a fine white horse and sweep you away. You waited a long time. When that young Atwood showed up, with his smooth talk and his fancy car and winnin' smile, you were like a nice, ripe peach, just ready to drop off the tree. And you did drop. You dropped good and hard. But that was not—"

"Mama—"

"Pardon me. I believe that I was still speaking."

"Fine. Speak. Finish."

"What I'm saying is—and you *are* listening, aren't you?"

Joleen gritted her teeth. "I am, Mama. I am listening."

Camilla's eyebrows had a skeptical lift—but she did continue. "What I'm saying is that what happened with Bobby Atwood was not it—was not love. And Dekker and Stacey, well, that was certainly *something,* but it wasn't *it,* either. Not the real, true, deep lifelong passion I am talking about. Not what I had with your daddy. Not what DeDe has with Wayne."

"Mama. Some people never find that kind of love."

"We are not talking about some people. We are talking about you. And Dekker. My first baby. And my best friend's little boy."

"Well, maybe you have to stop thinking of us that way—as your baby and Lorraine's little boy. We are grown people now. We have a right to make our own decisions about life. And about who we will love."

"I never said that you didn't. I just don't like this." Camilla looked into her cup again—and then sharply up to snare her daughter's gaze. "Something else is goin' on here. I know it. I can feel it."

Joleen kept her face composed—and told some more lies. "Nothing is going on, Mama. I don't know what you mean."

"Oh, you do. You know. There is something…." Camilla pushed her cup to the side and leaned across the table. "Is it…those Atwood people? You went off alone with them, didn't you, before they left the wedding Saturday? I saw you go inside with them."

Joleen opened her mouth to let out more lies. And then shut it. Camilla would have to hear the truth about the Atwoods sooner or later.

"Yes," Joleen said. "They wanted to talk to me."

"About…?"

Sam was too quiet. Joleen stood.

"What is it now?" muttered her mother. But Camilla had had three children of her own. She nodded. "Go on. Check—and then get right back in here."

Joleen went through the dining room. She found her little boy sitting on the hooked rug near the big window at the front of the house, playing with the wooden blocks one of the uncles had given him for his first birthday six months before.

Sam looked up. "How," he said, beaming proudly at the crooked stacks of blocks in front of him.

"Yes," said Joleen, her chest suddenly tight. "A very fine house." She would do anything—*anything,* including telling her dear mama a thousand rotten lies—to keep her boy safe, to be there whenever he needed her. To get to see his face now and then when he smiled like he was smiling now.…

She took in a deep breath to loosen those bands of emotion that had squeezed around her heart. Then she asked slowly, pronouncing each word with care, "Come in the kitchen? With Grandma and me?"

He shook his head and loosed a string of nonsense syllables.

"You mean, you want to stay here?"

"Pway."

She wanted to scoop him up hard against her heart,

to hug him until he squirmed to get down. But no. He was content, sitting on her mama's rug, playing with his house of blocks. Why ruin that?

"Okay. Be good."

"I goo."

Her steps dragging, Joleen returned to the breakfast nook. She slid back into her chair. "He's fine."

"All right. What did the Atwoods want to talk with you about?"

Joleen took a fortifying sip of her coffee. And then she told her mother everything that had transpired in her father's study before the Atwoods took their leave.

When she had finished, Camilla picked up her coffee cup, started to sip, realized it was empty and set it back down—hard. "Oh sweetheart, the nerve of those people."

"I hear you, Mama."

"I did not like that Robert Atwood. Right from the first I saw that he would be trouble. Thinks he's a cut above, doesn't he? That he's better than the rest of us. And the woman, Antonia? Well, I'm willin' to admit I felt sorry for her. Scared of her own shadow, and wearing *mauve,* of all colors. Much too cool for her. Just faded her right out to nothin' at all. She needs a bright, warm palette, to bring out that peach tone in her—"

"Mama."

"Oh, well, all right. I'm rambling and I know it. It's just, what else can I say, but how dare they?"

"I asked myself that same question."

Camilla folded those beautiful hands on the tabletop. "I think I am starting to understand it all now. You and Dekker have been scheming. You've decided that the two of you getting married is somehow going to help you keep the Atwoods from stealin' our Sam."

Joleen gulped. "No, Mama. Of course not. You asked me what happened with them, and I told you. It's got nothin' to do with Dekker and me."

"Oh, sweetheart. You are such a bad liar. You shouldn't even try it."

Joleen only wanted to get out of there. "I am marrying Dekker, Mama. That is all there is to it."

"But you don't *love* him—not the way you need to love the man you bind your life with."

Joleen stood. "I am saying this once more. I want you to listen. I do love Dekker. And Dekker loves me. We are getting married as soon as possible, and we are going to be happy. You just wait and see."

"But you don't—"

"Mama. Enough. You have said your piece, and I have heard it. This decision, though, is mine to make."

Camilla was shaking her head, her mouth all pursed up, brow furrowed. At that moment she looked her age—and more. She said, very softly and with heavy regret, "I know I was never the mother I should have been."

Joleen glared down at her. "You are *my* mother. If I was startin' all over, and God gave me a chance to choose, you are the one I would pick in an instant."

"Oh, baby…"

"Do not start in cryin' on me, Mama. I just don't have the time or the patience for that right now."

"I only…I wanted so much *more* for you."

"Well, this is about what *I* want. And I want to marry Dekker. I want to make a life with him." It surprised her, how firm she sounded. How secure in her choice.

On the counter, the coffeemaker made a gurgling sound, and somewhere outside, a leaf blower started up.

Camilla's tears spilled over, they trailed down her soft cheeks. "Well, I have told you my feelings on this."

Joleen held her ground. "And I have said what I will do."

There was a box of tissues, ready and waiting, in the center of the table. Her mother yanked one out. "I love you, baby."

"And I love you, Mama."

"And no mistake—" Camilla had to pause, to blow her nose. Then she started again. "No mistake is so big that love can't find a way to make it right in the end."

Chapter 7

Joleen fitted in her blood test later that day. The lab said she would have her results by Thursday. That night she and Dekker decided they would marry on Friday afternoon at the Oklahoma County Courthouse.

Joleen called DeDe in Mississippi.

"Oh, I cannot stand it," DeDe wailed when Joleen shared the news. "You are my sister and Dekker is the only brother I have ever known and if you two are getting married on Friday, Wayne and I are comin' home right now."

Dekker got on the line with her and managed to calm her down. He told her they would miss her, but on no account would he allow her to cut her honeymoon short. He finally got her to promise to stay in Mississippi for another week as planned.

Camilla, Niki and Sam would attend the short ceremony. As for the rest of the family, Joleen told them that she loved them all dearly, but she and Dekker could only have so many guests at the courthouse.

"Well then, do not have it at the courthouse, hon," argued Aunt LeeAnne.

Joleen explained that she wasn't quite up for planning another big wedding so soon after the one she'd put together for her sister. She said that she and Dekker just wanted to get the formalities over with and start living their lives side by side.

They all said they understood. But they didn't. Joleen could see it in their eyes.

"We *have* to do *something*," Aunt LeeAnne insisted. "Just a little family get-together when you come home from the courthouse. At least we can have that."

So it was agreed. After the civil ceremony, the cousins and uncles and aunts would be waiting at Camilla's. They would have chips and dips and little sandwiches with the crusts cut off. They'd bring a few wedding gifts and they'd offer their heartfelt congratulations.

At the courthouse both Niki and Camilla cried a lot. Camilla had no reservations about explaining to Joleen why she was crying.

"Because another of my babies is saying 'I do.' Because I know there is more goin' on here than I have been told about. Because, well, I do feel that I have been cheated of giving you the kind of wedding DeDe had, a real *family* wedding, which you know I believe every woman deserves…and because I wish my best friend could be here on this day of all days—but I know, if Lorraine *were* back with us again, she'd just be headin' off to jail. And that plain breaks my heart."

By then the whole family had learned the truth about Dekker's real identity.

And they hadn't found out quite the way Joleen and Dekker had intended.

* * *

Dekker had left his apartment Tuesday morning to find five reporters lurking outside. They all wanted to interview him, to get the first statements from the long-lost Bravo Baby. Dekker told them to get lost.

He got a call from his brother an hour or so after he chased the reporters away. Jonas told him that the story had broken in Los Angeles that morning. He urged Dekker not to let it bother him. He said it had been bound to leak out sooner or later.

"As a Bravo," Jonas warned. "You'll have to get used to being in the spotlight now and then."

"No, I won't," said Dekker.

Jonas laughed and assured Dekker that the whole thing would blow over eventually.

By Wednesday the wire services had gotten hold of it. The tale of how Dekker Smith was really Russell Bravo of the fabulously wealthy southern California Bravos made the second page of the *Daily Oklahoman*. And everyone in the family had been able to read all about it for themselves.

So part of the reason that Camilla cried through Joleen's wedding was because she had recently learned that her best friend in the whole world had not been Dekker's mama, after all, but the accomplice of the evil uncle who had stolen him from his *real* mother—who, as it turned out, had died just a few short months ago, never having seen her precious second son again.

Niki cried for her own reasons. Because her big sister and her beloved Dek were getting married, and because her mother was crying, and because...well, just because.

Dekker had found the time to go out and buy Joleen a ring. It was so beautiful—two curving rows of diamonds set into the band, surrounding a single large marquise-cut stone. He kissed her after the judge pronounced them man and wife—a light kiss, hardly more than a gentle brushing of his mouth across her own.

Right then her mother and sister burst into renewed sobbing. Joleen and Dekker turned from each other to try to settle them down.

They all went back to Camilla's house together, in the beautiful new silver-gray Lexus that Dekker had bought the day before. Two cars filled with reporters followed along behind.

"Ignore them," commanded Dekker, his voice a low growl.

Joleen granted him her most unconcerned smile. "No problem." And it wasn't. For her. She was a little worried about her new husband, though. Since Tuesday, news people seemed to be popping up wherever Dekker went. He was getting very tired of it.

"You go on in," he said when they got to her mother's. "Give me a minute."

Joleen put her hand on his sleeve. "What are you going to do?"

"Have a few words with the media."

"What will you say?"

"That I'd appreciate a little privacy on my wedding day."

"Don't you think that it might be better if—"

"Jo. Go in. I won't be long."

She could tell by the thrust of that cleft chin of his that it would get her nowhere to keep after him, so she got her son from his car seat and herded her mother and sister toward the front door.

The aunts and uncles and cousins and lots of finger

foods were waiting inside. Joleen moved from one set of loving arms to the next, getting kissed and congratulated by one and all.

"Well, don't you look beautiful," said Aunt LeeAnne, stepping back to admire Joleen's ivory-colored streetlength silk sheath and the short, fitted jacket that went with it.

Joleen thanked her aunt and kept an eye on the front door until Dekker slipped through it a few minutes later.

"How did it go out there?" she asked him, when she finally got him aside for a moment.

He shrugged. "They said they would leave."

"They're gone, then?"

"I have my doubts. They all have this kind of glassy-eyed, hungry stare when they deal with me. To them, I'm not even really human. I'm just a story they'll do anything to get. Maybe I should have listened to you and left it alone—and don't give me that I-told-you-so look."

"I'm sure I do not know what look you are talkin' about."

"The one on your face right now."

She made a show of crossing her eyes—and then grew more serious. "Did you tell them straight out that we just got married?"

"Hell, yes. They followed us from the courthouse, and that leads me to believe they probably already knew—which is just fine. Let Robert Atwood read all about how you've married the famous—and rich—Bravo Baby, let him think about the ways it will mess up his plans. Let him—"

"Hey, you two," called Uncle Hubert from over by the big bowl of sparkling-wine punch that Aunt Catherine had made. "Stop that whispering. Get over here with the rest of us. Time for a little toast…"

"Yes, come over here right now." Camilla paused to sob and dab at her eyes with a tissue. "We want to wish you both the best of everything."

Camilla cried until six-thirty. But then the doorbell rang. It was one of Wayne's bachelor uncles from the wedding the week before—the one who had stayed so late last Saturday night. The uncle, whose name was Ezra Clay, did not come empty-handed. He had a gift for the newlyweds and a huge bouquet of tiger lilies for the mother of the bride.

At the sight of her admirer, Camilla ran upstairs to freshen her makeup. When she came back down, she took Ezra Clay's hand and led him to the kitchen. They stayed in there for quite a while. When Joleen went in to hunt down more pretzels, her mother and Wayne's uncle were standing close together at the counter, a tall crystal vase in front of them. Half the lilies stood in the vase, half lay in wait, bright splashes of sable-spotted gold, on the counter.

Camilla chose a flower from those waiting on the counter, clipped the stem at an angle with her gardening shears, and carefully propped it up in the vase. Then she leaned close to Wayne's uncle and whispered something.

The uncle laughed, a low, intimate sound. Camilla laughed, too, and leaned close again to whisper some more.

Joleen watched them from the corner of her eye as she got a fresh bag of pretzels from the cupboard by the stove. Ezra Clay could have been anywhere from forty-five to sixty. He had intelligent dark eyes and nice, broad shoulders. He owned a couple of ice-cream store franchises, Joleen thought she remembered Wayne mentioning once.

Could this be the man who would convince her mother to settle down at last?

Sure. And maybe tomorrow the sun would set in the east.

Joleen closed the cupboard door. Whether Ezra Clay lasted in her mother's affections or not, Joleen was grateful to him. Camilla had not shed a single tear since he'd walked in the front door.

Romance, Joleen thought wryly, did have its uses.

Dekker, Joleen and Sam left the party at a little after nine. The reporters—who had *not* gone away when Dekker asked them to—snapped pictures when the newlyweds emerged from the house, their flashes explosions of blinding light in the warm autumn darkness. Then they jumped into their cars, ready to give chase.

Dekker swore under his breath as he swung out of Camilla's driveway. "They said they'd leave us alone for tonight, damn it."

"Well, they are not doing it." Joleen fastened her seat belt. "Take your own advice and ignore them."

Dekker muttered a few swear words under his breath. Joleen pretended not to hear. She smiled and waved at the family members who had gathered on the porch to watch them drive away.

"And how the hell am I supposed to see to drive?" Dekker grumbled as they took off down the street. He had to squint through the words Just Married, which Bud and Burly had scrawled on the windshield in shaving cream. There Goes the Bride was written on the rear window. And a bouncing row of tin cans clattered along behind them.

Joleen brushed the birdseed from her hair. "It's three blocks to my place. Take it slow and we'll make it okay." They'd chosen to stay at Joleen's house for the wedding night. First thing in the morning they were leaving for Los Angeles.

As soon as they turned the corner and all the waving relatives disappeared from sight, Dekker swung over and stopped at the curb.

"What now?" Joleen demanded, as one of the reporters' cars slid in behind them and the other rolled past the Lexus and nosed in along the curb just ahead.

Dekker whipped out his Swiss Army knife—the one with three blades, a corkscrew and just about every other tool known to man tucked inside. "Be right back."

"Dekker—"

He was out of the car before she could tell him to stay where he was. She watched him circle around to the rear bumper, where he crouched, disappearing from her line of sight. When he stood again, he had the cans, still hanging by their strings.

He came back to the front of the car and presented them to her. "Here. Do something with these."

Like what? she thought, but decided not to ask. She took them and set them on the floor next to her door. They rattled together as Dekker swung away from the curb. He passed the car in front before the reporter at the wheel had the wherewithal to shift into drive.

"I thought you said you couldn't see," Joleen reminded him as the powerful car picked up speed.

"I'm managing."

"Lord, I hope so."

"And this baby handles like a dream."

"Oh. Good news to all of us, I am sure...."

Sam laughed in pure glee from the backseat. He let out a string of almost-words, followed by a rousing, "Vroom-vroom-vroom!"

Joleen clutched the armrest and thought of all the times she'd suggested her friend ought to get himself a new car. And now he had done it. She could almost wish he hadn't.

But then again, his old Road Runner, which still sat beneath the carport outside his apartment building, boasted 383 cubes on a V-8 block—a fact he mentioned often and with considerable pride. If he'd been driving it right now, they'd be going at the same speeds—and the ride would have been a whole lot rougher.

They barreled around a corner, tin cans rolling at her feet. "Dekker..."

He wasn't listening. "Very fine," he murmured, "like a knife through warm butter..."

In seconds they reached another corner and spun around it. Joleen shoved the cans out of the way, braced her feet more firmly and told herself she ought to be grateful he hadn't bought that Ferrari he'd mentioned Wednesday.

"Maybe later," he'd decided, after considering the Ferrari. "First, I want to get us a nice family car."

The Lexus was a four-door. In Dekker's mind, that made it a family car, though clearly, what it had under the hood would stack up against that old Road Runner of his any day of the week.

They took two more corners at speeds faster than Joleen wanted to think about. Then at last Dekker applied the brakes. "Well?" he asked.

She glanced behind them. The dark street was deserted. "You lost them."

"Vroom-vroom-vroom," said Sam.

Dekker readjusted his rearview mirror. "You haven't seen any of them hanging around your place, right?"

"No, I have not."

"Good. Then maybe they haven't figured out where you live yet. Which means we'll be left alone tonight. And tomorrow, we are outta here."

"I cannot wait." She gave him a look, one that told him just what she thought of his driving so fast.

He grinned back at her, not sorry in the least.

Dekker drove around—at a sedate speed—for another fifteen minutes. "Just to make certain I shook those fools."

The dashboard clock said it was 9:33 when he pulled up in front of the tidy one-story house that Joleen had been calling home for a little over a year.

"We'd better hide this car," he said. "If our 'friends' decide to cruise the neighborhood, it would be a dead giveaway."

So Joleen got out and moved her own car from the small detached garage at the side of the house. Once Dekker had parked in the vacant space, she went to get Sammy. "And put those tin cans in the recycling bin," she said as she leaned in the car to free her son from his safety seat.

Dekker, who stood behind her at that point, made a put-upon sound in his throat and muttered, "What? You? Anal?"

She pulled her head out of the car just long enough to make a face at him before she reached back in to scoop Sammy out of the seat and into her arms.

* * *

Joleen's house was very much like a lot of the smaller houses in Mesta Park. A classic prairie cottage, it had no hallways. Living room, dining room and kitchen opened into each other, a bedroom off each. The single bath was tucked between the two back bedrooms.

Joleen had the room off the kitchen and Sam had the one in the middle. The largest bedroom, in front, with a nice window facing the porch but without direct access to the bath, served as her guest room. Dekker carried his overnight bag in there as Joleen took her son with her into her own room. She swiftly changed out of her wedding dress and into a pair of capris and a crop top.

Then Sammy had his bath. He went right down when she put him to bed, turning his face toward the wall and sighing in tired contentment. Joleen tiptoed from the room, switching off the light and pulling the door quietly closed behind her.

She found Dekker sitting in the kitchen, his back to the window, at the old pine table she'd picked up at a yard sale and refinished herself. He'd changed clothes, too. Now he wore faded jeans and an OSU T-shirt.

She tipped her head at the open Rolling Rock in front of him. "I see you managed to find the beer."

He picked up the bottle and toasted her with it—then set it down without drinking from it. "What a damn day."

"You said it." She got herself a Coke from the fridge and dropped into the chair across from him. "At least Uncle Hubert didn't get falling-down drunk."

"That's true. We need to be grateful for small favors. But I have a request."

"Name it."

"Can we stop having weddings for a while?"

She raised her right hand, palm out. "I do solemnly swear. If there is another weddin' in the next five years, we will not have a thing to do with it."

He leaned back in the chair, crossed his feet in front of him and tipped his beer at her again. "But what if it's cousin Callie's?"

"Callie is on her own."

"You think I believe that? If Callie and that cowboy tie the knot, you'll be planning the menu and helping her pick out her long white dress."

"Think what you want."

"And what about Niki?"

"What about her?"

"What if she decides to get married?"

"My baby sister is thirteen. I will not *allow* her to get married in the next five years."

"Maybe Camilla—"

"Dekker. *Please.*"

"I think she likes the ice cream man. A lot."

"She likes them *all* a lot. But they never do last, and you know that as well as I do."

"Who's the cynical one now?"

"I'm not bein'—" She cut herself off. Something had happened in his face, though his body remained just as before, slouched in the chair, totally relaxed.

"Don't tense up," he said low. "Pretend nothing has changed."

"Well, all right." She sat back herself, crossed her own ankles and drank from her Coke.

He winked at her. "You're a champion."

"Thank you. And what, by the way, is going on?"

"Keep your eyes on me."

"Okay..."

"I heard something. I think there's someone outside the window behind me—and don't shift your focus there."

"You mean—?"

"Reporters. It looks like they've found us, after all. But don't say it—don't say anything about it. Whoever's out there won't be able to hear much through the window, but the view of your face through those lace curtains should be pretty good, considering that the overhead light is on and the shades are up."

She understood. Whoever it was might be able to make out her words as her lips moved—though why it should matter, she wasn't quite sure.

Dekker said, "I want to give our uninvited guest a little taste of his own medicine. And do not start frowning. Please."

She put on a big smile.

"Don't overplay it."

She toned it down.

He shifted forward, drawing his legs up and resting his forearms on the table. "Lean toward me."

Still grinning—but not too hard—she mimicked his pose, which brought their noses within inches of each other. "Now what?"

"Now, I want you to kiss me."

Joleen almost blinked—but stopped herself in time.

"Just do it," Dekker whispered.

"But—"

"Humor me."

"What good is—"

"Jo."

That was all he said. Her name. It was enough to re-

mind her of the trust she put in him, of what a true friend
he was and always had been.

She would jump off a cliff for him if he asked her to.
What was a kiss compared to that?

She leaned even closer.

And their lips met.

His lips were soft. Warm. She wondered if hers felt
cool to him. And then she thought of their brief kiss at
the courthouse.

This made it two times.

Two times in her whole life that she had kissed
Dekker's mouth—and both of those times were on the
same day, their *wedding* day.

His mouth moved against hers. "Close your eyes."

It was a most ticklish feeling, talking together, with
their lips touching. She couldn't help smiling. "Dekker,
I know how to kiss."

"Do you?"

"Yes, I do."

"Well, okay then. Prove it."

Joleen rose to the challenge, letting her mouth go soft
and her eyelids drift down.

Several seconds passed. Very lovely seconds.

Dekker's mouth opened slightly against hers. She felt
the warm flick of his tongue.

It was…shocking.

Dekker's tongue. Touching the moistness just inside
her lips.

Shocking.

But not the least bit unpleasant.

Some part of her mind rebelled. This, after all, wasn't
what the two of them were about. Not Joleen and Dekker.
Brushing kisses—quick, fond pecks on the cheek—those

were all right. But nothing mouth-to-mouth. Nothing involving wetness. Nothing including tongues.

However...

Somebody ought to teach those reporters a lesson. And this would do it—though she wasn't quite sure how.

But Dekker knew. And that was good enough for her.

She sighed.

He made a low, teasing sound in his throat and went on kissing her. With tenderness. And considerable skill.

Not deeply, though. He never did more than skim the secret flesh right inside her mouth.

Not deeply...

A memory flared, bright as those photoflashes on her mama's front porch earlier that night.

Herself at the age of eleven. Spying on a sixteen-year-old Dekker, who was with Lucy Doherty, his first serious girlfriend.

They were kissing, Dekker and Lucy. Sitting on that little iron bench in the corner of Lorraine's backyard, kissing long and deep and slow. Joleen, behind the fence next door, could see them through the space between the fence boards.

So strange. All these years later. Here she was, her mouth against Dekker's mouth. Thinking of him kissing Lucy Doherty, of her own naughty young self, with her snoopy little nose pressed to the fence.

The way he'd kissed Lucy, now *that* had been a deep kiss.

Joleen was starting to wonder what it might feel like if Dekker were to kiss *her* deeply when she realized he was pulling away.

She sighed for the second time and let her lashes drift open.

His blue, blue eyes gleamed at her. "Good job."

"I aim to please." The words came out as a throaty purr. Did she intend them to? She wasn't sure. "Um, what now?"

"Now, we get up from this table and we go into your bedroom with our arms around each other. We want it to look as if, when we get in there, we're going to do what newlyweds usually do."

What newlyweds usually do...

The words set her pulse throbbing. Which was so silly. They were not *really* going to do what newlyweds do.

They were only going to make the reporter think that they would.

Why are we doing this, really? she wanted to ask. But she didn't quite dare. She still faced the window, and the light overhead seemed way too bright, too revealing. Whoever was out there might know what she said. That would ruin Dekker's plan—whatever his plan was, which she didn't know yet.

She didn't want that, to ruin her friend's plan—her friend who, as of tonight, was her husband, too....

But then, not *really* her husband. At least, not in *that* way.

"Ready?" he asked.

She swallowed. Nodded.

He held out his hand to her.

She laid hers in it—her left hand, the one on which she now wore the shining band of diamonds he'd given her at the courthouse. Holding on, he rose and came around to her side of the table, his eyes locked with hers the whole time.

He pulled her out of the chair and wrapped an arm

around her, tucking her in close to the side of his big, hard body. It was six steps to her bedroom door. He flipped the wall switch as they passed it. The kitchen went dark. He drew her over the threshold, kicking the door shut behind them.

She started to reach for the light switch, but he caught her hand. "No. Not the overhead light…" His breath teased her ear.

He left her, a shadow moving on silent feet, drawing the shades. Since her room was at a back corner of the house, there were two windows, one on the left wall next to the bed and one to the right of the headboard.

She remained at the door, waiting.

"And now?" she whispered, when both shades were lowered.

She heard a click as he switched on her bedside lamp. In its soft glow, he returned to her, took her shoulders in a gentle grip.

She frowned up into his shadowed face. "Dekker, what—?"

"Wait here. By the door. Don't get in front of the lamp. The light should draw him, but he shouldn't be able to see anything, really."

"But what are you going to *do?*"

Again, he refused to answer. "Wait here. I won't be long."

"But—"

He touched her mouth for silence. "Just wait."

She rolled her eyes at him and shrugged.

"Is that a yes?"

So she gave him the nod he seemed to require.

He went out through the other door—the one that led

to the bathroom and Sammy's room and from there, to the dining room.

Joleen slid to the floor. She wrapped her arms around her drawn-up legs and propped her chin on her knees.

Great. Now she got to wait, while Dekker played detective.

And what was the *point,* she wanted to know?

He'd already asked those news people to leave. It hadn't worked. He'd tried ditching them. Without success.

What else could he do?

She realized what and started to stand again.

But no.

She sank back down. She had told him she would wait here. Okay, she would wait.

And if he got himself into a fight tonight, he'd better be prepared to hear a few harsh words from her later. Because she would be sharing with him a large piece of her mind.

Dekker pushed open the door to Sam's room and froze, listening.

Once he heard the shallow, even breathing that told him Sam was fast asleep, he moved forward. He stopped at the door to the dining room. The faint sliver of brightness beneath it confirmed what he remembered; there was a light on in the front of the house, the floor lamp Joleen had switched on low when they first came in the front door. Other than that—and the lamp in Jo's room—the house was dark.

Good.

Dekker opened the door and slid through it, pulling it silently closed behind him. Keeping near the wall, he went beneath the arch into the front room, where that single lamp burned. He'd left the guest room door ajar. He ducked through it.

The shades were up in there. Dekker flattened himself against the wall by the window that opened onto the front porch. He waited.

Nothing. No sounds or movements beyond the window. He hoped that meant the porch was deserted, that the damn reporter was on the prowl around back, trying to get a look in Joleen's bedroom window, to steal a shot of the famous Bravo Baby making love to his bride.

The window creaked a little as Dekker slid it up. He slipped back into the shadows, waited some more. He heard only innocent noises: a horn honking a block or so away; wind chimes on the porch next door; the intermittent bark of a lonely dog in the distance.

Dekker counted to three hundred. Slowly. Then he moved into the window again, to unhook the screen. It swung out. He held it clear and went through.

The porch provided no surprises. Keeping as much in the shadows as possible, Dekker moved down to the opposite end, by the front room, and slid over the rail to the ground. The night was clear, bright with stars. The waning moon rode high, and there wasn't much cover on that side of the house. But he was in luck. No reporters lurked there.

Maybe they'd given up and gone away.

Or maybe they had moved around to the back of the house where he had hoped to lure them.

Swiftly and silently he covered the distance from the front porch to the back. He pressed himself to the wall at the end of the house and stole a look around the corner.

Yes.

The soft glow from the lamp in Jo's room showed him a figure—male—in dark pants and shirt, perched on the side rail of her small back porch, craning to see through the narrow slit between the blind and the window frame.

Perfect, thought Dekker. Off balance, with his back to me.

He slid around the corner and made for the porch steps.

His target barely had time to turn and grunt, "Huh?" before Dekker grabbed his arm, twisted it up behind him and yanked him down from the rail and hard back against his own body, keeping the arm up at an unnatural angle—and getting a nice, tight lock around the neck.

The camera around that neck swung as Dekker's captive struggled.

"Easy," Dekker whispered. "I'm not going to hurt you. We're just going to have a nice little talk."

The body in his grip stopped fighting him. "Whatever you say…"

Dekker knew that voice. He murmured a low oath. "Pollard."

"Got me."

"I thought you were a reporter."

"'Fraid not."

"What the hell are you doing here?"

"Man's gotta make a living, Smith."

Dekker gave his captive's arm a slight upward push. Pollard let out a sharp grunt of pain. Dekker whispered, "Who are you working for?" As if he didn't already know.

"Look. Could you ease off on the arm a little?"

"I want some answers."

"You'll get them. Just back the hell off."

Chapter 8

Joleen heard a thud on the back porch. And then faint scuffling sounds, followed by the mutter of low voices.

Dekker had found his man.

She listened for the heavy thumps and pained grunts that would have indicated a brawl in progress. She simply was not going to put up with any brawl on her back porch.

But no such noises occurred. So she kept her word and waited there on the floor of her bedroom, her back against the kitchen door, her knees drawn up to her chest.

Dekker returned to her the way he had left. He appeared in the doorway to the bathroom.

She gave a push with her feet and slid upright. "Well?"

He pulled the door closed behind him. "For the moment our visitor is gone. Too bad we all know he won't stay that way." Dekker held out his hand. "I confiscated this." A memory card sat in his palm.

Joleen stared at it and thought about the long, sweet, not-deep-enough kiss she and Dekker had shared at her kitchen table—the kiss, she reminded herself, that had been purely for the reporter's benefit. She wondered how many shots the man had taken through the kitchen window. Not that it mattered now, since Dekker had the memory card.

Dekker turned from her. He broke the card in half and dropped it into the wastebasket by the closet door.

Joleen went to the bed and sat on the edge. "I can see what you mean, about those reporters." She flopped onto her back with a sigh. "They get old real fast."

Dekker was silent.

She lifted her head off the bed and frowned at him. "What?"

"That was no reporter, Jo."

She hauled herself to a sitting position again. "Then what?"

"P.I.," he said flatly. "Name's Pollard. Dickson Pollard. Used to be on the OCPD. Now, he's on the payroll at Ace Security, the biggest—and some say the best—agency in the city."

Joleen felt her skin crawl. "Robert Atwood." Righteous indignation burned along her every nerve. "Robert Atwood hired him to spy on me."

"Jo. It's not exactly a big surprise."

"That man has probably been takin' pictures of me for weeks, hasn't he? Peeking in my windows, spying on my life."

"Look at it this way. The situation hasn't changed. You just know for sure now, that's all."

She scowled at her friend. "Why doesn't that make me feel any better?"

He came and dropped down beside her on the bed. "Because it's a violation of your privacy, of your right to lead your life without people who mean less than nothing to you—total strangers—poking their damn noses in it." There was heat in his voice.

She found her own anger had worn itself out. Weariness took its place. She leaned her head on his shoulder. "I think now I understand a little better how you've felt the last few days, with all those reporters following you everywhere you go. It's not fun."

"No. It is not."

"And I guess, even though you took the card from his camera, that detective will still be reporting what he saw to Robert Atwood."

Dekker made a low noise of agreement. "No way to stop him—short of keeping him captive or murdering him."

"But that's good, right? Robert Atwood will read in the papers that we are married. And Dickson Pollard will report that he saw us acting like newlyweds."

"Exactly."

They sat for a moment without speaking.

Finally, Dekker muttered, "I'll bet you're beat. We should go to bed." He started to stand.

She realized she didn't want him to go.

And, now she thought about it, he probably *shouldn't* go.

She grabbed his hand before he could get away from her. "Dekker…" He let her pull him back down beside her. "It just occurred to me. Maybe you ought to sleep in here—I mean, in case that Pollard guy comes back. If you're sleepin' in the guest room, won't that cause suspicion, about the two of us, about whether our marriage is the real thing or not?"

"I'll keep the light off and the shades down. You do the same. If Pollard does come back tonight, he won't have a clue where either of us is sleeping."

That made perfect sense. She felt foolish, suddenly, for suggesting otherwise. She just knew her face was cherry red.

"And after tonight," he added, blessedly oblivious to her embarrassment, "for two weeks, we won't be here to spy on. When we get back we'll find a new house. I'll make sure security there is state-of-the-art."

She forgot all about her red face. "We're going to move?" Joleen loved her little house. Her uncle Stan, who made his living buying rundown houses, repairing them, and then selling them again, had found it for her. Uncle Stan had also made sure she got a great price and small mortgage payments. She'd put in a lot of time and tender loving care to fix it up just the way she wanted it. "We didn't talk about moving."

"No, but we will have to move."

"*Have* to?"

He lifted an eyebrow at her. "You have a problem with moving?"

"I, well, I suppose I thought that you could just…" She let the sentence trail off.

He finished it for her. "Move in here?"

"Is that so impossible?"

"Come on, Jo. You've got one bathroom—accessible only through your bedroom and Sam's."

"We could add another bath."

"Why not buy a bigger house, something more suited

to the three of us? We can afford it. We can afford any damn house we want."

"But…" she began, then didn't really know how to go on. What he said did make sense.

"Jo." He was shaking his head at her. His eyes looked so soft. "I know you love your house. But there are going to be changes. You have to accept that."

She folded her hands in her lap and stared down at them. "You're right. And I…I want us both to be happy with this marriage of ours." She raised her head, gave him a smile. "We should live in a house we've chosen together."

Now his expression was the next thing to tender. "Did I ever tell you I like your attitude?"

"Some call me anal. Can you believe that?"

"Never." He cupped the back of her head in his big hand and pressed his lips to her forehead. When he pulled away and met her eyes again, she could still feel that kiss on her skin, a sensation of sweet warmth and gentle pressure.

He stood. "So who gets the bathroom first?"

"Be my guest."

"I'll be three minutes…max."

"No hurry."

"I'll just go in and out through Sam's room."

Awkward, she thought. This is awkward, the two of us, married but *not* married. Will it always be this way?

No, she told herself. Of course not. They would grow accustomed to living in the same house, to each other's day-to-day ways. They'd be like roommates, eventually. Roommates, only better. Because of the bond that had made them family to each other long before their marriage. Because they were the dearest of friends.

And their moving would ease the awkwardness, too. With a bigger house they could each have a lot more privacy.

"Jo?" He was staring down at her, waiting for her to answer him.

What was the question? "Oh. Sorry. Go ahead. Through Sam's room." He turned to leave her—and she stopped him before he could open the bathroom door. "Dekker."

He faced her again, lifted an eyebrow in an expression that said, *What now?*

She shouldn't have stopped him. Why had she done that? "Never mind. Go to bed."

"Not yet. You've got something on your mind. What?"

"It's stupid…"

"What?"

"Well, um, remember Lucy Doherty?"

He was frowning, puzzled. And why shouldn't he be? Lucy Doherty was a page from the distant past. She had gone away to college over a decade ago, married some med student and moved to Colorado, if Joleen remembered right.

"What about her?" he asked.

"Was that…were you in love with her?"

He folded his arms over his broad chest. "Weird question."

She shrugged, to show him that she agreed with him. It *was* a weird question, and she shouldn't have asked it. She wished she hadn't.

But she had, so she might as well get his answer.

Not that he would give it easily. He said, "I was sixteen years old."

"Meaning…?"

"I don't get it. What made you think of Lucy?"

"Oh, I don't know…" *Liar,* a critical voice inside her head accused. *You are a stone liar.* "I was just wondering…" *Wondering while you kissed me, remembering you and Lucy, the way I spied on* you *kissing* her…

Yes. That was the truth of it. His kiss had reminded her of watching him with Lucy. But she simply could not make her mouth say that truth.

Why not? She could—and usually did—tell Dekker anything and everything. But somehow, she couldn't bring herself to tell him this particular truth, not right now, not tonight.

You do not *tell him everything,* that critical voice insisted. And the voice was right. Somehow she'd never gotten around to telling him how she'd spied on him with Lucy, though it had happened almost fifteen years ago, was a meaningless incident, really, nothing to make a big deal over.

Well, and now she considered the question, why *should* she have told him that? It *was* years and years ago. Before her father died, when she had felt…safe. Secure enough with her world and her place in it to do naughty things now and then. She had as good as forgotten all about it.

Until tonight. Until Dekker had kissed her. Not deeply. But long…

"Jo, are you all right?" He was watching her too closely, that frown of puzzlement still creasing his brow.

She drew herself up. "I am fine. And it is late. Go to bed."

He lingered for just a moment, on the verge of saying more. But then he only muttered a good-night and left her, shutting the door carefully behind him, so that all she heard was the tiny click as the latch caught.

Joleen turned off the lamp—Dekker had said they should keep the lights off—and she kicked off her shoes and stretched out on her bed to wait for him to have his turn in the bathroom.

A minute or two later she heard him in there, heard the water running, heard the toilet flush. He finished, as he'd promised, in almost no time at all.

There was silence from the other side of the door. The faint clicking sounds from the early-model digital clock on her nightstand seemed suddenly very loud.

She should get up, wash her face, brush her teeth. But she just lay there, staring into the darkness.

Joleen lifted a hand, touched the pads of her fingers first to the space between her brows and then, very lightly, to her lips. Her eyelids drifted down.

She turned on her side and snuggled into the pillow.

An interesting way to spend a wedding night, she thought as sleep came creeping up on her—alone in her own bed, touching the places her absent bridegroom had kissed....

Chapter 9

By morning the reporters had discovered the address of the Bravo Baby's bride. A caravan of them followed the Lexus all the way to the airport.

Dekker didn't try to reason with them. He didn't yell at them to get lost. He didn't even rev up the Lexus and leave them eating his dust.

When Joleen praised his self-restraint, he replied with obvious satisfaction, "Where we're going, they won't be able to get to us."

Joleen began to understand what her husband meant, when they arrived at the airport and she learned that Jonas Bravo had sent a private plane for them. More than a plane. A jet.

"Jonas offered me the use of one of his planes when I flew home last week," Dekker said. "I turned him down, told him a commercial flight would do just fine. And then I ended up spending the night at O'Hare, holding up DeDe's wedding in the process. Not this time. If I have to learn to live with reporters tailing me everywhere I go, damn it, I'll get there fast and in comfort."

They landed at Los Angeles International Airport at just a little past noon. A long, black limousine was waiting to take them to Jonas's house in Bel Air.

Angel's Crest looked like the villa of some Mediterranean king. Of pinkish stone, with a red tile roof, the house crowned a hill at the end of a long curving drive lined in stately palm trees. From the back, which was visible most of the way up the drive, it was all carved stone archways, jewel-paned glass and glittering fountains. Also in back, across a spacious courtyard from the house itself, a rectangular swimming pool tiled in cobalt blue sparkled like a huge sapphire, catching and throwing back the golden rays of the southern California sun.

The limousine topped the hill and drove around to the front, where the view was simpler than on the way up. The facade consisted of two wings of that pinkish stone, each with a double row of large windows, upstairs and down. The wings flanked an imposing portico a story taller than the rest of the house. The portico boasted a row of smooth stone pillars and a mosaic-tile floor.

Beyond the giant, studded mahogany front door, a beautiful black iron staircase curved upward toward an arched ceiling three stories above.

"Palmer," said Dekker to the man who answered the door. "How are you?"

"I am quite well, sir. Yourself?"

"Fine. This is my wife, Joleen."

"Hi." Joleen held out her hand.

Palmer hesitated only a fraction of a second before clasping Joleen's fingers and giving a quick squeeze. "A pleasure, Mrs. Bravo."

Sammy, who'd been clutching Dekker's index finger and staring wide-eyed until then, stepped forward. "I Sam."

The butler gazed down at him and spoke gravely. "How wonderful to make your acquaintance, young man." Palmer glanced up and met Joleen's eyes. "Miss Mandy will be so pleased to find she has a..." He paused, stuck on the exact nature of the relationship.

Joleen came to his aid. "Nephew. Mandy is Sam's aunt. Stepaunt, I guess, if you want to get specific about it."

"Yes, of course. Her nephew. That's right." Palmer gestured toward the curving staircase. "May I show you to your rooms?"

Dekker asked, "My brother...?"

"He should be here soon, with Mrs. Bravo—that is, the *other* Mrs. Bravo. They've requested a late lunch—at two, in the small dining room, if that will suit you?"

"Sounds great."

"You remember the way to the nursery?"

Dekker said he did.

"If the boy is agreeable, you could take him there before proceeding to the dining room. Amanda's nanny, Claudia, will watch them both while the adults enjoy a more leisurely meal than would be possible with the little ones in attendance."

Since Sam was usually pretty good in new situations, Joleen gave a qualified yes. "We'll try it. Kind of play it by ear. See how he takes it."

"Whatever you decide. Just an option, you understand." Palmer led them up the stairs and down a couple of hallways, finally stopping to usher them into a spacious bed/sitting room. "I hope this will do."

The room took Joleen's breath away. Lush floral fabrics covered the sofas and the bed. Gold-threaded brocade curtains spilled to the floor around the ceiling-high arched windows. A heavily carved gilt-framed mirror hung over a fireplace with a mantel that looked as if it might have once graced the private rooms of some decadent French king. Glass doors opened onto a terrace, which overlooked the city far below.

Joleen found herself staring at the bed. It was huge, king-size at least, silk pillows piled high against the padded satin headboard. It was also the only bed in the room.

"The closets and bath are through there." Palmer gestured toward a door on a wall perpendicular to the one that led out to the hall. "And a room for the boy…" He strode over and opened a third door. "I had a bed with rails brought in—or is Sam still in a crib?"

"He's been in a bed for a couple of months now."

"Excellent. You'll find a large bin of toys suitable for a boy Sam's age in there, as well."

Sam picked up the important word, *toys,* and made a beeline for the room that had been set up just for him. Joleen followed as far as the door. She saw white-trimmed forest-green walls, a dark green rug on the burnished wood floor. It was cozy and inviting. And Sam was already digging into the toy box.

Joleen turned back to the adults in the main room. "It's just great," she said to Palmer. "You have thought of everything." Well. Everything except the fact that she and Dekker slept in separate beds…

The butler nodded. "Also, there's a smaller bath, on the other side of the child's room."

"Thanks, Palmer," Dekker said.

"You are quite welcome, sir. Your bags will be brought up right away."

Palmer left them.

Joleen felt Dekker's eyes on her. "One bed," she said softly.

"Yeah." His smile was rueful. "I noticed that."

"I take it you didn't tell your brother about our… situation?"

"That's right. Though I trust him." That was a rare thing, coming from Dekker. He was so cautious. He hardly trusted anyone.

"You know him that well? In the few days you spent here?"

"Yeah. I think I do. It's crazy, I know. A lot of it's just…a sense I have of him. An instinct. But there are also his actions. Like the way he handled himself when he tracked me down back home. He told me the facts straight out, no hedging around. When I refused to believe him, he didn't argue, just gave me his card, with all his private numbers on it, so I could reach him any time I wanted to. When I showed up here a few days later, he was ready for me. He's a very busy man, but somehow he found time for me. A lot of time. That's how he's been with me. Never pushing me, but right there, prepared to face whatever needed facing, as soon as I was willing." He sent her a sideways look. "And I want to talk to him, about the problem with Robert Atwood. If that's all right with you."

"You think he could help us?"

"I think he has resources and…methods of action at

his disposal that we wouldn't even dream about. I have no doubt he could crush Atwood like a bug, if it came to that."

Joleen looked at her friend with alarm. "*Crush* him?"

"I meant financially, that Jonas would know how to ruin him."

She sent a furtive glance toward the other room and lowered her voice so her son wouldn't hear. "I'm not having any part in crushing Sammy's grandfather, financially, or otherwise, no matter how rotten a human being he might be."

"Settle down, Jo. I said Jonas *could* crush him, not that I'd ask him to. I was trying to make the point that Jonas might provide other...options. Other ways to approach the problem."

"Oh." She dropped onto one of the beautiful sofas and stared up at him, contrite. "Sorry. I'm edgy, I guess. The plotting and planning just never seem to end."

"I only want us to be as prepared as we can be."

"I know you do. And I'm grateful, I really am." He was a wonderful friend to her. The very best. She straightened her shoulders. "All right, then. I agree. We'll talk to your brother."

"Good—but I still think we should keep the exact terms of our marriage to ourselves, the same as you did with Camilla."

Joleen had given him a complete report of her conversation with her mother. "I don't really think it's the same. You know how Mama is. Sometimes she talks too much. It's different if your brother can keep the truth to himself."

Dekker shook his head. "Why lay that on him? Why make him responsible for keeping our secrets? No. If we're going to do this, we have to do it right. Everyone has to believe we are married in *every* way."

But we are *not* married in every way, she thought, irritation rising again. Really, all they did lately was scheme. And since last night—their wedding night—it seemed that they were constantly dealing with the issue of sex, with the fact that they weren't having any and no one was supposed to know that they weren't.

Which was what they'd agreed on.

She'd better remember that.

Chin up, she told herself. It's a reasonable plan and we're going to stick to it. Stop feeling all put-upon and focus on solving the problem at hand.

She spoke briskly. "Okay. We have more of us than beds to sleep in. What do you think we should do about it?"

"I can take Sam's room. And he can sleep in here with you."

That sounded like a sensible solution. "Okay, that should—"

Someone tapped on the outer door. Dekker went and let in two maids who were carrying their luggage. "Just put it all right there." He indicated a spot near the door to the closets and the bath.

Dekker waited until the two women had left them alone again before he turned to Joleen. "On second thought..."

"What?"

"This house is crawling with service staff. If we sleep in separate rooms, my brother might never know—but the maids will."

She didn't see how the maids would find out anything. And she also didn't see that it mattered—which must have shown on her face.

He made a low, impatient noise in his throat. "Jo. They make the beds. They change the towels, empty the wastebaskets. They see everything. No matter how careful we are, after a couple of days, they will get the picture that you and Sam are sleeping in here—and I'm in there."

"Oh, come on. Does it really matter what the maids know?"

"Use your head. Why would we let some stranger in on a secret we're not willing to share with my brother or your mother?"

Scheming, she thought again. Plotting and planning. And always having to make sure everyone thought they were lovers when they were not.

"What is the maid gonna care?"

"The maid might care a lot. If the right person got to her. If she was paid enough to share what she knows."

"This is too much. You are kiddin' me."

He just looked at her, wearing that stony expression he got when he was not going to budge about something. She threw up both hands. "Well, fine. So what do we do?"

"Sam will have to stay in the other room. And the two of us will sleep in here."

Her heart did a funny little stutter inside her chest. "Together?"

He gave her a lazy grin. "Is that a request?"

She saw that he was teasing her, and felt relief—didn't she? "Very funny."

He was all seriousness again. "You get the bed. I'll take one of the couches. I'll just use a pillow and a blanket, and I'll put them away every morning before we go down to breakfast. All my things, though, will be in this room, with yours. We'll share the main bathroom. That should be enough to make it appear that we're also sharing the bed." He paused, then prompted, "Well? What do you think?"

"I think that you have been in the detective business for way too long."

"Maybe I have. That doesn't change the situation we have to deal with here. What do you say?"

What *could* she say? He was probably right. He usually was, in matters of this kind. "Okay, okay. We'll share this room. But I'm smaller than you. I'd probably be more comfortable than you would on the couch."

"Offer again, and I won't say no."

"We'll switch off. That's fair."

"Can't argue with that."

"Mama." Sam came toddling through the door to the smaller room. "Potty?"

He was in training pants. And he was doing just great, too. Day by day, the accidents were fewer and farther between.

"Right this way." She caught his little hand and led him back through his room to the bath on the other side.

They took Sam to meet Mandy and her nanny before they went down to join Jonas and his wife. Mandy was a beauty, with thick black curls and dark eyes.

She fluttered her impossibly long eyelashes at them, then picked up a stuffed dragon and bopped Sam on the head with it. Sam grabbed it away from her and bopped her right back.

They stared at each other for a long and dangerous moment. And then they both grinned.

Mandy turned for the stacks of blocks in the corner. Sam waddled right along behind her.

"He'll be fine, *señora,*" promised the pretty young nanny.

Joleen's gaze was still on her son. "Sammy, we'll be back soon."

Sam didn't even glance her way. He was already squatted on the floor, helping Mandy add to her stacks of blocks.

Dekker muttered, "That kid really misses you when you go."

"No separation anxiety," she told him loftily, turning to look him square in the eye. "That is a good thing. My son is secure with his world and his place in it."

Dekker kept a straight face, but those midnight eyes were gleaming. "I never doubted that."

"You'd better not." She reached out, took his arm.

It was such a simple gesture, something she'd done a hundred times before.

But this time it was…different. A tiny thrill passed through her, a shiver laced with fire. And she found she was all too aware of the feel of his forearm under her hand, the texture of the hair there, the warmth of his skin, the hard muscle beneath.

And Dekker had picked up her reaction—though it was achingly obvious he didn't understand it. He frowned down at her, baffled. "Jo?"

She laughed and tossed her head—to clear it of this sudden crazy notion that touching Dekker excited her.

"You okay?" He was eyeing her with extreme wariness.

She flashed him her brightest smile. "Better get downstairs, don't you think?"

"But are you sure you—"

"Dekker, let's go. Your brother is waiting."

Jonas Bravo looked a lot like Dekker. Uncannily so, Joleen thought when Dekker reintroduced them. He had those deep-blue eyes that looked black as midnight from certain angles. And that cleft in his square chin.

The two were built a lot alike, too—big—with thick, wide shoulders and muscular arms. So odd she hadn't noticed the resemblance that first time she'd met Jonas, a couple of weeks ago, when he and his wife had shown up at her mama's door.

But she'd been so distracted that day, with all the details that went into planning a wedding. And she hadn't been looking for Dekker's long-lost big brother to come knocking out of nowhere. She'd believed as she'd always believed: that Dekker was Lorraine Smith's beloved only son. And she had *seen* what she believed.

Amazing how much things could change in the space of two weeks.

Joleen had liked Jonas's wife right from the first. At second meeting, she saw no reason to alter her opinion of Emma Bravo, who had chin-length hair the color of moonbeams, a taste for bright colors and tight, short skirts—and a smile as big as Texas, which was her home state.

Dekker teased Emma that he'd missed her the last time he'd been in town.

The beauty mark by Emma's red mouth disappeared as she grinned. "Jonas and I had a few things to…work out." She put her hand lightly on her husband's arm. The two shared a look that made the air shimmer with heat.

Jonas said, "She's decided she'll never leave me again."

Emma's smile was slow and knowing. "He is stuck with me now."

Joleen thought she'd never seen a man so happy to be stuck. And she felt a little stab of something that just might have been envy.

She heard her mama's words in her head. *Passion and excitement. And magic. I want those things for you—and I want them for Dekker, too….*

It was about as clear as the view through the window that looked out on the pool that Jonas and Emma had all those things. And more.

Joleen slid a glance at Dekker, who was looking at the other couple right then. And she couldn't help thinking of that moment upstairs in the nursery, when she'd taken his arm and shivered at the feel of him under her hand.

Had that really happened?

Well, of course it had.

She knew it had.

But what did it *mean?*

Oh, well, what a silly question. She knew what it meant.

Something had changed. Something had…shifted. It had started last night, with the long, sweet kiss at her kitchen table, the kiss he had intended only for the benefit of the man watching them from outside, the kiss that, Joleen was reasonably sure, had meant very little to her lifelong friend.

Too bad she couldn't say the same thing for herself.

Since that kiss, she had started seeing her best-friend-turned-husband in a whole different light. They'd barely been married for twenty-four hours. And already she was changing her mind about a few things.

Changing her mind in a large and scary way—which

was probably the reason she'd felt so edgy, back in their bed/sitting room, when they got into it, *again,* on the issue of sleeping arrangements.

She was starting to wonder why they didn't just forget all about this big secret they were keeping. If they went ahead and slept together, there wouldn't *be* any secret to worry about. They would be married, in *every* way. It wouldn't matter who spied on them, who made the bed, or who changed the towels in the bathroom. It wouldn't matter if reporters or private detectives crept around outside their windows trying to get a glimpse of what was going on in there. All anyone who watched them would find was a pair of newlyweds doing exactly what newlyweds do.

But there was a big problem with that idea: Dekker himself. She recalled the baffled look he had given her when she'd touched him and felt what she'd always sworn she didn't feel—not with Dekker, not with her dear, dear friend.

He just didn't get it, didn't see what was happening to her.

He didn't *want* to get it.

Not that she could blame him. It wasn't part of the deal, for her to go and get turned on by him. She'd told him it would take her *years* before she'd allow herself to get involved with a man romantically again.

And he'd made it so carefully, painfully clear that he wasn't interested in anything like that, either. That he didn't believe he would *ever* be interested.

Dead meat, he had called himself. Emotional dead meat when it came to man-woman love…

What did that *mean,* exactly? She should have probed further on the subject, that night a week ago, when they'd first cooked up this marriage scheme in her mother's dark backyard.

Was he...did he mean that he *couldn't?* That he wasn't capable, physically, of making love? Was it possible that the scars Stacey had cut into his heart went that deep? That he couldn't even share pleasure with a woman anymore?

Looking back on a few things Stacey had said during the really rough time at the end of their marriage, well, maybe there *had* been some problem in that area. Back then Joleen had chalked up those remarks to Stacey's natural tendency to overdramatize every little thing. And Stacey had been so...messed up, by then. So terribly confused and out of touch with reality. She had said a lot of things that bore no relationship at all to the truth.

So most likely Dekker had meant it more in the *emotional* sense. That, emotionally, he wanted nothing to do with man-woman love or anything that went with it. That *was* how he'd put it: *emotional* dead meat—or had he?

Had *he* been the one to use the word, *emotional?* On deeper reflection, she couldn't be sure. It might have been Joleen herself, putting her own spin on what he had told her.

Down the table Emma laughed. She was talking about the business she owned, a pet grooming shop in Beverly Hills. She and Jonas were making plans to open more of them.

And Dekker had turned. He was looking at her now. He had one brow lifted. Joleen knew he was wondering what she could possibly be thinking about. She sent him a quick, tight smile, shifted her glance away, picked up her fork and turned her attention to finishing her meal.

At least, she pretended to concentrate on the food.

But her mind really was a thousand miles away, tracking the past—the events that had shaped them. The people who had made them what they were.

Well, not *people*. One person.

Stacey…

Chapter 10

Dekker rarely would talk about Stacey. But Joleen knew most of the story, anyway.

After all, Stacey had been Joleen's friend first. And when things got bad, Joleen was the one Stacey came to in her misery, the one Stacey confided in.

And Stacey had not always been so...difficult. So desperate and sad. At the beginning, well, she was really something. So much fun...

Like a sudden light in a dark room, blinding but welcome. That was Stacey. Joleen had been drawn to her from the moment they met—at Central States Academy of Cosmetology, when they were both nineteen.

There was something purely magical about Stacey. Something bigger than real life. It was as if she wove a spell, with the music of her laugh and the aura that surrounded her, an aura of excitement and...what? *Specialness,* maybe.

Stacey was everything Joleen wished she could let herself be. Stacey never had small emotions. She cried and laughed with total abandon. She never fretted. Never worried—or that was how she came across at first. She and Joleen were about the same size, both had brown hair and dark eyes. But the resemblance ended there.

Stacey was a little like Joleen's mother and sisters. Prone to making big drama out of the smallest events. Stacey loved roller coasters, for heaven's sake. And she had a *tattoo,* which had seemed to Joleen to be so wonderfully brazen and daring. At tattoo of a blood-red snowflake, low down on her back, so low down it was really more on her bottom—the left side, just above the dimple.

"Snowflakes are the most perfect, most beautiful thing in nature," Stacey told Joleen. "And no two of them are ever alike. And they don't last, they are gone in a moment, melting on your tongue. Except for *my* snowflake. I'll have it my whole life."

Which, as it turned out, hadn't been all that long.

The truth was, Dekker and Stacey were a disaster together. Their love was hot and passionate and all consuming. Their marriage had been a runaway train—something big and powerful and out of control, plummeting down from the crest of a high mountain, headed for a crash of stupendous proportions.

And Joleen was the one who had introduced them. On Easter Sunday. At her mama's house.

· Stacey didn't have any family to speak of. Her parents had divorced when she was seven. Her mother had remarried and lived in Colorado somewhere. Stacey didn't know where her dad was. She hadn't seen him in ten years, she said. Stacey said she loved how, even

though Joleen's dad had died, the family hadn't broken
up. Joleen and her mother and her sisters still shared the
family home. Joleen had aunts and uncles, from both
sides, and they all got together on a regular basis. Stacey said she *longed* for that kind of family connection.

Stacey came for dinner that Easter, when she and
Joleen were both nineteen. And Dekker came, too.

He'd been a little late, as Joleen remembered it. He'd
had his own place for four or five years by then. But he
was a dutiful son and would often visit his mother—or,
rather, the woman they had all believed at the time was
his mother.

And he would always try to make it over for family
events. Then again, he *had* been ambitious back then.
Totally dedicated to getting ahead. He'd worked long
hours with the OCPD, and sometimes he just couldn't
get away.

He had come to dinner that Easter, though. He had
walked into the house and set his eyes on Stacey, and
that was that.

"Who's your friend, Joly-Poly?"

Joly-Poly. He used to call Joleen that, back then. She
hated it. Joly-Poly. Roly-poly. They sounded way too
much the same. And roly-poly, everybody knew, meant
fat—which Joleen was not. Or it meant those little gray
armadillo-backed bugs that squeezed up into a tight little
ball if you touched them.

She'd answered him grudgingly. "This is Stacey. And
you'd better be nice to her."

"Oh, I will. Real nice. As nice as I can be."

Joleen had seen it all, then. In the way Dekker was
looking at Stacey—and the way that Stacey was staring back at him, all that specialness, that magic she had,

shining in her eyes. Zap. Hit by the thunderbolt, like in that old movie, *The Godfather,* both of them. Goners.

They were married six weeks later. And almost immediately things had started going wrong....

"Right, Jo?" she heard Dekker say.

Joleen blinked. "I...pardon me?" She gave her husband her brightest smile.

He looked at her as he had in the nursery—as if he was worried about her. And as if she made him a little bit nervous.

But that look only lasted a fraction of a second. She doubted their hosts had even noticed it.

"I said, the reporters don't bother you, the way they get to me."

She picked up her water goblet and sipped from it, giving herself a minute to pull her wandering mind fully back to the here and now. "That's right." She set the goblet down. "But then, I've only had them tailing me since yesterday. I'm sure it's not gonna take long until I'll be as fed up with them as Dekker is."

Emma sighed. "When Jonas and I got married, it was the same. I couldn't take a step without tripping over some newshound."

"It became necessary," Jonas said, "to throw the hounds a bone."

Dekker took his meaning. "A press conference."

"Right. We'll set one up for Monday or Tuesday. You talk to them on your terms, in a formal setting. Tell them how happy you are, how much in love, whatever you're willing to let them know. The point is, you can plan ahead what you're going to say to them. *You* control the situation. Give them enough to make a decent story and they'll leave you alone—for a while, anyway."

"At this point, I'll try anything," said Dekker.

"As I said, we'll set it up ASAP."

Dekker slanted Joleen a look. She read the question in his eyes. He was wondering if she was ready to talk about the Atwood situation.

Joleen nodded. "Might as well get it over with."

Emma laughed. "What is this? Get *what* over with?"

Dekker said, "We have…another issue we could use some advice on."

"Tell us."

So Dekker told them. He did the job much more simply and efficiently than Joleen could have managed—only leaving out the connection between their sudden marriage and Robert Atwood's ultimatum. And, of course, the depressing details of their sleeping arrangements.

Joleen felt the eyes of her host and hostess on her more than once during the telling. And she had a sense that they both easily deduced what Dekker was leaving out—well, maybe not the secret of their nonexistent sex lives, but certainly the fact that they had married to give Joleen a better defense against Robert Atwood's potential claims of her unfitness as a mother.

"It sounds to me as if you've made all the right moves," Jonas said when Dekker had finished. "Stay married—happily, of course. Provide the best of everything for that little boy. And by that I mean a good, stable, loving home as well as all the obvious things that your money will buy. If you do all that, I'd say that bastard can't touch you."

"I thought so, too," Dekker agreed.

"I think we should go ahead and see Ambrose on Monday, though," Jonas said. "I'm about 99 percent certain he'll tell us there's nothing else to do until Sam's grandfather makes his next move. But there's no harm in checking with him, in case there's something we're not seeing here."

Emma must have noticed Joleen's questioning look. She explained, "Ambrose McAllister handles all the personal legal matters for the Bravo family. He's been doin' it for more than thirty years. He is the sweetest, dearest man. And smart as they come, too. You will love him."

Joleen tucked her napkin in at the side of her empty plate. "I truly do appreciate all this."

Emma grinned. "No thanks are needed." She pushed back her chair and stood. "Now, let's head on upstairs. I have a nephew up there and I want to meet him."

It was the kind of day Joleen had read about and seen in movies: a real California day. Not a cloud in the sky and seventy-eight degrees at four in the afternoon.

Emma suggested it might be fun if they all went on out to the pool. She said they didn't need to go back to their rooms to change.

"You all can just choose what you need from the cabanas. Palmer always keeps them stocked like a department store, with everything from bathin' suits in all sizes to air mattresses, goggles and snorkeling gear."

Joleen laughed. "What about sunscreen?"

"Honey, that's in there, too. Name your brand."

So they all trooped out to the pool area, which had three cabanas, one for men, one for women—and one that was done up just like the poolside bar at some fancy hotel. Emma even went and got her dogs—a couple of cute and very well-mannered miniature Yorkshire terriers that she explained had first belonged to Jonas and Dekker's mother, Blythe.

The dogs sat in the shade of the loggia, which was a long colonnaded back porch beneath the big terrace off the master bedroom suite. The dogs looked so sweet and eager, wagging their tails and panting with happiness, as if just being there tickled them pink.

The humans, on the other hand, suited up and swam in the cobalt-blue pool. Mandy and Sam splashed around on inflatable toys in the shallows, with the nanny there to tend to their every whim.

With Sam so well taken care of, Joleen even dared to stretch out on an air mattress and close her eyes for a few minutes. It was a little bit of heaven, just floating there in the blue, blue pool under the paler blue of the California sky.

But then she felt the slight tug on the side of the mattress and knew without opening her eyes who it was.

She didn't move, didn't speak. Kept her eyes shut. Maybe, if she didn't acknowledge him, he would just swim away. For several long and lovely minutes, she had not even thought of him. It had been real nice, for a change, not to have her lifelong-friend-turned-husband-turned-object-of-impossible-desire dominating her every thought.

But then he had to go and dribble cool water over her sun-warmed thighs.

"Dekker," she muttered, "I am tryin' to relax here."

More water dribbled over her. She opened her eyes—just to slits, enough that she could see he was scooping water into his palm and pouring it on her in a trickling stream.

"Stop," she said.

He didn't.

She turned her head and met those eyes that, right then, seemed to just about exactly match the cobalt blue of the pool. He was grinning, like a naughty kid up to mischief and enjoying it.

"What part of 'stop' was unclear to you?"

The grin faded. "Something's bugging you." He spoke low, for her ears alone. "What?"

"Nothing is—" She cut herself off. Lately, she'd been telling way too many lies. But not to Dekker. She never lied to Dekker. Was she going to start now?

He was waiting, treading water inches from her air mattress, dark hair slick and shiny as the pelt of a seal, water drops gleaming in his brows and lashes, dripping in little rivulets down the strong column of his neck.

A forbidden urge assailed her—to lean close, stick out her tongue, lick the water right off his neck, then slide her tongue upward, over that wonderful dent in his chin and straight to his lips.

"Damn it, Jo. What is going on?"

She snapped her guilty gaze away from his mouth— and up to meet his accusing eyes. "I…" She sent a swift glance around them. Jonas and Emma were sitting side by side, on the edge at the deep end, dangling their legs in the water, with eyes only for each other. The kids and the nanny paddled happily in the shallows.

No one was looking at them. But still, it was hardly the time or the place to talk about this—if there even was such a time, such a place…

Trailing gleaming drops of water, Dekker lifted a hand and clasped her arm just below the elbow. It was a touch intended to reassure, she knew. A touch that meant, *I'm here. You can trust me. You can talk to me.*

But it didn't work.

Because heat went zinging through her, a bullet of longing, ricocheting up to her shoulder, zipping back and forth around her heart and then zooming on down to her belly—and lower.

"Don't!" She jerked away.

Dekker stared at her for a long, awful moment. It was a stunned, angry stare—and an injured one, too, as if she had done more than jerk away from him. As if she had slapped him right across the face.

Then he turned around in the cool, clear water and swam away from her.

Chapter 11

Something had happened, with Jo. Something was wrong. Dekker didn't know what.

She wouldn't tell him. Once she gave him the brush-off, there in the pool, she started avoiding him. Avoiding his eyes, avoiding physical contact.

Around six, when the nanny took the kids in to feed them, Jo excused herself, too. She vanished into the house for the good part of an hour. The rest of them were just coming inside when she appeared again, freshly showered, smelling like flowers, wearing a clingy scoop-necked dress the same golden-brown color as the lights in her hair when the sun got caught in it. The dress skimmed all her curves and fell to just above her ankles.

Emma said what Dekker was thinking. "Girl, you are lookin' good."

Joleen smiled her thanks at the compliment, and then

Emma explained that she and Jonas were going to have to leave their guests to their own devices for a while. "We have *got* to freshen up." Emma slid her husband a sly look. The glance he gave her in return made it pretty clear that more than freshening up would be going on as soon as he got his wife alone. "Dinner in the small dinin' room at eight-thirty. We'll have drinks in the living room off the grand foyer, at eight—that is, if that's all right with the two of you?"

"Sounds great," Jo answered.

"Yeah, great," Dekker muttered, instantly wishing he could call the words back, try them again, make them sound a little more upbeat.

But he wasn't feeling all that upbeat at the moment. Damn it, he wanted to know what was eating Jo.

And Emma and Jonas didn't care about his bad attitude, anyway. Right then, as far as those two were concerned, the rest of the world flat-out did not exist. Emma curled her hand around her husband's arm and led him away.

Which left him and Jo, standing there alone just beyond the set of French doors that led out to the loggia. It was a chance, he realized, to find out what her problem was.

But before he could say a word, she started giving him orders. "Go on up and have your shower," she instructed, as if he were some kid who had to be reminded when he needed a bath. "I'll see how Sam's doin'." She turned and walked away from him.

He should have stopped her, should have said, *Hey, wait a minute. What the hell is going on here?* But he didn't. He just stood there, wishing he could strangle someone, watching her walk away. That damn dress clung to her backside like poured honey. And it had a slit, too. Right up the back, all the way to her knees. He could see the smooth, ripe skin of her calves as she moved. He must have stood there for a good sixty seconds, till she was way out of sight, staring like a long-gone fool at the place where she had last been.

He just wasn't used to this—to Jo shutting him out. Not in the past few years, anyway. Yeah, when she was a kid she used to put on attitudes with him. She would get all insulted at something he'd said. Wouldn't tell him what he'd done to make her mad, or anything sensible like that. She'd just get steamed up and not speak to him for days or even weeks.

Which hadn't bothered him a whole hell of a lot back then. She was a kid and she had more to deal with than any kid should, after her dad died. He figured she had a lot of frustrations bottled up, from always having to be the responsible one in her family. And he figured he could take it if she wanted to exercise her frustrations on him.

But the days of her putting on attitudes with him were behind them. Had been for a long time. Or so he'd thought until this afternoon—when she'd given him attitude to spare.

Why? He needed to get to the bottom of it.

That night, he decided. When they were alone, after the drinks and the dinner and all that, when they finally went up to bed. She'd have a hard time evading him then, since they would be sleeping in the same damn room.

The hours seemed to crawl by until that time came, even though Jonas and Emma were terrific hosts and the food was exceptional. After the meal they went to the media room, where they watched a bizarre but entertaining film about aliens—both the illegal variety and the kind from outer space. Emma explained that Jonas had been the movie's major backer. The filmmaker was evidently Jonas's close personal friend.

Joleen sat at Dekker's side through both the meal and the movie. She laughed in all the right places. She chatted easily with his brother and Emma. She even talked to *him,* now and then, soft little murmurings. Things like "Please pass the bread" and "Thank you" and "Excuse me," when her napkin slid off her lap and she bent over to get it and her leg brushed his under the table.

She never would look at him, though. Not *really* look at him. Her eyes were always sliding away whenever he tried to snare her glance.

So all right. Later. He'd deal with her later. When they were finally alone.

At a little after midnight they said good-night to Jonas and Emma. They stopped in at the nursery to get Sam, who'd already had his bath and been dressed in his pj's. The little guy had fallen asleep in a nest of pillows on the floor of the playroom. Dekker carried him back to their own rooms, where Jo tucked him into bed. She tiptoed from the smaller room and quietly shut the door.

It was time, and he knew it. Time to confront her. Time to get whatever it was out in the open where they could deal with it.

But there was a slight problem.

He did not have a clue where to begin.

She said, "You go ahead. Use the bathroom first."

"No. It's all right. I can wait."

"No really, you go on."

They stood there, in the area between the foot of the bed and the grouping of big, soft, gorgeous sofas, staring at each other.

Finally she let out a sound—a small noise in her

throat that spoke of pure impatience with him, with the situation, with who the hell knew what all. "Oh, all right, Dekker. I'll go first."

"Good," he said, his tone as gruff and fed up as he felt right then. "Do it."

She turned for the big closet and dressing area that led to the bathroom, and when she got in there, she shut the door behind her. Which left him alone in the bed/sitting room, staring at the shut door and facing the bleak truth.

He just…didn't know how to get through to her.

She was the talker, damn it. She was the open one, the easy one, the one who never hesitated when it came time to hash something out.

He never had to do more than lift an eyebrow or mutter, What? And she would be telling him any and everything she had on her mind.

So what the hell had happened? What had gone wrong? Had he *done* something to get her mad?

He couldn't think what.

However, somehow, since late this afternoon, muttering What? and raising his eyebrows had gotten him exactly nowhere with her. He'd even gone so far, down there in the pool, as to ask her directly what was going on. For that, he got half a denial.

At least she'd done that much. Stopped herself in mid-lie. He could do without hearing lies from her mouth.

Dekker stalked over to one of those big, beautiful couches and dropped into it, swinging his feet up and plunking them down on the gleaming wood of the inlaid coffee table. He looked at his shoes, though he wasn't really seeing them.

He was thinking that Jo had damn well better *not* start telling him lies. He'd had enough lies in his life. Enough lies and enough sulking. Enough of the kind of woman who needed more of everything than he could ever give. The kind of woman who made him feel that he was lacking, somehow, that he couldn't quite cut it—as a husband, as a man, as a caring human being.

The kind of woman that Stacey had been.

Hell, was he cursed or something? He couldn't help but start to wonder. Right now, it seemed as if all he had to do was marry a woman to turn her into a—

Dekker shut his eyes.

No. Not right. Not fair.

Jo was not Stacey. Not in a hundred thousand years.

And Stacey, well, in the end, no matter how mixed-up she'd been, and no matter how exhausting the emotional chase she had led him, he *had* chosen her, loved her, pursued her. Married her.

And he'd been no more ready to be a husband than she had been to be a wife. They'd made a royal mess of it. She had wanted his undivided attention, twenty-four hours a day. She'd wanted him to live, sleep, eat and *breathe* Stacey. And for a while he had given her just what she wanted.

But he was a man with a plan then. He had things *he* wanted, too. Like to make detective, which meant time away from Stacey. Which made Stacey very unhappy.

He learned, as time went by, that Stacey not only *wanted* his attention. She needed it. Craved it. The way a drunk needs his bottle, the way a junkie requires a regular fix.

And damn it, he was not a bottle of scotch. He was not a hit of smack. He just couldn't do it, feed that hunger of hers indefinitely.

He knew now he should have tried to get her some help. But at the time, it was hard to see anything very clearly. At the time, his reaction had been to pull away.

And the more he pulled away, the more she *needed*. The more she cried and ranted and raved, accusing him of not loving her, not wanting her, not *being there* for her.

She staged some crazy stunts in her ongoing quest to get his undivided attention.

She'd tried getting him good and jealous.

If they went out to dinner, she'd flirt with the guy at the next table, so charmingly—and so blatantly—that the guy would get up and follow her when she went to the women's room. They would end up in the parking lot, Dekker and his wife's new admirer, duking it out— or at least, that's how it went the first four or five times she pulled that one.

But eventually Dekker got wise. As soon as she had picked out a sucker at another table, he would get up and leave her there.

So she changed tactics. She became totally devoted to him. She drowned him in her damned devotion, hanging on his every word, cooking lavish meals. She developed a kind of radar about those big meals of hers. Whenever he was working an important, time-consuming case, she would cook a lot of them. He would work late and miss them. And she would be crushed.

The total devotion lasted for a long time. And then, after one of their big fights when he didn't show up to eat another of her gourmet feasts, she disappeared. He came home the next night and she was gone. She left a note on fine linen stationery scented with her perfume. It said she "couldn't take it anymore." She "wasn't sure if she could even go on."

That note scared the hell out of him. She'd done some crazy things, but she'd never hinted at suicide before.

He was frantic, certain she meant to do something

to hurt herself and desperate to make sure that she was all right. It was two in the morning.

He'd gone straight to Jo, pounded on the door of her mama's house, where she was still living then, not giving a damn if he woke up Camilla and the other girls.

But the others didn't wake. Or if they did, they stayed in their beds. Jo was the one who came to the door in her pajamas and robe, rubbing the sleep from her eyes.

He'd demanded to know where his wife was.

Jo pulled him inside, led him to the kitchen, made coffee and set a steaming mug of it in front of him.

Then she said she didn't know where Stacey had gone.

"She was here, then? You talked to her?"

"Drink your coffee, Dekker. Settle down."

"Did you *ask* her, try to find out where the hell she planned to go next?"

Jo dropped into the chair across from him. She stared at him for a moment that seemed to stretch out for at least a year. At last she nodded. "Yes. Yes, I did ask her."

He fisted his hands to keep from lurching across the table, grabbing her out of that chair and shaking her until everything she knew came spilling out. "And?"

"Oh, Dekker, what she said to me was between us. I just don't know if I should be talkin' to you about it. I don't know if it's the right thing to—"

"Tell me, damn you. I have to know."

Jo folded her hands on the table and looked down at them. Now she was shaking her head. "Stacey said... she said she couldn't trust me. She said that I would only end up telling you." Jo looked up then, a sad little smile curving her mouth. "It's strange, you know? But you and me, we go back such a long ways. You are *fam-*

ily to me, Dekker. And Stacey, well, she is a dear, dear friend. I love her and I *hurt* for her, for everything she's goin' through. But it is not the same. And she *knew* that. Better than I did, I guess, until she said it to me...." Her voice trailed off. She was looking at her hands again.

Impatience tightened inside him like a fist. "Said *what* to you?"

Her head snapped up. Shadows haunted her eyes and her mouth trembled. "Oh, I don't—" She cut off the protests herself that time. And she told him, "Stacey said that my basic loyalty was to you. That when you came here lookin' for her, you would get me to tell you whatever I knew, no matter if I swore to her that I would never betray her trust."

"It's not betraying her trust if you talk to me. You know it's not. She's not thinking clearly. And I have to find her. You have to tell me whatever you know."

"I don't really know anything, honestly. She was here. She was upset. She would not say where she planned to go next."

"Why the hell didn't you call me the minute she walked out your front door?"

"She asked me not to."

"And you did what she asked?" He sneered those words, glaring at her. "Damn it, what are you, a stone idiot?"

She didn't rise to the bait. Even worried sick over his missing wife, he noticed that. She only met his gaze across her mama's breakfast table, her own eyes steady, her expression soft and sad with understanding.

Yeah. What really stuck with him, looking back now on that grim night, was how hard Jo had tried to make it easy on him. She hadn't fought back when he had insulted her. She hadn't ranted at him, though she could have made a case in her own mind that he deserved to hear a little ranting. She hadn't laid it on him hard, saying it was for his own good. She hadn't copped a single huffy, holier-than-thou attitude.

Because by that night, Jo had grown up. The touchy, insecure teenager was gone. Somehow, while he hadn't been looking, while he'd been busy reeling through his life, trying to get ahead on the OCPD and be Stacey's husband at the same time, Jo had become a woman—and the kind of woman who refused to judge others, who could take a few verbal blows from a friend in need without feeling she had to retaliate.

She'd put it to him so gently, chosen her words with great care. Stacey had cried on her shoulder, she'd said. Stacey had talked about how things weren't working out.

But Jo's sweet kindness to him that night hadn't kept him from knowing what had really gone on. He knew his wife too well, knew that Stacey would have wailed and moaned. She would have called him a hardhearted SOB who refused to love a woman the way she needed to be loved.

"She'll be all right, Dekker," Jo had promised him. "She'll come back. I know she will...."

And she had come back. Six days later. Looking like hell, like she'd been at some weeklong party somewhere doing things he was probably better off never knowing about.

But alive. In one piece.

There had been a big scene, another in the infinite chain of big scenes. At the end she had begged him to take her back. She'd sworn she would never pull anything like that again.

And she hadn't.

Next, she started calling him at the station, leaving messages with the dispatcher.

"Please. You have to help me. Tell him he has to come home immediately. It's an emergency. It's life and death...."

The dispatcher would radio him and he would go charging back to the house—to find her sitting on the couch in a sexy nightgown, ready to show him her snowflake tattoo.

By then he had zero interest in her tattoo. Or in any part of her pretty, scented, smooth little body. He didn't want to make love with her. He didn't know if he would ever want to make love with her again—or with any woman, for that matter. The equipment, it seemed, had stopped working.

And he really didn't give a damn. A sort of numbness had set in. Which was okay with him. Numbness was a big improvement over the grueling agony of loving Stacey. It was a relief, more than anything. He was through, done, finished. No longer able to rise to the occasion.

His body was telling him something. It was time to surrender the field, to give up on the impossible task of trying to love a woman who could never get enough.

He found himself an apartment and moved out.

There were more big, teary scenes. For Stacey, anyway. He opted out of them. He would hang up the minute he heard her voice on the phone, hear her moaning and sobbing and begging him to give her just one more chance. He would refuse to open the door when she came pounding on it, calling his name, demanding that he open up and talk to her.

She had needed help. She had needed help every bit as much as a drowning woman needs someone to throw her a lifeline. But he'd been no help at all to her. He'd been too desperate himself—to keep from going down with her.

Jo had done better with Stacey—been more of a friend than he had ever been a husband. She'd thrown the damn lifelines. She'd taken Stacey to a counselor and arranged for her to join some kind of group therapy sessions. But Stacey had screwed it up. She would miss her appointments with the counselor. She wouldn't show up at group. The counselor had finally dropped her. The group had voted her out.

And she'd kept calling him, begging him, pleading with him to come back to her.

Her final call to him wasn't that much different from some of the calls that went before it. By then, it wasn't anything new when she said that she couldn't take it anymore. That if he didn't talk to her, she was going to end it.

He wasn't there to take that call. She left her last message for him on his answering machine. In it, she accused him of all the same old things—of deserting her, of not loving her, of not being there when she needed him most. She cried that she had had enough, more than she could take, of life and everything that went into it. She said she would wait ten minutes and if he didn't get back to her, she was swallowing a bottle of pills and she was going to bed. For good.

By the time he got that message, seven hours later, she was deep in the coma from which she would never wake.

The door across the room opened.

Jo came padding through it, barefoot, wearing a white cotton robe that reached her knees. Her face was scrubbed clean of makeup, and her hair curled, soft and full, around her heart-shaped face.

"Your turn," she said, her tone too bright—forced. Not right.

"Jo."

The tight little smile she was giving him vanished. She hovered there, several yards away from him, near the end of the huge bed. Those big brown eyes were bigger than ever right then, dark and soft and full of all the things that, for some reason, she wouldn't tell him.

It came to him, hit him all over again, as if for the first time, in a flash of painful insight that constricted his throat and made his chest feel too small for the heart trapped inside it.

She was *his* lifeline. As much as she'd ever tried to be Stacey's. She had saved him from going down after Stacey died. She had come to him with her casseroles and her perky talk, with her insistence that he get out of the apartment, go to a movie, to a car show, to art festivals on the lawns at OCC, to flea markets at the state fairgrounds. She must have hauled out the damn *Sunday Oklahoman* every week for three or four months, there, and scanned all the ads and articles, picking out places she could drag him to. And then, after she picked them out, she worked on him, gently and without mercy, never giving up until he would finally agree to go there with her.

That was a friend.

They didn't come any better.

And he couldn't bear...this distance. This *strangeness,* between them.

He swung his feet off the coffee table and stood. He

still didn't know how to make her talk to him, how to get rid of whatever it was that had come between them.

But the distance. He could do something about that. He could close it.

He went to her. She watched him coming, eyes that couldn't get any wider, somehow doing just that.

When he stood about two feet from her, where he could see the gold flecks in those wide, wide eyes, smell soap and a faint, sweet perfume—and peppermint toothpaste, when she let out a long, jittery breath—he made himself ask her. Again.

"What the hell is it? What's bothering you?"

She lifted a hand and put it against her throat. He saw the war going on inside her. She was thinking up lies, deciding whether or not to try running them past him.

He shook his head at her, slowly, tenderly. "Don't do it. Don't lie to me…"

She took that hand from her throat, waved it, as if she didn't know what to do with it.

He caught it. She stiffened. He thought, for a split second, that she would do what she had done to him down in the pool: jerk away, whisper hotly "Don't!"

But no. She caught herself. Her lashes swooped down. She dragged in another long, shaky breath and let it out with great care. Deliberately she twined her fingers with his.

Better, he thought. Now we're getting somewhere.…

Her lashes fluttered up. She looked at him anxiously. "Let's…um. Could we sit down, do you think?"

He almost smiled. "Yeah. I think we could." The bed had no footboard, just the big padded satin affair at the head. "How about right here?" He sat on the end of it and pulled her down beside him. She came somewhat reluctantly, as if she'd thought better of the idea, but didn't know how to get out of it now.

It didn't matter if she hesitated, he told himself. She *did* sit. Beside him. She had laced her fingers with his. And now she would tell him what the hell was happening with her.

She spoke. "Um. Dekker…"

He gave her hand a reassuring squeeze. "Those are very nice feet you have. But do you think you could make yourself look at me?"

She did it, with obvious effort. "I…" She let out a small, anguished-sounding moan. "Oh, I just can't. I really can't, Dekker. Please try to understand…."

"Can't what?"

"Can't…talk about this, not right now. Please. Just don't make me. If you would only…"

"What? If I would only what?"

"Just…believe me when I tell you, it is not your fault. It is nothin' you have done. It is *my* problem. And I am going to handle it the best way I know how."

"Which is?"

She pulled her hand from his, waved it in the air some more. "No. I mean it. You have got to give me a little time here, okay?"

"Time for…?"

"To deal with it. To…work it out in my mind."

He almost demanded, *Work* what *out?* But he shut his mouth over those words. She was asking for time.

As her friend—hell, as her *husband*—it was his duty to see that she got what she needed. He owed it to her, for the sake of all that they were to each other, to wait until she felt that she could tell him this deep, dark secret of hers.

After a minute of strained silence, he muttered, "All right," then added more forcefully, "When?"

"When what?"

"When can you talk to me?"

She looked absolutely miserable. He wanted to grab her and…what? Pull her close. Protect her forever. Promise her that everything would be okay.

And then force her, somehow, to tell him. All of it. Whatever it was that she thought was so awful she couldn't even share it with him.

Nothing could be that awful. She ought to know that. There was nothing she could tell him that he couldn't take.

And besides, if she *did* tell him, well, maybe he could fix the problem, could *make* it okay.…

But no.

He was not going to grab her. He was going to remember, to keep foremost in his mind all that she had done for him. Always, if he possibly could, he would honor her wishes.

He waited.

Finally she told him in a small, unhappy voice. "Soon. I promise. I will work this out and then we will talk about it."

"Soon," he echoed, wondering with a stab of impatience what exactly she meant by that.

"Yes." She was looking at her feet again, her voice small, sad and lost. "Soon…"

Chapter 12

Dekker took his turn in the bathroom and then they went to bed—Joleen *in* the bed, Dekker on one of the couches across the room. Joleen had a hard time getting to sleep. She wondered if Dekker was awake, too. Not a sound came from his side of the room. Could be he was just a very silent sleeper.

Or maybe he was lying over there on the cramped sofa in the dark, wondering what her problem was and when she would finally break down and tell him.

Oh, she didn't think she ever could.

How would she do it? How would she…get her mouth around the words?

Well, Dekker, the problem is, I have got the hots for you….

Not.

Or *I have rethought this whole separate beds thing,*

*and I have changed my mind about it. I would rather
you just come on over here and climb into bed with me
so that I can jump your bones….*

*I mean, that is, if you would like your bones jumped
by me. Would you? Could you…?*

Right.

No. Better to wait. At least for a while.

Maybe a way to tell him would come to her. Or maybe
these crazy new feelings she had for him would just…
go away. Maybe she'd get used to them. Learn to live
with them, to *cope* with them….

Oh, who did she think she was kidding?

Even if she woke up tomorrow and discovered that
these irksome new longings had vanished with the light
of day, Dekker was still going to want to know what it
had all been about.

But that would be all right, wouldn't it?

If only she didn't *feel* this way, if these little shivers
and flashes of heat would just stop quivering through
her when he touched her, when he *looked* at her, when
she looked at *him,* then they could laugh about it.

They could agree that it had only been a kind of temporary insanity. They could talk it over and come to
some nice, neat, safe conclusion. They would decide
that it was probably brought on by all the stress in the
past few weeks. Good old Jo had just snapped for a little
while there, gone delusional, imagined that she wanted
more from Dekker than he would ever be willing to give.

She turned over, adjusted the covers, smoothed out
her pillow, tried not to sigh. She had a *little* time, anyway. Before he would start pushing her again to tell him
what was going on in her head.

Maybe, in that time, some workable solution to this predicament would occur to her.

She sent a silent prayer to heaven that that might be the case. And after the prayer she lay very still, hoping sleep would find her.

It did, but not until a number of endless hours later.

Joleen woke with a start. It was morning. She had that where-am-I feeling. This was not her house, not her bed....

She was lying on her stomach. She lifted her head from the pillow and squinted at the satin headboard. "Ugh."

Before she could think better of the move, she rolled over and sat up.

That was when she saw Dekker. He was up—barely—standing over in the sitting area, wearing nothing but a pair of boxer shorts, folding up the blanket he had slept under. His hair was squashed on the left side, and he had a sleep dent on his cheek.

He looked...really good, in just his boxer shorts, as good as he'd looked yesterday, at poolside, in those swim trunks he'd borrowed from the men's cabana. He had powerful legs, that narrow waist, those heavy, wide shoulders corded with muscle.

And there it was—that shivery, infuriating thrill, zipping through her again.

So much for the false hope that it would all be over in the morning.

"'Mornin'."

He returned the greeting, then gestured toward the bathroom. "You want to...?"

"Are you, uh, plannin' to take a shower?"

"The thought had crossed my mind."

"Well, maybe, if I could just—"

"Go ahead."

"I will only be a minute."

"No big rush."

But she did rush. She rushed in there and she used the toilet and she washed her hands and she rushed back out. "Thanks. Your turn."

He laid the folded blanket over his arm, picked up his pillow and headed for the dressing area. When he got in there and shut the door, she sank to the edge of the bed with a tiny moan.

Oh, she hated this, all these stilted exchanges over the big, important issue of who would use the bathroom when. It was all so…dumb.

There was plenty of room in there, after all. That bathroom was like everything else at Angel's Crest. Fit for a king—and for his queen, too. That bathroom had two sinks, two showers, a huge tub with massaging jets and two commodes, each in its own little marble-walled cubicle. If they were *really* married, if they were doing *all* the things that married people do, they could go in there at the same time. They could each do whatever they needed to do without one of them in the least inconveniencing the other.

Or, if they only didn't have to *pretend* that they were *really* married, then she could share Sammy's bathroom, and Dekker could have the king-size one all to himself.

But no. They weren't *really* married and the maids could not be allowed to discover such a shocking fact.

She let out a huffy little breath—and decided she was making way too much out of this.

"Lighten up, girl," she said to the empty room. "It will all work out. Just give it time."

They shared the morning meal in the breakfast room, all four adults and the children, as well. Jonas suggested they fly to Las Vegas. "Just a day trip, the four of us. What do you think?"

"Jonas finds gambling relaxing," Emma said.

"That's right, I do. But if you two would rather do something else, just speak up."

Dekker said the idea was fine with him, and Joleen agreed that she would love to go. It sounded wonderful, she said.

Wonderful in more ways than one, she was thinking. They'd be good and busy, exploring the casinos, making their way among the crowds. There would be zero opportunity for private conversation. No time for her and Dekker to be alone, no time to dwell on the painful new awkwardness between them.

Leaving Sam and Mandy in the capable hands of the nanny, they headed for the airport at a little before eleven. The flight, in one of Jonas's aircraft, took hardly any time at all. They spent the better part of the afternoon wandering from one huge pleasure palace to the next. Jonas and Dekker played craps. Emma and Joleen yanked the one-armed bandit and tried a few hands of blackjack.

Some time after four they were recognized by an intense-looking fellow in plaid shorts with a fancy camera hung around his neck. Within ten minutes they had two other men a lot like the first one following after them.

"Time to go home," Jonas said wearily.

By seven they were back at Angel's Crest. They visited the nursery, then the four of them shared a late, light supper out on the loggia with the lights of L.A. and the blue of the Pacific spread out in a glittering panorama below.

The two couples retired to their rooms at nine-thirty. Dekker and Joleen stopping by the nursery to collect a sleeping Sam.

Once Sam had been tucked into his bed, there was the grueling who'll-use-the-bathroom-first routine to get through.

"Just go ahead."

"No, really, it's—"

"I mean it. Go on."

So Joleen went first. She took care to get the blanket and the pillow from the closet area on her way back out to the main room, since it was her turn to take the couch.

Dekker went into the dressing room as soon as she emerged from it. The minute the door closed behind him, she flew around the main room, turning off all the lights save one lamp beside the bed.

Then she plunked her pillow on the end of a sofa and lay down. Holding one side of the blanket and kicking the rest of it into place with a bicycling motion of her feet, she settled the blanket over her. She turned over on her right side, with her back to the room.

And she heaved a heavy sigh. Dekker was fast, when he used the bathroom getting ready for bed. She had wanted to be on the couch, under the blanket, in a position that would clearly signal she was on her way to sleep, before he returned. And she had succeeded.

Dekker emerged from the bathroom about three minutes later. She heard the whisper of his feet across the rug—and then nothing. He had stopped, was just standing there, midway between the dressing room door and where she lay on the sofa.

Joleen lay very still under her blanket, her eyes shut, willing him to say nothing, to go over to the bed and get into it and just…let it be.

She didn't quite get her wish. He swore. And he said her name.

She did not breathe. She did not move.

She was handling this all wrong and she knew it. She was hurting her dearest, truest, lifelong friend, leaving him to worry and wonder what could possibly be the matter with her.

But she couldn't bring herself to tell him.

And at the same time, she just didn't know how to pretend with him. How to act as if everything was normal, when it *wasn't* normal, when she was a wreck of unsatisfied yearning inside herself.

Just *wanting* a man shouldn't mess everything up like this. But somehow, it did. She couldn't relax with him, couldn't really *talk* to him. Not now. She knew that if she even tried, it would all come pouring out. She would embarrass herself and put poor Dekker on the spot.

She also knew the time was fast approaching when she would have to do just that.

But now all she wanted was to put it off. Avoid the inevitable. For a few days, a few hours, however long she possibly could.

She heard movement. He was walking away from her. He had given up, for now, on trying to talk to her.

There was a soft rustling—the blankets on the bed. And then a click as the room went dark.

On Monday, Jonas and Emma both had to work. Joleen spent a lot of that morning and afternoon in the nursery with the children, then later she gave the nanny a break and took them out to the pool. She didn't see much of Dekker, didn't know how he occupied himself.

Apparently, he had decided to give her what she'd said she needed—time and space to deal with what was bothering her.

At four, though, they were both due at the offices of Jonas's lawyer. They rode there together, in one of the long, black Bravo limousines. It was a silent ride. They looked out the smoky glass of the car's windows and avoided each other's eyes.

When they got to the offices of McAllister, Quinn and Associates, Attorneys at Law, a pretty, beautifully dressed secretary showed them to a conference room. Jonas and Ambrose McAllister joined them a few minutes later. The attorney, who was tall, white-haired and soft-spoken, listened to the same story Dekker had told Jonas and Emma two nights before.

When Ambrose had heard it all, he told them what Jonas had thought he might. He said they had done all that could be done until Robert Atwood made his next move.

"I want you to contact me immediately when that happens," Ambrose McAllister said. "We'll see what, exactly, we're going to be dealing with, and I'll advise you from there. Now. Is there anything else I can help you with? Anything at all?"

Dekker said he'd been thinking about changing his name, legally, to Bravo. "After all, it's my real name, anyway."

Ambrose nodded. "And did you want to go back to Russell, as well?"

"No. I've been called Dekker so long, I don't think I want to try getting used to another first name."

Joleen felt relief when he said that he'd keep his first name. She might eventually become accustomed to calling him Russell, but somewhere in the back of her mind, he would always be Dekker to her.

And, apparently, to himself, too.

"A name change is a pretty straightforward procedure," Ambrose said. "It is handled, though, in the state of residence. Were you planning to make your home here, then, in California?"

Dekker said that no, they'd be living in Oklahoma.

"Then I'll be glad to refer you to a good attorney there."

Dekker shook his head. "I can handle that." In his line of work, he knew quite a few lawyers. "Just wanted you to point me in the right direction."

They rode down in the elevator with Jonas, who had a limousine waiting to take him back to his offices at Bravo, Incorporated. Joleen and Dekker returned to Angel's Crest, went their separate ways, meeting again in the living room off the grand foyer when Palmer served the predinner drinks.

At ten-thirty, they said good-night to their hosts and climbed the curving staircase. They stopped in to pick up Sam, carried him to their rooms, put him to bed.

Then Dekker said, "I'm not really tired right now. Think I'll go out for a while."

Go out where? she thought.

But she didn't ask. She didn't feel she had the right, since she had spent the better part of the past few days trying to figure out ways to avoid him. What could she offer him right now, anyway, if he stayed here with her? Good company?

Hardly. All the old easiness between them was

gone—burned away, it felt to her, by the heat of her un-spoken desire.

She thought of Stacey, who had pretty much gone off the deep end over Dekker. The poor man. When women fell for him, it really messed up his life. His first wife had made him into her obsession. And now his best-friend-turned-second-wife wanted him so much she didn't dare let herself even talk to him.

"All right," she said. "Good night, then."

He gave her a brief nod in response and then he was gone. She got ready for bed and slipped between the covers.

She must have been asleep when he came in, because she had no idea what time that was.

The next day at four, in a big meeting room at the offices of Bravo, Incorporated, in downtown Los Angeles, they held the press conference.

Joleen and Dekker sat at a long table together, holding hands—Jonas had advised that—and sharing a microphone, which Jonas had suggested, as well. He said people naturally tended to be nervous in the glare of the lights, under the eyes of so many prying news people; they drew into themselves.

"If you use one mike, you'll have to sit close together. You'll be turned toward each other, leaning in. Body language sends a powerful message and we want yours to have 'happy newlyweds' written all over it."

Jonas sat on Dekker's left, with his own microphone, ready to jump in if things got too rough.

Dekker gave a short speech about how much it meant to him to have found his real family at last. Then he explained that he'd grown up next door to Joleen, in

Oklahoma City. They'd been friends all their lives. And recently they'd realized that they both wanted it to be more. They had married four days ago. He also said he had a stepson named Sam, the "greatest little guy in the world."

He said he couldn't be happier, leaning toward her as he said it, to speak into the mike, holding her hand as his brother had advised him to do. His hand was warm, enclosing hers. Hers felt small. And cold at first. It warmed, though, wrapped in his. She stared at his mouth as he spoke, at the cleft in his chin, thought about all the years she had known him—her whole life. For Joleen, there had never been a world that didn't have Dekker in it.

Her throat closed up, right there, in front of all those news-hungry reporters, while Dekker said how happy he was and she stared at the cleft in his chin. She felt an insistent pressure behind her eyes....

She could have slapped her own self right smack in the face. She *never* cried. She couldn't afford to. In her family, *someone* had to keep her head at all times.

Dekker finished speaking. Then came the questions, fast and furious, all the reporters vying to get Dekker's attention. Some of the questions were awful. Dekker handled them with a steady voice and a direct stare.

"How does it feel to be raised by your own kidnapper?"

"I didn't know she was my kidnapper. I believed she was my natural mother. She treated me well—better than well. The woman pretty much dedicated her life to raising me."

"We understand that Lorraine Smith is dead. What would you say to her, if she were still alive today?"

"She's not alive today, so I guess I don't have to figure out what to say to her."

"Your first wife died tragically, didn't she? I wonder if—"

"My first wife is not why we're here today. Next question."

At the end, the press wanted more details of the honeymoon. Were the bride and groom going anywhere else on their wedding trip, after their stay at the fabulous Angel's Crest?

Dekker answered that one with an outright lie. "No, we'll spend our entire honeymoon here in Los Angeles. We're enjoying our visit with my brother and his wife."

Joleen couldn't blame him for lying. No doubt the news people would eventually track the famous Bravo Baby down wherever he might go. But why draw them a map?

Then again, she thought, maybe it wasn't a lie. Last week Dekker had mentioned spending the second half of their honeymoon in Hawaii. But since then, he hadn't said anything about where they would go next. Maybe in the last few discouraging days he'd decided they might as well just stay in Los Angeles until it was time to go home.

And maybe he was right. Here, the distance and the silence between them was almost bearable. They had Emma and Jonas to distract them. Sam had Mandy to play with and the nanny to look after him whenever Joleen wanted a break from the full-time job of caring for a toddler.

It would have been fun, before, just the three of them. Building sand castles on some silvery beach, catering to Sam—and just being together, talking easily about anything and everything the way they always used to do.

But now? No. Not much fun at all. Not with this silence yawning between them. Not with the secret she wouldn't share. Not with her impossible yearning eating her up every time she looked at him....

"It went well," Jonas said, after the press conference was over. "Very well. You have the knack for handling yourself in the spotlight, Dek."

"It's a knack I wouldn't mind never using again."

That night, when they went to their rooms, Dekker said he was going out again.

She longed to ask, *Where will you go? What will you do? When will you be back?*

But she kept all the questions locked up inside. She knew if she asked them, she would only be opening the door for him to ask questions of her. She still was not ready for that.

"Well, good night then...."

"Yeah. Good night, Jo...."

Dekker went outside by a set of stairs that led down to the huge back patio. As he emerged from the stairwell and shut the door behind him, he spotted one of Jonas's bodyguards, in the shadows beneath a palm tree about ten yards away.

Dekker waved. The guard raised a black-gloved hand in response.

That's me, Dekker found himself thinking, as he watched that shadowed hand saluting him through the darkness. That's me. Just two weeks ago.

So strange. His life now. It was as if he had crossed some invisible line. Gone over to the other side.

Before his brother had found him, Dekker was often

the one standing in the shadows, peering in on the lives of others. Watching. And sometimes watching *over*. He'd taken a bodyguard assignment or two in the couple of years since he'd set up his agency.

Dekker strode aimlessly across the patio, to the edge of the cobalt-blue pool. He stared out over the lights of the city, the ocean beyond.

But he wasn't really seeing them. He was thinking. Thinking that now everything had changed. Now he was the Bravo Baby. The Bravo Baby all grown up.

Someone worth watching. By reporters and syndicated press photographers. By his brother's bodyguards.

By Atwood's detectives hired to get the dirt on Jo.

Jo...

How did that happen? What was she doing, creeping into his mind now?

He'd come out here, after all, to get away from her. From her silence. From the thing she couldn't make herself tell him. The thing that had no substance yet stood, impenetrable as a thick plate of shatterproof glass, between them.

He sat down on the edge of the blue, blue pool, slipped off his shoes, peeled off his socks, rolled up his trouser cuffs and dangled his legs in the water. It felt good, warm and satiny, against his skin.

He heard footsteps behind him, recognized the quiet, firm tread.

He turned. "Jonas."

His brother had changed clothes since they all went upstairs. He wore loose cotton slacks and a light shirt, unbuttoned. He was barefoot. He dropped down next to Dekker, rolled up his slacks and swung his feet into the water.

Dekker glanced back over his shoulder—at the terrace of the master suite. From that terrace, anyone sitting at the edge of the pool would be in plain view. "Been watching me, big brother?"

Jonas chuckled. "You were down here last night, too." He let a moment elapse, then asked carefully, "Anything...the matter?"

"Yeah. But I don't want to talk about it."

"Sure?"

"Positive. But thanks."

"If you change your mind..." Jonas let the thought trail off, which was fine with Dekker. He got the message, and he appreciated the offer.

Not that he'd be taking his brother up on it.

They sat for a while, feet in the water. Dekker became more aware of the city noises, distant but ever-present: the faint wailing of sirens, the whoosh of traffic so constant it sounded like the faraway roar of a waterfall. A smell of smoke hung in the air, barely detectable, but definitely there.

Finally Jonas suggested, "How about a couple of games of eight ball?" There was a pool table in the game room, on the first floor of the huge house behind them, right next-door to the media room.

Dekker shook his head. "Go on back to Emma. Get some sleep. I know you have to work tomorrow."

"You are no fun at all."

"Go on. Get lost."

Jonas pulled his feet from the water, rolled down his pants legs and stood. "There ought to be something profound I could say before I go."

Dekker looked up at his brother, watched the pool

lights play on the face so much like his own. "Not necessary."

"When I was six, before our evil uncle messed everything up, there were so damn many things I was going to do for you, say to you, *teach* you. And look what happened? You went and grew up without my help."

Dekker felt himself smiling. "I guess it's a major responsibility, huh? Being a big brother."

"Words like *'daunting'* come to mind. At six I was ready. Now, well…"

"You're doing great. I mean that."

"Sure you won't let me beat you at pool?"

"I said get lost. I meant that, too."

Dekker watched his brother until he disappeared through one of the French doors that opened onto the loggia. Then he turned back to his somber contemplation of the city lights spread out below.

The next morning at breakfast Emma had an announcement to make. "Jonas and I have finally decided on the perfect wedding present for you two."

Dekker set down his fork. "Wait a minute. You've given us our present. This visit. It's a thousand times more than enough."

Emma shook a finger at him. "No, it is not. There is more. And you are getting it."

"Sounds like a threat."

"It is a visit to heaven."

"Heaven?" Joleen asked with a laugh that Dekker read instantly as faked. "Did you say—"

"You bet I did."

"Emma," said Jonas. "I think you'd better explain a little further."

"Well, all right. I will." She beamed first at Dekker and then at Joleen. "You two are leaving Friday for La Puerta al Cielo—that's Doorway to Heaven and it is a five-star resort Jonas owns, right at the tip of the Baja Peninsula. And did you notice I said 'you two'?"

Dekker nodded. Joleen was quiet. He glanced her way and noted with a tightening in his gut that apprehension had drawn a line between her brows.

Emma chattered happily on. "I said 'you two' because Sammy will stay here, with us. You will never be more than a quick flight away, if he needs you. And the two of you will get to do what newlyweds are supposed to do—spend seven long, lazy days and beautiful balmy nights with only each other to think about."

Chapter 13

"What are we going to do now?"

Joleen asked the question in a low, tight voice. It was some time later. Jonas and Emma had left for the day, and the nanny had taken the children back upstairs.

Dekker set down his coffee cup without drinking from it. It seemed crystal clear to him what they would do now. "We're going to Baja."

"But we can't just—"

"Why not? They're all supposed to think we're happy newlyweds, remember? And this is the kind of trip happy newlyweds would jump at."

She looked away. "Well, I...I think I'll have to tell Emma that though there is nothing I would love more than a week alone with my new husband, we just are not going to be able to go."

"Why not?"

She coughed, nervously, into her fist. "I'll say that I don't think I can leave Sam for all that time."

"You'll *say* that."

"Yes. I will."

"You'll *say* it, but it's not the truth, not the real reason you don't want to go away with me."

That gave her pause—though not for long. After a moment or two of heated silence, she said carefully, "Sam is only a year and a half old, and it makes perfect sense that I wouldn't want to go away for a whole week without him." She was watching him sideways, as if she didn't quite dare to look him square in the eye.

He dared. He stared at her dead-on. He was so damn sick of whatever had gone wrong with her, whatever had made her stop wanting to be with him, to talk to him. He hated this, whatever it was.

And he wanted it gone.

He said, "So it makes perfect sense. Fine. That doesn't mean it's true."

"Dekker, I don't think it matters what—"

"Let me ask you directly. If you said that you couldn't make yourself leave Sam here for a week, would it be true?"

"What does it—"

"So it would be a lie, wouldn't it? Because Sam would do just fine without you for a week. He's a well-adjusted kid. You said it yourself—zero separation anxieties. And he's made himself at home here. He likes the nanny and he likes playing with Mandy. And he will be safe. You know it. Safe from harm. Safe from that SOB grandfather of his. Because if there's anyplace in the world that no one could touch him, it's right here at Angel's Crest."

She started to speak. He went on before she could get

anything out. "On the other hand, if he *did* have a problem, if something came up, if he got sick or whatever, we could be back here in a matter of hours."

"Dekker, I don't—"

He cut her off that time with a short, chopping motion of his hand. She turned to follow the direction of his gaze. A maid carrying a silver coffeepot came toward them through the archway that led to the kitchen. She brought the pot to the table, refilled their cups, scooped up a few empty dishes and then left them the way she had come.

As soon as she was gone, Dekker stood. "Let's talk about this upstairs."

Joleen stared up at him.

She wanted to scream—just throw back her head and let out a long, loud wail. She felt so…trapped.

Trapped. And frustrated.

And confused.

And dishonest.

And just plain terrible about herself.

She spoke in a charged whisper. "I am fed up with worryin' about what the maid thinks. I do not *care* what the maid thinks."

His gaze bored through her. If looks could burn, she would be nothing but cinder and ash.

"Upstairs," he said. "Come with me. Now."

He confronted her as soon as they got through the door of the room they had been forced to share.

"You've had three days," he said, shoving the door shut. "Three days to 'think it over,' three days to 'deal with it'—whatever the hell 'it' is."

She put up a hand, palm out, to keep him at bay.

"Please. Can't you just wait?" She backed away from him. "Can't you just let it be, let me work this out in my own time?"

He went after her, each step slow and deliberate. "No. I can't take this anymore. There is no damn thing in the world you could say to me that I can't deal with, can't find a way to understand."

She reached the center of the room, between the bed and the sitting area, and she hovered there, emotions chasing themselves across her pale face—indecision, anger, outright misery. "I just don't... I can't—"

He didn't stop until he was right in front of her. "You don't what? You can't what?"

She wrapped her arms around herself, shook her head, her eyes too big, too sad, too hopeless. "Oh, Dekker..."

And something snapped inside him. He grabbed her by the shoulders, his fingers digging in. "What, damn it? What?"

She winced.

They both froze, staring at each other. Remorse burned through him. If he had hurt her...

He uttered her name on a ragged whisper, tried to pull her close.

"No!" She jerked away, gasped, put her hand across her mouth.

All he wanted was to reach for her again—to yank her against him, to *make* her take the comfort he needed to give her.

This was going nowhere. Better to get out.

He started to turn.

"Wait." She grabbed his arm. "Oh, wait..." She let go, with a swiftness that stunned him, as if to touch him burned her. But then she gave a small cry. "Oh, please.

I hate this, too, I hate what has happened between us. I hate it as much—no, *more*—than you do. Oh, Dekker, don't go...."

He faced her. And he waited. A kind of grim acceptance had settled over him. He saw no reason to push her further for answers. Either she would tell him. Or she wouldn't—and he would turn around once more and this time he *would* leave.

Her face, so pale a moment before, flooded with color. "I...can I ask you...?"

"Anything." It came out a growl. "You know that."

"The other night. Friday, our weddin' night?"

"Yeah?"

"When you—" she hesitated, swallowed, as if the next word almost choked her trying to get out "—kissed me. At the table, in front of the window, when we thought a reporter was—"

"I remember, Jo."

"Okay. Well, Dekker, um...you..." She ran out of words, lost her courage again.

He couldn't stop himself from prompting, "I...?"

"Well, you—" She sucked in a long breath and let it out in a rush. "I felt your tongue, Dekker. You used your tongue. A little. You did."

He thought he understood then. He felt like a worm. "It was a sleazy move, huh? God. I am so sorry. You probably think I'm putting the moves on you, taking advantage of our situation to—"

"No. Wait."

"What?"

"Please. Don't be sorry."

"Huh?"

"I do *not* think that you are putting any moves on me."

"You don't?"

She shook her head. Her soft cheeks were the deepest pink he had ever seen them. "I just…I want to know, um, why you did that?"

He was completely in the dark all over again. "Wait a minute. For three days you've hardly spoken to me…because you wanted to know why I used my tongue when I kissed you…and you were too embarrassed to ask?"

She clasped her hands in front of her and stared down at them as if she were trying to see through to the bones. "No. No, that's not it."

"Then *what?*"

She lifted her head, cried, "Oh, I am getting there. I am *trying* to get there. If you would just—"

He patted the air between them, palms out. "Okay. Sorry. Take your time. It's okay…"

"I…"

"Yeah?"

"I just want to know why you did it. That's all I'm asking right now."

"Why I…used my tongue when I kissed you?"

"Yes. Exactly. Why?"

He studied her face for an endless moment as he realized he didn't have the faintest idea. "I, uh…"

"Yeah?"

"I wanted the kiss to look convincing to the guy outside the window. I did what I had to do to make it that way." Hadn't he?

"But your *back* was to the window. Whoever was out there couldn't tell if there were…tongues involved, or not."

He wondered, vaguely, if he'd ever had such a strange

conversation as this in his life. "Hell, Jo. It seemed natural, I guess. A natural thing to do, in that situation."

"Natural?"

"Yeah. We were playing our parts, right? The bride and groom on their wedding night."

"But you never, I mean, all these years we have known each other. All my life…"

"Yeah?"

"You never did anything like that with me before."

"Right. I didn't. And I apologize. I went too far and I—"

"Don't apologize. *Please.*"

"But I—"

"Did you like it?" The words came out in a rush. Her astonished expression said it all. She couldn't believe she had said such a thing.

He quelled the sudden urge to grin. "Well, yeah."

She was frowning—a very intense sort of frown. "Are you sure you understood the question? I asked if you liked—"

"I got it. You asked if I liked kissing you, with a little bit of tongue involved." Her face, if possible, got even redder than it was already. "And I said yeah."

"It was enjoyable for you, kissing me that way?"

"Didn't I just say that?"

"Yes, I thought you did. I wanted to be sure."

"Okay, then. You can be sure."

She unclasped her hands, looked at her palms as if she couldn't decide what to do with them next. Then she whirled away, strode to the bed and dropped to the edge of it.

He approached cautiously. "Mind if I…?"

"Of course I don't. Sit."

He sat. Beside her.

"Dekker…"

He made a low noise, to let her know he was there, and that he was listening.

"Something has…happened to me. Something I never expected. Something I never *imagined*…" She looked down at her feet and added in a tiny voice, "Or at least, I don't *think* I imagined." She let out a tiny groan. "Oh, I don't know. I don't know if I can bear to tell you…to ask you…" She shook her head slowly, wearily, back and forth.

He waited. What else could he do-at that point? Maybe Atwood had somehow managed to get through the extensive security network his brother employed at Angel's Crest, managed to get through and threaten her somehow. Maybe she had some incurable disease.

It didn't matter. Whatever it was, as soon as she told him, they could face it together.

"I don't know how to say it," she murmured. "Except to just *say* it…"

"Good idea."

She drew herself up and looked straight at him. He had never seen her look so determined—or so lost.

She said, "Dekker, I…I *want* you. I know this is a lot to ask, but do you think, maybe, that we could make love together?"

Chapter 14

It was not what he'd expected. Not by a long shot.

And he must have looked as thunderstruck as he felt, because she instantly jumped to her feet and started protesting. "Oh. Oh, look. Never mind." She threw up both hands. "Oh, why did I say that? I do not believe that I said that." She pressed her hands against her ears, as if by blocking out sound she could somehow take back the words.

Then she dropped her hands to her sides, heaved a big sigh and pleaded, "Oh, Dekker. Could we...do you think we could, um, pretend that I never said that?"

"Jo..."

"No. Now, you listen."

He looked at her levelly.

"Are you listening?"

He nodded, to show that he was.

And she asked again, "Will you *please* forget what I just said?"

She had to know the answer to that one. He said nothing, just went on looking her square in the eye.

A shudder passed through her. "Oh. Oh, this is awful. I never should have told you. You should have let me just—"

"Jo. Settle down. *Sit* down. Please."

She chewed on her lower lip for a moment, her sweet face contorted with distress. And then, with a little moan, she slumped back down beside him.

He gave her—and himself—a moment to regroup. Then, with some caution, he put his arm around her.

She let out a second small, agonized groan. He held on to her—but lightly. After another iffy moment, she relaxed and laid her head on his shoulder.

"Jo," he said softly. "This is not a terrible thing."

"Oh, well," she mumbled. "Easy for you to say."

He kissed the top of her head, gave her shoulder a squeeze. "We've been through so much together. We can get through this."

She gave a small humph. "How?"

Now she'd finally told him what she wanted, it all seemed very clear to him. Simple as adding one and one and coming up with two. "If you want this marriage to have sex in it, well, okay. That's fine with me."

She gave him a nudge with her elbow in the old, wonderful, teasing way. "Don't get too excited at the idea."

"I'm excited." And he was, suddenly—that hot, rising feeling.

She must have been looking down at his lap, because her head shot up. "Dekker!"

He spoke lazily, with some humor. "Well now, Jo.

If lovemaking's in the offing, a man will often become excited."

"Oh, really? Thanks for the tip."

"Anytime."

She looked…what? Doubtful? Concerned? He suggested tenderly, "Go ahead. Say it. Whatever it is."

"I just…I wasn't sure. I didn't know. If you would want to, with me. If you even *could*."

Even with all her hesitations and sighs, he took her meaning. "There was a while there, a few years ago, when I couldn't. But recently, I have noticed that the necessary equipment has started showing signs of life again."

She looked at him expectantly. And he decided that it was about time they went ahead and got it out there, said the name. Told the truth. "You heard about the problem from Stacey, right?"

Jo nodded.

"What did she tell you?"

"Oh, vague things. She never said it outright. But she hinted, once or twice, in the last few months you were still living together, that you were not able to, uh…"

"Get it up?"

She lifted one shoulder in a half-shrug. "I didn't take her too seriously. She said so many crazy things at the end. It got so I could never tell what she'd made up in her own confused, unhappy mind, and what had really happened. I learned that whatever she said, I shouldn't put a lot of store in it—but then, the night of DeDe's weddin', when you and I were talking about man-woman love…?" She let the sentence wander off, looked at him for confirmation.

He gave it. "Yeah, I remember."

"Dead meat, is what you said. That you were dead meat when it came to man-woman love."

"That's right, I said that—and?"

"Well, it kind of stuck with me. And later, after you kissed me at my house on our own weddin' night, after I started realizing that I would like it if you kissed me some more, I did get to wondering if maybe what Stacey said had been true."

"It was. I couldn't do it, couldn't make love with her, not there at the end. Maybe I still did love her, even then. It's hard to say. But I sure as hell didn't *want* her. I didn't even *want* to want her."

"Oh, Dekker. I am so sorry...."

He lifted his hand from her shoulder, laid it against her silky hair, felt the warmth of it, the tender curve of her skull beneath his palm. "There is no reason for you to be sorry."

"You never would have met her, if she hadn't been my friend."

"That hardly makes my bad marriage your fault."

"I wanted...to help you. To help *both* of you. I loved you both, so much, and you were both so unhappy, both hurting so bad."

"You did help." He clasped her shoulder again, gave it a squeeze. "You saved my damn life, after Stacey was gone. And you did all you could to help her, too. More than *I* ever did, that's for sure."

"No. I didn't."

"Yes, you did."

"It wasn't enough."

"Jo. With Stacey, nothing was *ever* enough."

She let out a small, mournful sound. "So sad..."

"Yeah. Yeah, it was. Real sad..." He insinuated his

hand beneath the warm, silky fall of her hair. She lifted her head from his shoulder and looked at him, mouth tipped up, dark eyes alight.

He wrapped his hand around the back of her neck. So good, he thought. To be able to touch her again. To let himself touch her in this whole new way. He brushed her lips lightly with his, felt her shiver slightly, beneath his hand.

It came to him that he loved the scent of her, that he always had and always would. She smelled of soap and shampoo. Clean. Fresh. With that tempting hint of flowers—and something more. Something that was distinctly Jo, something that, to him, would always mean all the good things, the sweetest things….

"Dekker?"

"Um?"

"Do you want to…right now?"

"Do you?"

"Oh, yes." Her eagerness enchanted him. But then she frowned. "I, well, I think it is only fair to warn you. I'm not all that experienced. It was only a few times, with Bobby. And I have to admit, those times weren't very good. I always thought that it *could* be, you know, good. But I didn't know what I was doin', and Bobby Atwood was…well, for a guy goin' nowhere, he was sure in an all-fired hurry to get there, if you know what I mean."

He kissed the end of her nose. "We'll work it out."

"I just wanted you to know."

He put his mouth on hers again, tasting. She sighed some more, her lips softly parting, inviting his tongue inside.

He could never have refused such a sweet invitation.

He tasted her, more deeply, sweeping the secret flesh

of her underlip, running his tongue over her pretty white teeth, and then meeting *her* tongue, which shyly darted back at first, then, hesitant but eager, came forward to rub against his own.

He guided her back, to lie across the bed with him. She went without hesitation, smiling against his mouth.

They lay there, kissing—long, lazy kisses. He was enjoying every sigh, every slightest hungry quiver of her body under his. He wanted to make it last, stretch it out into forever. To make it last for her sake, because she was Jo, because that fool, Atwood, hadn't had sense enough to love her the way she ought to be loved.

For her sake, and also for his own.

This, now—Jo's mouth under his, her sweet, soft body moving beneath his hands—this was a gift the likes of which he had never thought to know.

So damn many gifts she had given him, down all the years. Gifts of loyalty, gifts of time, the simple gift of her presence when he had been hopelessly lost and completely alone, when he had nothing to say and nothing left inside himself to give to anyone else. The gift of her insistence, her refusal to give up on him, that dogged stubbornness in her that made her stick with a friend till the end, no matter what.

So damn many gifts.

And now this…

He wanted to make it good for her, to show her what it *could* be, between a woman and a man, so that later, when the threat Robert Atwood posed to her had been effectively neutralized, when she was ready to move on to the kind of man she deserved, she'd go with confidence in herself as a desirable woman, with the full knowledge of how to take pleasure and how to give it back in kind.

He raised his head enough that he could look at her, at her flushed face, her kiss-swollen mouth. Her lashes fluttered up and her eyes were so dark and soft right then, he thought of summer nights or of falling, falling forever, but into a good place.

She asked his name, on a whisper of breath, and she raised a hand, brushed it lightly back from his temple, fingers stroking his hair, sliding against his scalp in a tender brand and then gone.

He lowered his mouth to the smooth space between her brows, murmured, "What?" against her skin.

But she had no real question, or if she did, it had already become unnecessary to ask it. Because she only closed her eyes again, stroked his shoulder, said his name once more, so low, on a moan.

He touched the side of her throat, felt the pounding of her pulse there. And then he pressed his mouth where his fingers had been, taking a long, lazy moment to taste the rhythm of her heart, smiling to himself when she sucked in a little gasp at the feel of his tongue on her skin.

Tenderly, still feeding on the pulse point in her throat, he let his fingers wander downward—but not too far. Just enough to cup his hand over one soft, upthrusting breast. She gasped again.

He raised his head and waited for her to look at him. Those lashes fluttered up. She gave him a smile—one that trembled at first and then bloomed wide.

He found he was as hungry to look as to touch. So he let his gaze wander down the curvy length of her, gently molding her breast at the same time, feeling the nipple pressing into his palm even through the layers of cloth that protected it.

She wore a T-shirt the color of a mango when you cut

it open, exposing the sweet meat inside. And a pair of trim green slacks that came midway between her knees and her ankles. Slip-on sandals on her feet.

She lifted her head to see what he was looking at.

He suggested, his voice gruff with arousal, "You could get rid of those sandals with no effort at all."

As he watched, she toed off one sandal and then the other. They thumped to the rug at the side of the bed.

"How's that?" she asked, a little breathless.

He looked into her face again, saw excitement and the glint of apprehension. "Perfect." He touched her mouth, with the pads of two fingers, then traced those fingers downward, putting his own mouth where his fingers had been, kissing her again, feeding on her mouth, drawing on her tongue until she surrendered it, gave it up, let him have it to suck on.

She moaned, and another of those long, hungry shivers went through her. He felt that shiver under his hands as it shimmered down her body.

Her body...

Strange. He'd known her virtually her entire life, remembered standing over her crib a few days after her birth, amazed at how ugly a baby could be, thinking that something so small and unappealing would need to be protected, knowing, even then, at the age of five, that he would always protect her, no matter what.

But her body?

Until lately it hadn't concerned him much. Oh, as she'd grown up, he'd been well aware that she wasn't the least bit ugly anymore, that she had all the right curves in all the right places. But her curviness, her womanliness, didn't seem to have anything at all to do with him or with their relationship to each other.

Until lately...

Lately—as in that dress the other night, the one that wasn't quite gold and wasn't quite brown, the one that hugged all those curves that weren't supposed to concern him. Yeah, he could still picture it, the way that dress had clung to her backside when she'd turned and walked away from him.

And in that swimsuit she'd found in the cabana that same day—it was turquoise and blue, with splashes of gold at the waist. She had stretched out on that rubber raft and floated there so peacefully. He'd known she'd wanted to be left alone, and he'd known he ought to let her have what she wanted. But he hadn't been able to resist the desire to get close to her. Eventually he had surfaced at her side.

At first she wouldn't look at him. She lay with her cheek on her arm, her head turned away.

Since she wouldn't look at him, he let himself look at her.

At her body.

The word "smooth" had come to mind. Smooth and soft. Warm. Touchable. Tiny hairs glinted like gold dust on the backs of her thighs.

He'd thought then that he did want to touch her— feel the warmth, the smoothness, the silkiness of those little hairs....

He wanted to touch her. And in much more than just a friendly way. He'd felt his body rising, responding to the sight of the woman that he wanted.

And it was okay to let himself want her. It was good to know that he *could* want a woman again—after all, for a while, there had been some doubt on that score.

Also, he had been certain, there in the pool, that he would never do anything about wanting her. They were friends, married for a time, because she needed to be married. But she herself had defined the terms, that night in her mother's backyard.

We are deep and true friends. But we are not lovers....

He'd dribbled that water over her thighs to force her to look at him—and also to watch the way it beaded up and glittered as it trickled over her skin....

"Dekker?" She was staring up at him now, stretched out with him across this bed he had never thought to share with her. He saw a hundred questions in her eyes.

For the first time as a man with her, he felt more than aroused. He felt...something hot and insistent, something very close to need.

He sucked in a long breath and thought about control—that he needed to exercise a little of it about now. He couldn't really have her now, be inside her, feel her softness closing around him. He would have to wait for that. This marriage of theirs was not forever. They couldn't afford to go making any babies together. And at the moment he had nothing to keep a baby from happening.

Then again, maybe she did. It was doubtful. But no harm in asking.

"Are you on the pill, Jo?"

Those eyes went wide again. She shook her head. "Oh, I didn't even think about that."

He smoothed his hand down her hair again, wrapped a coil of the silky stuff around a finger. "No diaphragm handy, huh?"

"Uh-uh." She started to sit up.

He clasped her shoulder. "Where are you going?"

"Uh, well, I thought, you know, that we'd have to wait until—"

"Please stay here. For a little."

"But we probably shouldn't—"

"We won't. Not until later. Not until tonight."

She swallowed. "Tonight?"

He nodded, thinking of what they *could* do now, that he could still give her pleasure, maybe get to see her face as a climax shuddered through her, certainly get to see her naked, here, in the warm light of a California morning.

The mango-colored shirt ended at her waist. Such a simple act, to insinuate his hand between it and the satiny skin of her belly. He pushed the shirt up, put his mouth there, on her stomach, swirled his tongue around her navel, then dipped it into that tender little groove.

"Oh!" she said, and "Oh!" again.

He pushed the shirt up farther. "Raise your arms." She did. He pulled the shirt over her head and then tossed it toward a chair a few feet from the bed. Her bra was bright pink, and her breasts swelled temptingly from the lacy cups. The thing hooked in the back, though.

He'd deal with it in a minute. He slid a finger under the button at the waist of the green slacks.

"Dekker Smith, what are you up to?"

"That's *Bravo,* or it will be soon." With a flick of his thumb, the button came undone.

She let out a small sound of distress as he tugged her zipper down. "Well all right then. Dekker Bravo, you are undressing me."

"That's right. Lift up."

"But you said that we—"

He put a finger to her lips. "Shh. Trust me?"

She gently pushed his hand away. "You know that I do."

"We'll be careful."

"Isn't that what men and women are always saying to each other, right before they get carried away and end up not being careful at all?"

"Maybe it is. But this is different. We're not kids. I have…some measure of control. I won't go any farther than we can afford to go. I promise you."

She looked at him, long and deep. "You're sure?"

Was he? Hell, yes. He was sure. He could do this. Touch. Taste. But not possess. "Positive."

"We're just going to…?"

"Play a little. Safe play. I promise. Later I'll go out and get us some protection. And then, tonight…" He let the thought finish itself.

"Hmm," she said, a pleased sort of sound, and then she put her soft hand on the side of his face. "Well, anyway. If something did happen now, we *are* married…."

"Nothing's going to happen," he vowed. "Nothing that will make babies. I swear it."

Her eyes probed his for another long moment. Then she said the word he was waiting for. "Okay."

It was all he needed to hear. He put his mouth back on hers and he kissed her, another endless, seeking, very wet kiss. As he kissed her, he undressed her, pushing those green pants off her hips and down, getting rid of her silky panties. And then, finally, taking away her bra.

She sighed and she moaned, and she pressed herself close to him, those beautiful bare breasts against his chest, her legs rubbing along his. He began kissing his way down her body, tasting her flesh, finding it so sweet and tender, so warm. So good…

He lingered at her breasts for a long time, sucking the hard little nipples into his mouth, rolling his tongue around them, loving the way she lifted her body, pressing it closer, giving him more….

He moved lower, down over her soft belly, to the nest of brown curls at the top of her thighs. By then all her initial apprehension had fled. She was openly, honestly needful, clutching his shoulders, making hungry, willing noises deep in her throat.

He loved that. Her very openness. She was just so… responsible, as a rule. Letting go rarely came easily to her.

Gently, he pushed her thighs apart and settled between them. She stiffened and she gasped when he put his mouth on her. And then she cried out.

And after that cry, she surrendered completely, opening wider, offering herself up to him, letting him do what he wanted, letting him taste her so deeply, he would never forget, never lose her completely. Always, in the most primal part of his consciousness, the taste of her would linger, imprinted on his senses, a branding on his soul.

She was wet and slick, dripping with her need and his hunger combined. She held his head, slim fingers splayed, gripping hard, pushing her body frantically against him. He held on, too, cradling her bottom in his hands, lifting her up like a cup to drink from, running his tongue over the soft, secret folds, latching on and sucking deeply, rubbing the swollen nub of flesh that was the center of her pleasure.

She said things, promised things, wild things. Things like forever. He took those promises for what they were: words of the moment, of her passion.

They did not have forever. But they did have right now.

And now was good enough—more than good enough. It was better than anything he'd ever expected. A gift.

The perfect kind of gift—given so freely and completely unsought. A gift he would save in his heart, even after he had to let her go.

The tiny, soft explosions started. He felt them, there, against his tongue.

He stayed with her, maintaining the secret, intimate kiss as the long shudders took her. She cried out again. And again. He held on, his mouth tight against her, tasting her woman's release, sharing her pleasure at its highest point, until she went lax with a heavy sigh and pushed at his shoulders.

"Oh. Stop…I can't…" He took pity on her then and broke the long, forbidden kiss. "Oh, come up here. Up here, to me…" Her hands weren't pushing anymore. They were pulling, tugging, urging him upward. He went to her, moved up her body. She wrapped those soft arms around him, and she buried her head against his neck.

"Oh," she said again. And then his name, over and over, a litany, a soft, tender chant. "Dekker, Dekker, Dekker, Dekker…"

He made a low, rough, questioning sound.

She chuckled. It was the naughtiest laugh he had ever heard. "What you did…I do not believe what you did…"

He smoothed her hair and he stroked her slim back and he held on, tight. She slid her leg between his, rubbing her body up close, as if she would melt right into him. When she got where she wanted to be, she went still.

They lay like that for a time, arms and legs entwined.

She was the one who moved first. She reached down between them and cupped her hand over his fly.

Molten heat went pouring through him. He pulled back enough to give her a warning look. "Better not."

Those big dark eyes gleamed at him. "Trust me." She stuck out that pink tongue of hers and moistened those soft, tempting lips. "Nothing's going to happen that will make babies. I swear it."

What else could he do?

He whispered, "Okay."

Chapter 15

The too-brief days that followed were magical, the nights pure enchantment. They were the kind of nights Joleen had never dared to imagine she might someday know.

They kept their word to each other, that first morning, played with each other, did the most shocking and incredible things to each other—but held back from making love fully.

In the afternoon Dekker went out and got what they needed.

And that night they were careful and quiet, with Sam so close, right in the next room. They engaged the privacy lock on his door and they held their hands over each other's mouths when one or the other got too carried away.

Carried away...

Oh, yes. That was the word for it.

Dekker plain and simply carried her away.

He kissed her and caressed her until her body felt as if all the nerves had been swollen, turned inside out, so that even the feel of the air on her skin was almost too pleasurable to bear. And when he came into her…oh, was there ever any feeling quite like that?

To hold him inside her, pushing in her so deep, reaching for the very center of her, surging toward her heart.

How could it be? *Dekker,* of all people. Here she'd grown up right next door to him and never known the things that he would someday do to her body, the wonder he would bring to her, the sweet, shattering spell he would weave on her senses.

Could they go on like this forever? Oh, probably not. But that was okay. Just to have this, for now, was more pure magic than Joleen ever would have asked of life.

Sammy put up no fuss at all when they left for the resort on Friday morning. He let Joleen kiss him goodbye and then he squirmed to get down.

"Pway, Mama. Manny…" He had Mandy's name by then, but without the *d.*

"He will be right here, *señora,*" the nanny promised. "I will take very, very good care."

Dekker took her hand. "Come on, Jo. The car is waiting.…"

La Puerta al Cielo. Doorway to Heaven.

And it was. The resort consisted of a spacious open-air lobby overlooking seven sugar-cube white buildings, two suites in each. On the grounds and near the buildings prickly flowering cactus, ironwood and palo verde trees grew. Gleaming little brooks, accented with miniature waterfalls, wound in and out among the desert blooms.

Doorway to heaven. Oh, definitely.

Their suite was twice the size of Joleen's house. The talavera-tiled bathroom contained a tub every bit as roomy as the one they'd left behind at Angel's Crest, a tub made for lovers. And the bathroom and the bedroom kind of blended together, so a person could step right through from bath to bed. Joleen and Dekker found this feature wonderfully convenient.

Even the floors of the place took a person's breath away. They were made of fossilized limestone from Yucatan, one of the attendants explained, inset with pebbles in intricate designs. *Tapates de piedras,* the attendant called them: "stone carpets," mosaic designs of fish and birds that made Joleen think of exotic and faraway places—Ancient Greece or maybe Rome.

They had an ocean-view patio, furnished with big white-cushioned rattan chairs, with a telescope in case they felt the urge to gaze more closely at the stars. There was a half-moon-shaped hot tub built into the patio wall, and a set of stairs that spiraled upward to the roof.

And there was a bed on that roof. The first night of their visit, very late, they climbed those stairs and used that bed. It was more than the doorway to heaven that night. Lying there on the rooftop patio, with Dekker— *joined* with Dekker—that was heaven itself. The velvet night so warm and sweet around them, and the stars so close she felt she could reach out and grab a handful, cool silver light to carry with her when they went back downstairs.

He pressed so deep into her, and then withdrew, and

then, slowly, filled her again. She sighed and moved with him, accepting him, losing him, calling him back to her once more. She thought of the ocean, sliding up on the shore, ebbing away, only to return again, over and over, the rhythm endless. And endlessly sweet...

The next day, near twilight, they walked on the beach, which was gold as the pelt of a lion, the sand so fine, silky as bath powder. They watched the evening light soften, watched the sky turn pink and then the sea. Slowly, magically, it all deepened to indigo as the night came on.

Then they went back to their suite and they made love some more.

The days seemed to flow, one into the other. Two days. Three. Four. Five...

Except for missing Sam, she could go on like this forever.

But time did not stand still for them. Friday came. They flew back to Los Angeles. Sam ran to her when she went to him in the nursery. He clung to her.

For about five minutes.

Then he was squirming to get down, calling for "Manny."

They stayed the weekend with Emma and Jonas, spending lots of time with the children, in the nursery and out by the pool. Then, when the nights came, heaven was waiting all over again.

Monday they boarded one of Jonas's jets and took off for home. Joleen felt a little sad to leave the magic of their honeymoon behind.

But there was so much to do, their whole lives to live. They would start looking for a house immediately, and Joleen would have to find the right day care, and of course things would be hectic at the salon. She'd have a lot of catching up to do, after two weeks away.

And Dekker had started talking about expanding his detective business. He wanted to find a bigger, nicer office in a better building than he was in now. He'd hire some office help, start looking for a couple more good investigators.

"What I'm talking about," he said, "is starting over from the ground up." He'd been running things by the seat of his pants up till now. For their honeymoon he'd just locked everything up and made sure the answering machine was on. If he expanded, he'd have people to cover for him whenever he took time off.

It would be a whole new ball game, he said. And he seemed to be looking forward to it, to using some of the money he'd inherited and making A-1 Investigations into the biggest and best agency in the city.

There would also be the Atwoods to deal with. But that didn't worry her so much anymore. Once she found the right day care, she would be ready. Ready in every sense of the word to deflect whatever accusations Robert Atwood tried to throw at her. Especially now that she and Dekker shared a bed. Let Bobby's awful father send his detectives around to spy on them. Those detectives would see a couple who were married in every sense of the word.

The Bravo jet touched down at Will Rogers World Airport at a little after one in the afternoon. They got all the way to Joleen's house in the Lexus without spotting a single reporter on their tail.

It had been so relaxing at Angel's Crest and in Baja. No reporters ever got past the gates at the Bravo mansion. And the exclusive resort was the same. At La Puerta al Cielo, any nosy person wanting to sneak a peak at the spectacular grounds—or at the lucky few who enjoyed such luxury—was simply turned away by the security guard at the front gate.

Now that they were back home, they'd probably have to deal with the media again, at least to some extent. But not yet. Joleen decided to enjoy the privacy while it lasted.

Joleen's little house seemed somehow to have grown even smaller after the lavish accommodations they'd enjoyed for the past couple of weeks—smaller and a little bit worn. That threadbare spot on the arm of her easy chair hadn't seemed quite so obvious to her before. And she'd never really noticed how many scars and scuffs marred the surface of her big round oak coffee table.

Still, this little house *was* home—and would be until they found a new one. She felt a rush of affection for the place. She also felt chilly. The weather had turned. The sky outside was a sheet of gray, the temperature in the forties, a misty rain falling. Dekker checked the furnace and fired it up.

Sammy had eaten on the plane and was more than ready for his nap. Joleen put him down. He was out almost the minute his little head hit the pillow. She turned from his bed to find Dekker waiting in the doorway to the dining room. She pulled the door closed as she crossed the threshold and went to him, sliding her arms around his hard waist.

She tipped her mouth up. He took it. They shared a long, slow, lovely kiss.

He was the one who broke it. "You're shivering."

"Umm. Heater's on, though. In a few minutes, I'll be just fine." She stretched up, planted another kiss on those wonderful lips of his, a quick one, that time. "Hungry?"

"Always." The corners of his mouth curved up in

a lazy smile. He cupped her bottom and pulled her in tightly against him, so that she could feel just how hungry he was.

She tried to look reproachful, though her every nerve had set to humming with naughty anticipation. "You know I meant for lunch."

He bent his head and nibbled at her neck. "*I* didn't."

She tried not to moan. "I thought…didn't you say you had to get over to the agency?"

"Soon…" He breathed the word against her skin.

She felt his tongue, sliding along the skin of her throat, followed by the light scrape of his teeth. She did moan then.

He pretended she had actually said a real word. "What was that?"

"I think…"

"Yeah?"

She reached around behind her and grabbed one of the hands that held her bottom. "You had better come with me." She pulled him toward the kitchen—and the door in there that led to her bedroom.

They were passing the phone on the kitchen wall when it jarred to life. They both jumped, froze, looked at the phone and then at each other. The phone rang again.

Joleen did not want to answer. Neither did Dekker. She could see that in his midnight eyes.

But their honeymoon was over. They were back in real life now. They had to start dealing with all the usual responsibilities again. And besides, she thought rather smugly, once they closed their bedroom door of an evening, they could head straight for heaven. And they could go there every night, with little chance of interruption.

Dekker was watching her face, reading it, she knew. He saw that she would answer the call. So he did it for her, snaring the phone off the wall in the middle of the third ring and holding it out to her.

She pressed it to her ear and heard her mother's voice. "Joly? Baby? Is that you?"

"Hi, Mama."

"How long have you been home?"

"Not long. Twenty minutes or so."

"I left a message for you to call me as soon as you got in."

"Sorry. I haven't checked my messages yet."

"Well, never mind. I have reached you. Did you have a good time?"

"I did. A wonderful time."

"And Dekker?"

Joleen hooked a finger in the belt loop of her husband's faded jeans. She gave a tug to get him up nice and close, then planted a quick kiss right on the dent in his chin. "Dekker had a fine time, too—everything okay? At the shop? At home?"

"Everything is fine. No problems. Is Dekker there with you now?"

"He sure is."

"And our Sammy?"

"We just put him down for his nap."

"Good—I want you to stay right there, both you and Dekker. Do not go anywhere."

Now, what was going on? "But Mama, what—"

"Don't start askin' questions. It will all be explained."

"You know, Mama, I hate it when you get mysterious on me."

"One hour, okay? Don't either of you go anywhere for sixty full minutes. Give me your solemn vow on that."

"Mama—"

"Joleen, I want to hear your promise."

"All right, all right. I promise. An hour."

"Dekker, too."

"But—"

"Ask him."

Joleen blew out an exasperated breath and put her hand over the receiver, "Mama wants to talk to us. I don't know what about. She says she'll be here within an hour and she wants us both to promise to wait here till she comes."

He shrugged. "Tell her we'll be here."

Joleen spoke into the receiver again. "All right. We'll be here."

"Good." The line went dead.

Joleen held the phone away from her ear and glared at it. "I hate when she does stuff like this."

Dekker chuckled. He took the phone and hooked it back on the wall. Then he pulled Joleen close. She rested her head against his heart and grumbled, "Kind of spoiled the mood, didn't she? How can I drag you back to my room and have my way with you when Mama could be knockin' on the door any second now?"

He lifted her chin with a finger. "Buck up."

She pulled a sour face. "Isn't it nice to be home?"

"Maybe I'll take a sandwich, after all…."

So they had lunch while they waited.

Joleen got some bread from the freezer and opened a can of tuna. Dekker had a Rolling Rock and she had a Fresca over ice.

When they'd eaten the sandwiches, Joleen rinsed the dishes and put them in the dishwasher. Then she sat back down with Dekker at the table. He nursed his beer, and she ended up getting herself a second Fresca before they heard the doorbell ring.

Camilla hardly gave the bell a chance to finish chiming before she was poking her head in the door and calling out, "Hel-lo!"

Joleen and Dekker got up and started for the living room. Three steps later, as they cleared the doorway to the dining room, they saw that Camilla wasn't alone.

Antonia Atwood stood at her side—and a much different Antonia than the mouse in mauve who had attended DeDe's wedding three weeks before.

The faded brown hair had been artfully permed and colored and beautifully cut in a soft chin-length style. And the face...

Why, it was a *pretty* face now, cleverly enhanced by a deft hand. The effect was not of a woman made up, but a woman at her best, her eyes wide and bright, her cheeks flushed with healthy color, her mouth soft and inviting and subtly red.

And Antonia's taste in clothes had changed, too. What she wore now suited her perfectly. Simple lines, the best fabrics: a silk shirt the color of a ripe peach, linen slacks in honey tan.

Joleen knew instantly who had wrought this amazing transformation. She confronted the culprit. "Mama. Tell me you are not the one. Tell me you have not had this woman over at the salon."

"Well now, baby, I can't tell you that. Because the truth is, I have. We have become real close in the last two weeks, Tony and I, and—"

"Tony?" Joleen could hardly believe her ears. "You call her *Tony* now?"

"That's right. I do. And I want you to settle down, you hear me? Don't go jumpin' to any conclusions until you understand all that has happened while you were away."

It was a reasonable request, and Joleen knew it. She commanded, in a controlled tone, "Talk, Mama. And make it good."

But Antonia was the one who spoke next. "Please," she said, her wispy voice changed somehow, sounding so much stronger, so much more sure than before. "Let's start with the most important point, with the reason that I am here, now, in your house."

That sounded like an excellent idea. "Well, fine. You tell me. Why are you here?"

"Because I want you to know that I have done what needed doing. I have stood up to my husband for the first time in our thirty-plus years together. There will be no lawsuit. No one is going to try to take Samuel away from you."

Chapter 16

Joleen's legs had gone suddenly wobbly. "I don't...I can't believe that you—" What was she trying to say? Whatever it was, it had flown clean out of her head.

Her mother said, "Honey, you look like you could use a chair. You come on in here and sit down."

Dekker had her by the elbow. He guided her into the living room and eased her into the chair with the threadbare spot on the arm.

Once he had her settled, he frowned down at her. "What can I get you? What do you need?"

"Nothing." She reached out, touched his arm in reassurance. "I'm okay." He still looked way too concerned. She spoke with more force. "Seriously. I am fine." As she said the words, she found they were true. The shock of what she'd just heard was passing.

Dekker moved to the side, but stayed with her, next to her chair.

She sat up straighter. Her mother and Antonia Atwood stood, side by side, across the oak coffee table. It was a united front if Joleen had ever seen one.

And Camilla had the strangest expression on her face. She looked at Dekker and she glanced at Joleen and then quickly looked back at Dekker again. "Hmm," she said softly. "Oh, yes. Oh, my, yes."

Whatever her mother was mumbling about, it could wait. Joleen wanted a few answers. And she wanted them now.

"All right," she said. "I am listening. I hope that one of you plans to explain what has been happening around here."

Camilla stopped glancing back and forth between Joleen and Dekker. She cleared her throat. "Well, I suppose you could say it all started two days after you left for California."

Antonia nodded. "That was when I went to speak with your mother at the salon."

Camilla grinned. "I ordered her out, at first."

"But I was persistent."

"You certainly were." The two women shared a smile that could only be called fond.

Then Antonia looked at Joleen again. "I approached your mother because, by the time I got up my courage… by the time I finally accepted the fact that I would have to take action, that I could not allow things to go on as they were, you and your new husband had gone out of town. It was all over the newspapers, about your marriage—" she glanced up at Dekker "—and about you, Dekker, about what you'd learned of your real background." Her eyes met Joleen's again. "And Robert was furious. He had talked to our lawyer, of course, and been told that your marriage and your new husband's wealth would make things a lot harder for him. Pretty much impossible, really, was what the lawyer said…"

Antonia paused. A small sound of distress escaped her. "Oh, my dear Joleen, the whole time, even before your sister's wedding day, when Robert first told me what he planned to do, I knew it was so very, very wrong. I'd seen you with Samuel, seen with my own eyes what a fine mother you are. And I also knew…" She hesitated, as if whatever she meant to say was just too difficult to admit.

But then she forged on. "I knew that Robert and I had not been the parents to our darling Bobby that we should have been. That Bobby had grown up to be… weak. And irresponsible. That what he'd done to you, leaving you all on your own with a baby to raise, was unforgivable. And yet, there you were, reaching out to us, offering us a place in your little boy's life. I did admire you. So much. But Robert—" Antonia hung her beautifully groomed head. "Oh, I don't know. I just don't know about that man."

"Now, now, Tony." Camilla wrapped a comforting arm around the other woman's shoulder. "It is going to be okay, now. You know that. It will be all right."

Antonia sent Camilla a grateful glance, then turned to Joleen again. "Oh, I wish you could understand, though of course I know I cannot expect you to. My husband could not bear to admit how totally we failed, with our son. And he would have given anything for what he will never have—another chance. He was—he still is, really—terribly confused. He convinced himself that he could somehow start all over. That it was his duty to steal your son from you and raise Samuel the way he knew, deep in his heart, that he should have raised our Bobby." Antonia's eyes had a faraway look, at that moment. Faraway and infinitely sad.

She seemed to shake herself. "But that was then. Now, as I told you, there is no way he will even *try* to take Samuel away from you."

Joleen leaned forward. "You sound so certain about that."

"I am. Very certain. You see, after I talked with Camilla…" Antonia paused to fondly pat the hand that clasped her shoulder. "I went to Robert and I told him that there would be no custody battle. That if he tried such a thing, I would not only leave him, I would be there, in court, to testify in your behalf." A bleak smile lifted the edges of Antonia's mouth. "He was not happy with me. I spent two nights at your mother's house, as a matter of fact, to give him a chance to cool down a little. But we are…working on our problems now. And it looks as if we may come through this together, still married to each other, after all.

"Joleen." Antonia pulled away from Camilla. She took a step to the side, as if she would go on around the coffee table, come to where Joleen sat in the comfy old chair. But then she stopped herself. "I hope someday you can bring yourself to forgive me. And maybe eventually even find it in your heart to forgive Robert, too. I should have come forward sooner. I know that. I am so sorry, not only for what my son did to you, but also for all those terrible things Robert said to you the day that your sister was married. And beyond that, for the constant anxiety you must have suffered in the past few weeks, believing you would be facing a long, drawn-out court battle. I wanted to try to call you, as soon as I'd confronted Robert…"

"But I stopped her," Camilla said, sounding thoroughly pleased with herself. "I wanted you to have that time away." A knowing gleam lit up the big brown eyes. "I can see I was right, too—that your little getaway has been very good, for both of you. And, anyway, the news was right here, waitin' for you, when you got home. Oh, it is all going to work out, now, isn't it? It is all going to work out just fine." Now those brown eyes were brimming.

Joleen said, "Mama," in a warning tone.

"I won't," vowed Camilla. "I will not start in cryin' right now. You do not have to worry. You have my word."

Joleen turned her gaze to the woman at her mother's side. More than a good haircut and a few makeup tips had happened to Antonia Atwood. A much deeper change had taken place. Here was a woman who had finally stood up for what she believed in. The quaking mauve mouse was no more.

Slow down here, a more cynical voice in the back of Joleen's mind cautioned. A little suspicion is healthy. This could be a trick, some new angle Robert Atwood has decided to try against you, a clever way to get you to let down your guard.

But Joleen didn't believe that. How could she?

Just looking in Antonia's eyes told the real story. Bobby Atwood's mother had taken a stand. And she would not be backing down from it.

Joleen said, "Thank you, for this. For doing the right thing. For…coming to me now."

Antonia dipped her chin in a nod of acknowledgment. "It's not enough. But it is a start. And I also want you to know that arrangements have been made for you to get the financial support Bobby should have provided when he learned there would be a baby. It will be a considerable amount of money. Our family lawyer will be contacting you in the next few days to discuss all the details."

Joleen opened her mouth to protest that she didn't need any money. But she shut it without speaking. It wasn't *her* money, after all. It was Sam's, and he did have a right to it.

The grandmothers left a few minutes later, after Camilla extracted a promise from Joleen that she and Dekker and Sam would have dinner at her house that night.

As soon as she let the two older women out the front door, Joleen turned to her husband. "Well. What do you think of that?"

He shrugged.

She peered at him more closely. "All of a sudden you are very quiet."

"What is there for me to say?"

Something had changed. She couldn't put her finger on what. "Is something wrong?"

"Not a thing."

It came to her what was probably bothering him. "You don't trust her."

"No, that's not so. I think she was telling the absolute truth. I think Robert Atwood knows now that he doesn't have a prayer of taking Sam away from you, not under any circumstances."

Joleen realized she'd been holding her breath. She let it out in a rush. "Oh, Dekker. I believed her, too. But I couldn't completely allow myself to think that we were in the clear until I could hear it from you. I know, sometimes, I can be kind of a fool about trustin' people."

"You are no fool, Jo. And you're right about this. That woman's on the level. I'd stake my whole, newly acquired, totally unearned fortune on that."

So silly, but right then, she felt hesitant about going to him, putting her arms around him, laying her head against his heart. Why? "You know, you do seem kind of distant."

He shrugged again. "Just preoccupied. I should get over to the agency, check my messages. Who the hell knows what I've got there that I need to deal with."

Well, she was not allowing this strange feeling of distance that had popped up out of nowhere to get between them. She moved forward, wrapped her arms around his waist and put her head where she wanted it—against his broad chest. "I'd like to keep you here forever."

She felt his chuckle, a deep rumble against her ear. Was it just a little forced?

He kissed her, on the crown of her head, a sweet, warm pressure, his lips against her hair. And then he was taking her by the arms, setting her back from him. "Gotta go."

"But I—" She stopped herself from begging him to stay a few minutes longer. For heaven's sake, the man did have a business to run. He'd been totally hers for over a week now. And she was spoiled. Now they were back home, she was going to have to get used to giving him a little space.

She thought of Stacey and almost shivered, though the heater had done its job and the house was now cozy and warm. She was not going to become the kind of wife that Stacey had been—clinging and needful, never letting him have a moment to himself.

She put on a bright smile. "Well, go on, then. You get to work."

He turned from her. She trailed after him and stood there in the open doorway, the chilly air outside bringing up the goose bumps along her arms, watching as he hurried away from her down her front steps.

He called sometime later. She wasn't sure exactly when. She and Sam were out picking up a few groceries at the time. He left a message saying he had even more to deal with at the agency than he'd anticipated. He wouldn't be making it back for dinner at Camilla's. He didn't know when he'd get in.

And she shouldn't wait up for him.

She could hear it in his voice. Something *was* bothering him, in spite of his earlier denials.

She tried to call him. At the agency, and on his cell phone. She got voice mail both places. She tried his apartment. Same thing.

Well, fine, she told herself as she put away the wedding gifts Camilla had left in the guest room for her while they were gone. He had to come home eventually. And she *would* insist they talk about it as soon as he did. However late it ended up being, she would be waiting up.

Right after dinner Camilla asked Niki to take Sam upstairs and keep an eye on him for a little while. "And you," she said to Joleen. "You come on with me."

"Mama…"

"Don't you 'mama' me. Come on. This way." Camilla grabbed Joleen's hand and dragged her toward the study, shutting the door behind them once they were inside.

Camilla folded her arms across her middle. "You've had a frown between your brows all evenin'. And Dekker is missing. I can hardly keep up with all the changes around here lately. I want you to tell me. Just tell me straight-out. What has gone wrong now?"

Joleen spoke with measured calm. "Dekker is not missing. He has work to do. He's been away for two weeks and—"

Camilla waved a slender hand. "Don't give me that. There is somethin' wrong here. I can see it in those eyes of yours. And I do not like it. This afternoon I was feelin' so good, too. I actually thought all of your problems were solved."

"Mama—"

Camilla shook her head. "No. Wait. Let me say what I have to say."

"But—"

"I mean it. Let your mother talk."

Joleen let out a groan and dropped into one of the soft, old chairs. "Oh, go ahead. As if I ever could stop you."

Camilla narrowed her eyes and pursed up her mouth. "Don't get righteous on me now, not after the way you have lied to me."

"Mama—"

"Shh. You think I wasn't bound to get it all figured out? You think your mama is a fool, she can't add two and two and come up with four? You two, you and Dekker. I know what you did, schemin' together, deciding to marry to keep Robert Atwood from having any chance of stealing Sam. I had it figured out from the first, even though you lied right in my face and said it wasn't so. I knew. A mother knows. And by the time Tony came looking for me at the shop, I'd done a little deep thinkin' on the subject. And it had come to me that maybe you and Dekker were not such an impossible pair after all."

Joleen shifted in her chair. "Oh, now, what is that supposed to mean?"

"It means, I got to thinking how it was for you two. That maybe it wasn't a problem of there being no spark between you, but that over and over again life had got in the way of you findin' out what you were to each other—first, with your daddy dying, God rest his sweet, sweet soul."

Joleen leaned forward. "Daddy dying? What does that have to do with—"

"Joly honey, you got so responsible after Samuel passed. You had no time for the love that was waitin' for you. And then, along comes that poor, pretty, mixed-up Stacey, getting between you and Dekker, snatchin' him away from you before you even knew he was yours in the first place. And then she hurt him. Hurt him down to his very soul. And after Stacey, well, there was that foolish, handsome Atwood boy. And then that boy dumped you and you had Sam. And by that time both you and Dekker had convinced yourselves that you were immune to love.

"But you know what I told you, that morning after you announced to the family that you and Dekker were tying the knot. It was the truth, what I told you. There is no mistake so big that love can't find a way to make it right in the end.

"Once I saw the truth about the two of you, I knew what you needed. A little time, in close quarters, away from it all. And that is why I didn't let Tony call you with the news that the custody battle was off. I wanted the two of you to have that time. I wanted you to have the chance to find out that you are not immune to love, that you love each other, in a soul-deep, man and woman way."

Camilla parked her hands on her hips and let out

a hard huff of breath. "And it worked, didn't it?" She waved a hand again. "You don't even have to answer. I saw you two together today. And there it was, at last. The fire, as well as the tenderness. You two have it all— or, at least, I could have sworn you did this afternoon."

Camilla fell silent. The beloved, shabby room seemed to echo with everything she had said.

Joleen swallowed the lump that had formed in her throat. And then she jumped from the chair.

"Oh, Mama…"

"Come here, baby. Here to me…" Her mother's arms were waiting. They closed around her.

"Oh, Mama. You are so right…"

"Well, of course I am, baby."

"But…something *is* wrong. I don't know what. He got so far away, all of a sudden, right after you and Antonia left this afternoon."

"You have told him, haven't you? You did say the words?"

"The words?"

Camilla took Joleen's face in her hands. "Honey, I mean, have you told him that you love him—as a *man?* Have you done that?"

Joleen swallowed again.

And her mother dropped her hands, stepped back and sent a look of pure exasperation heavenward. "Oh, well, I should have known. You haven't even *told* him."

"But, Mama, you don't know how it has been. We've been so happy, just livin' every minute for all it was worth. I didn't even think about telling him, about sitting him down and saying, 'Look, I love you. You are the only man for me.' It didn't even seem necessary to say it in words. Everything was going so wonderfully. It's been so beautiful. So right."

"It is necessary," her mother said softly. "He needs to hear that you love him, and he needs to hear it from your mouth."

"Yes. Yes, of course. I can see that. I can see that now."

"Tell him."

"I will."

"As soon as he has sense enough to come home to you."

"I promise."

"And then find out what happened this afternoon that made him pull away."

"Oh, Mama. I…I worry—"

"That is not news, baby. Since your daddy died, you have worried way too much."

"I mean, I worry that he'll think I'm like Stacey, clinging to him, making *demands* on him that he can't handle."

Camilla took her by the shoulders then and gave her a shake. "You listen. You listen to me. You are not Stacey. You never were and you never could be. You are a strong and self-sufficient woman who knows what she wants out of life, not to mention how to go about gettin' it. And Dekker knows that about you. He probably knows it even better than you do. Never, ever is he going to confuse you with that poor, troubled girl. Do you understand?"

"Yes, Mama. I do."

"Talk to him. Stick with him. Get *him* to talk to *you*."

Chapter 17

Dekker surprised her.

In spite of that message he'd left, saying he would be in late, he was waiting on her front porch, one leg slung up on the railing, when she got home from her mother's. A quick shaft of pure gladness passed through her at the sight of him, hunched down in his leather bomber jacket against the bite of the chilly night wind. And then apprehension rose up, tightening her stomach, making her heart beat a little faster than before.

He had his own key. She had given him one a year ago, when she first moved in. It bothered her—a lot—that he hadn't used it. It seemed as if he made a sort of statement, by not letting himself in, by waiting out here in the cold and the dark like a stranger, like someone who didn't have the right to enter her house when she wasn't home.

When he saw her drive up, he jumped down from the

porch and jogged over to pull open the garage door for her. She drove her car in, got out and went to get Sam from the backseat.

Dekker waited for her to emerge and then lowered the door. She turned for the back steps, carrying her sleeping son on one shoulder.

When Dekker fell in beside her, she asked, carefully, "Why didn't you let yourself in? No need to sit out here in the cold."

He didn't answer. His silence, to her, seemed ominous. She sent him a glance. And for that she got a shrug that might have meant anything.

They went up the back steps. "I'll just put Sammy down," she said once they were inside.

"Fine."

She left him, turning the light on as she went out of the room.

She took Sammy to the bathroom and got him to use the toilet. Then she put him to bed, taking off his little jacket and his shoes and socks, but leaving him in his clothes so as not to wake him any more than she had already.

Once she'd tucked him beneath the covers, she kissed him, on his soft little cheek, taking comfort from the contact. Then she smoothed his hair off his forehead, whispered a good-night he did not hear and tiptoed from the room.

Dekker was waiting for her at the kitchen table. He had not helped himself to a beer, had not even taken off his jacket.

They looked at each other for a long, bleak moment. There were maybe four feet between them. But the look in his eyes told her it might as well have been a thousand miles.

Where have you been? she was thinking. What's the matter? What has gone wrong? The questions echoed in her head, but somehow not a one of them made its way out her mouth.

He was the one who spoke first. "I have a few things to say. A little...explaining to do."

She had to cough before she could get words out. "I...um, all right."

He tipped his head at the chair across from him. "Will you sit down?"

She slid into the chair, folded her hands on the tabletop.

"Well," he said, and cleared his throat.

She licked her lips, tightened her folded hands. She longed to tell him what was in her heart. But he had asked to go first. And she would give him that.

"Damn," he muttered. "Where the hell to begin..."

"Just—"

"What?"

Her mouth felt parched. She had to force the words through all that dryness. "Go ahead. It doesn't matter... where you start."

"How about this afternoon?" His voice was hard, heavy with sarcasm. "How about that? How about Antonia Atwood, showing up here, proving that all you had to do was wait a little, and there would have been no threat to Sammy."

She didn't quite see what he was getting at. "All right," she murmured. "What about Antonia? What about this afternoon."

He made a low noise, one of pure impatience. "Oh, come on. You know what. This afternoon proved that we never needed to get married in the first place. And we wouldn't have. If I hadn't pushed you into it, it never would have happened. You would have had to get through a nerve-racking week or so. And then Antonia would have stood up to that husband of hers and everything would have worked out all by itself. But I couldn't leave it, couldn't let the problem take care of itself. I had to...turn your life upside down. And for what? It's a very good question, don't you think?"

She still didn't know where he was leading her. But she could see very clearly that wherever—*whatever* it was—he was blaming himself.

"Dekker, you had no way of knowin' what Antonia would do. And you did not *push* me into our marriage. I was willing, more than willing. We both know that I was."

"Sure you were. Why wouldn't you be? We've been... such good friends. So...close."

"Why do you say it like that? Like there's something wrong with what we have been to each other? There is nothing wrong with you and me, together. Our friendship has been one of the best and most important things in my life."

"You trust me."

"I do. Absolutely. With my life. You know that."

"Well, yes I do know that. And I have to tell you, I lied in that message I left for you this afternoon."

"You lied..."

"That's right. I haven't really been at the agency. I've been at my apartment. Sitting. And thinking. All afternoon. Into the evening..."

"Thinking about what?"

He looked at her, a hard, unhappy look. And then,

abruptly, he stood. "Look. What's the point of this? We don't really need to go into all the gory details."

"Yes, we—"

"No. We don't. The deal is, you don't need to be married to me anymore. The deal is, you never did."

She stared up at him, her heart feeling as if it was just shriveling down to nothing inside her chest. "What are you telling me, Dekker?"

"I am telling you that I'm going to give you that divorce we talked about at the first. The divorce we agreed we would get when Robert Atwood was no longer a threat to you. I'm telling you that I'm setting you free. Right away."

"But Dekker. I don't want to be free."

He stared at her with something that looked almost like pity. "Jo. You just don't get it. You don't even know… what you are. The kind of woman you are. The kind of man you deserve. Who have you been with? That idiot, Atwood. And me. You can do better. You *will* do better."

She could not stay in that chair. She leaped to her feet. "I keep trying, trying to say it, to tell you how I really feel. I think I am sending out a very clear message. But somehow, you are not receiving. I will say it slowly. And I will say it clearly. Dekker, there is no one—*no one*—who is better than you."

He only shook his head.

She felt as if she was slipping down a hill, grabbing at rocks and bushes, trying her hardest to halt the fall. And not succeeding. So she blurted it out. "Dekker, I love you. I love you with all of my heart. You are my husband. And I'm glad, so glad that you are. I don't care how we got to it, what little lies we had to tell each other to give ourselves permission to take the big step. We're married. I want us to stay that way. I love you and I don't want anyone else."

For half of an instant she thought she had him. Something like hope flared in those deep-blue eyes. But then hope faded. His eyes went flat. He spoke low. "You say that because it's not in you to say anything else. You are loyal to a fault."

"Dekker, I say it because it is the truth!"

"Don't you get what I'm telling you? This whole thing, you and me, our wild time in Baja, I think…I wanted that. I think I wanted it bad. I think I've wanted it for a long time now, with you, and I've been looking for a way to give myself permission to have it."

"So? What's wrong with that?"

"I told you. You can do better. Damn it, I *love* you. I want the best for you."

"You love me." Her shriveled heart expanded to hard-beating life again. "You said it. You heard yourself. You admitted that you love me."

"That is not the point."

"Oh, yes. It is. It is exactly the point." She started for him.

He threw up a warding-off hand. "Stay there. Don't come any closer. I want you to have the best life can give you. And I am not it."

She stayed where she was—but she spoke with the absolute conviction of the love that she bore him. "Oh, yes you are. There is no one better, truer, more *right* for me than you."

He looked at her as if she had lost her mind. "What are you talking about? Look at my damn life. I mean, who the hell am I, anyway? I can't help but wonder— and you should wonder, too. My 'mother,' in reality, was

my kidnapper. In a way, my whole life has been a lie.
I married a woman with serious emotional problems.
And then, when things got tough, I turned my back on
her. She committed suicide. And I almost gave up completely. I left the department, just walked away, kissed
all my ambitions and dreams goodbye. I would probably
be dead myself now, if not for you. I run a two-bit detective agency over a coin laundry in a badly maintained
building downtown. And a few weeks ago I found out
who my real family is, I found out I happen to be a very
rich man. But that's all I've got going for me, and that
just dropped into my damn lap. I am a—"

That was it. All she could take. She cleared the two
feet that stood between them and clapped her hand over
his mouth. "You shut up, Dekker Sm—" she caught herself "—Dekker Bravo. I will not hear such things from
you, such lies, such a terrible, cruel twisting of the truth.
I am sorry, so sorry, about Stacey. About the hell she
lived in, in her own mind. And the hell we both know
she put you through. You could not have saved her. Nobody could have saved her—except Stacey herself. And
she…well, she did not manage it. And that did almost
kill you. Because you loved her. And you *hurt* for her,
for all she was, for all she could have been, for all she
could not get past.

"But what happened to Stacey was not your fault.
And you only hurt yourself more, hurt everyone who
loves you, by not letting her go, not forgiving yourself
and getting on with your life."

He grabbed her then, grabbed her by the arms and
hauled her up against him. His eyes burned into hers.
"You can say that. You can say that, because—"

"Because it is true," she said right into his face, pressing herself closer, harder, tighter to him than he was already holding her. "Because I love you, I love you with all I have got in me to love. I love you as my dearest, closest friend. As my husband, the one I want to share my life with. And as the lover who sets my body on fire."

"Don't," he said, the word desperate, low, very rough. His hands hurt her, his fingers were like bands of steel on her arms.

And she didn't care, she could take the pain. All she cared about was that he never, under any circumstances, let her go.

"Don't?" She handed the word right back to him. "Don't what? Don't tell you the truth? Don't ask you to stop lying, putting yourself down, trying to turn away from me and calling it for my own good? What are you saying, you are not good enough? Who has been the man in my family for ten years? Who shows up to fix the faucet when it won't stop leaking? Who bails my crazy sisters out of jail? Who shows my little boy, by example, every day, what it is to be a man, to be the one we all can count on?"

"Jo, I—"

"Nope. Not. Wait. Oh, you have made me good and mad, Dekker Bravo. And as for your life being a lie, well, maybe Lorraine did keep a terrible secret from you. But everyone knows how much that woman loved you. She loved you more than her own life. And what about us, huh, what about all us Tillys and DuFraynes? What you have, with the family, well, that is no lie. You had a pretty good childhood, all in all. And I think I ought to know, bein' as how I was there."

"Jo…"

She realized she was crying. Crying. She couldn't

believe it. She *never* cried. The tears dribbled down her cheeks. She would have swiped the damn things away with a vengeance if he hadn't had such a tight grip on her arms.

"And besides." She had to pause to sniff good and hard. "Besides, poor Lorraine is like Stacey. She's gone from us now. Time to forgive her. Time to move on. The sins of the past have been set right, I would say, as much as they ever can be."

He said her name, again, in a whisper this time. And then he released his cruel grip on her arms. He cupped her face, hands gone suddenly so very tender, and rubbed at her tears with his thumbs. "Damn it…"

Oh, he was losing it. She could see it in those beautiful blue-black eyes. He was wanting her, she could feel that as she pressed herself so close against his body. He was…giving in, though he kept fighting it, giving in to love…

She stretched that little bit closer, just close enough to brush her lips against his. His breath caught.

She whispered against his mouth, "What are you talking about? Who do you think you are kidding? I deserve better, you say? Better than you? So what will that mean, then, if you do let me go? If we get that divorce and I start in with other men, trying to find with another what I've already got with you? Are you going to stand still for that, for some other guy putting his hands on me? Is that what you're telling me, you're going to sit by and watch me get *what I deserve* with some other man?"

He swore again, this time a word that burned her ears when she heard it.

She kept right after him, utterly shameless, pressing her breasts up to his chest, her hips to his thighs, letting the tears stream, unheeded down her cheeks. "Tell me, Dekker. Try to tell me that lie…."

That did it. His control broke. He took her mouth, hard. With a glad, triumphant cry, she parted her lips and sucked his tongue inside.

He wrapped his arms around her so tight, it knocked the breath from her body. Then he started walking her backward, across her kitchen floor. He turned into her bedroom, shoved the door shut with his heel.

His hands were all over her. And she gloried in every hungry, grasping touch. They tore at each other's clothes, not bothering to take them off completely, only what they had to get rid of to get to each other.

He unhooked her bra, yanked her shirt up, latched that hot mouth of his onto her breast. She left him his jacket and his shirt, but went right to work unbuttoning his jeans, shoving them and his boxers down enough to free him.

The flared slacks she wore were something else again. They had to come all the way down and off, along with her panties.

She felt the air against the flesh of her legs. She was naked from waist to ankles, though her shoes and socks were still on.

He lifted her. She went with a glad cry, wrapping her legs around him, sliding her wetness down onto him, taking him inside.

He groaned. She took his mouth, took that groan into herself. He surged upward, filling her.

She stilled, opened her eyes, saw *his* eyes gleaming at her through the gloom of her dark bedroom. "Say it," she commanded. "Say you love me. Say it now."

He swore again.

She did not waver. "Say it."

He groaned again. And he gave her what she wanted. "I love you." He swore once more. "Love you, love you, love you, Jo…"

"Say you'll stay with me. Never leave me. Be my husband. Forever. As long we both have breath in our bodies, you will be mine and I will be yours."

"Jo…" He pressed up into her.

She shook her head, refusing to move with him. "I know it. I know it already. You are mine and you are not going to leave me. Because I know you. You wouldn't… do this, with me, now. Under no circumstances, but most especially not like this, without any protection. You wouldn't. Unless you had completely surrendered. Unless you finally understood exactly where you belong."

"You are killing me…"

"No. I am loving you. And I…I want you to—I *beg* you to—say it." He shifted beneath her, just the tiniest bit. "No! Don't you move. Not until you say it."

He made a guttural sound, something dragged up from the depths of him.

Tenderly she put her hand across his mouth. "Oh, say it. Please, please say it…"

He moaned.

"Yes. You can. You can say it to me.…"

"I will…never leave you. I will…be your husband…"

"Forever."

"Forever. As long as we both have breath in our bodies… I am yours, Jo. Always. I am yours.…"

"Oh," she said. "Oh, yes…that's it. That is exactly it."

He pushed into her, hard.

"Yes! Oh, Dekker, yes…"

And the rest was pure magic. Hard and frantic. Wild and wet and fine.

When at last he slumped, spent, against the door, she whispered her love tenderly. He whispered his back to her.

He staggered to the bed with her and carefully laid her down.

They were naked in no time. He came into her waiting arms. She pulled the covers over them. They lay awake for another hour or two, whispering softly, sharing secrets and plans.

And then, wrapped up close and warm, together in the truest sense—man and wife, passionate lovers, the very best of friends—they drifted off to sleep.

They bought a seven-bedroom house, right next to Mesta Park in Heritage Hills. It was a beautiful old place with lots of interesting woodwork and lustrous hardwood floors, high ceilings and crown moldings and fine beveled glass in the windows.

The yard was a good size, had a pool and a brick fence around the perimeter, with an iron gate across the wide driveway. The fence and the gate went a long way toward discouraging the prying eyes of the press. And anyone the fence and gate didn't take care of, Dekker's pricey security system did.

In April, they threw a big party, for family near and far. It was a housewarming and also an opportunity to renew their wedding vows.

Bravos came from all over—Emma, Jonas and Mandy from Los Angeles, of course. And Marsh Bravo— Dekker and Jonas's cousin—and Marsh's family, too. They lived in Norman, just a twenty-minute drive from

Oklahoma City. Marsh was the evil Blake's son, the one who had found the first clues to the terrible deed his father had done. And there were more. Some second cousins, from Florida and from Northern California—a pair of sisters, with their husbands and children. And from Wyoming, three other second cousins, and their wives and sons and daughters, as well.

There were a lot of Tillys, of course. And all the usual DuFraynes. And Antonia and Robert Atwood. Antonia positively glowed, and Robert stayed close to her, clearly smitten in spite of himself with his newly confident wife.

After a particularly gruesome binge around Christmastime, Uncle Hubert had joined Alcoholics Anonymous. He was sticking with it, too, attending meetings regularly, drinking only ginger ale at social occasions. So Joleen didn't have to worry about taking care of him as the party progressed.

But there were plenty of other crises to deal with. Niki had found her first boyfriend. They were having some kind of fight. Niki kept bursting into tears at regular intervals. And DeDe was pregnant. She had trouble holding her food down, threw up on the back patio and then ran, mortified and sobbing, into the house. She locked herself in the upstairs bathroom and it took both Wayne and Joleen to coax her out.

Then there was Mama, who had a new boyfriend with whom she flirted and carried on in a shameless fashion. This was the third or fourth since the ice cream man back in October. They just never lasted. But Camilla claimed she was happy. And Joleen had to admit that she did seem to be, especially now that she and Antonia were so close. The boyfriends might come and go, but when Camilla Tilly found a true woman friend, it was always for life.

Dekker and Joleen renewed their vows after darkness fell, by the golden light of several rows of pretty paper lanterns strung from tree to tree, under the steady silver glow of a glorious full moon.

And as Dekker Bravo promised anew to love, honor and cherish Joleen for the rest of their lives, it came to him that the past truly had been put to rest. When he looked into his wife's loving eyes, all doubt was vanquished. He knew exactly who he was.

The stolen Bravo Baby had found his way home at last.

* * * * *

A frequent name on bestseller lists, including the *New York Times*, **Allison Leigh** says her high point as a writer is hearing from readers that they laughed, cried or lost sleep while reading her books. She credits her family with great patience for the time she's parked at her computer, and for blessing her with the kind of love she wants her readers to share with the characters living in the pages of her books. Contact her at allisonleigh.com.

Look for more books from Allison Leigh in Harlequin Special Edition—the ultimate destination for life, love and family! There are six new Harlequin Special Edition titles available every month. Check one out today!

THE BILLIONAIRE'S
BABY PLAN
Allison Leigh

For my husband.

Prologue

"Good news." Lisa Armstrong sailed into the living room of her brother Paul's Beacon Hill town house, waving a newspaper over her head like a flag. "All of that sweet-talking to the features editor I've been doing the past few months are finally paying off. The paper's going to do a twelve-week series on families seeking alternative methods of conceiving, and the Armstrong Fertility Institute is going to be prominently featured." She felt her brilliant smile wilt a little when she finally focused on her brother's unsmiling expression. "This is good news," she reminded him. Her gaze switched to Ramona Tate's pretty face. "All human interest and all good press for the clinic. Nothing for you to have to spin into something more palatable."

But Ramona did not look overjoyed, and as the institute's public-relations magician—not to mention her brother's fiancée—she ought to have, particularly considering the tap-dancing she'd been having to do for too long now.

Lisa slowly lowered the paper and tossed it onto the coffee table. She'd been a little late to the sudden gathering her brother had called, and his spacious living room suddenly felt as if it was closing in on her.

Thoughts that her brother and Ramona had called the get-together to announce that they'd finally set a date for their wedding fizzled. There wasn't a speck of joy on the faces of any of the handful of people gathered there.

She looked back at Paul. "What's happened?"

"Derek has resigned his position as CFO of the institute." Paul's voice was even, but oddly flat.

"*What?* Why?"

"The financial audit that Harvey Nordinger conducted turned up serious discrepancies."

"Which, as CFO, our silver-tongued brother should be dealing with," she countered readily. She already knew the audit that Paul had instigated had shown less than satisfactory results.

Paul's lips twisted. "*I* told Derek to resign, Lis."

She felt the air leave her lungs in a whoosh. She sank down onto the arm of the couch, staring. "But he's part of this family." And the family *was* the institute. It had been since their obstetrician father, Gerald, had established it more than two decades earlier, expanding it from its roots as an innovative fertility clinic into one of the world's premier biotech firms in the areas of infertility and genetic testing.

Paul, the eldest, was chief of staff. Derek, Paul's twin, served as the CFO and Lisa, the youngest, was the administrator. Only Olivia, their other sibling, remained uninvolved in the day-to-day operations of the clinic.

Paul let out a rough sigh and raked his fingers through

his hair. He shared a look with Ramona. "If Derek weren't family, we'd be prosecuting him."

Lisa blinked. "Excuse me?"

"He's been embezzling from the institute. Harvey's proved it."

She gave a disbelieving laugh. "Harvey's wrong. I know you trust him implicitly, Paul, but he's wrong." She looked around the room, from face to face. Ted Bonner and Chance Demetrios, the shining duo that Paul had lured away from San Francisco to head up their research operation. Sara Beth, who was not only the institute's head nurse, but also Lisa's best friend and Ted's bride. They all, along with Ramona, were eyeing Lisa with something akin to pity. "He has to be," she insisted. Derek might be Paul's twin, but she was the one who felt closest to him.

And everyone there knew it.

Unease was blooming in her throat. Derek had his faults, certainly. But they all did. And most of those faults were centered on their unswerving commitment to the institute. "Derek wouldn't steal from his own family."

"I'm sorry, Lisa. He—" Paul broke off, his jaw clenching. Ramona slid her slender hand over his shoulder and his jaw slowly eased. His hand covered Ramona's. "He admitted it," he finished gruffly.

His words fell like stones.

Lisa's throat slowly tightened and her nose started to burn.

She wanted to argue.

To convince him that, somehow, it was a terrible mistake.

But how could she? The truth was written on his face.

He cleared his throat. "The reason why I wanted everyone to meet here, instead of at the institute, is because I want to make certain none of this gets out. Not to any of the staff or the patients, but especially not the media or—"

"Daddy," she finished, her voice going hoarse. Until his declining health had forced his retirement, the Armstrong Fertility Institute had been Gerald Armstrong's life. "He can't find out. It'll kill him."

"Which brings us to the next point of all of this." Lisa didn't see how it was possible, but Paul looked even grimmer. "Finances. We barely have enough operating capital left to keep our doors open through the quarter. As it is, we'll have to cut our budgets to the bone. If we lay off—"

"No." Lisa shoved off the couch like a shot, wrapping her arms around her waist. "The second anyone gets wind of layoffs, the reporters will be back on us like sharks." She shook her head. "Only this time they'll have real blood to find. There has to be other ways for us to cut expenses. I don't know about everyone else, but I'll stop taking a salary—"

"Lisa—"

She ignored him. "—and we'll get together a prospectus. We'll get a loan."

"No bank is going to touch us in the condition we're in and we wouldn't be able to keep Dad out of it."

"Then private investors," Lisa countered, feeling more than a little desperate. She may have missed out on the medical brilliance gene that Gerald had passed on to Paul, but she considered herself a decent administrator. It was the only thing about her that she felt certain her father was proud of. It was her one part in ensuring that her father's life's work lived on.

Yet she hadn't known what Derek was doing.

"We've never had investors before," Paul said.

"Pardon me for saying so, but you've never needed investors before," Ted inserted quietly. He let go of Sarah Beth's hand, which he'd been holding, and stood up. "However, it does give me an idea…"

Chapter 1

Lisa stepped out of the cab and onto the sidewalk, staring at the narrow entrance of Fare, complete with uniformed doorman, ahead of her.

Why a restaurant?

Not for the first time since she'd flown from Boston to New York City was she still puzzling over the choice. Even though the meeting had been arranged by Ted Bonner, its purpose was business. Not social.

Thank heavens.

She realized the doorman was staring at her, and with a confidence that she didn't feel, smiled at the man and strode across the sidewalk, unfastening the single button on the front of her black-and-white houndstooth jacket when he ushered her into the softly lit restaurant before silently departing.

The shadowy hostess station was unattended and she waited in the hushed silence. There was a faint strain of music, but it was subtle and nonintrusive.

Waiting to be shown to the table was okay with her. She didn't want to be there anyway. But she'd promised Paul.

She swallowed.

This is just another meeting with a potential funder. Investor.

Her mind debated the term.

She was used to meeting with funders. Usually representatives of a philanthropic or scientific foundation to discuss research grants that the institute was seeking.

This…this was another kettle of fish, entirely. And even though it had been her idea to use investors to solve their current dilemma, she'd never in her wildest imaginings thought she'd be meeting this particular one.

She smoothed her hand over the wide belt of her high-waisted slacks and buttoned her jacket again. Switched her slender, leather briefcase from one hand to the other.

The meeting that Paul had called earlier that week replayed in her mind. She'd never seen her ever-confident, ever-capable big brother actually question whether or not the institute could survive at all and that—as much as the reason why—still had her deeply shaken.

"The gentleman is waiting for you."

Lisa blinked herself to the present where an exotically beautiful girl dressed in a narrow black sheath was smiling patiently, her hand extended slightly to one side.

She undid the button again, gripped the handle of her briefcase more tightly in her moist hand and stepped forward.

She spotted him immediately.

The "gentleman" whom Lisa would never have termed as such.

Rourke Devlin.

Billionaire venture capitalist. A man who never had to worry about finding funding for his own work because he *was* the fund. He was Ted Bonner's friend. And even though she could appreciate that fact, could appreciate the generosity he'd shown to Ted and Sara Beth during their trip to newly wedded bliss, she couldn't envision anything productive coming out of this encounter.

He was dark. Powerful. Arrogant. Rich as Midas.

And as frightening as the devil himself.

Rourke didn't even rise as she approached his small round table situated in the center of the exclusive, small restaurant. But his black gaze followed her every step of the way.

She felt like a lamb sent to slaughter and damned Derek all over again.

She might have promised Paul that she'd do her best on this meeting despite her personal reservations, but it was because of Derek that this meeting—or any of the other half dozen that she'd frenetically set up for the following week—was necessary in the first place.

A black-clothed waiter had appeared out of nowhere to pull out the second chair at the table for her.

She thanked him quietly and took her seat, tucking the briefcase on the floor next to her. There were plenty of tables surrounding them, but none was occupied. Only Rourke's, sitting here, center stage like king of the castle. "I've read reviews of Fare," she greeted him. "The food is supposed to be magnificent."

"It is."

Hardly a conversational treasure trove. She hoped it wasn't an indicator of how the rest of the meeting would go, but feared it probably was. Despite Ted's insistence that Rourke was open to meeting with her, she couldn't help but remember her encounter with him months earlier at their Founder's Ball—and the single dance they'd shared—as well as his seeming disapproval at the time of the institute in general. "The view is lovely."

He didn't turn his head to glance at the bank of windows overlooking a pond surrounded by trees that were just now beginning to show the first hint of coming autumn. "Yes."

In her lap, her hands curled into fists beneath the protection of the white linen draping the table. All right. Forget pleasantries. She'd just get to the point. "I appreciate you meeting with me."

He lifted a sardonic eyebrow. "Do you?"

She studied him, wondering not for the first time exactly what it was about the man that seemed to place him on a different plane than others.

There were plenty of men as powerfully built. Plenty of men who possessed strikingly carved features and well-cut, thick black hair. All it took was money to buy the fine white silk shirt he wore with such casual ease. There was a single button undone at his tanned throat; a charcoal-gray suit coat discarded over the back of his chair.

He exuded confidence. Power. And he looked at her—just as he had on the other few occasions they'd been in one another's company—as if he knew things about her that she might not even know herself.

Which mostly left her feeling as if she were playing some game in which she didn't know the rules.

She moistened her lips, realizing as she did that it was an indicator of her nervousness, particularly when his gaze rested on her mouth for a moment. "I know your time is valuable."

The waiter had returned and was silently, ceremoniously presenting, then opening a bottle of wine. The cork presented and approved, the first taste mulled over, the crystal glasses partially filled. Lisa had been part of the production hundreds of times and wondered silently what any of them would say if she told them she would have preferred a fresh glass of iced tea. Wine always went straight to her head.

And it didn't take her MBA to know that she needed all of her faculties in prime working order when it came to dealing with Rourke Devlin, who hadn't volunteered even a polite disclaimer about the value of his time.

But she said nothing. Merely smiled and picked up the glass, sipping at the crisp, cool Chardonnay. It *was* delicious. Something she might have chosen for herself if she were in the mood for wine. But she would have pegged Rourke as a red wine sort of man. To go along with the raw red meat those strong white teeth could probably tear apart.

"I told the chef we'd have his recommendation," Rourke said. "Raoul never disappoints."

"How nice." She really, *really* wished they were meeting in his office. This just seemed far too intimate. Additional diners around them would have helped dispel that impression. "Isn't Fare usually open for lunch?" It was well past noon. And the reviews she'd read about the place had indicated it took months to get a reservation.

"Usually."

Which explained *so* much. She lifted the wineglass again and thought she saw the faintest glimmer of amusement hovering around his mobile lips. And it suddenly dawned on her why they were in a restaurant and not his office.

Because he'd known it would set her on edge.

She wasn't sure why that certainty was so suddenly clear. But it was. She knew it right down in her bones. And the glint in his eyes as he watched her while he lifted his own wineglass seemed to confirm it.

She set down her glass and reached down to pull a narrow file out of her briefcase. "Ted gave you some indication why we wanted to meet with you." It wasn't a question. She knew that Ted Bonner had primed the pump, so to speak, with his old buddy, when he'd arranged the meeting once Paul had jumped on the bandwagon of approval. "This prospectus will outline the advantages and opportunities of investing in the Armstrong Fertility Institute." She started to hand the file over to Rourke, only to stop midway, when he lifted a few fingers, as if to wave off the presentation that they'd pulled together at the institute in record time.

Not that he could know that.

Ted wouldn't have told the man just how desperate things had become. Friendship or not, Dr. Bonner was now a firmly entrenched part of the Armstrong Institute team. And *nobody* on that team wanted word to get out about the reason underlying their unusual foray into seeking investors. Their reputation would never recover. Not after the string of bad press they'd already endured. Their patients wouldn't want their names—some very well-known—associated with the institute. And without patients, there wouldn't just be layoffs. The institute would simply have to close its doors.

Damn you, Derek.

She lowered the prospectus and set it on the linen cloth next to the fancy little bread basket that the waiter delivered, along with a selection of spreads.

"Put it away," Rourke said. "I prefer not to discuss business while I'm eating."

"Then why didn't you schedule me for when you weren't?" The question popped out and she wanted to kick herself. Instead, she lifted her chin a little and made herself meet his gaze, pretending as if she weren't riddled with frustration.

He was toying with her. She didn't have the slightest clue as to why he would even bother.

And she also left the folder right where it was. A glossy reminder of why they were meeting, even if he was determined to avoid it.

He pulled the wine bottle from the sterling ice bucket standing next to the table and refilled her glass even though she'd only consumed a small amount. "Have a roll," he said. "Raoul's wife, Gina, makes them fresh every day."

"I don't eat much bread," she said bluntly. What was the point of pretending congeniality? "Are you interested in discussing an investment in the institute or not?" If he wasn't—which was what she'd *tried* to tell Paul and the others—then she was wasting her time that would be better spent in preparation for meeting with investors who were.

"More bread would look good on you," he said. His gaze traveled over her, seeming to pick apart everything from the customary chignon in her hair to the single silver ring she wore on her right thumb. "You've lost weight since I last saw you."

There was no way to mistake the accusation as a compliment and her lips parted. She stared, letting the offense ripple through her until she could settle it somewhere out of the way. "Women can never be too thin," she reminded him coolly, and picked up the wineglass again. Might as well partake of the excellent vintage since it was apparent that he wasn't taking their meeting seriously, anyway.

No doubt he'd agreed simply to get Ted off his back.

"A ridiculous assumption made by women for women," Rourke returned. "Most men prefer curves and softness against them over jutting bones."

"Well." She swallowed more wine. "That's something you and I won't have to worry about."

He looked amused again and turned his head, glancing at the bank of windows. His profile was sharp, as defined—and cold—as a chiseled piece of granite. His black hair sprang sharply away from his forehead and the fine crow's-feet arrowing out from the corner of his eyes were clearly illuminated.

Unfortunately, they didn't detract from the total package.

"The view here *is* good," he said. "I'm glad Raoul went with my suggestion on the location. Initially he was looking for a high-rise."

She wanted to grind her teeth together, as annoyed with her own distraction where Rourke-the-man was concerned as she was with his unpredictability. "I didn't know that restaurants were something you invested in. Techno-firm startups seemed to be more your speed. Aren't restaurants notoriously chancy?" She lifted a hand, silently indicating the empty tables around them.

"Venture capitalism is about taking chances." He selected a roll from the basket and broke it open, slathering one of the compound butters over half. "Calculated chances, of course. But as it happens, in the five years since Raoul opened the doors, I've never had cause to regret this particular chance." He held out the roll. "Taste it."

She could feel the wine wending its heady way

through her veins. Breakfast had been hours ago. Wait. She'd skipped breakfast, in favor of a conference call.

Which meant drinking even the tiniest amount of wine was more foolish than usual.

Arguing seemed too much work, though, so she took the roll from him. Their fingers brushed.

She shoved the bread in her mouth, chomping down on it as viciously as she chomped down on the warmth that zipped through her hand.

"Good?"

Chewing, she nodded. The roll *was* good. Deliciously so. It only annoyed her more.

She chased the yeasty heaven down with more wine and leaned closer to the table. "Obviously excellent bread and wine isn't always enough to ensure success, or this place *would* be busting at the seams."

"Raoul closed Fare until dinner for me."

She blinked slowly and sat back. "Why?"

"Because I asked him to."

"Again…why?"

"Because I wanted to be alone with you."

A puff of air escaped her lips. "But you don't even like me."

Rourke picked up his wineglass and studied the disbelieving expression of the woman across from him. "Maybe not," he allowed.

Lisa Armstrong had looked like an ice princess the first time he'd seen her more than six months ago in a crowded Cambridge pub called Shots where he'd been meeting with Ted Bonner and Chance Demetrios.

He'd had no reason to change his opinion in the few times he'd seen her since.

"But I want you," he continued smoothly, watching

the sudden flare of her milk-chocolate eyes. "And you want me." He'd known that since he'd maneuvered her into sharing a single, brief dance with him months earlier.

Her lips had parted. They were slightly thin, slightly wide for her narrow, angular face, and a shade of pale, delicate pink that he figured owed nothing to cosmetics.

And he hadn't been able to get them out of his mind.

Obviously recovering, those lips pursed slightly. Her eyebrows—darker than the gold that covered her head—returned to their usual, level places. Her brown gaze was only fractionally less sharp than it had been when she'd first sat down across from him. But a strand of hair had worked loose of that perfect, smooth knot at the nape of her neck and had curled around her slender neck to tease the hollow at the base of her throat. "You have an incredible ego, Mr. Devlin."

So he'd been told. By foes, friends and family alike. He pulled his gaze from that single, loose lock of hair that tickled the visible pulse he could see beneath her fair, fair skin. "I don't think it's egotism to recognize facts. And you might as well make it Rourke."

"Why?" She didn't seem to realize she'd reached for the other half of the roll he'd buttered and flicked a glance at it before dropping it back on the small bread plate. "Are we going to be doing business together after all?"

His inclination was to admit that they weren't.

But he also had plenty of good reasons to want to ensure that Ted Bonner and Chance Demetrios were able to continue their work without any more hitches. Investing in anything that Ted was involved in would be a good bet.

But through the Armstrong Fertility Institute?

Not even Ted knew why that particular idea was anathema to him.

Maybe it was small of him, but he wasn't ready yet to release Lisa Armstrong from this particular hook. He was enjoying, too much, having the ice princess right where he wanted her.

He hid a dark bolt of amusement directed squarely at himself.

Nearly where he wanted her.

"Our salads," he said instead, glancing at Tonio, their waiter and Raoul's youngest son, as he approached with his tray.

He could see the ire creep back into Lisa's eyes.

She controlled it well, though. Merely smiling coolly at Rourke as Tonio served them. He wondered if beneath that facade she would have preferred giving him a swift kick or if she really was that cool, all the way through.

It would be interesting to find out.

Interesting but complicated as hell.

He picked up his fork, his appetite whetted on more levels than he presently cared to admit. "Eat," he said when she looked as if she weren't even going to taste Raoul's concoction. He hadn't been exaggerating when he'd observed that she'd lost weight.

At the Founder's Ball in her floaty gown of slippery brown and white that had hugged her narrow hips and left the entirety of her ivory back and shoulders distractingly bare, she'd felt slender and delicate in his arms.

Now, even with the thick weave of her jacket and the wide-cut legs of her slacks, he could tell she was even thinner.

She took her work to heart.

He could have told that for himself, even if Ted hadn't mentioned it.

Often in the office before anyone else arrived. Often there later than anyone stayed.

For Ted to even *notice* something like that, beyond his Bunsen burners and beakers, was something. He'd said she was a workaholic.

Ironically, that gave her and Rourke something in common.

She was poking at the tomato salad and he was glad to see that some of it actually reached her mouth. His sister Tricia would take one look at her and want to fatten her up with plenty of pasta.

"How long have you and Dr. Bonner been friends?"

He had to give her points for adaptability. He'd expected to receive a mostly chilly silence for his autocratic refusal to discuss what they both knew she'd traveled to New York City to discuss. "Since we were boys."

Her gaze flicked over him. "I find it hard to envision you as a boy. Were you schoolmates?"

He almost laughed.

Ted Bonner had grown up with wealth and privilege. Rourke and his three sisters might have had the same, if their father hadn't walked out on them when they were young. Instead, the Devlin clan had gone from being comfortable to being…not.

They'd been locked out of their fine Boston home with no ceremony, no explanations.

He'd been twelve years old.

For a while, his mother had struggled to keep them in Boston. He and his sisters had switched from private to public schools. They'd moved into a basement apartment a lifestyle away from what they'd been used to.

But in the end, within a handful of years, Nina Devlin had simply been forced to move them all back to New York where they'd moved into the cramped apartment above the home-style Italian restaurant his grandparents owned and operated.

And Rourke's father? He'd landed in California with a surgically enhanced trophy wife who'd been fewer than ten years older than Rourke.

He'd seen them only once. When he'd been twenty-three and had raked in a cool million over his first real deal.

That was when Trophy Wife had indicated a considerable interest in Rourke's bed and Dad had claimed Rourke was a chip off the old block.

He'd never seen either one of them again.

"Ted and I were in the same Boy Scout troop," he told Lisa, fully expecting the surprise she couldn't hide. Before they'd left Boston, his mother had chugged him across town to keep him involved in the troop that he'd been drafted into by his father, before he'd skipped. Rourke had hated it until he and Ted had struck up an unlikely friendship.

"*You* were a Boy Scout."

"Trustworthy, loyal, helpful, friendly—" He broke off the litany of Scout law when she snorted softly.

"Sorry," she said, but aside from the bloom of pink over her sharp cheekbones, she didn't particularly look it. "I just have a whole mental image of you wearing khaki shorts and merit badges." The tip of her tongue appeared between her pearl-white teeth. Then she laughed softly, and shook her head. "A considerable change from your usual attire."

He dragged his gaze away from the humorous stretch of her lips only to get caught in the sparkle of her eyes.

He tamped down on the heat shooting through him.

He hadn't seen her smile, really smile, since that first glimpse of her at Shots when she'd been laughing over something with her friend Sara Beth.

Glancing at Tonio, who immediately cleared away their salads, Rourke picked up the prospectus. "The Armstrong Institute's been plagued with bad press," he said, breaking his own trumped-up rule of no business over lunch. "Questionable research protocols. Padded statistics."

"Both allegations were proved false. By none other than your Scout buddy, Ted."

"Yet the bad aftertaste of innuendo remains."

The sparkle in her eyes died, leaving her expression looking hauntingly hollow. "That's a little like blaming the victim, isn't it? The Armstrong Institute has never operated with anything less than integrity. Nor has any of its staff. But we're to be held accountable now for someone else's shoddy reporting?"

"Integrity." He mulled the word over, watching her while Tonio returned again with their main course of lobster risotto. "Interesting choice of words."

Her gaze didn't waver as she reached for her wineglass again. "I cannot imagine why."

She would be a good poker player, he decided. Not everyone could baldly lie like that without so much as a blink. She was even better at it than his ex-wife had been.

But for the moment, he let the matter drop. "Eat the risotto. It's nearly as good as my mother's."

She picked up her fork and took a small bite. Poked at the risotto as if moving the creamy rice around her plate would be an adequate substitute for actually eating. "Investment in the Armstrong Fertility Institute would be along the line of similar projects for Devlin Ventures. You've had great success in medically related firms."

"None of which was family controlled," he said flatly. "I don't do family-owned businesses."

"You invested in Fare."

"I'm a *partner* in Fare."

Lisa's gaze finally fell, but not quickly enough to hide the defeat that filled it. She set down the fork with care. Dabbed the corner of her lips with her linen napkin before laying it on the table. "I believe I've wasted enough of your time. Clearly you agreed to this meeting only because of your friendship with Ted." She pushed her chair back a few inches and picked up her briefcase as she rose. Her gaze flicked back to him for a moment. "Please assure Raoul that my departure is no reflection on his excellent meal."

She turned away and started to leave the dining room.

"I'm surprised you would give up so quickly," he said. "So easily. I would have thought you were all about duty to the institute."

He saw her shoulders stiffen beneath the stylish jacket. She slowly turned, clasping the handle of her briefcase in both hands in front of her. "I am. And that duty dictates that my time is better served on prospective investors. Not dallying over amazing risotto and good wine with a man who has a different agenda. Whatever that may be."

He had no agenda where the institute was concerned. With the single exception of his unwelcome attraction to *her,* anything to do with the Armstrong family put a vile taste in his mouth.

"The institute is on the brink of financial collapse," he said evenly. "I'm not in the habit of throwing away good money."

"The institute is experiencing some financial hiccups," she returned coolly. "Nothing from which we cannot recover. And if you didn't have some burr under your saddle that I still fail to understand, you'd be able to recognize that fact, too."

"That's what you really believe." It was almost incomprehensible. The losses that the institute had incurred were nearly insurmountable.

Her chin angled slightly.

Too thin. Too tense.

But undeniably beautiful and certainly dutiful to her cause.

"Fine. We'll meet in the morning."

She lifted an eyebrow. "Where? Your favorite breakfast shop?"

He very nearly smiled. The ice princess did have a claw or two. "My office. Nine o'clock."

Her eyebrow lowered. Her eyes flared for a moment. She nodded. "Very well."

"And don't be late. I'll be squeezing you into the day as it is."

"I'm never late," she assured him and, with a small smile, turned on her heel and strode out.

He watched her go, waiting to see if she'd glance back.

She did. But not until she was nearly out of sight. He still managed to hold her gaze for a second longer than was comfortable.

Her cheeks filled with color. This time when she turned to go, there was a lot more *run* in her stride.

How far would duty take her?

He picked up his wine, smiling faintly. It would be interesting finding out.

Chapter 2

"Of course he's going to invest." Sara Beth Bonner's voice was bright and confident through the cell phone's speaker. "Why else would he ask you to come to his office this morning?"

"I don't know." Lisa shook her head, glancing from the phone that was sitting on the vanity in her hotel room, to her reflection in the mirror. She'd already smudged her mascara once and had had to start over. She didn't have time to mess up again, or—despite her falsely confident assurance to Rourke the day before—she would be late for their appointment that morning. "I know he's an old friend of your brand-new husband, but the man's a player. I don't *know* what he wants."

"Ted keeps saying Rourke is rock-solid."

Lisa made a face at her reflection. The man *was* rock-solid—she'd found that out for herself when they'd danced together at the Founder's Ball. But that, of course, wasn't what Ted meant. "Just because Rourke was Boy Scout material once, doesn't mean he still is."

"What does Paul say?"

Lisa decided her mascara was finally acceptable and closed the tube with one hand while reaching for her lipstick with the other. "The same thing. That of course I can convince Devlin to jump on board." She smoothed the subtle pink onto her lips. "Unfortunately, Paul doesn't seem to grasp the fact that such blind faith only makes the pressure worse."

"It's not blind faith," Sara Beth assured her. "It's confidence. Come on, Lisa. Don't start doubting yourself now. You can do this."

"When did you trade in your nurse's uniform for a cheerleader's?"

"Hmm." Laughter filled Sara Beth's voice. "I wonder how Ted would feel about me in a short little skirt, waving pom-poms around."

Lisa groaned. "Newlyweds," she returned. "Listen, I've gotta run. My flight gets in around three so I'll probably see you at the institute before you get off. Shift, I mean."

"Nice."

"What are friends for?" She disconnected the phone, but she was finally smiling.

Thank goodness for Sara Beth. Her friend never failed to cheer her up.

She smoothed her hand once more over her pulled-back hair and pushed the phone into the pocket of her briefcase. She hadn't come to New York the day before prepared for an overnight, which had necessitated a quick trip out to find something suitable to wear for today's meeting because she refused to meet with Rourke again looking like day-old bread.

Since she'd already spent a small fortune on her Armani ensemble for the debacle of the day before, her personal budget was definitely taking a hit. But the black skirt she wore with the same black jersey tee from yesterday looked crisp and suitably "don't mess with me" teamed with the new taupe blazer. She looked good and wasn't going to pretend that it didn't help bolster her confidence where the man was concerned.

She pushed her bare feet into her high-heeled black pumps, snatched up the briefcase and hurried out the door.

The morning air was brisk and breezy, tugging both at her chignon and her skirt as she waited for the cab that the doorman hailed for her.

The traffic was heavy—no surprise—and she wished that she hadn't taken time to phone her mother that morning. It would have been one less item taking up time, and it wasn't as if Emily Stanton Armstrong had had anything helpful or productive to say, anyway.

The only thing that Lisa had in common with her mother was a devotion to the man they had in common—Gerald. The great "Dr. G." She'd given up, years ago, trying to understand what made her mother tick, much less trying to gain her approval. Emily already had the perfect daughter in Olivia, anyway. Olivia was the wife of a senator, for heaven's sake. Jamison Mallory was the youngest member of the U.S. Senate and the eldest son of Boston's most powerful family. He might as well be royalty. And he was probably headed for the White House. Olivia and Jamison had even recently adopted two children who'd lost their own parents, completing their picture of the perfect family. Rarely did a week pass when Lisa's sister and brother-in-law weren't featured in either the society section or the national news.

Not that Lisa was jealous of her older sister. Olivia looked better—happier—now than she had in years. Lisa just never felt as if they were quite on the same page. The things they wanted in life had always been so different.

She sighed a little, brushing her hands nervously over her skirt. She *had* to pull the institute out of the fire.

The cab finally pulled up in front of the towering building that housed Devlin Ventures. A glance at her chunky bangle watch told her she had nearly ten minutes to spare.

Perfect.

She quickly paid and tipped the driver and left the cab, weaving between the pedestrians on the sidewalk to enter the building. Gleaming marble, soaring windows, shops and an atrium filled with live trees greeted her. It was impressive, and if she'd had more time, she probably would have wandered around the first floor, just to explore. But since she didn't, she aimed for the information desk that ran the length of one wall.

In minutes, she possessed a visitor's pass that got her through the security door that wasn't even visible from where she'd entered, and had bulleted dizzyingly to the top floor of the building in an elevator that went strictly to that floor, and that floor alone.

Devlin Ventures wasn't merely an occupant of the building.

It was the owner.

She barely had time to smooth her hand over her hair and run her tongue discreetly over her teeth to remove any misplaced lipstick before the elevator doors opened and she stepped out onto a floor that was as calm and soothing as the first floor had been busy and vibrant.

For some reason, she hadn't envisioned Rourke Devlin as a man to surround himself with such a Zen-like environment.

A curving desk in pale wood that matched the floor faced the elevator and she stopped in front of it. "Good morning," she told the girl sitting there. "I'm Lisa Armstrong. I have an appointment with Mr. Devlin."

The model-thin girl consulted something behind her desk, and seemed to find what she was looking for. "I'll show you to his office." She rose and swayed her way along a wide corridor. At the end, she turned, hip jutted, and lifted a languid hand. "Cynthia is Mr. Devlin's assistant," she said. "She'll see to you now."

Lisa found herself facing a woman who was as unattractive as the receptionist was attractive, right down to the heavy black-framed glasses that did little to disguise a hawkish nose. "Good morning."

Rourke's assistant gave her a short glance. "Mr. Devlin is unavoidably detained. I'm afraid he can't see you as scheduled."

Lisa felt her chest tighten. Dismay. Annoyance. Disappointment. They all clogged her system, jockeying for first place. "I'm happy to wait," she assured her.

Cynthia gave her an unemotional stare that told her absolutely nothing. "If you wish." Her gaze drifted to the collection of low, brown leather chairs situated near the windows.

Taking the cue, Lisa headed toward them. The view would have been spectacular if she had been in the mood to appreciate it.

Would Rourke stoop to blowing her off like this, without so much as meeting her face-to-face?

It didn't seem to fit, but what did she know?

The man was impossibly unpredictable.

She set her briefcase on the floor beside one of the chairs that had a view of the important one—the entrance, so she wouldn't miss spotting Rourke when he came in. If he came in.

The minutes dragged by and she tried not to fidget. She was used to being *busy,* not cooling her heels like this. But she sat. And she waited and she watched.

Several people came and went. She honestly couldn't tell whether they were members of Rourke's staff or visitors. Cynthia of the ugly glasses seemed to treat them all in the same way.

Nobody came to sit in one of the other chairs near Lisa, though. And after at least an hour of sitting there, she pulled out her BlackBerry. Answered a few dozen e-mails. Listened to even more voice mail messages. Her secretary, Ella, confirmed that she'd successfully rescheduled the appointments that she'd originally had on her calendar for that day.

The last message was from Derek.

As soon as she heard her brother's voice, her teeth felt on edge. She skipped the message, neither listening to it, nor deleting it.

Her fingers tightened around the phone and she turned to stare out the windows.

How could her brother have *stolen* from the institute—from his own family—the way he had?

How could she not have realized? Suspected?

She should have just deleted the message. There was nothing Derek could have to say that she wanted to hear.

Not now.

Unfortunately, beneath the anger that bolstered her was a horrible, pained void that she couldn't quite pretend didn't exist.

"You waited."

She jerked her head around to see Rourke standing less than a foot away. The phone slipped out of her hand, landing on the ivory-colored rug that sat beneath the arrangement of chairs. "We had an appointment." Her voice was appallingly thick and she leaned forward quickly to retrieve her phone.

He beat her to it, though, and she froze, still leaning forward, her face disconcertingly close to his as he crouched there.

He slowly set the phone in her outstretched palm, but didn't release it even when her fingers closed around it. His dark, dark gaze roved over her face.

She felt almost as if he'd stroked his fingers along her temple. Her cheek. Her jaw.

"What's wrong?" His voice was low. As soft as that never-there touch.

Everything.

The word nearly slipped out and, realizing it, she quickly straightened. The phone slid free of his grasp; once again hers alone. She tucked it into her briefcase. "Other than enjoying the view for the past two hours? Not a thing."

His expression hardened a little, making her realize—belatedly—that it had been softer after all. For a moment. Only a moment.

He straightened. "You should have rescheduled."

Cynthia was at her desk, but that was a good thirty

feet away. Still, Lisa kept her voice low. "And waste another morning?"

"For someone courting my financing, you're sounding very waspish."

The damnable thing was, he was right. And if he were anyone else, she would have sat there all day, happily, and still had a smile on her face when he finally got around to meeting with her.

"I'm sorry." She rose. "It's not you." Not entirely, anyway. "And of course, if you would like me to reschedule, I'll do so."

He studied her for a moment. "I have to make a small trip today."

Even prepared for it, she felt buffeted by more dismay.

But before she could formulate a suitable reply, he'd leaned over and picked up her briefcase. "Come on."

He was heading for the elevator, not even stopping to speak to Cynthia along the way. Lisa had to skip to catch up with him and stepped onto the elevator when he held it open for her. "You don't have to escort me from the building to make sure I leave," she said when the doors closed on them. He held the briefcase away from her when she snatched at it.

"I'm sure you learned somewhere along the way that you get more flies with honey," he observed.

"Fly strips work amazingly well, too," she countered and folded her hands together. She was *not* going to play tug-of-war with the man where her own briefcase was concerned.

His lips twitched.

For some reason the descending elevator seemed to creep along, in direct contrast to the way it seemed to have shot her to his floor when she'd arrived. He turned and faced her, leaning back against the wall that was paneled in gleaming mahogany with narrow mirrored inserts. "You look nice today."

Her lips parted. She blinked and looked up at the digital floor display above the door. Thirty. Twenty-nine. Twenty-eight. "Thank you." He looked nice today, too. Mouthwatering nice.

Which was a direction her thoughts didn't need to take.

"Did you sleep well?"

Even more disconcerted, she slid him a quick glance, then looked back up at the display. "Yes, thank you. My hotel was comfortable." It was hardly The Plaza, but then she was on an expense account. Unlike her wardrobe, the cash-strapped institute would foot the bill for this little junket. As such, the room was moderately priced and not entirely conveniently located. She glanced at her watch. "My flight leaves this afternoon."

Twenty-four. Twenty-three.

"Do you ever wear your hair down?"

"I beg your pardon?"

He pushed his hand in his trousers pocket, dislodging the excellent lay of his black suit coat. "It's long, isn't it?"

Eighteen. Seventeen.

"A bit," she allowed, trying to figure out what angle he was coming from.

"I've never seen you wear it down."

She huffed a little, exasperated not just with him, but with the eternal slowness of the elevator. "Since you've seen me only a handful of times, is that so surprising?" She didn't like—or trust—the faint smile hovering around his lips. "If we're going to be asking for personal information, then what was it that had you—" her voice dropped into a toneless imitation of Cynthia's "—unavoidably detained?" She raised her eyebrows expectantly.

"My mother was in the hospital last night."

Stricken, her eyebrows lowered. "Oh. I'm sorry." She looked more closely at him. He didn't look unduly upset. His suit was as magazine-perfect as always, his eyes clear and sharp; he didn't look as if he'd spent the night in some hospital waiting room. "She's all right?"

"A sprained ankle that they thought might be broken."

"Oh. That's good then. Well. Not good that she has a sprain, of course. But—" She realized she was babbling and broke off.

Fortunately, the elevator finally rocked softly to a stop and the doors slid open. He waited for her to exit first but he still held her briefcase. And continued to do so, either oblivious to, or choosing to ignore, her awkward gestures of taking it back.

They were nearly to the main entrance and he was still in possession of it when he spoke again. "Your security pass."

She'd completely forgotten it. She unclipped it from her lapel and dropped it off at the desk, then rejoined Rourke where he was waiting. "I didn't realize you owned the building," she said, holding out her hand for what seemed the tenth time. "It's quite an impressive space."

He glanced around. "It'll do." Then he took her hand, as if that was what she'd been waiting for, and tugged her through the doors.

Feeling as if she'd dropped through the looking glass, she couldn't do anything but follow.

Outside, the breeze had picked up, but the sun had warmed, foretelling a perfectly lovely September day. She caught her skirt with her free hand before it could blow up around her knees. "I'll contact your assistant to reschedule."

"No need. Come with me." He released her hand, and touched the small of her back, directing her inexorably toward a black limo that was parked at the curb.

She tried digging in her heels, but that was about as effective as holding down her skirt against the mischievous breeze, and before she knew it, she was ensconced in the rear of the spacious limousine.

With him.

And what *should* have felt spacious…didn't. Not when his thigh was only six inches away from hers and she could smell the heady scent of him. Fresh. Clean. A little spicy.

"Mr. Devlin—"

"Rourke."

A jolt of nervous excitement whisked through her. Maybe all wasn't lost, after all.

On the other hand, maybe he was merely planning to drop her at her hotel.

The teeter-totter of possibilities was enough to make her dizzy and answers were the only thing that would solve that. So she obliged him. "Rourke." Warmth bloomed in her cheeks at the feel of his name on her lips. "Where are you taking me?"

"Greenwich."

"*What?* Why?" It would surely take an hour each way, and that was if the traffic didn't get heavier.

But he just lifted his hand, putting her off as he put his vibrating cell phone to his ear.

She fell silent and sank deeper into the butter-soft leather seat, crossing her arms and kissing goodbye any chance she had of making her flight home on time.

He was still talking, so she reached for her brief-case—at last—and pulled out her own phone, sending a quick message to Ella that she'd need to move back her flight. Again.

Then, leaving that to her trusty assistant, she scrolled through her e-mails—two from Derek which she ig-nored as surely as she'd ignored his voice mail—and then dropped the phone back into her briefcase in favor of looking out the window.

She was even beyond trying to puzzle out what Rourke was up to, because she just ended up with a headache, anyway.

He stayed on the phone the entire drive—his voice low and steady as he discussed some upcoming media launch—and she found herself struggling against drows-iness. When the car finally turned up a long, winding drive bordered by immaculate lawns and massive shrubs, some still blooming, Rourke finally put away his phone.

They passed an island of tall, slender cypress trees bordering a flowing fountain, then a terraced swimming pool, and after rounding yet another curve in the drive, came to a stop in front of an immense Tudor mansion.

"It's beautiful." She couldn't stop the exclamation when they stepped out of the car. "Who lives here?"

"My mom." He didn't head toward the grand entrance, fronted by a dozen wide, shallow stone steps, but instead to a smaller, more unobtrusive door well off to one side.

She hurried after him, her heels clacking against the pavement.

He stopped and waited until she caught up to him, and they went in through the door. "You grew up here?" Her voice echoed a little in the long, empty hall they found themselves in.

"Hell, no." He reached back and grabbed her hand unerringly—sending a shuddering quake through her that she tried to ignore—then turned and left through another door that led outside onto a stone terrace.

She immediately heard the high-pitched squeal of children's laughter and Rourke let go of her hand just in time to catch up the little girl who aimed for him with the speed and accuracy of a heat-seeking missile.

It was all Lisa could do not to gape as his face broke into a full-blown smile while he swung the blond-haired imp up in the air, earning another peal of squealing laughter from her. She caught his face between her star-fish fingers and pressed a smacking kiss against his lips. "What'd you bring me?"

Rourke laughed outright and hitched the little girl on his shoulder, tickling her knees beneath the short hem of her miniature white tennis dress. "This," he told Lisa, "greedy little one is my youngest niece, Tanya. Say hello to Ms. Armstrong, munchkin."

"Is she your girlfriend?"

Lisa nearly choked, particularly when Rourke sent her a sidelong look. "Does she *look* like she's my girlfriend?"

The little girl's eyes were just as dark as Rourke's; a startling contrast considering the golden curls spilling around her head. And they focused on Lisa with an un-nerving intensity. "Maybe," she determined. "But I'm gonna marry Uncle Rourke, anyway. He's mine."

Lisa couldn't help but smile. "I see."

"I'm five, so I gotta wait a while. But you can still play with him," Tanya said generously. Her hand patted Rourke's head as if he was a particularly good pet. "I'm not very good yet." She pointed toward the tennis court on the far side of yet another swimming pool. There were a half-dozen kids trotting around the court, batting tennis balls back and forth more like ammunition than in any semblance of a real tennis match.

Trying not to blush—because the second Tanya had said *play,* her uncle had given Lisa a look that left her feeling scorched—she caught at her blowing skirt again and focused anywhere other than on Rourke. "Are those your brothers and sisters?" She nodded toward the other children.

"They're my cousins. I'm a lonely only," Tanya said so pathetically that Lisa had to bite back a laugh.

"Lonely my foot," Rourke chided, lifting her off his shoulder and flipping her heels over head before setting her on her feet. "Where's your grandma?"

"Aunt Tricia said she hadda sit in the shade with her foot elevatored." She gestured toward the lagoon-shaped swimming pool where several lounges and chairs were arranged around tables shaded by large beige market umbrellas. If it weren't for the thick border of trees well off in the distance that were showing faint shades of fall, it would have seemed like the middle of summer.

"Run ahead and tell her I'm here with a guest."

Tanya immediately turned on her little sneakered feet and raced across the stone courtyard, dashing down the terraced steps and across the lawn toward the pool.

Lisa caught at her drifting skirt again. A rerun of her trousers from the day before would have been smarter. "Rourke, you could have just said you wanted to check on your mother. I would have understood the need to reschedule our meeting." If anything, his evident concern for his mother made him seem much more human than she'd previously suspected.

"Rescheduling isn't necessary."

The teeter-totter was back in full force. "Because…?" She trailed off warily.

"Because I already know what I need to know." He lifted his hand in a wave when a petite woman appeared from beneath one of the umbrellas and started toward them. "That's Tricia. Be prepared. She likes bossing everyone around."

Her jaw tightened. He was being deliberately obscure. "Runs in the family, evidently," she murmured.

But he just grabbed her wrist and strode off again, pulling her with him whether she wanted to go or not and not releasing her until he met his dark-haired sister and swept her into an unrestrained hug that surprised Lisa all over again.

Then he held out his arm toward Lisa, introducing them. "This is my sister Tricia McAllister. Trish, this is Lisa Armstrong."

Feeling awkward, Lisa stuck out her hand. "It's nice to meet you."

Tricia had the same scrutinizing black eyes her brother possessed and they were clearly speculative as she looked from Lisa to Rourke and back again. "And you," she returned, exchanging a quick handshake before addressing her brother again. "Cara and Lea are bringing lunch down any minute now. It's so lovely out, I said we had to eat outside. So come say hello to Mother and then pull two more chairs over to her table." She headed off.

Rourke caught Lisa's eye. "See?"

"Is she the oldest?"

"Of my sisters, yes."

Which, she assumed, meant he was older than they were. "Brothers?"

He shook his had. "Until Trish had her third kid—

Trey—I was the only guy in the group, save a couple of brothers-in-law." He wrapped his hand around her elbow, steering her toward the tables beyond which the pool shimmered like pale clouds floating in liquid silver. "Now smile and stop looking like you're heading to your own execution."

"I'm sorry. But I feel like I'm intruding here."

"It's just family."

"Right. Your family." The back of her neck itched. "I'm here on business but they probably think this is social." At least that was what the speculation on Tricia's face had indicated.

He lifted an eyebrow. "So?"

"So—" She broke off, her hands flapping uselessly. She'd left the briefcase—along with her means of contact with the outside world—in the limo. And with each step they took, her heels sinking into the still-lush lawn, she felt as if she was getting further away from that familiar world in favor of this resortlike home. "It's…it's not."

"You'll have your money. All of it. Now relax." Completely disregarding the shock that had her legs nearly going out beneath her, his steps didn't hesitate as he continued pulling her toward the others. "Think of us as one happy family."

Chapter 3

All of it?

Lisa barely heard anything after those three little words. She supposed she must have functioned through the meal—carried from the house by Cara and Lea, who turned out to be Rourke's other sisters. Rourke sat her across from his mother, Nina. She had one bandaged foot elevated on a second chair, a position that didn't prevent her from busily working the colorful blanket she was crocheting. Like a general maneuvering her troops, Tricia called in all the children from the tennis courts, directing them around the two other tables even as she tossed out introductions that Lisa had no hope of following.

Not when *all of it* kept circling in her head, even trumping that ironic "happy family" comment.

He couldn't have meant it literally. Could he?

Before she knew it, the meal was done, the oddly

prosaic plastic plates and utensils disposed of and after being indulgently waved off by Nina Devlin, Lisa found herself walking through an honest-to-goodness hedge maze with Rourke while three of his nieces—Tanya in the lead—raced ahead of them.

"What exactly do you mean by *all of it?*" she finally asked.

They'd both left behind their jackets at the table. He'd rolled the cuffs of his white shirt up his forearms. Even his tie was gone. And at her abrupt question, he stopped and looked at her. The hedge was tall enough that it couldn't be seen over, but not so high that it felt claustrophobic. She could hear the high-pitched little-girl voices ahead of them, and still feel the breeze tugging at her chignon and her skirt.

But when he focused his attention on her face just then, they might as well have been locked together, alone, in a four-by-four vault. "I mean *all of it,*" he repeated as if she were witless.

Which was pretty much how she felt. Ultimately, the institute needed millions, and the most practical solution—if the least desirable—to that would have been from multiple sources. Not even Ted had really believed that Rourke would consider covering their entire need. "But—"

He lifted a hand, silencing her. "This isn't up for discussion. I'm willing to invest as much as it takes, but I'll be the only investor. No others."

Her blood was zipping through her veins more quickly, excitement making her pulse pound. This was it, then. Truly it.

The answer to a prayer.

"Are you agreeing because of your friendship with Ted?"

"Does it matter?"

She slowly shook her head. "What matters is the institute."

"Right." His lips twisted a little. "As it happens, I do want to see Ted and Chance have every opportunity available to them. And Ted won't leave the institute."

Her shoes crunched on the smooth gravel of the path as she took two steps one way, then back again. "You asked him?"

His eyes glinted, reminding her needlessly that—indulgent uncle or not—he was a calculating businessman. "Of course."

She swallowed. Paul had courted Ted and Chance away from San Francisco. With the institute in its currently precarious position, could she blame them if they were courted away from *them?*

"Ted flatly refused, though," Rourke added. "Wouldn't even consider any of the institutions I brought to his attention. Which is good. Because without Bonner and Demetrios I wouldn't touch this with a ten-foot pole." His eyes narrowed. "I know the numbers, Lisa. More importantly, I know why."

He couldn't possibly know that Derek was the cause. But she knew that before the *t*'s were crossed and the *i*'s dotted, he'd have a right to know the truth. For now, though, she chose to skirt it. "With such a level of financial commitment, are you expecting to be more hands-on in a functional capacity?"

He looked darkly amused. "Afraid I'm going to want to set up an office next to yours?" They turned another corner of the maze.

"Of course not," she blithely lied. The Armstrongs ran the Armstrong Fertility Institute. If she had anything to say about it, that was the way it would continue. "Naturally, you'll want some assurance that your investment is protected, so I—"

"It'll be protected all right. Just not by my regular presence during your management meetings. I'm not interested in telling you what staff to hire and fire or what sort of patient load every physician should maintain or what research protocols should be followed. The institute already knows all that."

Given the grim set of his mouth, she wasn't certain if there was a compliment in there or not.

She was leaning toward *not*.

"Then what, exactly, *do* you mean by protection?" The institute had been in successful operation for more than two decades. With the exception of their run of bad press during the past year, the only instance of mismanagement was what they were dealing with now.

Of course that instance was a freaking whopper.

"I mean *you*."

She frowned, trying—and failing—to decipher his meaning. "I have no intention of deserting the institute," she assured him. She'd had plenty of offers in the past few years, offers she'd never taken seriously, because her heart was in Cambridge, firmly entrenched in her family's calling. "I'll be there as long as there's a light-bulb burning."

He shrugged. "That's up to you."

Which left her more confused than ever. But a clatter of gravel heralded the giggling trio as the girls ran past them on their way back out of the maze and Lisa waited until they were gone again before speaking. "We're talking in circles, Rourke."

But he didn't answer immediately.

Instead, he closed his hand over her elbow and led her around another corner.

They'd reached the center of the maze where four short benches sat on each side of a square, tiered fountain.

It was charming and very serene.

And without the presence of his nieces, very, very private.

Rourke let go of her elbow and faced her. "I want an heir."

She did a credible job of hiding her astonishment. "And you want the institute to assist with that? We specialize in IVF but we also have an excellent history with surrogacy." Or maybe he had a girlfriend that not even little Tanya knew about.

For some reason, her mouth tasted a little acid over that thought.

"I know."

Relief coursed through her. At least now she felt as if she understood what he was aiming for. He'd said he wanted an heir. A child. They could help to make that come about. "Confidentiality is sacred at the Armstrong Fertility Institute, Rourke. You don't have to worry about that. And honestly, my brother Paul might want to brain me for saying this, but you don't have to agree to invest this heavily just to be assured of that. In comparison, those fees would be—" She broke off, shrugging. Because, truly, those fees would be less than minuscule to a man of his significant wealth. "As for the surrogate, if you have someone in mind, our attorney will walk through the entire process with both of you. And if you don't have someone in mind, we have—"

"I do. You."

It took her a minute to realize what he'd said.

She pressed her hand to her chest, a disbelieving laugh on her lips. "You want *me* to be your surrogate?"

"No," he said evenly. "I want you to be my wife."

She felt the blood drain out of her head. Disbelief morphed into anger.

Clearly he wasn't serious. Nothing since she'd stepped into Fare for that farce of a meeting the day before had been serious.

Not to him.

Her hands curled at her sides. "I cannot believe I let myself take this seriously. When, obviously, this is all just a game to you. What is it, Rourke?" She spread her arms. "Do you have some particular ax to grind or are you just bored?"

He ignored her. "I figure a year, maybe two at the outside. That's comfortable enough to have a child within that time. After which you can go your way and I'll go mine. The child, of course, will be with me at least half the time. I'm not ignorant that two parents are better than one. If you choose to exercise that role, of course. If not—" He shrugged. "I'll be just as happy to have him or her full-time. As you've seen for yourself there's plenty of other family around."

She gaped. "You plan to push this theoretical child off on your mother to care for, just so you can have yourself an heir?"

"Of course not." He looked impatient. "My mother obviously adores her grandchildren, but I don't expect her to raise them. My mother lives here, but this is my home."

"But you have a penthouse in the city." The glorious penthouse that Sara Beth had raved over nearly as much as she'd raved over Ted, who'd romantically swept her there while he'd been courting her.

"And a lakeside loft in Chicago and a cabin in Colorado and a house on an Oregon cliff. All of which are beside the point. In exchange for your…contribution… the institute will receive all the funds it needs to climb back out of its hole and stay there."

"How generous." Her voice dripped sarcasm. "If you're serious—and frankly, I'm having a hard time with swallowing that—what on God's green earth would lead you to think that I'd be agreeable to this?"

"You told me yourself you're dedicated to the institute."

"Dedicated, yes. Insane, no."

"Then when you get back home, you'd better tell everyone at the institute to polish up their resumes."

"I'm sorry to bust your egotistical bubble, Mr. Devlin, but you are not the only player in the investment game. I'll find new investors. *Real* ones." Investors who weren't out of their minds. "Nobody at the institute is going to have to lose their jobs. Nobody!"

"If you don't agree, there's not an investor in this country—or beyond—who'll want to touch the Armstrong Fertility Institute when I'm finished." His voice was low. Flat. "Everyone—and I mean everyone—will know how badly your own brother embezzled from the company. Derek couldn't even stick to just draining from your operational funds. He had to take from the research grants, too. And he did it for *years,* right under your noses. You think you weathered tough times when the institute was accused of using unauthorized donor sperm and eggs? When you were accused of inflating the in vitro success ratios? That was a cakewalk. You don't have only patients to lose. You've got the respect of every medical and scientific community to lose. Everything your father ever worked for." His black gaze didn't waver. "The institute won't just disappear quietly into the night like a fine business that has seen a natural end of life. It'll blow up and the toxic fumes will never fade. Not even your very capable P.R. fixer, Ramona Tate, will be able to spin you out of this."

The chicken salad they'd had for lunch swirled nauseatingly inside her. "How did you know about Derek? From Ted?" She would have staked her reputation on Ted's loyalty to the institute.

She *had* staked her reputation on it.

The look Rourke gave her was almost pitying. "Ted Bonner has never betrayed anyone or anything, least of all the Armstrong Institute."

"Then how did you come across such privileged information?"

"There are some things that even the venerable Armstrong family can't hide," he said, leaning toward her. "Do you really think that I would consider investing in the institute without knowing exactly what I'd be getting into? I made it my business to know as soon as Ted called to set up a meeting with you. I didn't get to where I am by being naive, Lisa."

"Did you get there by resorting to blackmail to get what you want?" She was shaking and very much aware that he hadn't answered her. "Or are we just special that way?"

His smile was cold. The wolf in full, ravenous mode, greeting Red Riding Hood right at the door. "Oh, princess, you are definitely special. And don't consider it blackmail when we're all getting something we want out of the deal."

Fury bubbled inside her, vibrating through her voice. "You met me yesterday with no intention of investing."

He didn't deny it.

"So what happened between yesterday and today? Some angel visit you in your dreams and tell you it was time for an heir?" She struggled to keep her voice down.

His gaze drifted from her face, down her body, and back up again. "Something visited me in my dreams," he allowed.

There was no mistaking his implication and she flushed so hard, she was practically seeing him through crimson.

Or else that was her fury.

She'd never been so close to losing control. She wanted to yell and pound her hands on something.

He would make a satisfying target.

She took a deep breath, waiting until her vocal cords didn't feel as if they were strangling her. "I have no intention of being your broodmare, and even less intention of allowing you to ruin my institute!"

"You might want to think about it," he suggested, when she turned on her heel and started walking away from the fountain. "I'll give you until tomorrow afternoon. That'll give my media director time to leak the... appropriate news."

He'd been talking with his media director for much of their drive to Greenwich. She felt even sicker. She looked back at him. "Appropriate."

"Don't agree to my...proposal—"

"Proposal!" She snorted. "Insane proposition, maybe."

He barely paused over her interruption. "—and it'll be just as I've described. A hailstorm of disaster will come down on the institute by the time people tune into the evening news. But if you do agree, I'll work equally hard at ensuring the world never knows what sort of thievery you have going on in your family. And the only thing in the news will be a human interest blip about our upcoming marriage."

She hated, absolutely hated the fact that there was a stinging burn deep behind her eyes. There was no way she'd show any sort of weakness in front of this man. "Why should I trust you?"

He held up his hand. "Scout's honor."

She stared at him, her hands curling and uncurling at her sides. "I've never come as close to wanting to hit someone as I am now."

"Your brother Derek would make a better target." His voice was flat. "He's the one who put you in this position."

And how badly she wanted to be able to deny it.

But she couldn't.

Derek. Her own brother. The one she'd always been able to turn to. He'd been the one to teach her to drive when her father was too busy to and her mother was disinclined to. He'd been the one to help her pass her high-school math classes, to whisk her away for a day of sailing when all the rest of her friends were primping for the prom that she'd never been asked to go to. She'd gone to the same university as he; he'd told her what teachers were good and which ones to avoid. He'd taken her out for her first legal beer.

And he'd been her biggest supporter when it came to

convincing their father that she—youngest of the Armstrong siblings—had what it took to become the head administrator of the institute.

She hated him for what he'd done to all of them. Couldn't understand how he could have done what he'd done.

And she wished like hell that she could cut off the memory of all that he'd meant to her.

"Come on, Lisa." Rourke's voice dropped gently; the predator sensing weakness. "It won't be so bad. A handful of years at the outside is all you'll be giving up. And in exchange, the institute will be set for the next fifty years when the next generation takes over. You can expand. Open another location on the west coast if you want. The sky will be the limit."

She didn't care about expansion. Or new sites. She cared about the site—the only site—they had. She cared about what it would do to her father if the institute fell from grace while it was under her watch. Gerald's health had been declining for years. She wasn't sure if he could survive such a mammoth, shocking disappointment.

She and Paul and the others at the institute had all agreed that it was best to keep Derek's horrible misdeeds from their parents. It wouldn't solve anything if they knew, and would only upset them.

She pressed her fingers to her temples.

But if Rourke was to be believed—if she didn't go along with his plan—there was no way that her parents wouldn't learn what Derek had done.

It was unbearable to even contemplate.

"My driver can take you back to your hotel," Rourke said, and she decided she was losing her mind to think there was a hint of compassion in his voice. "You have some thinking to do."

"According to you, there's no thinking to be done. Agree or suffer the consequences."

"The institute can't hide its financial precariousness much longer. Even if I did nothing, the truth would come out."

"But you're prepared to help it along." Her voice was thick. She looked at him, wishing she could understand what was ticking behind his impenetrable gaze. "And for what? What did we ever do to you?"

His eyes narrowed. "I don't like thieves."

"I don't like drivers who run red lights," she exclaimed. "But I don't take it so personally that I deliberately go hunting them down!"

"I didn't hunt you down, sweetheart. *You* came to me. I've just come up with a solution that benefits us both."

She shook her head. His gall was unbelievable. "You can whitewash it all you want, Rourke, but coercion is still coercion."

He sighed faintly. "The more you keep thinking along those lines, the harder this all will be. My advice to you is to focus on the advantages." His lips twisted a little. "That's what I'm doing."

She watched him.

The silence between them slowly ticked along, broken only by the soft gurgle of water spilling tranquilly over the edges of the fountain.

"I don't see why we would have to marry," she finally said. Maybe...*maybe*...she could tolerate being a surrogate mother for him. But that didn't necessitate a pointless marriage.

A glint sparked in his eyes. The wolf scenting blood. "My child won't be born a bastard."

She looked up at the blue sky, then back at him. "Come out of the Dark Ages," she said impatiently. "People hardly care about that anymore!"

"My mother still cares." His expression was inflexible. "I care."

So they'd all suffer through a sham of a marriage just so his heir wouldn't be born out of wedlock?

"I suppose I should be grateful you don't have some moral objection to divorce, too!"

"If I did, it went by the wayside well enough thanks to my ex-wife."

She'd been aware that he was divorced, yet her furtive research when she'd first met him hadn't managed to unearth any details about the woman. He'd been paired with dozens of women—from famous models to actresses to heiresses. But there'd definitely been no details of his former wife. "How long ago were you married?" Maybe he was nursing a broken heart and taking it out on her because she was female.

"A lifetime."

"Right." He wasn't that old. Only four years older than she. "What happened?"

"Nothing that concerns you."

"It does if I'm going to be putting your ring on my finger," she returned. "Since I assume, to go along with your other antiquated notions, that you'll be wanting me to wear one."

"You think it's old-fashioned for a couple to exchange rings along with their vows?"

She wanted to stomp her foot. Because she *didn't* think it was old-fashioned. She thought it was right and it was true and it was what people *in love* did. People who were committing themselves to each other for the rest of their lives.

Like Sara Beth and Ted had done. Like Paul and Ramona were going to be doing.

Certainly not for Rourke and her.

The very idea of it struck her as blasphemous.

"There is just one more detail," he added.

Her nerves tightened until they vibrated at a screaming pitch. "What?"

"The terms of our arrangement are to be kept private. As far as the rest of the world will know—including your family and your friends as well as mine—this will be a traditional marriage. Entered into for all of the traditional reasons."

She let out a disbelieving laugh. "Like what? Love? Who's going to believe that we're in love?"

His gaze suddenly focused on her mouth. His voice dropped. "I think we can be convincing enough."

She felt scorched and wanted badly to blame it on her temper. On the impossible position he was forcing her into.

But she was fresh out of strength to even maintain that simple of a lie to herself.

"What if I have a problem carrying the baby?" She tossed out the possibility with a hint of desperation. The fertilization itself wouldn't be a problem. Obviously. In vitro fertilization—IVF—was just one of the specialties at the institute.

But carrying the baby to term once it was implanted?

Her sister, Olivia, was proof that not every pregnancy made it to term. Who was she to say that she might not have Olivia's tendency toward miscarriage?

But even as she thought it, her common sense rejected it. Physically, Olivia was as delicate as an orchid. Her sister's body simply wasn't built to bear children. Lisa was about as delicate as an oak tree.

"You're in excellent health," he said. "There's no reason to believe you would have difficulty."

"How do you know I'm in excellent health?" Her jaw tightened. "Maybe I…maybe I have an STD!"

He laughed softly. "How long has it been since you've been with a man?"

She flushed. There was no earthly way that Rourke could know that she hadn't been involved with anyone—that way—since she'd been in college. Years. Followed by more years. "None of your business."

"It is when you're going to be carrying my baby inside of you."

Her knees felt weak. She moved around him—uncaring that he seemed to find amusement in the distance she kept between them—and sat down on one of the carved benches.

"It's academic, anyway," he commented. He plucked a leaf from the hedge nearest him and twirled it between his fingers.

A distant part of her brain envied him that ability to look so calm when everything was going to hell in a handbasket.

"It doesn't matter how many lovers you've had," he went on. "Or haven't had. You had your annual physical last month just like you've done for years. You're as healthy as a horse. You don't even have a prescription for birth control pills."

Her jaw dropped. "How do you know that?"

He just continued watching her. Leaving her with

mad scenarios of stolen medical files running rampant through her head. But that would have taken forethought, wouldn't it?

She eyed him, not certain of anything anymore. "You've thought of everything, I guess."

"And now it's time for you to do your thinking."

But she just shook her head and looked away from him. "There is no choice." And he knew it.

"You'll do what it takes to save the institute?"

He let go of the leaf. Her eyes watched it swirl around in circles until it landed on the gravel between them.

"Yes." She looked up at him. "You've got a deal."

Chapter 4

Rourke watched the limousine bearing Lisa in the rear seat drive away from the house.

A part of him was elated.

An equal part of him was disgusted.

Not with Lisa. She'd done exactly what he'd expected her to do. His personal dealings with her might have been counted on one hand, but he knew she was singularly dedicated in her goals where the institute was concerned. Agreeing to his terms had been her only option.

He wished that the elation could edge out the disgust if only for a moment or two.

"Where'd Lisa go?"

He looked over at Tricia, who'd walked around to the front of the house. "She has to catch a flight back to Boston."

After she'd agreed, she'd asked him about the rest of his plans.

And even though he had more than a few, he hadn't been able to heap them on top of her slightly bowed shoulders. So he'd lied. He'd told her that he would contact her later and they could iron out the details.

Her lips had twisted. But when she'd pushed off the bench, she'd stood tall and slender in front of him when she'd told him that she would use his limo then, after all.

Because she had work to get back to.

He knew there was no doubting that.

Even with him throwing money at the institute, it was going to take some real work to recover from the mess that Derek Armstrong had left behind.

He shoved his hands in his pockets, willfully pushing all thoughts of the man out of his head. He looked at Tricia. "What did you think of her?"

His sister—only two years his junior—looked up at him. "What do you think I thought? She looks like Taylor."

He turned to look back at the curving drive, though the limousine had already passed from sight. That had been his first thought, too, when he'd seen Lisa in Shots. That she looked like his faithless ex-wife. But the next time he'd seen her—when Ted and Sara Beth had eloped—he'd realized how superficial that first, startling resemblance had been. Oh, Lisa was still slender and leggy. A blonde with brown eyes and a face that was arrestingly sculptured with a reserved demeanor that just begged to be smashed.

"She's not Taylor," he told his sister. She might be an ice princess, but Lisa had a brain. And dedication, which she'd proved just that afternoon.

The only dedication his ex had was to herself.

"Well, obviously, I know that," Tricia said, rolling her eyes. "Just make sure you remember it."

"What else did you think of her?"

She eyed him more closely. With all the suspicion of a sister who'd endured plenty from him throughout their childhood. "She seems nice enough. A little cool, but I think that's probably because she's shy."

"Shy?" He shook his head, dismissing the notion. Lisa had confidence to spare. There was no room for shyness there. "Not a chance."

His sister huffed. "Why'd you ask if you're going to ignore what I think, anyway? Trust me. The woman has a shy streak a half mile wide. You just don't see it 'cause you're a guy. All *you* see are those long legs of hers and those big brown eyes."

He saw a lot more than that. He saw the means to his future. One that, for a long while, he'd given up on ever having.

He never thought he'd be in the position of hearing his own biological clock ticking, but that was where he was. There was a helluva lot of macabre irony that the situation caused by Derek Armstrong was now providing Rourke with the means to succeed in the one thing he'd ever failed at.

Or maybe, it was simply poetic justice.

Elation edged ahead at last, and Rourke dropped his arm over his sister's shoulder. "How fast do you think you can put together a wedding?"

Lisa stood on the front porch of her parents' home and took a deep breath. She'd barely landed in Boston when her cell phone started ringing with messages, but it was the one from her mother that had brought Lisa here this evening.

Nobody ignored Emily when she summoned you to a family dinner.

Not even when one had, just that day, been coerced into agreeing to marry a devil.

Blowing out a breath, she pushed open the door, entering the foyer where the scent of furniture polish and fresh flowers greeted her. Knowing that her mother wouldn't appreciate her arriving with briefcase in hand—tangible evidence that she was a business-woman and not a society wife—she left it on the floor next to an antique console table that held the cut-crystal vase filled with flowers and walked through the house that she'd grown up in.

She found everyone already in the drawing room. Her mother was sitting on the settee, her typical glass of sherry in her hand. Surprisingly, Gerald was out of bed and sat in his wheelchair next to the settee, sipping amber liquid from a squat glass of his own. Paul and his fiancée, Ramona, were standing close together near the bay window that overlooked the back of the estate. Her blond head was tilted close to his dark one and they seemed lost in their own world.

Derek was notably absent, for which Lisa was painfully grateful.

She was pretty certain that in her present mood, she would have lost her control altogether if she'd had to see him just then.

It was going to be difficult enough trying to sell the idea of her sudden "romance" with Rourke Devlin as it was.

She went to her father first, bending over him to kiss

his cheek. "Daddy. It's good to see you up. You're looking well." And he did. His shoulders weren't as broad and strong as they'd been before he'd become confined to his wheelchair and his face wasn't as fiercely handsome as it had once been, but he was still an impressive, dauntingly intelligent man.

And right now, that intelligence was peering out at her from her father's eyes. "You don't," he said bluntly. "What's wrong?"

"Nothing!" She straightened and managed a laugh. "Just too much to do and not enough hours in the day. That's what *you* always used to say," she reminded.

He lifted his glass, watching her over the rim. He didn't look convinced, but she turned quickly for her customary air kiss with her mother.

"You're late," was the only observation her mother had for her.

"I'm sorry." She looked over the back of the settee to find her brother watching her, his eyebrows lifted a little.

She could well imagine he was curious about the results of her New York trip. She shook her head ever so slightly, glancing back at her mother. "You know I was in New York for most of the day. I had to stop at the institute when I got back."

Emily's lips pursed. "I suppose that's why you didn't have time to dress more appropriately for dinner."

She was long used to her mother's disapproval and ignored it in favor of going to the gleaming wooden bar on the far side of the room. "I thought Olivia and her clan would be here, too," she said to no one in particular.

"She and Jamison had another function tonight."

And of course those functions would be important enough not to earn Emily's trademarked sniff of displeasure. "Too bad," Lisa said. "I was looking forward to seeing Kevin and Danny again." Since they'd joined the family, Lisa had been unfailingly charmed by the two sweet little boys her sister and brother-in-law had adopted. And right now, the three- and seven-year-olds would have provided a welcome distraction. "How long until dinner?"

She could hear her mother's sigh from across the room. "Long enough for you to have an aperitif."

As if to *not* have a predinner drink was the height of crassness.

Paul appeared beside her and pulled a wineglass from beneath the bar. "White?"

She stifled her own sigh and nodded.

He poured her a glass. "I'm sorry I was tied up with patients this afternoon and missed you when you got back." His voice was low. "How'd it go?"

Her fingers tightened nervously around the delicate crystal stemware. Her mother had switched her attention to fussing over Gerald, though Ramona was watching them. Lisa pulled her lips into a smile for her brother and his fiancée, lifting her glass a little as if in a toast. "We… um…we're not going to have to worry about that…small problem anymore. It's completely taken care of." Or it would be soon enough.

She took a hasty gulp, drowning her anxiety in wine.

"He went for it, then?"

He, of course, meant Rourke. "Mmm-hmm."

Her brother smiled. "I knew you could pull it off, Lis."

"There is one thing I need to tell you—" She broke off when they heard the chimes ringing from the front doorbell. Her first thought was that Derek was showing up, after all, but she quickly dismissed it. This was his childhood home, too. He wouldn't have stood on ceremony any more than she had. He'd have walked right on in.

"Go see who it is, Lisa," her mother ordered. "Anna is off today." Anna was her parents' housekeeper.

She didn't mind. It gave her an escape for at least a few minutes. She left her wineglass sitting on the bar and walked through the house back to the front door, pulling it open without so much as a glance through the heavily leaded sidelights.

Rourke stood on the porch. He was wearing a dark overcoat that made his shoulders look even wider than usual, and the golden light from the sconces positioned beside the massive door made his black hair glint.

She resolutely ignored the way her heart practically stood still and pulled the door shut a little behind her, lest anyone else's curiosity led them to the foyer. "What are *you* doing here?"

"Is that any way to greet your fiancé?"

The term jarred her. "What would you like me to do? Throw myself into your arms?"

"That'd be more natural, wouldn't it?"

"There's nothing *natural* about any of this." The magnitude of what she'd agreed to overwhelmed her all over again. As did the needlessness of it all. She stepped farther outside, nearly pulling the door closed entirely. "Why me?" she asked. "If you want a child—within the bounds of wedlock," she added quickly before he could interrupt, "why not just marry one of your other women?"

He smiled a little. "And what women would those be?"

The evening air was decidedly cool, but her limbs felt

decidedly not. "The women you date. Obviously." He was a seriously eligible bachelor. There was no question that the man had women in his life.

"Dating gets…messy."

Wasn't that what she believed, herself?

"This feels pretty messy to me," she countered.

"This is business. The terms are already outlined."

"A child is not a business."

"So says the woman whose entire life revolves around an institute that creates them."

"We're not cloning people, for heaven's sake! We're helping infertile couples achieve fertility." She went stock-still when his hand suddenly lifted toward her.

"This strand of hair keeps working loose of that knot you keep it in." His knuckles brushed the underside of her jaw as he ran his thumb and forefinger down the long, wavy lock.

It didn't seem to matter that he was wreaking havoc on her life. Just that faint touch made her bones feel like gel. "Wh-what are you doing here? For that matter, how'd you even know where I was?"

He wound the strands of hair around his finger. "Your assistant told me."

She jerked back, and he let her hair loose though he still left her feeling crowded on what was supposed to be a very spacious porticoed entrance. "What were you doing calling Ella?"

"Finding out your schedule, obviously."

"You should have contacted me."

He smiled faintly. "Somehow, I think Ella was more forthcoming than you would have been."

The truth of that stuck in her throat. "You said we… we would work out the details of our—" She couldn't even manage an appropriate word and just waved her hand instead. "Later."

"And now it's later. You're meeting with your family this evening. I figured it'd be logical for me to be here when you tell them we're getting married."

"Maybe I didn't plan to tell them this evening," she bluffed. Badly.

"I'd think you'd rather they hear it from you than from somewhere else."

"What'd you do? Issue a press release?" She hadn't really taken him seriously on that score.

"I've arranged for the ceremony to be held in New York at St. Patrick's Cathedral."

"What?" The cathedral was famous. It was Catholic. "I'm not Catholic." She hadn't even been to church in years. And he was a divorced man.

"I am."

She folded her arms tightly. "Aren't there…requirements to be met there? Marriage classes or something?"

"Ordinarily."

How simply he glossed over what she knew had to be an encyclopedia of protocols, and it was just another example that he wasn't any ordinary man. Not even an ordinary, wealthy man.

So she squashed the multitude of questions that her detail-oriented mind wanted answers for, and settled for just one. "Why do you want a church ceremony when you've already promised that our…union…has an expiration date?"

"That's a promise known only between you and me, remember? As far as anyone else is concerned, this is the real deal. Unless you're already chickening out."

She made a face. "I'm not chickening out." Not because she didn't want to back out. She did. But she wanted to ensure the institute's security even more.

"Good." He slid his hand inside the pocket of his coat and he pulled out a small, square jeweler's box. Without ceremony, he thumbed it open and pulled out a diamond ring. "Put this on."

She eyed the simple, emerald-cut solitaire. If this were a real engagement—if she were head over heels in love with the man—she would have been bowled over by its exquisite beauty. Something she would have chosen for herself—albeit a more modest-size stone—if she were given the opportunity.

But in that sense, there was nothing real about any of this.

She took the ring and slid it onto her left ring finger. The narrow band fit a little loosely and she nudged it with her thumb, pushing the weighty diamond to the center.

Beautiful or not, the ring felt more like a noose around her neck.

"I suppose you've already decided what date, too?"

"Next week."

She nearly reeled. "So soon?"

"I can fit it into my schedule now. And yours, as it happens, since you'll be able to cancel all of those meetings you have lined up next week with potential investors."

"H-how did you arrange the cathedral on such short notice?"

"I asked."

Panic bloomed inside her head. How could she ever be a match against him?

"Everything is already arranged," he continued. "The

ceremony will be at four. We'll have a small reception afterward at my penthouse. It's easier than finding another suitable venue, and Raoul will provide the catering. All you have to do is find a gown. We'll issue a few official photographs for the press, so keep that in mind."

"I'm surprised you didn't take care of the gown, then, too."

"Your taste is excellent. But if you prefer, I can make a few calls to some designers I know."

"Gosh. Thanks." She shivered and her sarcasm was shaky.

"You're cold." He suddenly pulled her close to him, wrapping his overcoat around her.

It was like being engulfed by a blast furnace. And for the life of her, she couldn't pull away.

"Better?" His voice dropped, whispering against her temple.

Her fingers curled against his shoulders, easily discerning the hard feel of him beneath the soft wool. No extra padding in that coat, at all. "Not really," she admitted.

"It won't all be bad. Have you seen the Mediterranean?"

She shook her head. She had to fight against the urge to lean against him. To just let him take her weight, and everything else on her plate....

But wasn't that what he was doing, anyway?

"I've arranged a private villa in the French Riviera for the honeymoon."

Honeymoon. She almost laughed. Or cried. Because he was covering all of his bases as far as appearances went. "I don't want to be away from the office for even a week."

"You will be, and it'll be three weeks."

Her gaze flew to his. "That's impossible. I can't just flit off for—" She broke off when the door behind them opened again.

"What on earth is taking so…" Emily's voice trailed off at the sight that met her. "Long?" Her eyebrows lifted in silent demand.

Lisa tried to untangle herself from Rourke's arms, but he wasn't cooperating. Which left her to peer over his shoulder at her mother. But when she opened her mouth to explain, nothing came. "I…I—"

"Blame it on me, Mrs. Armstrong," Rourke said smoothly. Without releasing Lisa, he tucked her against his side and turned to face Emily, his hand extended. "It's good to meet you again."

Again? Startled, Lisa looked from his face to her mother's.

The insistent inquiry on Emily's face was replaced by surprise. And no small amount of confusion. "Mr. Devlin. How nice to see you."

"Your mother and I were on the same charitable board a few years ago," he told Lisa. The smile he directed at Emily was both rueful and charming. "I'm afraid I forgot to mention it before." He looked at Lisa, the very picture of devoted man. "We've been busy with…other matters."

Her cheeks burned. She wondered if he'd studied the way Ted Bonner was always looking at Sara Beth, because he had the whole besotted thing down to an art. She glanced at her mother, who was now eyeing her with even more surprise.

"*You* are…seeing…Rourke Devlin?"

She would have had to have been a stone to miss her mother's implication.

Her chin lifted. She smiled a little and let her left hand slide down to the center of Rourke's chest. There was no way that her mother could miss the diamond on her finger. "Yes."

Emily's lips parted. She blinked a little. And Lisa knew that she probably should be ashamed of enjoying, just a little, the sight of her mother so obviously at a loss for words.

"I hope you don't mind that I didn't speak to you and Dr. Armstrong before now," Rourke smoothly stepped into the verbal void. "But your daughter has a way of making me forget all convention."

Lisa nearly choked over that.

But Emily was recovering quickly. Her smile was still more than a little puzzled. Proof that she couldn't understand what appeal Lisa might have for a man like him. But she stepped back in the doorway, extending her hand. "Of course we don't mind," she was saying. "Lisa is an adult. She makes her own decisions. Now come in out of the chill. We've got most of the family here," she continued when Rourke let go of Lisa and nudged her back inside the house. "Though it would have been perfect if Derek and Olivia could have been here for such an announcement." She gave Lisa a censorious look, as if Lisa had deliberately chosen the timing to annoy her.

But there was nothing but delighted pleasure again in Emily's face when she pushed the door closed and tucked her arm through Rourke's to lead him through her graciously decorated home.

Following behind them, Lisa blew out a silent breath.

At least now she didn't have to figure out a way to break the unlikely news that she was going to marry the man.

In that, she supposed she ought to be grateful.

"Everyone, look who's here." Emily's voice had taken on a cheerful slant by the time they entered the drawing room. "Darling." She went first to Gerald. "You remember Rourke Devlin, don't you?"

Rourke shook the older man's hand. "It's good to see you, Dr. Armstrong."

Gerald waved that off. "Gerald," he insisted. "And of course I remember the last time." He sounded irritated that Emily might suggest he wouldn't. "He was at the Founder's Ball. Lisa, get the man a drink." He gestured to the leather chair that until a few years ago, had been his own preferred perch. "You've met my eldest son, Paul, and his fiancée?"

Aware of the surprised looks that were passing between her brother and Ramona as the two greeted Rourke, Lisa went to the bar. She couldn't very well ask Rourke what he preferred to drink—presumably that would be something a "normal" fiancée would know—so she poured him a glass of the same wine she was drinking.

Though, as she carried it over to him and he tugged her down onto the arm of the chair and held her there with his implacable hand around her hips, she was rather wishing that she'd chosen a much stronger drink for herself. Instead, she held her own glass with tight fingers and it was then—seemingly all at once—that the rest of them noticed the ring on her finger.

Ramona gasped.

Paul muttered an uncharacteristic oath.

And Gerald just slapped his hand on his thigh. "Well, my God, Lisa-girl. Aren't you full of surprises!"

She smiled, hoping it didn't look as weak as it felt,

and avoided her brother's eyes. Of all those present, he was the one least likely to be convinced about her and Rourke's sudden match. "Wait until you hear Rourke's plans for the wedding," she said and smiled down at her intended bridegroom with a sudden hint of sadistic relish.

Let *him* be the one to tell Emily Stanton Armstrong that the wedding was already in the works.

And she'd have no say in the details, whatsoever.

"My pleasure," he said smoothly. But instead of launching into the litany of wedding arrangements that he'd already, arrogantly made, he lifted her free hand and pressed his thumb unerringly against her erratic pulse.

Then he smiled a little and sent her brief little spurt of satisfaction packing when he pressed his mouth slowly, intentionally, against her palm.

She forgot about her mother and everyone else. Except Rourke. And the fact that he'd plucked all control right out of the hand he was kissing.

Chapter 5

"You look beautiful." Lisa's sister, Olivia, fussed for a moment with the lightweight veil that streamed down Lisa's back from the small jeweled clasp where it fastened around her low chignon. "This has got to be one of the most romantic marriages I've ever heard of." Her dark eyes met Lisa's as she squeezed her hand. "This has been a remarkable year. I'm so happy for you and Rourke."

"Thanks." Lisa stared at herself in the long mirror of the luxurious hotel suite where she'd spent the night before her wedding. She'd traveled from Boston just yesterday morning and, in the thirty-six hours since, had been pinned and tucked into the wedding gown that she now wore, and her body from head to toe had been primped and fussed over by a crew of hairdressers, masseuses and aestheticians. And not two hours earlier, all buffed and polished, she'd stood in her perfectly fitted ivory gown on the terrace of her beautiful suite for the formal portrait that her mother had insisted upon. She'd been catered to and fussed over, and if she'd been given her fondest wish, she would have been miles and miles away from all of it.

There was something really wrong with surrounding herself with all the trappings of a fairy-tale wedding when the reason for it in the first place was anything but a fairy-tale romance. Lisa kept waiting for someone to stop and point them out as the counterfeit couple that they were, only nobody did.

Not Rourke's family, who'd hosted the rehearsal dinner the evening before at an unexpectedly quaint, homey Italian restaurant that Lisa had learned had once belonged to his grandparents, but was now run by Lea, mother of the impish Tanya. And definitely not by Lisa's parents. Emily might have been frustrated by her inability to run what she considered "her" territory—her daughter's wedding—but she was nevertheless glorying in the fact that Lisa was making such an unexpectedly advantageous match.

Lisa dragged her thoughts together. "And, you know, thanks for being my matron of honor," she offered to her sister. Olivia looked ethereal in her close-fitting royal-blue gown. Thanks to being Mrs. Jamison Mallory, she hadn't needed to prevail upon any of Rourke's connections to come up with an outfit befitting the occasion. "I know it was short notice."

Olivia laughed a little. "I'm glad to do it, Lisa." She swept a slender hand down her tea-length skirt. "Actually, I assumed you'd want Sara Beth to stand up with you. You're so close."

Lisa would have been glad for her best friend's support even if Sara Beth didn't know the full details of her and Rourke's arrangement. But Sara Beth had already been with Lisa for much of the day. She'd arrived at the hotel that morning before the buffers and the polishers with a bottle of champagne and a determination to see Lisa through what she suspected wasn't the "perfect romance" that had been touted in the news as soon as the media got a whiff of Rourke Devlin's impending nuptials.

But now, Sara Beth was already at the cathedral, giving support to her husband who was serving as Rourke's best man.

"I love Sara Beth, too. But you're my sister," Lisa said.

Olivia looked touched. "Well. Don't make my mascara run now, when it's time for us to leave for the ceremony. I hope that Jamison hasn't let Kevin lose the rings." She turned to retrieve the orchid bouquets that had been delivered to Lisa's suite earlier. "He's so excited about being the ring bearer but I think a lot of it may have to do with getting to walk beside Chance's stepdaughter, Annie. He's fascinated with her red hair."

Panic rippled through Lisa's stomach, and it had nothing to do with either Kevin or little Annie. With Olivia's attention elsewhere, she quickly swallowed down the last of her champagne. Courage, even in liquid form, seemed definitely called for.

Then she hefted up her trailing gown and took her bouquet from her sister. Like it or not, it was showtime.

Rourke pulled back his cuff and looked at his watch.

"Don't worry." Ted clapped him on the back. "The Plaza is only minutes away. She'll be here."

"I know. I just want to get it over with."

Ted smiled. "And get on with the wedding night?"

Rourke didn't deny it. He hadn't told his old friend any of the details behind the sudden marriage; leaving intact Ted's assumption that Rourke's interest in Lisa had carried them away.

The pretense wasn't entirely a pretense, anyway. Since that night with Lisa at her parents' home, he hadn't seen her again until the previous day when they'd both put their signatures on his prenup before joining the rest of their families and friends for the rehearsal and the dinner following.

Holding her in his arms, dropping kisses on her lips. None of it had been a hardship and if anything, he *was* more than a little preoccupied with thoughts of what was to come after the "I do's" were said.

"Gentlemen?" The woman in charge of keeping them on time poked her head into the room where Ted and Rourke were waiting. "We're ready for you."

Ted grinned and gave him a thumbs-up before preceding him to the chapel. The organist was already playing when he and Ted lined up in front of the priest.

He was surprised to feel a jolt of nervousness when he turned to wait for his bride. It wasn't a common sensation. His mother sat in the front pew, beaming her pleasure at him. Behind her were his sisters and their husbands and broods. Tanya was bouncing in her seat, alternating between pouts and smiles. She'd given him hell the evening before for stooping to marry someone else before she became available.

Young Kevin Jamison appeared, his focus much more squarely on the pillow he was carrying which bore the wedding rings, than it was on where he was walking.

Fortunately, his sidekick, Annie Labeaux—who was practically preening in her ruffled yellow dress—knew her marks perfectly, and kept Kevin coming in a forward motion.

Then Lisa's sister appeared, gliding up the aisle like the dancer he knew she'd once been. Tanya bounced again and, despite her mother's grasping hands, managed to stand up on her pew to wave both hands at him.

He waved back, earning a soft chuckle from most of the guests. But he wasn't really listening because Lisa had appeared at the rear of the chapel.

Rourke was vaguely aware of Gerald accompanying her in his wheelchair along the aisle toward him. Vaguely aware of the change in the organ music. Vaguely aware that he was still breathing.

She was beautiful.

Draped in some airy fabric that cinched her narrow waist in bits of lace, managing to look painfully innocent and wrenchingly sexy at the same time.

Her eyes didn't meet his when she reached the end of the aisle. She kissed her father's cheek and his motorized chair silently left her side.

Leaving Lisa to *him*.

He could see her pulse beating at the base of her slender neck. See a similar beat in the smooth flesh between the modest *V* of her neckline. And he could feel it beneath his fingers in her hands after she handed off her bouquet to her sister and placed them, cool and slightly shaking, in his.

Later, he knew they'd both repeated the vows. Knew he'd pushed his platinum band on her finger and had donned the wider version of it for himself. He knew that she'd lifted her lips for his brief kiss when the priest called for it, and knew that she'd tucked her hand through his arm as they'd walked back down the chapel aisle.

He knew it, because the license was duly signed afterward, they blinked against the flash of a dozen cameras as they left the cathedral behind, and then they were inside his limousine, which was bearing them, right on schedule, back to his Park Avenue apartment. The rest of the wedding party and guests were following in a raft of identical stretches.

"So that's it," she said, as they left the cathedral behind. She was looking at her hands that were splayed flat on her lap, surrounded by the cloud of her long gown.

Probably looking at the wedding rings.

"That was just the start."

He watched her fingers curl into the airy gown until neither her fingers nor the rings were visible. She looked straight ahead at the smoked privacy window separating them from the driver, then turned her head to look out the window. Her veil was pulled to one side, exposing her pale nape and the small, lone freckle that graced the tender skin.

He would kiss that freckle soon enough. And every inch of creamy flesh that stretched down her spine. He wondered how long it would take to undo the dozens of tiny diamond-like buttons that stretched down the back of her gown. Wondered, too, what she would be wearing beneath it.

She looked at him suddenly, her eyes narrowed, as if she'd been reading his mind. But she quickly disabused him of that notion. "There's not going to be any photographers at your apartment, are there?"

"At the reception?" He shook his head. "No. Outside the building, though? Likely." There had been a few camped out there for the past several days, clearly documenting the somewhat surprising fact that Rourke Devlin's fiancée wasn't yet in residence. "Don't worry. You're the picture of a princess bride. Just look up at me adoringly as we go inside and everyone'll be happy."

She grimaced and looked back out the window again. "Everyone but us," she muttered. "Even my best friend doesn't know what a lie this all is. I hope you're planning on going to confession someday or that farce of a wedding ceremony will haunt us to hell."

He touched his finger to her arm, feeling her start, before he dragged it slowly down to her wrist. "That's how you saw it?"

She shifted, crossing her arms. "How could I not? It was a pretense. Love, honor and cherish?" She shook her head, the corner of her lips turned downward.

"You'll be my wife with all the respect that deserves. I'll honor you." And he'd cherish her body the second he had the chance. No question.

The line of her jaw was like a finely chiseled masterpiece. "You won't love me."

Love had never gotten him anywhere. "And you won't love me."

She slid him an icy look. "That's right. The sooner we get what we want out of this deal, the happier I'll be."

"Then we're in agreement." He held her gaze with his, even after the limo sighed to a stop in front of his building. "Now, are you ready to get on with this?" His driver opened the door next to him.

Lisa's gaze slipped away. She picked up her bouquet that had been lying on the seat between them and nodded.

He stepped out of the car, and turned to help her out.

She stuck out one slender foot, shod in delicate straps, and then the dress seemed to follow as she slid out of the vehicle.

It was like watching flower petals unfurl and he knew the photographers that—as predicted—were still camped out nearby would be snapping away.

The moment Lisa was standing beside him, he slid his arm around her waist and pulled her close. His mouth covered hers.

Her lips parted; he could taste her quick word of protest, but he ignored it. And then he could taste the faint hint of champagne on her tongue and then deeper, the taste of *her* as she was kissing him back.

"Time enough for that later." Ted's laughing voice barely penetrated the fog that was gathering in Rourke's head. The hand his friend clamped on his shoulder was more intrusive.

Rourke slowly pulled away.

Lisa's eyes were wide. Her cheeks were flushed.

Sara Beth danced around next to Lisa, sliding a short little capelike thing around her shoulders that matched Lisa's dress before scurrying her toward the building, chattering a mile a minute about God only knew what. Crushed orchids rained down from Lisa's bouquet onto the sidewalk as they went.

He forced a smile for Ted and the others who were rapidly disgorging from the stream of limousines but the only thing he really saw was the panicked glance Lisa tossed back at him the moment before she disappeared into the building.

Yeah, he'd given the photographers their money shot, but just then he wasn't certain who was paying the price.

* * *

Lisa leaned back against the elevator wall and stared at her hands. She hadn't even had time to get used to the weight of the engagement ring during the past week, and now there was another band there to add to the unsettling unfamiliarity.

"Some kiss."

She glanced up at Sara Beth, who was not doing even a credible job of sounding, or looking, casual.

Lisa pressed her lips together for a moment. She could still taste him. "Yes." She kept her voice low. The elevator doors were still open. There was no point in pushing the button for Rourke's floor, because that particular one required a key.

Sara Beth's voice was just as low. "Considering the steam radiating off the two of you, I would've expected you to look a little more…glowing." She plucked Lisa's somewhat smashed bouquet out of her hands and gently stroked her hand over the blooms. "Rourke's obviously crazy about you. But are you really okay with this marriage thing? It's awfully sudden."

"I told you back at the hotel that I was."

"Yes, and you were two glasses into a bottle of champagne before you managed to say that." Sara Beth lifted her chin and smiled a little stiffly when Emily and Ramona stepped onto the elevator followed soon by Gerald, whose chair was being pushed by Paul.

"I still don't know why Derek wasn't at the ceremony," Emily was complaining. "I've left him a half-dozen messages but he hasn't called me back."

"Maybe he had something else he couldn't get out of," Paul said, his voice even.

"Not even for his sister's wedding?" Emily shook her head, looking upset.

"It was short notice for everyone, Mother," Lisa reminded, hoping that would be the end of it.

She had made it a point *not* to invite Derek and, considering the number of phone messages he'd been leaving for her, had been half afraid he'd show up anyway. Unless he was living under a rock, he couldn't fail to have read or heard that she was marrying the handsome billionaire.

Then Ted arrived, holding up a key that he used to unlock the button for the penthouse floor. "Rourke's talking to security. They were supposed to have the elevators unlocked by the time we got here."

"No detail left unturned," Lisa muttered.

Her mother leaned over to pinch Lisa's cheeks and she jerked back. "Hey."

"You need some color in your cheeks," Emily defended. "You're almost as white as your dress."

"I think she looks perfect," Ramona inserted, giving Lisa a quick wink when Emily turned to fuss over Gerald.

The elevator let them off in a spacious, marble-floored hallway that possessed two grand doors at opposite ends. The door belonging to Rourke was obvious; it was opened and a sedately uniformed beauty stood beside it, bearing a silver tray of crystal champagne flutes.

It took only a moment for Lisa to recognize the girl as the hostess from Raoul's restaurant. "For the new Mrs. Devlin," she greeted her, holding out her tray.

Mrs. Devlin.

Lisa's hand shook as she took one of the exquisitely cut stems. "Thank you."

"For heaven's sake, Lisa, we're not going to stand out here." Emily glided past, taking a glass of champagne for herself and Gerald, and entered the apartment with none of the reluctance that Lisa was trying to hide.

The second elevator arrived with a soft chime and, half afraid it would be bearing Rourke, she gathered her dress and went inside.

Even though she had been prepped by Sara Beth, who had seen the place when Ted had brought her here for a romantic getaway, Lisa still wasn't prepared for her first sight of Rourke's city home.

In its way it was as grand as his Greenwich estate. But where that mansion looked to have been steeped in tradition, his penthouse dripped modernism from its bank of unadorned windows to the gleaming dark wood floor, and minimalist ivory-colored furnishings.

The only color of note came exclusively from the chest-high glass vases flanking every window that were filled with immense bouquets of purple irises that seemed to reach for the high, coffered ceiling. The flowers were repeated in squat glass bowls all around the spacious living area.

She didn't know what surprised her more. The sleek, urban decor, or the profusion of flowers that he'd clearly arranged just for the purpose of their so-called reception.

"I told you it was beautiful," Sara Beth whispered beside her. She tucked her arm through Lisa's and drew her through the living area that was long enough to encompass Lisa's entire town house, toward the terrace beyond the windows where the flowers were even more resplendent.

Stunned, Lisa slowly stepped outside. There were several tables set there arranged end to end and looking as if they'd come straight out of a photo shoot from a high-end wedding. Situated in the corner, there was even a harpist whose dulcet sounds trickled in the air. "Amazing," she murmured.

"Thanks." Rourke's sister Tricia crossed to the nearest table and needlessly adjusted the position of a gleaming silver dessert fork against the pristine white linen cloth covering the table. "I'm afraid my brother didn't give me much time to pull things together."

Lisa started. "*You* did all of this?" She assumed that Rourke had simply thrown enough money at the situation to make things turn around on his dime-size schedule.

Tricia nodded. "Do you like? I wasn't sure about the color, but Rourkey said you were wearing purple the first night he saw you."

Lisa's capacity for speech deserted her. Whether because of hearing him called *Rourkey,* or that he'd remembered what she was wearing that night in Shots all those months ago.

Seeming to notice her muteness, Sara Beth squeezed her hand. "It's all so beautiful," she answered into the silence.

Tricia smiled, obviously pleased. "Wait until you see the cake that Raoul's wife made. It's a thing of beauty." She leaned forward suddenly and gave Lisa a quick hug. "And before everything gets too crazy, welcome to the family."

Thoroughly discomfited, Lisa hugged her back. "Thank you." But as she straightened, she spotted Rourke, who'd arrived, seeming to bring up the tail end of their modest gathering of guests.

Fortunately for Lisa, Tricia immediately slid into general mode at the sight of her brother, and she simply went where she was directed—namely to one of the chairs at the center of the long tables.

It was easier than having to think, particularly when she was already consumed with the effort of maintaining a smiling facade in the face of all the good wishes that heaped upon her head.

Hardest, though, was when Nina Devlin—clearly fighting tears—was the last to offer a toast to their marriage. "It just took falling for the right girl to get my son properly down the aisle. I couldn't be happier to have such a beautiful girl as a new daughter." She sniffed and lifted her glass, her damp eyes looking right into Lisa's. "To you and my son. Take care of the love you have found. Take care of each other." She grinned suddenly. "And take care of the grandbabies I'm hoping you're not going to wait too long to give me!"

Laughter rounded the table as glasses softly clinked yet again and the breeze whispered around their heads, making the purple flowers marching down the centers of the tables dance.

It would all have been perfect.

If it had been real.

Rourke leaned close to her, his lips grazing her cheek. "Drink, for God's sake." His voice was soft, for her ears alone.

She smiled brightly and drank.

She turned her lips toward him for a glancing kiss whenever one of his sister's mischievous kids tapped their water glasses with a spoon. She pushed a few bites of Raoul's excellent food into her mouth when it seemed expected. She stood in front of the beautiful confection of a cake that Raoul wheeled out to cut the first slice to share with Rourke. She went through the motions with a smile on her face until she wanted to scream. But she didn't drop that smile until hours later, when the last guest had finally departed and even Raoul and his son, Tonio, and daughter, Maria, had left through a separate entrance off the kitchen that Lisa had yet to even see.

Only then, when it was just Rourke and Lisa left in that high-ceilinged living room scented by irises and filled with the soft sounds of a low guitar, did she finally, finally let the smile fade.

Her cheeks actually hurt.

She pulled off the fine shrug that matched her gown and dropped it on the end of one of the couches before sitting down to peel her feet out of the strappy designer torture devices otherwise known as sandals and wriggled her toes.

"Everyone seemed to enjoy themselves." Rourke slid off his jacket and tossed it next to her.

She automatically reached for it, her fingers smoothing out the finely pinstriped charcoal over the back of the couch so it wouldn't wrinkle. "Everyone but us."

His smile was faint. He pulled on his tie. "I wouldn't have minded everyone leaving an hour sooner than they did, but I thought it was okay. Food was good."

She realized she was staring at his strong throat where his fingers were loosening the collar of his shirt and quickly looked away. "Raoul doesn't disappoint." Though she would have been hard-pressed to remember what the menu had been.

She pushed to her feet only to nearly trip over her gown when she walked toward the windows. She lifted her skirts. "This is quite a view you have here. The skyline. The park."

"It's a place to sleep."

She made a soft sound. How easily he dismissed the million-dollar view. "Right." Her fingers toyed nervously with the diamond hanging just below her throat. The necklace had been a gift from her father when she'd graduated from college. Aside from Rourke's rings, it was the only other piece of jewelry that she was wearing. From the corner of her eye she saw him toss his tie aside as cavalierly as he had his jacket.

It made her even more acutely aware of how alone they were.

"That was, um, nice news Chance shared before they left," she said, feeling a little desperate. "About him adopting Jenny's daughter, Annie." Not until she'd seen Rourke slapping Chance on the back and kissing Jenny's face had she realized he was almost as good a friend with Chance as he was with Ted. She was still wearing her veil and the whisper-light silk tulle tickled her back. She reached back to unfasten it. "She's a sweetie."

"Yeah, she is. Chance'll be a good dad. He and Jenny are great together. Here. Let me."

A sharp wave of unease rolled through her. She sternly dismissed it. Theirs was a marriage of convenience. It didn't involve sex. Just because *she* couldn't get her mind off it didn't mean a thing.

She swallowed and turned her back toward him. "It's got more pins in it than you'd think," she warned.

"I'll find them." His fingers grazed against her head.

She closed her eyes, trying not to jump like some virgin on her wedding night.

It was almost laughable.

She wasn't a virgin, though she might as well have been for all of the experience she didn't really have.

And it was her wedding night.

But for them, those two things were not even relevant. It wasn't as if they'd need to sleep together to make a baby. They had the institute for that.

With surprising gentleness, he worked the handful of pins free, then unfastened the jeweled clasp of the veil and handed it over her shoulder to her. His bare forearm brushed against her.

When had he rolled up his shirtsleeves?

Feeling treacherously close to the edge of hysteria, she took the veil and quickly stepped away. "Bath and a bed," she blurted, only to feel her cheeks turn hot. "That's, um, that's what I think I need." She waved her hand, which also managed to wave the floating, silky veil. "Just point the way. I'll find it."

He looked amused. "Bedroom's down that hall."

"Great." She took a step only to tangle her bare foot in her skirt again. She hauled everything up in her arm. "Um…thanks." Her cheeks went even hotter. She was acting like an absolute idiot and knew it and before she made a bigger spectacle out of herself, she nearly ran down the hall. She found the bedroom with no difficulty, and closed herself behind the door with relief.

The furnishings there were just as sleekly designed, with a mile-wide pedestal bed and nightstands that seemed to grow right out of the wall on either side of it. There were acres of unused space, yet the room didn't feel stark or barren. Maybe because of the large fireplace that was opposite the bed, or the expanse of windows— again unadorned—that lined one wall.

Behind one of the doors the room possessed, she found her suitcase sitting on a luggage rack in the siz- able closet. The closet then led to the en suite bathroom that, even in her exhausted state, was enough to make her swoon a little.

She flipped on the water over the massive tub and tossed in a generous measure of amber-colored salt from one of the heavy crystal containers decorating one corner of the stone ledge surrounding it. Immediately, lush, fragrant bubbles began to bloom beneath the rush of water and she reached for the buttons on the back of her dress only to realize with chagrin that there was no way that she would be able to undo enough of them on her own to even get the gown past her hips. Not even sliding her shoulders out of the narrow, fancily knotted chiffon that served as straps helped.

"Great." She eyed herself in the reflection of the wood-framed mirror that hung above the rectangular-shaped vessel sink. Her eyes looked wild and, thanks to pulling the pins from her veil loose, her hair was falling down.

"Lisa?"

She jerked, staring at a second door that led into the bathroom as it slowly opened. "What?"

Rourke stuck his head through. "I figured you'd need help with the dress."

She hated, absolutely hated, the fact that he'd realized that problem, too. But she walked over to him, presenting him with her back. "I do."

"Not the first time you've said those words today." His fingers grazed her back between her shoulder blades.

"Not the first time I didn't want to say those words today, either," she pointed out coolly. "Just get on with it." She pressed her hand against the bodice of the dress to hold it in place against her breasts as, centimeter by centimeter, she felt it loosening at the back.

"You know that telling me something like that just makes me want to take my time, right?"

She ignored him. It wasn't so easy, however, to ignore the feel of his fingers moving against her back. Even with the corset she wore beneath the gown, every grazing touch left her feeling branded.

She nearly laughed. Branded by his touch and shackled by his wedding ring.

He'd reached her waist. Another inch and she would be free of the dress, and of him. And, please God, the disturbing sensations roiling around inside her.

She held her breath, waiting. And the second she felt that bit of release, she started to step away.

But Rourke's hand slid right beneath the fabric of her gown, circling her waist. His palm pressed flat against the satin covering her belly as he tugged her back against him. "I've been wondering what was under the gown."

She could feel his shirt fabric against her shoulder blades. It was maddening. But what was more maddening was her weak longing to lean against the hard muscles she could feel beneath that shirt. "I *beg* your pardon?"

He laughed softly. "Let go of the dress." He didn't wait, but tugged the bodice out of her lamentably lax grip.

The gown slid to a fluffy cloud around her ankles, leaving her standing there wearing nothing but the white satin and lace corset and matching thong. And his hands.

Her frantic gaze landed on their reflection in the mirror, only to get caught in the snare of his gaze.

Never looking away from her, he lowered his head and pressed his mouth to the nape of her neck.

She swayed. His fingers splayed wider against her.

Thumbs brushing against her corset-contained breasts. Little fingers sliding against the thin elastic of her insubstantial panties.

Desire wrenched through her, hot and wet and aching.

She drew in a hard, quick breath. She pushed away his hands and stepped out of the cloud to snatch it up against her. "This isn't part of the deal. I'm not…I'm not h-having sex with you!"

He tilted his head slightly, his eyes narrowing. "We're married now, Lisa *Devlin*. So tell me. What the hell do you think *is* the deal?"

Chapter 6

Lisa stared at Rourke. "Do we have to rehash it all? You want a child. I want to keep the institute from closing its doors." She lifted her hands. "And here we are."

He watched her for a tight, seemingly endless moment. "My child isn't going to be conceived in a petri dish."

Her stomach tightened. She advanced on him. "And just what is *that* supposed to mean?"

He had the gall to laugh. "I know you're not that naive."

She jabbed her finger against his chest. "I am *not* sleeping with you."

He grabbed her hand, holding it aloft so that her rings winked in the light, sending prisms around the room. "It's too late for reneging now. You agreed."

"I agreed to be a surrogate for you. I didn't agree to be your whore!"

"You agreed to be my wife." His voice turned as flat as his eyes had gone. "To bear me a child. I never once said it would be the product of in vitro. And make no mistake. If I was going to treat you like a whore, I would've just taken you the night of the Founder's Ball and left the money on your nightstand."

"I don't know what infuriates me more." She finally managed to snatch her hand away from his hard grip. "Your absolute arrogance in thinking I would have slept with you that night, after sharing one dance with you, or you pretending now that this is what I agreed to! The Armstrong Institute specializes in IVF!"

"I didn't *marry* the Armstrong Institute!" His voice rose. He inhaled sharply. Let it out more slowly. "Obviously—" his voice was more controlled, even if his teeth were bared "—we're at cross-purposes, here." He suddenly moved, making her jump.

But he only moved past her to turn off the gushing water taps. "We'll conceive the baby in the normal way. I never said—or implied—otherwise."

She crossed her arms over the crumpled bodice of her dress, trying not to tremble.

She failed miserably.

"You know I *believed* otherwise." Her voice was stiff.

He lifted a sardonic brow. "Do I?"

She racked her brain. Surely they'd covered this. Hadn't they?

But the sinking sensation in her belly gave leeway for doubt to creep in.

She'd assumed.

And now, faced with his implacable certainty, she realized how badly she'd erred.

He did expect to sleep with her. To conceive a child, just as nature intended. And she…heaven help her…

she had agreed to his terms without ever clarifying this most salient point.

"Rourke—" She barely managed to voice his name. "Honestly, we barely know each other. I didn't...I mean, I don't—"

"Save it." He lifted a weary hand. Ran it down his face. "You and I both know it doesn't matter *how* long we've known each other. It's enough. But it's been a long day. So take your bath."

She swallowed hard and couldn't prevent slanting a gaze toward the door through which he'd entered. Did it lead to his bedroom?

To his bed?

"And...and then?"

His black gaze raked over her. "Don't worry, princess. The mood's definitely passed for now."

She wanted to sag with relief but pride kept her shoulders more or less straight.

"Our flight leaves tomorrow morning." He went to the door. "But make no mistake, Lisa. Once we're in France on our *honeymoon*—" his lips twisted "—I expect to make this marriage a real one. I suggest you spend the time between now and then getting accustomed to the idea."

Then he left, closing the door softly, but finally, behind him.

She sank down on the wide ledge of the bubble-filled tub, her fingers still clutching the fabric of her wedding gown.

She was shaking. And she very much feared that it wasn't horror over her mammoth-size misunderstanding where her wifely duties were concerned.

It was anticipation.

And where was that going to leave her, once her purpose had been served?

* * *

The answer to that question was still eluding her when they boarded Rourke's private jet the following morning. And when they landed in Nice that night.

Rourke was no particular help. Aside from introducing her to his flight crew when they'd boarded the plane, he barely spoke to her once they were in the air.

Mostly, he spent the time on the phone. And most of that time he spent pacing the confines of the luxuriously equipped airplane. The only time he sat down in one of the sinfully soft leather seats was when Janine or Sandy, his two flight attendants, served them their meals.

She could almost have let herself believe that what had happened in his apartment the night before had never happened at all.

Almost.

Instead, her traitorous eyes kept tracking his movements about the cabin, willfully taking note of the sinuous play of muscles beneath his black trousers as he paced, of the way his hands gestured as he spoke, tendons standing out in his wrists where he'd rolled up the sleeves of his black shirt shortly after takeoff.

Now, they were gliding silently through a star-studded night as they left the airport behind in a low-slung sports car that offered very little space between her and Rourke, at the wheel.

There was no driver. No flight crew.

Just…the two of them.

And all too easily, her senses were filled with the memory of his lips brushing against the nape of her neck, his hands sliding over her.

In the faint glow of the dashboard lights, she could see that hand capably curled over the steering wheel.

She bit her lip for a long moment and opened her window a few inches to let in the rush of night air but it wasn't anywhere near cool enough to suit her.

"You all right?"

"Just a little tired." It wasn't entirely a lie. Despite traveling in the cradle of luxury, the flight had still taken hours. Add in the time difference and it meant it was nearly midnight there. "I thought it would be cooler outside."

"Weather around here is pretty temperate year-round and August wasn't long ago. There's still heat lingering. Might even find the water still good for swimming." He glanced at her, then back at the road. "We'll be on a private beach."

She lowered the window another few inches, wanting the wind to blow away the ideas *that* caused.

The road they were driving on was narrow. Winding and, aside from the gleam of moonlight, very, very dark. They might have been the only two people left in the world.

"My father took me to Paris once," she desperately interrupted the insistent images filling her head. "I was still in college." It was the first time he'd included her in such a manner and she'd been thrilled to accompany him to the medical conference. "But we were so busy that I never had a chance to leave the city."

"Busy doing what?"

She was vaguely surprised that he even responded. It seemed unlikely that he was as tensely nervous as she. But still, conversation was better than silence, and it might keep her imagination under some control. "Keeping up with my father, mostly. He was presenting some new research at a conference." She thought back, remembering. "He was amazing."

She hadn't been offended to be the one fetching him water or carrying his papers. And when he'd included her in his conversations—had actually seemed proud of her when she'd offered some thought or opinion—she'd felt as if she'd accomplished something truly great. "It was the first time he actually treated me like an adult."

She felt Rourke's glance, but he didn't comment as he slowed the car to turn up a steep drive that seemed to appear out of nowhere. A dimly lit gate swung open for them, and once they were through, the road became even more winding and narrow.

Yet he navigated it all with obvious ease.

"I take it you've been here before."

"Mmm."

She chewed the inside of her lip. "With a woman?" She hated acknowledging the need to know.

His hesitation was barely noticeable. "None I've been married to."

She couldn't tell if it was amusement in his voice or irony.

But there was no time to dwell too long on wondering what woman—or women—had been here with him, because he pulled to a stop in a small stone-paved courtyard. "This is it."

There was not much to see beyond the low lights that were bright enough only to point out the perimeter of the courtyard and light the way along a narrow walkway. She climbed out of the car while he was pulling their suitcases out of the trunk that had probably taken some mathematical genius to fit inside in the first place, and even though she held out her hand to take some of her own smaller items, he just ignored her and loaded the straps up on his own muscular shoulders.

She wouldn't have thought the man would ever carry his own luggage.

"This way." He headed toward the walkway. "Watch your step. The lighting is pretty dim and the pavers might be uneven."

As she followed him, she also noticed that the bushes lining the walk were overgrown, which didn't help the going any. She was glad she was wearing flats, though her gauzy ankle-length skirt wanted to snag against the overgrowth. Before long, they passed through an archway that led into another courtyard and he unlocked a wide, tall door, and led her inside.

Given his taste in homes, she shouldn't have been surprised by the luxury that met them when he began flipping on lights as they passed through the entrance hall to a living area that rivaled his New York apartment for size. But after the rustic entryway, nevertheless, she was.

In his apartment, everything had seemed angular. Here, everything was arched—the doorways that were flanked by marble columns and the windows that were covered with shutters. The floors were gleaming stone and the furnishings all seemed to be done in soft browns. It was cool and elegant and expensively beautiful and she couldn't help but wonder if the paintings that hung on the smooth, ivory walls were originals.

He dumped their luggage on the floor and crossed the long room to push open the shutters guarding the tall arch-shaped windows there. "I told Marta—the housekeeper—that we wouldn't need her until tomorrow." Lisa realized they weren't windows at all but doors, when he pulled them right open letting in the fresh night air. "Come out and see the view."

Nerves jumping anew, she followed him outside onto a deep terrace guarded by a majestic stone balustrade that faithfully followed the steps that crisscrossed from this level to two lower ones, and finally the ghostly white sand that led to the silver-white glisten of the sea. "It's breathtaking," she admitted.

"Wait until you see it at sunrise."

"Sunrise?" She shook her head. "Thank you, no. I prefer to be sleeping at that hour."

His white teeth flashed in a quick grin that caused her heart to smack around even more than the view had. "Some things are worth getting up for at that hour."

She couldn't form a response to that to save her soul.

And he knew it.

His grin deepened as he turned to go back inside. "I'll show you the rest of the place."

Aside from the main living area, "the place" included two kitchens, one media room, an office that Rourke said was equipped with every convenience, and a total of six bedrooms.

"This one has the best view," he said of the very last one they came to.

And she could certainly see why.

The wide four-poster bed was positioned opposite a bank of windows that he immediately set about un-shuttering. They'd gone down a short flight of stairs to reach the room and it looked out the same direction as the living room, sharing that stellar view of the Mediterranean.

It didn't take a genius to realize *this* was the room he was expecting they would share. The room. And the bed.

She kept her eyes strictly away from that particular

item and went into the adjoining bathroom. Even that had windows that opened up to the view.

She pressed her palm to the knots in her belly and returned to the bedroom.

Rourke, done with the windows at last, watched her for a moment. "Marta will unpack everything in the morning. Do you want one of those suitcases for tonight?"

She hadn't considered herself a normal bride. She hadn't packed a trousseau. No sexy little negligees designed strictly for the purpose of enticing an eager groom. No fancy little ensembles to parade around in during the day. She'd packed what she'd had in her closet.

The only thing new that she'd worn in the past two days had been her wedding gown.

And everything beneath it.

Her mind shied away from those thoughts.

"I just need the overnighter. The small one. But I can get it…" She was already speaking to an empty room and could hear the sound of his footsteps on the half-dozen stairs that would carry him back to the living room's level.

She let out a shaking breath, looking around the room again.

The bathroom had possessed several mirrors, but the bedroom itself contained none and for that she was grateful. There were two large armoires on each side of the room and a bureau in the arching hallway that opened into the adjacent bathroom. She peeked inside each, finding them all empty.

Rourke still hadn't returned, so she opened one of the French doors and went outside onto the terrace.

If she looked up and to her right, she could see the

terrace level off the living room. If she looked down and to her left, she could see the lowest terrace, which could be reached by another set of stairs. But the terrace on which she stood was the only one that possessed a setting of deeply cushioned chaises and chairs positioned beneath a tall pergola. Long, pale drapes hung down the colonnades, drifting softly in the night air.

She couldn't help the sigh that escaped. It was all so impossibly beautiful.

If he chose a place like this for a honeymoon with someone he didn't remotely love, what would he do for someone he did?

"Here."

She whirled on her heel, pushing aside the disturbing thought. What did she care what he'd do for someone he loved?

Rourke stood in the deep shadow of the doorway, holding out her small case. She went to him and carefully lifted the strap away from his hand before sidling past him into the room.

Now what?

She was so far out of her element she didn't have a clue. She twisted the leather strap in her hands. "I—"

"I—"

They both broke off.

He lifted an eyebrow, but she just shook her head, mute all over again.

"I have some calls to make."

It was the last thing she expected him to say. "It's the middle of the night."

"Not in New York." He started to leave the room again. "It's going to take me at least a few hours so if you're hungry, I'm sure you can find something in the kitchen."

"I don't cook."

He glanced back at her. "Don't, or don't know how?"

Her cheeks went hot. "Does it matter?"

He shrugged and she felt positive it was her fanciful imagination that colored his faint smile with a shade of indulgence. "Cooking isn't part of the job description. But this place is always stocked with fruit and breads. Even someone who doesn't cook won't starve."

Job description.

Her hands curled so tightly, the leather strap dug into her palms. "I suppose *you* want something to eat."

His eyes were unreadable. "I'll manage."

Then he turned and left her alone and she almost wished she had jumped on the idea of preparing them some sort of meal. Because now all she was left with was that wide bed behind her and the sense that she was expected to prepare herself for it.

And for him.

Nerves spurred her into motion and she dumped her overnighter on the bureau. She needed to stop thinking like some Victorian virgin. She was a modern twenty-first-century woman, for God's sake.

She yanked open the case and unloaded the few items inside. The travel bag containing her toiletries, the over-size Bruins jersey that she preferred to sleep in, and a pair of clean, thoroughly utilitarian white cotton panties.

Not a speck of lace or ribbon or silk in sight.

Sadly, she didn't know if she'd have felt more confident if there had been. Probably not.

She was far more comfortable in a suit sitting in a

boardroom debating business practices than she was in a nightgown waiting for a man....

She had a few hours, according to what he'd said, but instead of attempting another bath when the memory of her last attempt was so fresh in her mind, she unpinned her hair and took a short, steaming shower and tried not to think about the fact that the slate-tiled enclosure was certainly roomy enough for two.

When she got out, she wrapped her wet hair in one of the plentiful plush terry towels, slathered lotion on her arms and legs—just like she did every time she showered, she justified—pulled on the jersey and bikini pants, and, feeling like a thief in the night, crept her way through the villa to the nearest kitchen. There was, indeed, a wide assortment of foods already available.

She selected a crusty roll and a handful of green grapes and turned to go back to the bedroom. But the chilled bottle of wine that had already been opened caught her eye, and she grabbed that, too, as well as one of the wineglasses that hung from beneath one of the whitewashed cupboards. Feeling even more thieflike, she stole back to the bedroom, carefully skirting around the office.

But her footsteps dragged to a halt when the low murmur of Rourke's voice through the partially closed door shaped into distinguishable words. "Call the publisher," he was saying. "Tell him if he doesn't squash the story, I'll personally call on every corporate advertiser they've got and he won't like the results."

One of the grapes rolled out of Lisa's hand and she silently darted after it, catching it just before it rolled down one of the steps.

She looked back and saw Rourke watching her, his phone still at his ear.

She flushed a little. "I was hungry after all."

His gaze settled on the wine bottle, looking amused. "And thirsty?"

"This *is* France. And the bottle was already opened."

"You don't have to defend yourself to me." He abruptly turned his attention back to the phone. "You're damn right I'm serious." His voice was sharp, obviously intended for his caller. "If you can't accomplish this, I'll hire someone who can." He went back into the office, closing the door behind him.

Lisa scurried down the steps to the bedroom feeling a little sorry for whomever was on the other end of that call.

She quickly demolished the bread and grapes even before she finished half a glass of wine. She pulled out her own cell phone and started to dial Sara Beth twice.

But she didn't want to burden her friend with foolishly panicked calls. Aside from Rourke's insistence that nobody know the true details of their agreement, Sara Beth's new husband was Rourke's friend and Lisa was loath to put her problems between them. Particularly when Lisa suspected that Sara Beth was already concerned.

So she put the phone away.

She paced around the bed, avoiding it as if it was poisonous, until finally, annoyed with herself, she yanked back the creamy silk bedspread and bunched up a few of the bed pillows behind her back. She pulled out the suspense novel that she'd brought with her, but reading it now was just as big a pretense as it had been on the plane, and she finally tossed it aside.

A part of her wished Rourke would just return and put an end to this painful waiting, once and for all.

But he didn't return. And the time display on her cell phone told her that not even an hour had passed, anyway.

She got out of bed, grabbed the bedspread off the bed and carried it, along with her wine, out onto the terrace. There, she wrapped the bedspread around her and stretched out on one of the chaises to stare into the dark, gleaming mystery of the Mediterranean sea. And there, finally, for the first time since she'd met Rourke in Raoul's restaurant, she felt herself begin to relax.

She never noticed when Rourke eventually came to the door of the bedroom and looked out at her to find her head bundled in terry cloth towel and her body wrapped in silk.

Because she was fast asleep.

Rourke sighed faintly and picked up the wine bottle from the wrought-iron table beside her and gave it a shake. Empty. There was still a good measure of liquid left in her glass, though, and he finished it off.

Then he leaned over her and scooped her, bedspread and all, off the chaise.

The lopsided towel unwound from her head, falling to the ground and her long hair tumbled free, damp and tangled, against his shoulder. He went stock-still, though, when her nose found its way to the hollow of his throat and her hand slid over his shoulder.

"I hope you didn't fire the guy on the phone." She sighed so deeply he felt her warm breath on his throat and fast heat pooled low in his gut.

The last thing he wanted to think about was his conversation with his media director, who'd called to warn him that some reporter had been nosing around, tying together the coincidence of Derek Armstrong's resignation as the institute's CFO with a reported sighting that he'd checked into an exclusive detox center in Connecticut on the very same day that his sister married Rourke. "I didn't fire him." He turned sideways to carry her into the bedroom and nudged the door shut behind them. Then he settled her on the mattress.

"'S good." She turned on her side, kicking at the confining bedspread until one long, slender leg was freed, then tucked her hands beneath her cheek.

He reached back to turn off the bedside lamp, plunging the room into darkness that was relieved only by the slant of moonlight through the windows. "Sleep tight, princess," he murmured and started to turn.

"Where're you going?" She pushed up on her elbow. Her wildly tangled hair streamed over one shoulder and the shirt she was wearing had slipped off the other.

To hell, he thought.

He reached for his belt and pulled it free. "Nowhere."

In the faint light, he could see her slowly close her eyes and she lowered her head again.

Even before he climbed into bed beside her minutes later, he knew she was once again fast asleep. He still scooped her against him. And when she didn't try to roll away, didn't do anything but offer a deep exhale that seemed to press her body more closely against him, he slowly pressed his lips to her fragrant hair and closed his eyes.

Who knew that hell could be so close to heaven?

Chapter 7

It was the rattle of china that finally dragged Lisa out of the comforting oblivion of her warm cocoon.

She opened her eyes, squinting against the bright sunshine that filled the room, getting a glimpse of the deepest blue sky she'd ever seen through the windows, as well as the attractive brunette who was settling the tray on the nightstand beside Lisa's head.

"Monsieur Devlin said you might wish for some coffee," the girl said in heavily accented English.

Lisa nodded, only to wince at the dull pain that reverberated through her head at the motion. She pushed up onto her elbow, gingerly taking the cup and saucer that the girl had filled and was holding out to her. "Thank you. Are you Marta?"

"Mais non, madame. Je suis Sylvie." She quickly rounded the bed to the other side of Lisa and began

straightening the pillows there, sweeping her hands deftly over the tumbled bedding.

Lisa eyed her, warily trying to see beyond the pain in her head to her memory of the night before. She'd eaten a little…Rourke had been on the phone…the wine…the chaise.

Her stomach clenched as she recalled the sensation of floating, his arms around her.

He'd obviously slept in the bed.

But had they done anything else?

Was it possible they'd made love and now she couldn't even remember it?

Feeling as if she'd fallen down the rabbit hole, she rubbed her hands over her eyes. Surely she'd remember…

"I can bring madame *les croissants et les fruits?*"

"No, thank you." She pushed the rattling cup and saucer onto the nightstand before she managed to spill the steaming brew all over herself and the bed, and sat up on the side of the mattress. "Can you tell me where Mr. Devlin is?"

The girl dimpled. "Swimming, madame. As he does every morning when he stays here."

Lisa pushed off the bed, yanking the hem of the jersey down around her thighs, and strode over to the French doors that were opened to the warmth of the morning sun. Ignoring the clanging inside her head at both the motions and the unrelenting sunlight, she went out onto the terrace and, sure enough, she could see Rourke's black head bobbing in the blue, blue sea.

"In case you wish to join him?" Sylvia appeared silently beside her bearing a plush white robe.

"I'm not exactly wearing a swimsuit."

The girl merely smiled. "Nor is he, madame."

Lisa snatched the robe and yanked it on, covering her jersey as well as her self-consciousness. "Thank you, Sylvie."

The girl tilted her head slightly, managing to look amused and sly at the same time, before she disappeared back into the house.

Maybe Rourke didn't need to *bring* women to this place if the lovely Sylvie was already at his beck and call.

Annoyed with herself for even wondering, she stomped barefoot down the steps to the lower terrace. Her feet met the coarse sand, slowing her speed considerably, but she made it to the towel that he'd dropped in a heap just beyond the water's reach.

He obviously knew she was there. He waved an arm, gesturing for her to come in.

In answer, she gathered the robe around her and sat down on top of his towel.

Despite the distance, she could see the flash of his teeth. Then his head disappeared beneath the surface of the glimmering water, reappearing again a moment later, considerably closer to shore. Before long, he was rising up altogether as he walked through the chest-high water as one hand slicked his hair back out of his face. Then the water was at his waist.

His hips.

She shaded her eyes, ostensibly from the sunlight, but just as much to hide the effort it took not to drop her jaw and just stare, when he kept right on coming. All warm, tanned flesh stretched over long, roping muscles.

Warm, naked flesh.

Not even being forewarned was enough to prepare her.

He walked right out of the sea like some pagan God

with water streaming down his corrugated abdomen, his thighs. His...everything.

And he didn't stop until he was less than two feet away. "My towel," he finally prompted.

Flushing, caught staring, she shifted off the towel and practically threw it at him.

Not bothering to hide his smile, he easily caught it and ran it down his chest. She was almost pathetically grateful when he wrapped it around his hips because she wasn't sure she would ever regain the art of breathing if he didn't.

"I met Sylvie." It wasn't at all what she should be saying, much less in such a waspish tone.

"I told her to make sure you had coffee before noon. Figured you'd need it after last night." He stretched out on the sand beside her, his head propped on his hand. With his hair slicked back from his face, he looked even more devilish. Black eyes bright, thick lashes clinging together with sparkling water drops, the whisper of a sardonic grin hovering around his mobile lips.

"Is *she* one of the women you've been here with?"

The slashing line beside his lips deepened. "She's a child."

"She didn't look very childish to me."

He tugged at her robe's belt until it came loose. "Mrs. Devlin, are you sounding jealous?"

"Certainly not. I just don't want to be embarrassed by coming face-to-face with one of my *husband's* lovers while on my honeymoon."

He gave a bark of laughter and captured her ankle in his hand. She nearly jumped out of her skin and wasn't helped any when his palm began slowly running up her calf beneath the loose folds of the robe. "Sylvie is Marta's niece," he drawled, his gaze capturing hers and allowing no escape. "Marta is a longtime employee of the owner, who happens to be a good friend of mine." His warm, still-wet palm reached her knee and began inching along the descent of her thigh. "And while we're married, the only lover I'll have is you."

She clamped her hand over his wrist, stopping the progress of his utterly distracting hand before it crept any farther toward the hem of her hockey jersey. "*Have?* Does that mean we already—last night—" She broke off, miserably humiliated at even having to ask.

His eyes were inscrutable. "You don't remember?"

Her jaw tightened. "Obviously. Not."

He moved suddenly, and instead of her hand capturing his wrist, he'd pushed her down and pressed hers into the sand above her head while he settled over her. "Princess, you'll definitely know when it's the morning after."

She drew in a shuddering breath, excruciatingly aware of every solid, male inch pressed against her from breast to toe. "Then w-we didn't."

He lowered his head until his lips were a hairsbreadth from hers. "We did not," he said softly. Slowly.

She swallowed and a soft sound rose in her throat that was either acknowledgment or relief or despair. She wasn't sure and, at that moment, wasn't sure that she cared.

He ran his other hand down the side of her head, threading through the tangles in her hair. "And when we do, it's not going to be because you're down half a bottle of wine just so you can face being in my bed."

"There wasn't even enough left in that bottle for two glasses."

"And you have no head for even one," he pointed out softly. "I saw that the first day at Fare. But you're clear-headed now, aren't you." His lips slowly settled against hers; not exactly a kiss, not exactly *not* a kiss.

Whatever it was, it made her forget the dull throb behind her eyes.

It left her heart charging inside her chest.

It had her fingers curling and uncurling against the sand.

"It's broad daylight." Her lips moved against his, her whisper barely audible. "Anyone could see us."

He angled his head finally, moving until his lips tickled the lobe of her ear. "Private beach. Nobody's watching." His hand left her hair and slid over her throat, working the lapels of the terry cloth robe out from between them.

"But Sylvie. Marta."

"Know better than to look," he assured her. "And if they do, what will they see?" His hands slid beneath the jersey, drawing it up her hip and stealing her breath. "A husband and wife on their honeymoon."

She sank her teeth into her tongue when his fingers grazed the flat of her stomach, but a sound still escaped. And then he was moving again, his weight leaving her, only she was still pinned against the sand by the ungodly pleasure of his mouth pressing against her navel.

"Wait," she gasped, wrenching her wrists free from his grip to press her hands against his shoulders.

He barely lifted his head. His gleaming eyes looked at her. "For what?" Watching her steadily, he pressed his lips against her abdomen.

Her muscles jumped. She sucked in a breath. "I—" She had no answer. What *were* they waiting for?

Her nerve?

His lips inched higher. Pressed another kiss. Still he watched her.

His gaze was equally as disturbing as the feel of his

lips, warm and surprisingly soft, particularly compared to the tingling abrasion of his unshaven jaw against her belly.

He nudged the jersey fabric higher, followed by another kiss.

Nudged again, nearly over her breasts. She felt the breath of balmy air against skin that had never directly felt it. "I don't do this," she said faintly. "Roll around naked on the beach like in some movie scene."

"You're not really naked," he murmured. With excruciating slowness, he dragged the jersey against her agonizingly tight nipples until they sprang free. "Not yet."

Her lips parted, searching for breath that wouldn't come. Her heart raced dizzily. His gaze finally left hers to survey what he'd revealed.

His fingers balled the fabric in his fist. "Beautiful." His voice was low. Rough.

His head dipped again to taste, and her back bowed off the sand at the feel of his mouth capturing first one hard, tight peak, then the other. She felt drenched in fire. "Rourke—" She couldn't take it. "Please."

"That's the plan. Please you." He kissed his way up the slope of her breast. "Please me."

"No." She was shaking her head, even as he was pulling the oversize jersey over it. "I can't. Not like this." But her heels were dragging into the sand while her knees lifted and her traitorous thighs hugged his.

"Can't, or won't?" He braced himself on his arms, keeping from crushing her, but the dark swirl of hair on his chest was a crisp tickle against her breasts. His narrowed eyes searched hers.

She could feel him hard and heavy and waiting. The only things separating them were a loosely draped towel and her panties, both of which could be so easily disposed of.

And heaven help her, but she wanted those barriers gone. She felt hollow and achingly wet and he was the means to heal her.

She'd never wanted anyone like this. She'd known it ever since that single, unforgettable turn around the dance floor with him at the Founder's Ball, even while he'd been making caustic comments about the fancy party that test-tube babies had paid for.

But none of that came to her lips as she stared mutely into his eyes.

She felt the push of his chest in the deep breath he drew. Her lips felt swollen and tingled when his gaze dropped to them. He ran his palm along her jaw, moved his thumb over her lower lip.

A small part of her brain warned her that she was only imagining a tenderness in his touch. A larger part of her body wanted to just sink into it.

His gaze lifted again and caught hers. "What are you afraid of?"

It was the last thing she expected from him. Cool irritation. Arrogant demand. Not this unexpected, unwanted softly voiced insight.

"Tell me." His voice dropped even lower.

"Everything." The admission was nearly as much a release as the one her body was aching for him to give her. Hot tears suddenly leaked from the corners of her eyes. "I'm afraid of everything," she whispered again. "Everything's out of control."

"Everything?"

"You," she amended huskily. "You make me feel out of control."

He didn't smile. Didn't gloat.

And it was more dangerous than if he had, because *that* she could have shored up her defenses against.

Instead, he simply asked softly, "What's safer than losing control in the arms of your husband?"

She couldn't bear the gentle probing in his eyes and closed hers. "Nothing if we were an ordinary couple. Which we're anything but."

He was silent for a moment. A moment filled with the lap of water, the whisper of a breeze, and the weight of this man whose words did nothing to allay the desire still holding her in its grip. "Control's important to you."

She let out a careful breath. "Isn't it to you?"

"I'm a man."

Her eyes flew open. She stared, then laughed brokenly. "Right. And for a man—particularly a man like you—your need to stay in control is acceptable and expected. But because I'm a woman—" She broke off, shaking her head.

He nudged her chin with his thumb until she was looking at him again. "I know the reasons why I control the things I do. To achieve the things I want."

"And what you want now is a child. Which is the only reason you want me."

He shook his head slightly and smoothed his thumbs down the tracks of her tears. "That's not the only reason. I wanted you long before it occurred to me that we could help each other."

And it scared the living wits right out of her. Men like Rourke didn't want women like Lisa. They wanted beautiful, sexy, accomplished women. Women who were as comfortable in their bedrooms as they were in their offices.

"I told you it's all going to be all right." His mesmer-izing gaze held hers even when he pressed his mouth against hers in a slow, drugging kiss that had her bones melting all over again.

And just when she was on the verge of collapsing into it, to twine her arms around his broad, broad shoulders, and pull him down onto her, into her, he suddenly jack-knifed off her and grabbed her hands in his, hauling her up to her feet. "Come on."

She very nearly stumbled, taking a few steadying steps in the sand as he leaned down again to scoop up her jer-sey and his towel that had slipped free, giving her another heart-stopping view. He dropped the jersey back over her shoulders, slung the towel around his waist again, and shook the sand out of her robe before handing it to her.

Bemused, she took it and followed, unresisting, when he took her hand and led her back up the short stretch of sand to the stairs leading up to their bedroom ter-race. Expecting him to lead her right to that big bed that they'd shared but hadn't "shared," confusion joined the miasma of emotions swirling inside her when he just let go of her hand once they were inside, and headed to the dressing room.

She looked from his departing backside to the bed that Sylvie must have finished making after Lisa had gone down to the beach, and back again. But Rourke didn't return and a moment later she heard the sound of the shower.

She shoved her hands through her hair, fingers catching in the tangles, as she pressed her palms against her head.

She did not understand the man she'd married at all.

Before she realized it, her feet had carried her into the spa-like bathroom where steam was already forming against the clear glass shower walls. The steam had not, unfortunately, begun to cloud the mirrors and before she could demand to know what game he was playing now, she caught a glimpse of her reflection.

She cringed, nearly groaning right out loud.

She looked like something the cat had dragged in. Hair sticking out at all angles. Day-old mascara smudging shadows around her eyes.

Ignoring the distraction of Rourke's movements behind the cloudy shower glass, she snatched open her cosmetic bag. She washed her face. Brushed her teeth. And was just beginning to attack the snarls in her hair when Rourke shut off the shower and stepped out, again displaying that singularly unselfconscious demeanor as he stopped behind her, heedlessly dripping water everywhere as he slipped the comb out of her nerveless fingers.

She couldn't pretend that her face wasn't blushing fiery red, but she *could* ignore it. "The tangles will get worse if I don't get them out."

"Then sit." Rourke closed his hand over her shoulder when she stood there staring at him in the reflection of the mirror, and he nudged her toward the padded stool tucked beside the vanity.

Looking too surprised to protest, she sat and looked even more bemused when he stood behind her and lifted up the ends of her hair to start working the tangles free with the comb. "It's longer than I expected," he admitted.

Her brown eyes widened. "You thought about...my hair?" She sounded so disbelieving that he almost laughed.

At himself.

He'd thought about a lot more than her hair. And now she was his wife and he was no closer to having her than he'd ever been, because he'd realized that he couldn't force himself to force her to want him in return. "You always have it pulled up," he said.

She'd curled her hands together in her lap. Tightly. And was watching him in the mirror as if he were crazy. "What are you doing?"

Maybe he was crazy. His hands kept working, patiently making his way from the ends of her hair to the scalp. "Keeping you from ripping so much of your hair out that you're left half bald."

"Why?"

He nudged her head forward with a finger. "Because I want to. Blame it on my controlling nature."

She gave an exasperated humph. "Where'd you learn to comb out tangles?"

"My sisters are all younger than me," he reminded her. "Someone had to help my mother with them."

Her gaze caught his in the mirror and damned if he felt able to look away.

"I can't figure you out," she said softly.

She wasn't the only one. "I'm just a man." He finally, deliberately lowered his gaze back to her head. "I can ditch the towel if you need reminding."

She huffed softly again. "You could probably buy and sell small countries but you insisted on marrying me to keep your mother happy."

Not just his mother. He moved on to another satiny hank of tangled hair, not commenting.

"And here you are combing out my hair."

"That sounds more like an accusation than an observation." He draped the tangle-free length over her shoulder and moved to the next section. Her head tilted slightly, revealing that tantalizing little freckle.

His mouth felt dry. Here he was. Surrounded by the

ocean of her while thirst was slowly, but surely killing him off.

"You're close to your sisters."

"Mmm-hmm." She was an observant woman and it wasn't something he'd tried to hide.

"They all have children. Are you just trying to keep up with them?"

His lips twisted. Not with amusement. "I want kids. Not so unusual. Haven't you thought about having them?"

"Not until you forced me to think about it," she returned. "Now, I feel constantly confronted by it."

He didn't reply to that. He merely stroked the comb one last time through her waving hair that was now free of knots, and then handed it to her. "Get dressed. We'll go into town for lunch."

He left the bathroom and Lisa turned on her stool to watch him go to one of the armoires in the bedroom and pull out a lightweight shirt and pants. He was nearly fully dressed and she was *still* sitting there, trying to understand the odd progression of the day.

Trying to understand this man to whom she was now married.

Finally, he stopped in the middle of the bedroom. His white linen shirt was untucked over beige pants. With his black hair still damp and tousled and his unshaven jaw shadowed, he looked expensively casual—and seriously sexy.

And a large part of her was demanding to know why she'd had to go and ruin what had started on the beach.

"I don't understand you at all," she admitted, beyond caring at that point what sort of edge she was probably allowing him.

"What's to understand? I'm hungry." He pushed his feet into leather loafers, missing the face she made.

"I wasn't talking about the lunch plans." Which she knew he was well aware even before he straightened again with the faint smile back on his face.

"You need to stop thinking so much," he said.

"If I could stop thinking, we'd have been having sex down there on the beach." She flushed all over again.

His eyebrows lifted a little. He gestured toward the opened doors leading to the terrace. "Then we'll go back down there. We can always have lunch later—"

"No." She quickly pushed to her feet. She was afraid he was playing with her, but that didn't mean she trusted him not to put words to action.

She knew that the time would come—sooner rather than later—when she'd have to live up to her end of the bargain. He'd bought his way into her uterus, in exchange for saving that which mattered most to her. The institute.

But that didn't mean she was ready yet to face the fact that in the process, she'd also sold him a place in her bed.

"I have sand on my legs," she said, reaching for the door between them. "I need a shower before I dress." Before he could comment, she closed the door.

It wasn't a significant exercise of control, but it was better than nothing.

And when it came to Rourke, she needed every speck she could hoard.

Chapter 8

Once Lisa was showered and dressed in a strapless yellow sundress with her hair pulled back again in its customary—and safely familiar—knot, they drove down to the village and left the car parked in a picturesque cobblestone alleyway bordered by ageless stone buildings graced with iron railings and colorful flowerboxes and walked to the nearby open-air market. Rourke seemed very familiar with the merchants that they passed, smiling and laughing off comments with ease that her long-ago high-school French couldn't hope to keep up with.

She found she didn't much care, though, because she was too busy taking in the incredible sights that the tiny seaside town had to offer and then Rourke was guiding her to a collection of unoccupied tables situated next to a small building. As soon as she'd taken the sun-bleached chair that he held out for her, a wizened old man came out of the building, his arms outstretched in greeting. "Rourke," he called, smiling broadly. "Who iz zis beautiful woman you bring to me?"

Rourke closed his hand over her shoulder. "Tyrus, this is my wife, Lisa. We married a few days ago."

"Marriage?" Tyrus's wiry eyebrows shot up over his buttonlike eyes and then he grabbed up Lisa's hand, bowing low over it. *"Très belle."*

Too aware of the warm hand that felt wholly possessive on her bare shoulder, Lisa barely noticed the kiss that Tyrus bestowed on the back of her hand. "It's nice to meet you," she managed when the diminutive man had straightened again.

"Oui, oui." He was nodding over and over again. "I bring you wine," he announced suddenly, turning on his heel to hurry back to the building. "We celebrate!"

Rourke pulled out the chair next to her and sat down. Their knees brushed beneath the little round iron table and though her instinct was to shift her legs, she resisted, mostly because of the gleam in his eyes that told her that was exactly what he expected her to do. "Obviously people know you in the village, too," she said.

"I've been coming here for a lot of years." Looking idle, he threaded his fingers through hers and his platinum wedding band gleamed in the sunlight.

For some reason, she found herself feeling mesmerized by the sight and deliberately blinked, focusing instead on the prolific red blooms of the lush bougainvillea that grew against the whitewashed walls of the building next to their table.

"Something wrong?"

She shook her head. "What brought you here in the first place?"

"An old friend."

"The same friend who owns the villa?"

"Yes."

Her teeth worried the inside of her upper lip. "A woman?"

His thumb slid in slow circles over hers. "I think you *do* have a jealous streak."

"Not in this lifetime," she lied coolly.

"Here we are," Tyrus reappeared, holding a bottle and several glasses aloft.

"We need some lunch, too," Rourke advised, sitting back in his chair. "I figured we'd see Grif and Nora here already."

"They still come every afternoon," Tyrus assured him as he deftly poured the deep red wine and even before he'd finished, a shapely blonde girl appeared with a tray that she sat on a neighboring table before tossing her arms around Rourke's shoulder to give him a long kiss right on the lips.

Lisa's jaw tightened and she pulled her hand out of Rourke's. He didn't protest. But then how could he?

He had his arms full of French blonde who was all but sitting on his lap.

"Rourke?" Another voice interrupted them, and Lisa looked up to see an older couple crossing the narrow street toward them.

With a deep chuckle, Rourke finally set aside the pouting blonde. "Lisa, Martine," he introduced carelessly as she rose.

"Old *friends?*" Lisa lifted her eyebrows. Rourke laughed, which was no answer at all, but Lisa was glad to see the blonde move away and disappear into the small building. Tyrus just stood by, beaming.

"I thought that was you." The woman, gray-haired, chicly styled and with no hint of a French accent, reached them and took the hands Rourke held out, and lifted her cheeks for his kiss. "Why didn't you tell us you were coming?"

Lisa saw the look that passed between Rourke and the man accompanying her.

"He did, darling." The man, tall and balding, slid his arm over the woman's slender shoulders as he shook Rourke's hand. "I told you last week that he was coming to use the villa."

The woman frowned a little, then shrugged with a little laugh. "My memory," she dismissed and focused on Lisa. "Are you a friend of Rourke's?"

Lisa was getting the impression that Rourke had plenty of "friends" in this part of the world.

"You would be Rourke's Lisa," the man answered even before Rourke or Lisa could. He rounded the small table and took Lisa's hand in both of his. Kindness shined out of his bright blue eyes. "He's told us so much about you. I'm Griffin Harper," the man said to her. "And Rourke's not actually family, but Nora and I feel like he is, so I'm still going to say welcome to the family." He leaned over and kissed Lisa's cheek, giving her no room whatsoever for feeling awkward.

"Of course!" The woman—Nora—clasped her hands together. "How could I forget? You got married again." She darted around the table and enveloped Lisa in a quick, Chanel-scented hug. "If we'd have had more notice, we'd have come to New York for the ceremony. Honestly, I never thought he'd get over that unfortunate business with Taylor," she whispered.

Feeling more than a little bewildered, and definitely

self-conscious being at the center of this attention, Lisa looked to Rourke. He obviously hadn't heard Nora's comment, since he and Griffin were busy pulling a second table and chairs closer.

Martine appeared with more glasses, which Tyrus quickly filled before he lifted his own in a toast. *"Pour l'amour."*

"For love," Griffin repeated, smiling benevolently.

The fondness they all felt for Rourke was plainly evident and even though she felt a fraud, Lisa managed to smile and drink and even to eat the excellent bread and cheese that Rourke broke off and fed to her.

The attention he gave her clearly delighted his friends, but she wasn't so easily fooled.

He was doing it to get under her skin.

And unfortunately, was being all too successful at it.

Then, when he whisked her partially finished glass of wine away from her to replace it with a bottle of sparkling water, Nora gave a little gasp. "You're not drinking. Are you pregnant?"

The lively chatter gave way to dead silence as everyone turned their attention to Lisa and she felt heat creep up her cheeks. She wanted to crawl under the table and hide. "No—"

"Not yet," Rourke inserted. He lifted her hand, watching her boldly as he kissed her knuckles. "But we're not planning to waste any time getting you there, are we, sweetheart?"

Her face went even hotter. "The sooner the better," she returned sweetly.

Tyrus clapped Rourke on the back and then swept the blonde into his arms, pressing his hand against her abdomen. "Soon you'll have many babies like Martine and me."

Lisa was startled. Martine was Tyrus's wife?

"That's what we're hoping," Rourke drawled.

Lisa slid her hand out of Rourke's and reached for her bottled water. "How many children do you have?"

"Five," Tyrus said proudly.

Lisa barely kept her jaw from dropping. Martine didn't look old enough to have had five children. But then she didn't much look like a wife, given the way she'd planted that kiss on Rourke.

And judging by the amused glint in *his* eyes, he was probably reading her thoughts all too accurately.

She angled her chin and looked at the Harpers. "Rourke hasn't told me how you all met."

"Grif staked me when I first went into business for myself," Rourke answered. "I wouldn't be where I am now if not for him."

Griffin waved a hand. "An exaggeration. Rourke was always going places. Anyone who knew him could see that."

"Especially my niece," Nora added. Her gaze turned toward Lisa. "You could be her twin, you know."

Griffin laughed a little too heartily. "She's not interested in that, honey." He poured the last of the wine into their glasses and handed the bottle to Tyrus, who disappeared into the building again with Martine. "Is everything at the villa meeting your satisfaction?"

"As always," Rourke assured him.

Lisa could feel an awkward undercurrent, even if she couldn't interpret the cause. "The villa is yours?"

Nora nodded. "I've told Griffin that we should just sell it to Rourke. He's offered often enough. But my husband won't let it go." She smiled at him, wrinkling her nose. "Sentimental old fool that he is."

"We spent *our* honeymoon there," Griffin told Lisa. His hand was covering Nora's on top of the table.

It was very plain that they adored each other.

"He bought it a year later," Nora added. "Of course it needed a tremendous amount of renovations."

"Well, whatever changes you made, they were perfect. I've never seen such a beautiful place," Lisa said truthfully. "The terraces alone are—"

"Très romantique?" Martine had returned.

"Very…romantic," Lisa agreed. "But where do you stay if not your own villa?" She kept her focus on Nora, who seemed ever so much more pleasant than Martine and her voluptuous lips.

"We have an apartment here in the village. It's more convenient for us to be right here on a regular basis," Griffin told her. "We get back to New York only a few times a year, but that's where our main home is."

"My doctor is here in the village." Smiling, Nora rolled her eyes. "Grif is constantly shuttling me off to see him."

"Only because I want you with me as long as I can have you." Griffin cupped her cheek in his hand for a moment.

The moment felt intensely private to Lisa and she looked away, her gaze falling on Rourke.

His expression was hollow and, without thinking, she covered his clenched fist that rested on his thigh with her hand.

The feel of Lisa's hand on his drew Rourke's attention long enough for him to pull his dark thoughts out of the abyss where they'd fallen. She was watching him, her eyes soft. Concerned.

He loosened his tight fist and turned his palm until it met hers.

Her gaze flickered for a moment, but in the end stayed on his. A tentative smile fluttered around the corners of her soft lips and just that easily he was wishing strongly that they were back in the privacy of the villa.

He threaded his fingers through hers and she seemed content to stay that way until Tyrus brought lunch for all of them and she needed her hand to eat.

By the time they were finished, several hours had passed and the sun was even higher in the sky. Tyrus and Martine had been forced to leave the table in order to tend to the other customers who came to their bistro and Rourke could tell by the way Grif kept looking at Nora that it was time for them to be going as well, even though Nora kept dismissing the idea when Grif suggested it.

"As pleasant as this is," Rourke finally said with a deliberate grin, "this *is* our honeymoon. And I'm afraid my bride keeps me pretty bewitched." He rose from the table and went around to drop a kiss on Nora's softly lined cheek. "Take care of your old man, you hear?"

Nora laughed and patted his face. "That would be a switch, wouldn't it?" She looked across the table at Lisa. "Taylor, dear, you and Rourke have got to visit us more often. Particularly when those babies finally start arriving. I want to be around to play with my grandnieces and nephews."

Rourke caught the way Lisa's smile wobbled a little and wished to hell that he'd thought ahead to this before hustling her into the village where he'd known it was likely they'd run into the Harpers.

"Nora, this is Lisa, not Taylor," Grif said patiently.

Nora's brows drew together, her confusion plain. "I…

It is?" She looked at Lisa apologetically. "I'm so sorry, dear. You're a friend of Rourke's?"

"Yes," Lisa answered gently. "I'm a friend of Rourke's." She leaned over the table to clasp Nora's fluttering hands. "And I very much enjoyed meeting you and your husband."

The concern melted from Nora's face. "You are a dear." She looked up at Rourke. "I hope you realize she's a keeper."

Lisa's cheeks were pink as she straightened and sent him a fast glance. He slid his arm around her slender waist. "Don't worry, Nora. I know exactly what I've got."

He felt the way Lisa stiffened at that, but she didn't move away or say a word. Probably because she was too decent to cause Nora and Grif any concern.

Grif clasped Rourke's shoulder. "If we don't see you again before you head back to the States, we'll definitely see you in November at the awards gala in New York." His gaze switched to Lisa. "It's not every day that I get to present this guy with an award. I'm not going to let him miss it."

"It's on my calendar," Rourke assured him, wishing Grif would drop it.

But Lisa's interest was obviously already piqued. "What's the award for?"

"The G.R. Harper Philanthropic Award."

Lisa looked startled. "You're *that* Harper? There isn't anyone on the eastern seaboard who hasn't heard of that award."

Grif laughed. "My father instituted it. I'm just chairman of the family's foundation now. And thanks to guys like your husband who understand the importance of philanthropy, we're still in business helping thousands of people every year. But I'm preaching to the choir. You'd already know that."

Lisa smiled, no hint of the fact that she undoubtedly didn't, showing on her face. "Yes. Rourke is…quite something."

"And I wouldn't show at all if I could get out of it," Rourke reminded Grif.

"You'll show if only to shame other corporations into trying to win the award next year by giving even more money."

Since that was the truth of it, Rourke couldn't very well deny it. But at last, Grif dropped the subject and after a kiss on Lisa's cheek, he waved them off.

Lisa waited until they were out of sight of the bistro before she pulled away from him. "How much did you give?"

She would find out anyway when the awards deal rolled around, so he told her and her eyes widened. "Well. If you can give away that much, no wonder you can afford to fund the institute the way you are."

"Right. So can we drop it?"

"What makes you uncomfortable about it?"

He exhaled. "I'm not interested in getting accolades for just doing what's right."

She fell silent at that, but he could feel the speculative glances she kept throwing him. And she didn't speak again until they'd reached the car. "Does Nora have Alzheimer's?" Her voice was quiet.

At least she'd dropped the award. "They discovered it about a year ago." He pulled open her car door for her.

She sank into the seat and looked up at him. "I'm sorry."

"I believe you actually mean that." He could see it

in her eyes that, in the sunlight, looked like translucent coffee.

Her lashes swept down suddenly, hiding those eyes altogether. She looked away and he thought briefly of his sister's claim that Lisa was shy. He'd dismissed it out of hand at the time, but maybe Tricia hadn't been so far off the mark, after all.

Lisa's fingers were smoothing the buttercup-yellow fabric of her dress over her legs. "Of course I mean it. It's perfectly clear that they're devoted to each other."

"They are." He rounded the car and slid behind the wheel and started the engine. "Not that they haven't had their trials, but they've always worked through them." He sighed deeply. "This one, though—" He felt his throat tighten and gunned the engine around a corner. "I don't know what Grif will do without her when that time comes."

"Rourke—" her voice softened "—that could still be a long way off, yet."

He nodded. Hoped.

"Her medical care here is good? I mean, this is a very small town. Wouldn't a larger facility have more treatment options?"

"The doctor she sees is an expert in the field. He focuses primarily on research and development. A lot like Ted's functions at the institute. The man's supposed to be a genius and this is where he wants to work. So... this is where they've stayed. And Nora is comfortable with him."

"Which is important to Griffin." She shielded her eyes from the sun with her hand as she watched him. "And they're both important to you."

"They've been good friends."

"Did you meet them because of Taylor?"

Given Nora's comments, he'd figured that question would come sooner or later whether he liked it or not. "No." It had been the other way around.

"So are you going to tell me who she is, or do I have to guess?"

He flexed his fingers around the steering wheel. "I imagine you've figured it out."

"She's your ex-wife." Her tone had cooled again. Sympathy no longer evident. "Whom I evidently resemble. A lot."

"My very *ex*-wife who bears a passing resemblance," he said abruptly. "You interested in seeing Nice? It wouldn't take long to drive there."

"And yet you *claim* you were never at the villa with her." She ignored his attempted side trip—both verbal and literal. "Seems unlikely when the place belongs to her aunt and uncle."

"I was never at the villa with Taylor," he repeated evenly. "Not before we married, not during our marriage and sure in hell not after it was over."

"Why not?"

"What difference does it make? Just because I like the place doesn't mean she did."

"Who wouldn't like it?"

She sounded indignant, and he almost wanted to laugh. "Let's just say that the villa was a little too laid-back for her tastes." Those had run more toward glitter and excitement versus peaceful tranquility. And he really didn't want to talk—or think—about his ex-wife any more than necessary.

"So how *did* you meet the Harpers?"

He slanted a look toward her. "You're very full of questions this afternoon. Why?"

That slender hand shading her eyes also shaded the expression in them. "We're married. People will expect us to know these sorts of things about each other." She hesitated for a moment. "If we're going to be…having a child together…we should at least have honesty between us. Know these sorts of things about each other."

"There's no *if* about it." Not anymore. Not thanks to the combined brilliance of Bonner and Demetrious.

"Fine. *Since* there will be a child, we should know this kind of stuff. Or at least make some attempt at knowing each other better if we want to make this work at all." Her chin lifted. "Or do you disagree?"

He didn't disagree. On the other hand, he was pretty curious why she was suddenly seeming as agreeable as she was. "Grif was a visiting professor in one of my sophomore university classes. Oddly enough, we hit it off."

"Why odd?"

He slowed to a stop at a crossroads. "Because I was cheating on an exam. Now, do you want to go into the city or not?"

"Why were you cheating?"

"Because it was easier than studying and I hated English lit. He should have kicked me out of the class."

"But he didn't."

"No. He didn't. And in the end, pretty much everything I know about being a decent man, I learned from him." He exhaled. "Grif wouldn't exactly approve of our arrangement."

"You knew what being good meant before you went to college. You told me you were a Boy Scout, remember?"

"A rotten one," he drawled.

"What happened to your father?"

"Enough questions for now. Nice or not?"

She looked one way down the empty road. Then the other. "Not."

He turned the car in the direction of the villa.

"Tyrus and Martine seem very friendly. Particularly Martine."

He hid a smile. Yeah, Martine had really bugged her. Not that it was unusual. Martine had a way of bugging most women. "They're interesting people. Tyrus used to own a five-star hotel in Paris."

"And his wife?" The last word had a decided edge to it.

"Adores him."

She huffed softly. "Really. She goes around kissing *everyone* like that? Or does she just reserve that particular greeting for you?"

"Admit it." He ran his finger down the nape of her neck. "You *are* jealous. First it was Sylvie. Now it's Martine?"

"Please. I just feel sorry for Tyrus."

"Tyrus is as proud of his attractive wife as he is proud of his hellion kids."

"And he doesn't mind that you and his wife are—" She gave him an eyebrow-arched look.

"Are nothing."

"Then what were you kissing her for?"

"Maybe you need glasses, princess. Martine was kissing me."

"You didn't exactly beat her off with a stick!"

"And offend Tyrus?"

She made a disgusted sound.

He laughed softly. "Martine kisses every man she knows. Tyrus doesn't mind because he knows he's the one she goes home with at night. And cheating for me extended only as far as English lit tests and that was a lifetime ago. I don't cheat on my women, nor do I share them."

"Is that supposed to be a warning or something?"

His humor dried up as rapidly as a desert rain. "Take it how you see fit. Once the terms of our marriage are met, you can do what you want." He was reminding himself as much as her.

"And if there's another man I want?"

"If there was another man you wanted now, we wouldn't even be here."

"You don't know that. You're the one with the money to save the institute."

"If you were truly involved with someone, you would have found another way than me."

"I think there may actually be a compliment in there."

He shrugged.

"Maybe there will be a man later on."

When a woman looked like Lisa there was always going to be plenty of men vying for that position. The thought was dark. "Don't expect me to come chasing after you."

"Why would you?" She dashed a lock of hair away from her cheek where it had blown loose from that infernal knot of hers. "It's not like you're in love with me."

"Wouldn't matter even if I were. If a woman betrays me, she can keep walking right out the door."

She slid him a long look. "Is that what Taylor did? Cheat on you?"

Bits of gravel spun beneath the tires when he turned

up the drive to the villa. He thought about not answering. Thought, too, about the logic in her assessment that there were some things they'd naturally be expected to know about each other. The reason behind the demise of his first marriage was probably one of those things. "Yes."

"I'm sorry."

He grimaced. "She wasn't."

"Would it have mattered if she were? How long were you married?"

"Four years. Not long enough for me to even consider forgiving that." The cheating wasn't the worst, anyway, though he had no intentions of getting into that. It was who Taylor had chosen to cheat *with*. And why. "And before you ask again, it was over nearly five years ago."

"Then you were married pretty young."

Out of college and on the way to his second million. "Doesn't excuse it."

She made a soft *hmm*. "I don't see how couples ever get over a betrayal like that, no matter how long they've been together," she added after a moment.

"Some recover from it. If they want to badly enough." He'd seen that in action. But then he didn't possess the same kind of fiber that made up a man like Griffin Harper.

And he'd never loved anyone the way that Grif loved Nora. Not even Taylor.

Lisa was shaking her head. "Not me. Lies are unforgiveable enough, but that strikes me as the very worst kind."

"Then we're more alike than either one of us thought."

She watched him for a long while. "That ought to be a frightening thought," she finally said.

"That there might be something we actually have in common?"

"Yes."

"But you're not frightened."

She sucked in her lower lip for a moment, leaving it distractingly moist. "No."

Then she sat back in her seat, leaving him with the disturbing knowledge that things would have been safer between them if she were.

Chapter 9

When they arrived at the villa, there was no sign of Marta or Sylvie and, contrarily, Lisa found herself wishing that there had been.

Because now, the silence only underscored her and Rourke's privacy.

Honeymoon privacy.

Maybe she should have told Rourke she wanted to go to Nice, after all.

Aware of his gaze on her like some physical thing, she crossed the living area to the doors and pushed them open, letting in the balmy, vaguely sweet-scented air. She toed off her espadrilles and walked out onto the terrace, and folded her arms over the top of the stone balustrade.

Below, the ocean glittered sapphire blue. Beyond the narrow line of beach, the hillside rose sharply, verdant with fat trees and tall palms.

"How could anyone *not* love this?" she wondered aloud. "It's so perfectly beautiful."

Rourke joined her at the rail. "Yes. It is."

But a glance at him told her he wasn't looking at the view, but at her.

There was no way to will away the flush that began climbing her cheeks. She turned her gaze resolutely back out to the sea. "Do you sail?" There were several boats out in the water.

"Occasionally. Are you shy?"

Her cheeks warmed even more. She tried a laugh, but it only came off sounding nervous. "What makes you ask that?"

"Tricia mentioned it. I told her she was off base."

"Well, there you go, then." What was the point of telling him that his sister was closer to the mark than he was?

His forearm was pressing alongside hers on top of the warm stone and it took every ounce of willpower she possessed not to move her tingling arm away from his. "When I was young, we went sailing as often as we could."

"Your family?"

She suddenly wished she hadn't even brought it up. That was what she got for trying to focus on something other than Rourke's overwhelmingly masculine appeal. "Derek," she admitted slowly. "Dad took me one time. It was Memorial Day weekend. Usually he was too busy to ever go, and my mother—" She shook her head. "Sailing wasn't exactly her cup of tea." Her lips twisted a little. "Would have mussed her hair."

"Like this?" Rourke tucked the strands of hair that had fallen loose from her chignon during the drive behind her ear.

She swallowed hard, unable to find her voice just then.

Rourke's hand went back to the railing. His forearm back to scorching hers. "What about Paul and Olivia?"

Her throat eased a little. "Paul had his own interests—usually his studies—and Olivia was always dancing." She didn't want to think about how much time Derek had always been willing to give her when she'd been growing up.

He'd been her pal, taking her sailing or to hockey games.

Her confidant, listening without judgment when she'd railed against Emily's stringent standards about the behavior of proper young ladies or when she'd been left alone on the night of every school dance because nobody had asked her out.

He'd even been her hero, helping her to see the value she had where the institute was concerned.

And now, she wanted to hate him for the position he'd put them all in. She did hate him. But she couldn't help still loving him.

"I can't believe what he did," she admitted. "Can't understand why."

The silence ticked between them, broken only by the hushed rustle of the palm fronds extending over the terrace. "He checked into a rehab center, if that helps you with the why."

Shocked, she looked up at Rourke. He was standing even more closely than she'd thought. "Rehab for what? When? And how do *you* know?"

"For what, I don't know. But it was Saturday. And that I know because my media director kept a story about it from seeing the light of day. I told you that I would do what I can to keep the institute and your brother's actions out of the press."

She remembered the bits of Rourke's phone conversation that she'd overheard the day they'd arrived. "I wasn't sure you'd meant it."

"I gave you my word."

This close, she could have counted every one of his thick, spiky eyelashes. "I've always thought you were impossibly arrogant." Her voice was little more than a whisper. "But I think there might actually be a wide streak of decency in there."

"And I used to think you were just an ice princess. Turns out that's just a mask you wear to keep anyone from seeing the heat that's inside. Same as this knot you wear hides those long, wild waves." He reached behind her head and she felt him pluck one of the pins out of her hair.

It dropped to the smooth stone beneath their feet with a soft ping. Soon, it was followed by another. And another.

Her mouth went dry. Her heart felt as if it was climbing up into her throat. "Do I remind you of your ex-wife? Is that what the attraction is?" She feared knowing the answer because she wasn't sure if it would even matter. Not with the way he made her heart pound.

"If you really reminded me of her, there would be no attraction," he said so flatly that she couldn't help believe him.

He pulled every pin from her hair, unwinding it and threading his fingers through it until it hung over her shoulders and down her back. When he seemed satisfied, his hands drifted to the buttons that lined the front of her snug bodice. His knuckles brushed against her as he deliberately undid the top one.

She exhaled shakily.

His head lowered. He slowly kissed the point of her shoulder, almost distracting her from the release of a second button. And a third. "Are you going to protest?" His words whispered against her neck, below her ear, more seduction than question.

Did she even want to? Hadn't she known this would happen when she'd declined driving to Nice?

"No." The word was barely audible.

"Good." Between them, she felt the bodice of her dress loosening. Inching downward.

A bird flew overhead, cawing loudly. She could barely hear the sound of the ocean above the pounding of her heart.

Then he slid one hand behind her head, catching the nape of her neck, his gaze locked on hers as he slowly pressed his mouth against hers and the only thing she knew then was the darkly seductive taste of him. The only thing she cared about was the feel of his hands on her.

He was devouring her by slow degrees and she didn't care.

He tore his mouth from hers, lips burning against her jaw, his breath as ragged as hers. He lifted his head, staring down at her as he took a step back. His hands were on her shoulders, fingers burning hotter than the sunshine.

Her loosened bodice fell away, the folds of her dress caught only by the swell of her hips. The sweet, warm air drifted over her bare breasts, her achingly tight nipples.

He twined his fingers gently in her hair, tugging her head back until she looked up at him.

"This is who I see when I look at you." His voice was low. Husky. "Fire in your eyes. Lips naked and soft. Skin warm and waiting."

"Then you're the only one," she admitted, feeling oddly thrilled. Wholly aroused.

"I could spend an hour or two explaining how wrong you are." His hands slid down her bare spine, pushing the dress beyond her hips, and the cotton crumpled around her ankles. Her feet. "But I've got better things in mind." He caught her hips and lifted her right off her feet and out of the dress.

She gasped and caught his shoulders more tightly.

"Put your legs around me."

Trembling wildly, she did, and he turned away from the balustrade to walk across the terrace. She pressed her head against his shoulder, agonizingly aware of the hard press of his chest beneath the soft friction of his linen shirt. He carried her down the steps to the lower terrace and nudged through the French doors of the bedroom.

It was cooler inside. And dimmer, thanks to the slant of the shutters on the windows. He left the door open and carried her to the wide bed, settling her in the center.

Her hands slowly fell away. She stared up at him as he began flicking open the buttons on his shirt. "I thought you were heading down to the beach." Her gaze felt glued to the expanding wedge of muscular chest he was revealing.

"Disappointed?" He reached the last button and tossed the shirt aside. His narrow belt jangled softly as he pulled it loose.

She swallowed. Hard. "Maybe," she admitted faintly.

His lips curved. His pants stayed where they fell, and so did the body-hugging boxers beneath. He bent one knee on the mattress, slowly moving toward her.

She knew she was staring, but there didn't seem to be anything she could do about it. Everything about him was hard. The muscles roping his shoulders. The ridges of his abdomen.

"We'll make love on the beach," he murmured, settling between her thighs where she felt that hardest part press insistently between them. "And anywhere else we want." His hands burned over her thighs, guiding them along his hips. "As often as we want."

Her fingers pressed into his chest. The swirl of dark hair there felt softly crisp against her palms. "You'll change your mind." The words came without warning, probably pushed out by the sudden tightness in her chest.

"I seriously doubt it." He turned onto his back, pulling her with him until she was draped over him like a wet blanket. "I've wanted you for months." His hands caught her face. Drew her closer. "Turn off that brain for a while, Lisa."

Her chest felt even tighter. "But I'm not any good at this," she warned miserably.

He didn't move a muscle. Didn't even seem to breathe for a moment. "I'm going to assume that some fool told you that. Because I know you're too smart to come up with such an asinine idea." His voice seemed to rumble up from deep within his chest, vibrating against her.

She straightened her arms, finding some distance between her racing heart and his. "But it's true. I'm not good with…with men."

He eyed her for a moment and even though she was shaking with desire, she still felt like a bug on the head of a pin.

And knew that she was the one who'd stuck herself there.

He pushed up on his arm suddenly, and without letting her go, pulled her with him up the mattress until his back was against the carved headboard. "No men," he said quietly. "Just one man." His hands slid slowly down her back, then slid up again. "Me." None of the fire had left his eyes but there was a watchfulness there that made her throat tight. "Are you afraid I'm going to hurt you?"

"No." Not in the sense that he meant.

"Are you a virgin?"

She shook her head yet again, this time flushing. "Of course not."

"When were you last with a man? Six months? A year? Two?"

"Seven." She was grateful that he didn't gape at her. "He was a guy in college."

"The only guy?"

She groaned and covered her face with her hand. "I should wear a muzzle," she muttered. "Then maybe my stupid tongue would stop getting in the way."

His chest lifted and fell with the choked laugh he gave. "I have plenty of thoughts about your tongue. None of them involves a muzzle, believe me." He pulled her hands away from her face. "There's nobody here in this bed but you and me. You have just as much control as I do." His lips twisted slightly. "More, when it comes down to it, because as much as I want you—and it's gotta be obvious as hell to you that I do—you're still the one who can say no."

Which she'd been doing all along. And which he'd actually been respecting, she realized, no matter what the terms of their agreement were.

"Will you trust me?" He tipped her chin up. "At least in this?"

"I want to," she admitted helplessly, surprising even herself by the truth of it.

"Good enough," he said softly. He slowly rubbed his thumb over her lower lip. "Kiss me."

She blinked. Moistened her lip only to taste the faint saltiness of the tip of his thumb. Her gaze flicked to his and she caught the flex of a muscle in his hard jaw.

Still he waited for her to make the move.

She leaned closer and brushed her lips across his. Felt the surprising softness, the unexpectedly lush curve of his lower lip. A faint sound rose in her throat and she sank a little deeper against his chest. Her hand roved over one wide, muscled shoulder; slid against the strong column of his brown neck and felt the push of his pulse against her fingertips.

That tattooing beat seemed as deeply intimate as the feel of his body pushing against her increasingly damp panties.

She grazed the tip of her tongue over his lip. Caught it lightly between her teeth.

His hands suddenly closed tightly around her hips only to ease off a second later.

What fascinated her more? That unexpected, uncontrolled motion? Or the very deliberate control he exercised over it?

She tilted her head slightly. Settled her mouth over his, tentatively tasting the inner curve of his lip, feeling the ridge of sharp teeth.

One of his hands shifted, slid over her rear, hovered over the elastic edge of her panties.

Her tongue found his and his chest expanded against her breasts. Like a needy cat, she felt herself arching against him, wanting more of that. Wanting more of his hands on the curve of her bottom, wanting more of the press of him between her legs.

She pulled her mouth from his, hauling in a shuddering breath.

"Tell me what you feel." His low voice was even huskier. More ragged.

"You," she breathed.

His teeth flashed. His fingers flexed against her spine. "Too obvious. *How* you feel."

He was in her head more than he was in her body. As little as a day—maybe even a matter of hours—earlier, and she would have shied away from that. From him.

She ran her hands down his arms, circled the sinewy wrists, then caught his hands. She drew them between them. Slowly pushed them flat and pressed her mouth to one palm, then the other.

Then she pressed his palms to her breasts.

"I feel empty," she whispered. "And I want you to fill me."

His hands cupped her breasts, shaped them. Thumbs roved over her drawn nipples, sending waves of need to the clutching space inside her. When his hands left her, she wanted to protest, but that desire died instead in the moist fire of his mouth closing over her while he shifted and bore her steadily down onto the mattress.

And then his tongue was branding a line down her abdomen, the edge of her underwear, and then beneath as he dragged the bit of cotton down her thighs and right off her legs.

Her hands frantically caught at his shoulders. "Rourke—"

He stopped. Looked at her. A dark angel in devil's disguise. "Yes?" The word whispered intimately against her.

She could barely breathe. "Yes," she sighed, and

nearly bowed off the bed with splintering pleasure when his mouth settled on her.

She was still quaking long moments later when just as deliberately, he kissed his way back up her belly. Over her breasts. Pressing his palms flat against hers, he slowly, inexorably pressed into her.

Filled her.

And even though she'd wanted this—wanted him— she hadn't expected to feel as if he were filling every cell that formed her, every thought that made her. She couldn't tell where she ended and he began. Couldn't tell if it was her body tightening all over again or his thickening even more with indescribable pleasure. Didn't know if it was the beat of her heart thundering against her breast, or if it was his. Didn't care that his name was a crying chant on her lips and loved it that her name was like a prayer on his.

Filling wasn't the right word at all, she realized faintly when everything they were coalesced into one…glorious…perfect…climax.

Joining was.

"So tell me about the idiot from your college days."

Her world had finally stopped spinning, righted once more even if a part of her wondered if it could ever really be the same. She'd regained the ability to breathe, as well, but Rourke's head resting against her breast was still a distraction.

She lifted his hand from her belly and toyed with his fingers, watching the play of light that slanted through the French doors catch in the platinum of their wedding rings. "I've forgotten all about him."

He laughed softly.

She found herself smiling, too. "He was in my economics class. His name was Skyler and I thought I was in love with him. He claimed he loved me, too, but after we slept together—mistake that it was—he dumped me. Said he needed a woman in his bed, not a stick who didn't know how to enjoy herself."

"What'd you do?"

"Besides believe him?" She shook her head. "I made such good grades that on the grading curve he ended up failing the class."

Rourke pushed up on his elbow. His hair was falling rakishly over his forehead. "Good girl." He kissed her arm. "And no man worth his salt should blame a woman for her lack of pleasure."

"Did you learn that bit of wisdom from Griffin, too?"

He shook his head, his grin quick and deeply wicked. "That came from a very smart cookie named Janelle who kindly introduced me to the ways of women."

She rolled her eyes. "And how old were you when this angel of mercy descended upon you?"

"Good choice of words," he drawled. "Sixteen. She was a much advanced twenty with an amazing arsenal of knowledge at her disposal."

She let out a huff and rolled onto her stomach. "Your mother would have been appalled."

"My mother never knew." He gave her a playful slap on the rump. "Get your lazy rear up. I'm starving."

She wanted nothing more than to sleep. "Typical."

"I *am* a man."

She couldn't help her smile, even if it did look goofy. "I noticed." She rescued one of the pillows from the foot of the bed where it had somehow ended up and tucked it beneath her cheek with a satisfied sigh. "You won't have to hunt or forage far, I'm sure. Not with Marta and Sylvie at your beck and call."

"Not quite. I told them we wouldn't need them after all while we're here."

Surprised, she opened her eyes and looked at him. "Since when?"

"Since you were in the shower this morning." With her hair streaming around her and her eyes looking slumberous and satisfied, it was all Rourke could do not to roll Lisa onto her back and make love to her all over again. Instead, he leaned over and satisfied himself by kissing the freckle on her neck and then the small of her back before sliding off the bed and moving away from temptation. "They made you feel self-conscious. So they had to go."

Not bothering with finding some clothes, he headed out of the room, carrying her bemused expression with him.

"You did pay attention when I said I couldn't cook," her voice called after him, "didn't you?"

He stopped and stuck his head back in the doorway. "You also claimed you were no good in the sack," he drawled. "Didn't believe you then. Don't believe you now." He yanked his head back from the doorway just in time to miss the pillow that she threw at him.

But he could hear her laughter as he headed away from the bedroom, and was smiling himself as he went.

While he might have sent Marta away, she'd still managed to leave an assortment of food in the fridge and he pulled out an apple and a bottle of water before going into the office, where he found a half-dozen messages on his cell phone. He returned only one, though, to Ted Bonner.

"Find the cure to cancer yet?" he asked when Ted picked up.

His friend's laugh sounded as if it were next door and not halfway around the world. "That's not the cure you used to be interested in."

Rourke supposed it was proof of how far he'd come since the day he'd learned that his and Taylor's failure to conceive a child hadn't been because of her infertility, but *his* that he could now laugh about it. "Believe me, buddy, I'm still interested. And grateful to be the first subject in your trial. First kid we have is gonna be named after you and Chance."

"Pity the kid if she's a girl, then. You're taking the compound?"

"As prescribed. And the vitamins. And eating right. Drinking plenty of water." He toasted his friend with the bottled water even though Ted couldn't see it. "Following all the protocols you've given me."

"We're going to have to expand the study, you know," Ted reminded him for about the millionth time.

"Say the word when you're ready," Rourke said, also for about the millionth time. "You know where your funding is coming from." And when a noninvasive, natural supplement hit the market to improve one of the causes of male infertility, they'd all be singing lullabies all the way to the bank. Nothing of which he and Ted and Chance hadn't already discussed at length. "So what'd you really call about, anyway?"

"Just wanted to share the good news. Sara Beth's pregnant."

"No kidding. Congratulations, man!" Genuine pleasure filled his voice.

"Yeah. I'm still wondering how it happened." Ted

laughed. "Well, you know what I mean. Don't tell your wife yet, though. Sara Beth wants to tell Lisa herself."

"No prob."

"Who knows," Ted went on. "If you and Lisa end up with that honeymoon baby you say you're hoping for, our kids could be in Scouts together someday."

"Yeah." Rourke slowly set the bottle down on the desk. A short while later, Ted hung up and Rourke left the office and the rest of his voice messages unreturned.

He walked back to the bedroom. Lisa wasn't lying in bed anymore, but he could hear the sound of the shower and he followed it into the bathroom, where he could clearly see her through the glass block of the shower wall.

He went over to the opening and looked at her lithe body, silky suds slowly sliding down her limbs while steam shrouded around her.

Her gaze warmed as she looked back at him.

"Want company?"

Her lashes dipped shyly, but only for a moment. Then she looked back at him and nodded.

And when he stepped into the steam with her, he knew he wasn't thinking about making a honeymoon baby any more than he'd been thinking about it earlier.

The only thing he was thinking about was Lisa.

And that most definitely hadn't been part of the deal.

Chapter 10

"Ohmigosh. Look how tanned you are." Sara Beth stopped in the doorway of Lisa's office at the institute and propped her hands on her hips. "Obviously honeymooning in the south of France for the better part of a month agrees with you."

At the sight of her friend, Lisa jumped from behind her desk where she'd been studying health insurance bids and went over to hug her. "Not as much as marriage seems to be agreeing with you," she countered, laughing. She stepped back to look over Sara Beth. "You're positively glowing."

Sara Beth's cheeks were almost as pink as the scrubs she was wearing. "Marriage is pretty good," she said, clearly understating. She stepped into the office and closed the door. "So tell me how the trip was. *Ooh la la* romantic? Hot monkey sex every time you turned around?"

Lisa headed back to her desk, ducking her head a little. "It was…pretty good," she returned.

Sara Beth let out a laughing groan. "Now that's just not fair." She leaned her hip on the corner of Lisa's desk. "At least—" she lifted her eyebrows "—tell me you didn't earn that tan sitting on the beach while you were poring over files from this place."

"I had fun," Lisa admitted slowly. Which wasn't at all what she'd expected.

Sara Beth lifted the glossy business magazine that was sitting opened on the edge of Lisa's desk, featuring a black and white shot of Rourke helping Lisa out of the limousine on the day of their wedding. *The Ties that Bind…or Blind?* was the article's headline. "Not every analyst thinks investing in the institute is the best business bet for Rourke. They are saying he did it for you."

"And Rourke's answer to that is in the article. The reporter tracked us down in France last week." After that momentous day when Rourke had turned her world upside down, the reporter's visit had been the sole intrusion of the life waiting for their return.

The rest of the time, she and Rourke had done exactly what most honeymooning couples did. They'd explored the countryside and strolled in marketplaces. They'd had lunch with the Harpers more than once, and even Martine had stopped greeting Rourke with that plastering kiss. They'd lazed on the beach and they'd even slept under the stars on the terrace outside their bedroom.

And they'd made love.

Again. And again. And again.

And if it weren't for the fact that Lisa had known that idyllic time would have to end when he returned to New

York and she to Boston, it would have been painfully easy to forget the reason they were there at all.

Sara Beth held up the magazine and read. "'Indulging my bride is my greatest pleasure, reports the newly wedded Devlin,'" she quoted. "'But nothing gets in the way of business. And the future of the Armstrong Fertility Institute is good business.'" She looked up. "Sounds great for the institute. What does the blushing bride think?"

Lisa lifted her shoulder. "Business *is* business. Just because we put these—" she lifted her hand, waggling her wedding rings "—on our fingers doesn't mean that's changed." He'd put her on the plane back to Boston where she'd get back to business and he'd stayed in New York where he'd get back to *his*.

They'd get together on weekends.

Sara Beth's expression had gone serious. "Then you *did* marry him for the money." She hopped off the desk before Lisa could form a reply. "I was afraid something was off even before the I do's. But everything happened in such a rush it was easy to buy into the whole sweeping-you-off-your-feet scenario. Tell me I'm wrong."

"It's not like that," Lisa protested. Not exactly. Not anymore. Not since she'd found the man beneath the money and he'd found the woman beneath the suit.

Sara Beth propped her hands on her hips, staring her down. "Are you in love with him?"

Lisa blinked, for some reason caught off guard. "Not every marriage is about love," she hedged. "There's mutual respect and common interests and—"

"Sex?"

Her cheeks suddenly blazed and Sara Beth, being

Sara Beth, didn't fail to notice. "You *are* sleeping with him!"

"Good grief," Lisa muttered, shaking her head. "Thank heavens you shut the door. Yes, I'm sleeping with him. He's my husband. He wants a child and he doesn't want to wait."

Sara Beth's long ponytail slid over her shoulder as she cocked her head, pinning Lisa with a studying stare. "What do you want?"

Keeping secrets from Sara Beth was nearly impossible. "I want what he wants," she said, which was close enough to the truth, wasn't it?

Sara Beth's eyes narrowed, but thankfully she didn't challenge that. "So, was he worth the wait after Skyler-the-Dweeb?"

Lisa's mouth opened. Closed. She blinked. "Definitely."

Sara Beth let out her breath in a whoosh and collapsed into one of the chairs in front of Lisa's desk. "Well, at least there's hope, then."

Lisa jostled the pile of bids into a neat stack. "Hope for what?"

"Your happily ever after."

She couldn't help herself. She laughed. "You are *such* a romantic."

"Yup." Sara Beth leaned back in the chair, her hands clasped over her tummy. "A pregnant romantic, as it happens."

Now it was Lisa's turn to stare. "What?"

"Dr. and Mrs. Bonner are pleased to announce the future arrival of baby Bonner." Sara Beth's smile positively dripped happiness. "It's soon, of course. And we weren't exactly trying, but then again, we weren't exactly *not* trying, if you know what I mean. And this isn't just another pregnancy scare," Sara Beth added, obviously no longer troubled by the time she'd feared she was pregnant, before Ted had proposed. "All tests positive and systems are a go." She grinned.

Sara Beth and Ted had been married barely half a year. They hadn't even been intentionally trying.

Beneath the cover of the desk, Lisa pressed her hand against her abdomen. There was no question that Rourke *was* trying to make a baby.

Yes, he was making certain that the process was mind-blowing, but she couldn't afford to let herself forget the underlying purpose.

For all she knew, she'd already conceived. She would probably know later that week, if her period arrived as usual.

And if she were pregnant, what would become of hers and Rourke's relationship? His real interest in her was her uterus, after all. And while she'd claimed to be just as anxious to get that accomplished as he was—because it meant getting closer to the end of their arrangement—a claim was all it was.

Pregnancy in theory was one thing.

Pregnancy in reality meant a child. Becoming a mother.

"Helloooo. Earth to Lisa."

She realized that Sara Beth had been talking to her and felt herself flush all over again. "Sorry?"

Sara Beth's eyes danced. "Reliving a little French bliss?"

Lisa ignored that. "So how are you feeling? You're going to be a great mother. And I—" she smiled, truly happy for her friend "—am going to make a great honorary auntie."

Sara Beth's smile trembled a little. "Yes, you are." She cleared her throat. "And aside from an occasional desire to throw up on a patient's shoes, I'm feeling marvelous. We haven't told anyone around here, yet. I wanted you to be the first to know."

"Okay, you've gotta stop or we're going to be blubbering idiots, here." Lisa snatched a tissue from the box on her credenza and swiped her nose.

"What about you and Rourke? Any possibility of a honeymoon baby?"

Lisa managed a nod and Sara Beth's eyes sparkled. "We could be pregnant together." She looked thrilled by the very idea of it.

"Rourke's coming to town Friday night for the weekend," Lisa offered, wanting to get off the subject of her becoming pregnant. "We should all get together then and celebrate your and Ted's good news."

"Perfect. You know, you sounded very married, just then." Sara Beth picked up the small clock sitting on the corner of Lisa's desk, then put it back and pushed to her feet. "That's the deal, then? You're in your separate cities during the workweek and together on the weekends?"

"We decided that before the wedding. I told you."

"Yeah, but…" Sara Beth wrinkled her nose. "I would sure miss Ted if we were apart every week like that. Although—" she lifted a finger "—all those special homecomings could have an appeal, too. Candlelight dinner. Sexy lingerie…" She grinned mischievously. "Of course, unless you've taken up shopping since you've been hobnobbing with the wealthy Côte d'Azur folks, I know for a fact that your drawers aren't exactly filled with those sorts of *drawers*."

Lisa deliberately made a face. "Don't you have a patient waiting?"

Sara Beth laughed and, with a wave, headed out of the office. "I'm done for the day just before lunch. Call me. We'll go shopping at my favorite lingerie store. You can get something totally out of character for you, and I can get something sexy to wear before I can't fit in it anymore!" Her rubber-soled shoes squeaked a little as she hurried down the corridor.

Lisa looked down at the papers on her desk, but her gaze fell on the magazine. She'd bought it at the newsstand on her way into work that morning and could have recited the article from memory by now.

Business is business. Rourke's words to the reporter might as well have been underlined and highlighted in neon for the way they seemed to jump out at her.

She'd been on the terrace, sitting at the table with the reporter and Rourke when he'd given the interview. She knew exactly what he'd said. The expressions on his face when he'd said them. And nothing in the article was a misrepresentation.

And she hadn't lied to Sara Beth. Business *was* business.

So why did Rourke's comment nag at her?

Annoyed with herself, she flipped the magazine closed and stuffed it into the bottom drawer of her desk. Her phone buzzed and she snatched it up. "Yes?"

"Had a lot of work piled up on your desk waiting for you?"

Something inside her chest seemed to squeeze at the unexpected sound of Rourke's voice. "Hi. And no, the pile hasn't been too bad." She glossed over the stacks of correspondence and reports and messages that she'd been wading through for two solid hours. "What's, um, what's wrong?"

His laugh was low and rasped over her nerve endings in a wholly disruptive way. "There has to be something wrong for me to call my wife?" His voice dropped another notch. "I *really* missed you this morning. Waking up without you in my arms was no fun at all."

Her mouth went more than a little dry. She glanced at the opened doorway of her office. Thankfully, her assistant, Ella, was busy with a telephone call at the desk she occupied outside Lisa's office. "I had to come back to work," she reminded him.

"I know." His voice suddenly sounded even nearer. "But one of the advantages of being the boss is that I can tell my business to follow—" he suddenly appeared in her doorway "—where I want it to go." He grinned faintly, snapping his cell phone shut.

She shot up from her chair so fast, it rolled back and banged the credenza behind her desk. "Rourke!"

"Is that a happy-to-see-me 'Rourke'?"

Her stomach jumped around giddily. "I didn't expect to see you until Friday night."

His lips tilted, amused. "I'll take that as a yes, because it suits me." He seemed to roll his shoulder around the door frame as he entered, and very deliberately closed the door behind him. "You look very…icy."

His eyes were anything but as he slowly advanced, and she moistened her lips, dashing her hands down the front of her pale gray suit. "Would you prefer I come to work in a red leather miniskirt?"

"Nobody'd get any work done if they saw the rest

of the legs you're hiding under these skinny skirts of yours." He hooked his arm around her waist and pulled her to him.

She supposed she should be a little offended at his macho tactic, but her heart was too busy jiggling around in her throat to worry too deeply. "What are you doing here?"

His fingers kneaded her hips through the fine wool suit. "Checking on my investment?"

She couldn't help the bubble of laughter that rose to her lips. "You're terrible."

His lips tilted. "That's not what you were saying last night," he reminded her, dropping a much-too-brief kiss on her lips. "Then it was more on the order of 'you're good, you're perfect, right there, oh, yes—'"

She clamped her hand over his mouth. "All right. Enough. This is a place of business."

"Where babies are made." He pressed a kiss to the palm of her hand before pulling it away and tugging her even closer until their hips met. "Coincidentally enough."

She sucked in a breath, nearly swaying. "How do you do it?" Her voice was breathless. "Make me want you like this?" They'd made love less than twelve hours ago. They'd returned from France in the afternoon, had dinner with his mother in the city, and before Rourke had driven Lisa to the private airfield where his jet was waiting to fly her back to Boston, had driven her mad in the foyer of his penthouse apartment.

They hadn't even made it as far as the bedroom.

"Lucky, I guess." His hands worked the buttons on her suit jacket, and delved inside to discover the camisole that was all she wore beneath it. Her nipple rose tight and eager through the thin, plain cotton and she had a fleeting thought of Sara Beth's lingerie shopping idea. "If we didn't need to meet with your management team in five minutes, I'd be asking if that office door has a lock on it."

"Management team." The reminder was almost as effective as a bucket of ice water. She met every week with her department heads. That day was even more important, since she was coming off a long absence, and they had to begin dealing with Rourke's influx of cash.

She hastily backed away from him, hurriedly redoing the buttons, a task that would have been much easier if her fingers weren't shaking and her body weren't yearning for his. "Is that what you really came for?"

"It's one of the reasons." He sat on the edge of her desk, watching her fuss with her jacket. "Not the only one."

She supposed she should be grateful for that.

She reached the top button of the jewel-neck collar and flipped the narrow silver necklace she wore out over it before picking up the leather-bound pad that held her agenda and meeting notes. "You didn't mention it before."

"You didn't mention the management meeting," he pointed out. "I learned that from Ella."

She stopped in front of him, holding her pad against her breasts like a schoolgirl. "Is this what it will be like? You going around me to find out about the operational matters of the institute? Pulling rank on me?"

"Don't get your panties in a knot," he drawled, looking amused. "Ella sent me your schedule first thing this morning the same way she'd been sending me your schedule before the wedding."

The explanation was perfectly logical but it still put

her on edge. She was way over her head when it came to him on a personal basis. She wasn't certain at all how she felt about him being underfoot here at the institute. This was her turf. Her comfort zone.

"Stop looking worried," he chided as he straightened. "I've told you that I had no problem with the way this place was being run to begin with. Except for the blind faith you all put in your CFO," he added pointedly. "All I want to do is observe and meet all the players." He held out one arm. "After you."

She gave him a narrow look, but aware of the time ticking and loathe to be late for anything, she stepped past him and headed out of the office.

The boardroom where they usually met was on the top floor of their building. When they arrived, Paul and Ted were already sitting at the enormous oval table dominating the center of the sunlit room. Ted got up, greeting Rourke with a wide smile and a clap on the shoulder and, leaving them to it, she assumed her usual spot at the table, glancing at the clock on the wall as the room quickly filled. At five minutes past, her gaze scanned those present. "Where's Dr. Demetrios?"

"Here." The handsome, swarthy doctor entered, his white lab coat trailing out behind him. "Got a mom-in-the-making getting prepped." His brown eyes sparkled with good humor. "So I'll give you about five minutes."

Lisa wasn't surprised. She well knew the doctor preferred to be bedside than boardroom table-side. "All right, then you and Dr. Bonner can report out first." She opened her pad and picked up her pen, taking an occasional note while Ted and Chance both launched into concise updates of their current work.

"We may be looking at an expanded study very soon,"

Ted concluded. "A natural supplement that increases sperm motility. Our early testing is looking really promising."

Lisa glanced up. This was news to her. "You've been doing testing?"

"With one subject." Ted looked slightly chagrined as his glance skipped around the room. "We were already involved in it before we started putting together our best-practices manual."

The manual had simply been a matter of avoiding the impression of lab irregularities. But she also knew that Ted wasn't likely to get into specifics during a regular management meeting. It wasn't as if the head of human resources or maintenance needed to know what innovative research paths they were heading along. They'd learned all too well over the past year how critical data security was.

She couldn't help feeling a buzz of excitement, though.

A new study.

Secure funding.

Her gaze tripped over Rourke's where he was sitting next to Paul at the other side of the table and warmth just seemed to bloom inside her bones.

Yes. Everything was going well.

More than well.

"Sounds good," she said mildly, ducking her head over her notes. "Back to the agenda, then. How many open positions are we still trying to fill?" She looked at the head of H.R., and the meeting proceeded without fanfare, breaking nearly two hours later.

Lunchtime.

The room quickly emptied as she rose from the table. Gathering her things, she watched her husband from the corner of her eyes as he and Ted talked, their voices too low to hear.

"How's married life?" Her brother Paul stopped next to her. "He treating you well?"

"Very." It was the truth, she realized. No matter what his motives were, Rourke did treat her well. They'd had their debates over the past few weeks. Politics. Hockey. Two people with opinions of their own were bound to. But he listened as well as talked. And he didn't judge.

It was a singularly disarming trait.

"You hear about Derek entering that program in Connecticut?"

"Yes." She tapped the end of her pen softly against the table that was striped by brilliant shafts of sunlight cutting through the floor-to-ceiling windows lining the paneled room. "Have you talked to him?"

Paul's lips twisted. "Ramona says I should. She would have lost her mother if it weren't for her finding her half sister to be a bone marrow donor. Now that her mom's finally on the mend, Ramona's more adamant than ever about family sticking together no matter what. But, no, I haven't talked to him."

"Do Mother and Daddy know?"

"I'm sure they do by now. They'll probably end up footing the bill." He sighed. "I'm supposed to believe in healing, but I'm not sure if that twin of mine even feels any remorse. At least Rourke has managed to keep it out of the papers. Only press the institute is getting again is good press. Finally." He suddenly pulled his phone out of his lab coat and checked the display. "I've gotta go. Patient's waiting." He squeezed her shoulder as he headed off.

Lisa looked over at Rourke again. He'd treated *all* of

them well. She swallowed the nervousness that wanted to rise in her throat and walked over to him and Ted. "Want to grab some lunch?" The casual question masked the silly trepidation she felt.

Rourke slid his arm over her shoulder in an easy move that nevertheless managed to make her stomach dance a little jig. "Wish I could." His fingers toyed with the bun at the nape of her neck, reminding her all too well of what usually happened when he started pulling the pins out of her hair...where it always seemed to lead. A shiver danced down her spine and the glint in his eyes told her he was well aware of the effect he was having. "But I can't."

She lifted her eyebrows, masking her disappointment. "The boss whose business follows where he wants can't take time to share lunch with his new wife?"

His fingers glided down the nape of her neck. Slipped beneath the collar of her jacket. If she wasn't mistaken, there was actual regret in his eyes. "I've got about ten minutes to spare with Ted—that new thing he's got brewing—and then I'm meeting with the mayor of Boston."

She started. He really *had* had other reasons than her for coming to town. "What for?"

"A construction project." He tilted her head and dropped a kiss on her lips. "Then I need to get back to New York. Cynthia's got my schedule slammed this week."

"You're still going to make it here for the weekend though?" She was painfully aware of Ted standing nearby and the obvious way he was trying not to listen— a physical impossibility, given his proximity—but was more concerned with the possibility that Rourke might *not* be able to return as easily as he'd claimed.

"Oh, yeah, Mrs. Devlin." Rourke glided his finger

along the satiny skin of Lisa's neck and watched the flare of her pupils that occurred in direct correlation to his touch.

It was damnably erotic.

"I'll be back." He pressed another kiss to her lips. A kiss that he ended too quickly, but wisely, given their audience and his time constraints.

And then he was striding out of the boardroom, Ted keeping up in his wake before he managed to forget that he *did* have a plate of responsibilities waiting for him, no matter how distracting he was finding his wife to be.

"You haven't told her," Ted asked quietly once they'd reached the privacy of his office. He unlocked a cabinet and pulled out a syringe.

Rourke didn't have to guess what Ted meant. "No reason to tell her."

He shrugged out of his jacket, loosened his belt and turned his back and felt the sting of the injection a few moments later. After several months of having his hip pricked by Ted's needles, the process was done in a matter of seconds and he was fastening his belt again, smoothing down his shirt and pulling on his jacket.

"That's a pretty big secret to keep from the woman you're married to. Think that's wise?"

"You've kept a secret or two yourself," he reminded Ted.

"Not anymore." Ted waved his hand. "Not that I've told Sara Beth that it's your butt I've been having to look at every month," he assured him. "You know that's confidential. But I have told her about the success we're having with the new regimen." He returned to the locked cabinet and retrieved a pill bottle that he tossed to Rourke. "Thirty-day supply. What's the point in keeping it from her? Lisa's a levelheaded woman. She sees situations like this all the time. And she's going to know the details of the treatment as soon as we expand it into an official study."

"She won't have to know that I was patient X." He slid the small bottle into his pocket. The second Taylor had found out it was *he* who was the failure in their baby-making department, she'd gone searching for more fertile pastures. Not that he considered Lisa to be cut from the same cloth as Taylor, but old habits died pretty damn hard.

The only ones who knew about his infertility were Ted—and by necessity his partner, Chance. And the only reason Ted knew was because one night, Rourke hadn't been as closed-mouthed as he usually was, thanks to the deep bottle of whiskey Ted had found him trying to drown himself in the day the divorce had finally become final.

It wasn't one of Rourke's prouder moments, but that particular cloud definitely had its silver lining. Because if he hadn't admitted his problem, there'd have been no reason for Ted to ever tell him about the treatment that he and Chance had already been trying to formulate. Or for Rourke to convince them that he was the perfect candidate to test it on once they believed they were on the right track.

Ted didn't exactly look convinced, but he let the matter drop. "The mayor of Boston, huh?"

Rourke shrugged more casually than he felt. "Just sounding him out on a new multiuse project. There are a couple other locations I'm considering, too."

"But if it were in Boston, you'd have to be around here at least part of the time getting it underway."

"Boston's a good city." He pulled open the door.

Ted grinned. "Particularly when that's where your wife lives, I'd think."

Rourke didn't deny it. He lifted his hand in a brief salute and made his way out of the building before he could fall to the lure of seeking out Lisa just one more time before he left. And it had nothing to do with the faint rattle of pills coming from his pocket.

He'd already become addicted to his cool-facaded wife.

And for the first time in his life, he didn't know what to do about it.

Chapter 11

Lisa glanced at the clock on her fireplace mantel.

Nearly eleven o'clock.

Rourke was supposed to have been there hours ago.

She exhaled, staring at the flicker of the two tall candles she'd lit at the center of the dining-room table. Surrounding the crystal candlesticks were baskets of no-longer-warm rolls, a salad that was twenty degrees past wilted and an eggplant lasagna that no longer steamed with an inviting aroma, but was going cold and sunken.

Sexy lingerie and candlelight dinners might be perfect for Sara Beth and Ted. But for Lisa and Rourke, it was turning out to be a foolish endeavor.

First of all, Lisa couldn't cook a decent meal to save her life. Oh, she'd tried. But the first effort was residing in the trash and what sat on the table now was courtesy of her decidedly frantic call to her favorite Italian restaurant.

While she'd been trying to blow out the stench of

burned garlic bread from the kitchen, they'd kindly delivered this once-beautiful feast with instructions that even *she* couldn't fail to follow.

And here she sat. Dressed in a filmy black nightie that Sara Beth had positively dared Lisa to buy, candles burned almost down to nubs, and no Rourke in sight.

She was much more annoyed with herself than she was with him. He'd only estimated his arrival when they'd talked that afternoon.

Not even talked.

Texted.

Which was the level that their communications seemed to have sunk to as the week had progressed since he'd shown up at the institute on Monday.

She was the one who'd gone all out with the foolish "welcome home" measures.

Boston wasn't even Rourke's home!

She finally blew out the candles, then rapidly cleared the table. Dumped the food in the trash where it joined the first attempt.

Staring down into the mess, she was appalled to realize there were tears on her cheeks.

She snatched a paper towel from the holder standing on her granite counter and swiped her face. Balled up the paper and pitched it in the trash.

A second later, she whipped the frothy, thigh-length concoction she was wearing over her head and shoved it on top of the food.

Turning on her bare heel, she stomped upstairs to her bedroom and yanked on an old college sweatshirt that reached her knees instead. Then she went into the bathroom and washed her face, twisted the hair that she'd left loose just to please him into a long braid, and went to bed.

She was *not* a lovesick bride and she'd better start remembering it.

Unfortunately, instead of closing her eyes and going to sleep, she lay there, staring at the clock on her nightstand, watching the minutes continue to tick.

That just made her feel weepy again, and after an hour, she finally shoved back the covers and went into the second bedroom that she'd set up as a home office. She sat down at the desk. Her calendar was open.

It was past midnight.

It was official.

They'd been married for four weeks now.

"Happy anniversary." She deliberately flipped the calendar closed. She turned on her computer. Read through a few dozen e-mails, two of which were from her mother about the never-ending details concerning Gerald's upcoming eightieth birthday party.

The light on her message machine was blinking, and she reluctantly hit the button, already braced for "motherly" messages there, as well.

She wasn't disappointed. She buzzed past her mother's voice reminding her that she'd assigned Lisa the duty of hand-addressing the birthday party invitations and tracking the RSVPs and that she'd better start looking for a gown for Paul and Ramona's Christmas Eve wedding, and she skipped past two more messages the second she heard Derek's gruff greetings. She knew that Paul had finally caved to Ramona's insistence that he at least talk to him. All Paul had said about the conversation, though, was that Derek still hadn't apologized for his actions. And until he could do that, Paul wasn't going to waste more time on him. He and Ramona had enough on their plate with their upcoming wedding.

"Hello, Mrs. Devlin." She started at the sound of Rourke's voice coming from the machine. *"I'm running late and you're not answering your cell. See you when I get there."*

"You called," she said to the machine, and just like that, her irritation dissolved, leaving her feeling teary all over again. Acting more like a teenager with her first boyfriend than a grown woman with a career-driven husband, she rewound the message and listened to it a second time.

Then she pulled out her briefcase and unearthed her cell phone that plainly showed her he had called.

Twice.

She dropped the phone on the desk and propped her head in her hands. "You are such a witch, Lisa Armstrong."

"Thought that was *Devlin* now."

She jerked and swiveled in her chair to see Rourke standing there. His jeans were washed nearly white and molded his hips and the thick ivory fisherman's sweater he wore made his shoulders look even broader and his hair even blacker. "How'd you get in?"

"You gave me the security code, remember? I came in through the kitchen." He dropped a very well-used duffel on the floor and stepped into the office, his gaze taking in the tall, mullioned window that overlooked her minuscule backyard, and the old library desk that consumed a good portion of the floor space. "Nice desk."

It was. She'd found it in a consignment shop years ago. "I didn't know you'd called," she said stupidly.

His slashing eyebrows quirked together. "My mother would like to think she raised me better than that. I'm nearly five hours late." He leaned over the chair, propping his hands on the sturdy, wooden arms and brought his head close to hers.

Close enough that she could smell the faint, heady scent of his aftershave.

"Don't you want to know why I was late?"

She was dissolving into a puddle way too easily with this man who'd manipulated her into marriage. "Business, I'm sure." She peeled his hand away from the chair so that she could sidle her way out of the chair past him.

He didn't let go of her that easily, though, and swung her around until she landed flat against his chest. "Yeah. The business of clearing the way to stay here for a few weeks at a stretch, rather than just the weekend."

Her lips parted. "What?"

"I'll make the trip back to New York if I have to, but for now at least, you're going to have to share a drawer or two." His hands slid slowly up and down her back. "So…what do you think?"

Even through her shock she was aware that he sounded diffident.

Which for Rourke was completely out of character.

And that was as alarming as the emotions coiling around inside her. "It doesn't matter what I think. You've already made up your mind, obviously." Made up his mind to change the rules of the game, since they'd already agreed to spend the workweek in their respective cities.

The question was why?

To hasten the chances of her getting pregnant?

His hands slipped down her waist. "I saw the garbage when I came in."

Her cheeks heated. "Dinner was ruined."

"I wasn't talking about the food."

Of *course* he would have to comment on the hank

of sheer fabric and ribbon that she'd shoved in alongside the eggplant. "I don't know what you mean," she lied blithely.

He snorted softly, a definite smile hovering around the corners of his way-too-sexy mouth. "Did you get that thing for me? A little…four-week anniversary gift?"

"Don't be ridiculous." For some reason, it threw her even more that he was aware of that small milestone, too. "I was…was…cleaning out my closet."

"Mmm. And that was the only thing to go."

He clearly didn't believe her. And why would he? She was a pathetic liar.

"Maybe you haven't figured it out, Lisa Armstrong *Devlin*." His hands slid around her waist, bunching up the fleecy sweatshirt. "But I find you insanely sexy. When you're buttoned up in your no-nonsense suits or when you're draped in expensive couture. If wearing a little piece of black nothing makes you feel good about yourself—and what we do together—then have at it. But make no mistake. Even when you look about sixteen, like you do now, you are attractive to me. Hell, all you have to do is simply exist—" she felt the stretched-out hem of the sweatshirt reach her thighs as he continued drawing it upward "—and I want you more than I've ever wanted anything."

"Even children?" She wanted to suck the words back in the second they slid out of her lips. "Don't answer that," she said quickly. There was no need for him to confirm what she already knew.

She was a means to an end for him. Without giving him the child he wanted, he wouldn't have any use for her. And once he did turn her into a mother—which was a state that was preoccupying her thoughts more and more with every passing day—her purpose for him will have been served.

"Fortunately—" he kept slowly bunching the sweatshirt upward and she felt cool air sneak over her bottom "—there's no need to choose." His warm fingers replaced the air, seeming to sear into her bare skin as he lifted her right off her feet. "Did you miss me?"

"I've been swamped at the office," she assured him coolly even while her hands were greedily snaking around his shoulders. "Thanks to your insistence that I be gone for a three-week honeymoon."

His lips twitched. He carried her around the duffel bag on the floor. "Bedroom?"

"End of the hall."

Her town house wasn't huge by any stretch. But it was in a neighborhood that she liked, and it was conveniently located to the institute. So she overlooked the drafty windows and the creaks in the floor, but as he carried her down the short hallway, she was enormously conscious of its shortcomings.

"My place is a lot different than your penthouse," she stated the obvious when he elbowed through the narrow doorway into her dimly lit, chilly bedroom. "Three mornings of waiting for the water heater to kick in will have you running back to New York."

"Don't count on it." He carried her to the shadowy foot of her antique four-poster and slowly lowered her until her bare feet met the braided carpet covering the hardwood floor. "This place smells like you."

There was probably a rule book somewhere that said she shouldn't be so easily disarmed. But she was, anyway. "And burned garlic bread," she added faintly.

His hands swept beneath the sweatshirt. "Just you," he assured her.

She sucked in a hissing breath when he tugged the garment over her head and his mouth dipped to the naked curve of her shoulder.

"You're shivering," he murmured. "It's cold outside."

The weather had changed. Autumn fully engulfing the city. But the rapidly cooling weather outside that managed somehow to sneak in beyond the brick walls of her town house wasn't what had her shivering now. "That's why I like the fireplace in here." She tugged at his sweater, much more interested in getting her hands beneath to the inferno of his flesh than she was in the temperature outside. "Lift your arms," she finally ordered.

His laugh was muffled in the folds of the sweater as he tugged it over his head and tossed it aside. But before she could press herself up close and personal to that hard, broad chest that she couldn't seem to get enough of, he'd tipped her off her feet again and easily nudged her into the center of her already disheveled bed. "Get under the covers. I'll make you a fire."

She scooted back on the mattress, happy enough to do that if he'd just hurry up and join her. "That's what I was kind of expecting," she said pointedly, lifting the blankets in invitation.

His gaze lingered on her bare body for a gratifying moment. Then he seemed to shake himself as he turned toward the fireplace that was in the corner of her bedroom, opposite the bed. "Have you had the chimney cleaned lately?" He crouched down and began pulling wood out of the fire basket next to the hearth, stacking it inside the firebox.

"Every year." Her eyes felt glued to the naked play

of muscles as he worked. "It might look old, but we're not going to go up in flames."

He looked at her over his shoulder. "I'm pretty sure we will," he drawled. He shoved some kindling under the stack of wood and pulled out one of the long matches she kept next to the wood.

In seconds, the flame was snapping hungrily at the kindling and he settled the iron screen back in place. Then he rose and turned to face her.

Even though they'd made love dozens of times now, her mouth ran dry as he finished undressing and there was no doubt in her mind as he climbed into the bed and drew her against his fully aroused body that he was interested in anything, just then, other than her. His hands were barely roving over her and she could feel the flames licking at her feet. By the time he pulled her, wet and aching, beneath him and sank so deeply into her that she couldn't help but cry out, she was heading straight for conflagration.

And even as she felt herself spinning wildly out of control, she clung to the fact that in this, at least, he was right there with her.

By the time Lisa woke, the logs in the fireplace were burned down to ash and sunlight was streaming through the twin windows on either side of the bed, shining right across the blanketed bumps of their tangled feet.

She looked at those bumps, feeling the warmth of his feet against hers beneath the blankets, the arm he had planted over her waist, keeping her backside tucked against him, and felt such a wealth of contentment that it was nearly overwhelming.

If she could have blamed it on the unheard-of presence of a man sleeping in her bed, she would have.

But it wasn't just any man.

It was Rourke.

She let out a long breath.

That week at work, she'd worried that having him in her home would feel awkward. It wasn't as if they were a world away in a Mediterranean villa where it had become easy to forget their real world. Their real lives.

This was Boston. Her home. It didn't get much more real than that.

And instead of feeling as if her space was invaded, as if he was taking over another area of her life—particularly knowing that he intended to stay for more than just a few days—she felt...content.

It ought to have confused the life out of her.

But lying there, feeling the steady rise and fall of his chest against her spine, Lisa couldn't summon up even the slightest confusion.

Only contentment.

It was nature itself that finally propelled her out of the warm nest of blankets and Rourke's arms.

The bedroom was at least ten degrees colder than it had been the night before, and she snatched up the first thing her hands encountered to drag over her head as she visited the only bathroom her upstairs possessed. Rourke's sweater.

The soft ivory knit hung over her shoulders and down to her knees and she couldn't help tilting her nose down to smell the scent of him in the weave as she cleaned her face and teeth and worked the remains of her braid out of her hair. A peek through the bedroom door showed her that Rourke hadn't budged since she'd left the bed, except to throw one arm over his head.

His hair—longer now than it had ever been since

she'd met him and showing a distinctly unruly wave—
was tousled over his forehead. During their honeymoon,
she'd gotten used to the sight—as well as the tantalizing
feel—of the dark blur of beard that always shadowed
his square jaw by morning and for a long moment, she
hovered there watching him sleep, a strange sort of tenderness invading her chest.

"If you're gonna stand there staring," his husky voice
eventually said, making her start, "come back to bed."

"Men your age shouldn't have so much stamina," she
retorted. "And it may be Saturday, but I have important
things to do."

He pushed up on his elbow and the bedding fell away
from his chest. "Honey, to a healthy guy who isn't quite
as old as you seem to think, in the morning, there ain't
nothing more important than that."

She forcibly dragged her gaze away from all that male
perfection on display and toyed with the too-long sleeves
of his sweater that hung below her fingers. "I have to
meet my mother and get some stuff for my dad's eightieth birthday party. Evidently, I'm in charge of hand-
addressing the invitations and tracking the RSVPs.
Making certain that everyone Mother wants there *is*
there." Emily would undoubtedly hunt down anyone
who didn't respond the way she wanted. All done in the
most steely-gracious way, of course.

"Have your secretary do it," Rourke suggested carelessly.

"It's bad enough having my mother push it off on me
without even asking if I had the time. I wouldn't dream
of pushing this off on Ella. And she'd quickly remind
you that she's my administrative assistant."

"Then have Cynthia do it."

"*Your* assistant? You're crazy. She scares me to pieces."

"She's a pussycat."

She hooted. "Maybe to you she is. Besides, she's in New York."

He bunched the pillow beneath his head again. "Then have fun meeting your mom."

Sudden inspiration hit. "You should come with me. Mother actually likes *you*." Emily would be thrilled at the notion that Rourke would be in town for days on end.

He slanted her a glance that gave new meaning to the phrase *bedroom eyes*. "Are you going to make it worth my while?"

"Bribery?" She leaned against the doorjamb. "I'd think a supposedly smitten—" she air quoted the word "—bridegroom would want to spend every possible moment with his new bride."

"Not when it's under the nose of Emily Armstrong," he returned wryly.

"Ah." She nodded, feeling a smile tug at her own lips, and crossed her arms. "You *do* really know my mother. Okay. Think of it as a philanthropic gesture. Doing a generous and kind deed for your wife."

He pulled the pillow over his head, lifting his hand in a stopping motion.

"You can't hide from it." She raised her voice. "I've already read about the awards ceremony being held next month and *all* about the noble deeds of this year's award winner." And been dauntingly impressed, wondering how he found the time to invest his *time* as much as his money. He'd not only funded several new shelters in the city, but he'd helped build them. Literally. With hammer and nails. He'd done the same with a new school for girls in Sudan.

But that was what Rourke did. Led by example.

He moved aside the pillow, giving her a baleful look that had her biting the inside of her cheek to hide her delight. It was so refreshing to see the ever-confident man even the slightest bit discomfited. Was it any wonder that she had to take advantage of it?

"If I go with you, will you not say another word about the award business until we actually have to show up at that damn dinner?"

"We?"

"You think I'm going to show up there alone?"

"Won't your family be there? Receiving the award is a big deal."

"Yes, they'll be there," he said, looking aggrieved. "And obviously, so will Nora and Grif."

She hid a smile and drew a cross over her heart. "All right. I promise not to mention it again. Although now I've got to add shopping to the list of things to get done. I assume the thing I'm not supposed to mention will be a formal occasion, and finding a suitable outfit is rarely accomplished in just one day."

"Fine. I'll go with you." His heavy-lidded gaze roved over her. "But first, you have to come here to me."

"I *was* going to fix you some coffee." It was one thing she could prepare faithfully without ruining. She bit the tip of her tongue for a moment. "Strong and hot, just the way you liked it in France."

"Strong and hot, yeah. But the coffee part is not on my mind at the moment."

She knew that. "It is on mine." She smiled slyly and turned to go down the hall.

"Come back here." She heard his footfall on the

creaking floorboards followed rapidly by a nasty curse. "Holy— It's *freezing* in here," he yelled.

Not at all his swell Park Avenue penthouse, which undoubtedly even had heated floors.

She glanced over her shoulder and giggled when she saw him coming after her, her grandmother's very faded wedding-circle quilt yanked around his torso. "Don't trip," she warned, dashing to the stairs.

She wasn't fast enough, though. Even hampered by a sixty-year-old quilt, he caught up to her before she reached the landing, scooped her right off her feet, and tossed her over his shoulder.

She found her nose abruptly up close and personal to his quilt-draped backside. "Hey." She wriggled her legs and his arm clamped down over her thighs as he strode back toward the bedroom.

"Caveman." She batted at his butt, but there wasn't much power behind it since she was giggling too hard. Then he flipped her off his shoulder and dumped her, bouncing, onto the bed and she couldn't help but laugh even harder. "What would the business world think if they saw you now?"

"That the caveman wants his woman." His dark eyes were wickedly intent as he threw aside the quilt and came down beside her, his mouth plundering his way to the valley between her breasts, right through the soft ivory sweater.

Her giggles died as she wrapped herself around him.

But what didn't die was the wistful thought that one day she might actually be his woman. For no other reason than that he wanted *her*.

Chapter 12

"Pretty swell invitations." Sitting across from Lisa two weeks later at the dining-room table in her town house, Sara Beth held up the engraved parchment. "As fancy as a wedding invite." She tucked the invitation carefully into its envelope, added the RSVP card and its little envelope, then handed it off to Lisa.

"Nothing but the best for my mother." Forcing a wry smile, Lisa crossed another name off the list, and started addressing the next envelope, only to have to toss it to the side with the other mis-starts when she began writing the same name that she'd just done. "If she knew I was already a week late getting them out, she'd want to skin me alive. Thanks for giving up your Sunday afternoon to help me, or I'd be even later getting them done." So far, thanks to Sara Beth's help, she'd gotten a quarter of the way through the hundred that were going out.

They'd be going even faster if she could get her mind actually *on* what she was doing.

"Ted's in the lab today anyway." Sara Beth tucked and sealed again, and set the finished envelope down. "It's not like you to procrastinate, though. Even when it comes to your mom. I'm guessing that's because Rourke has kept you pretty busy."

"And even after being back for three weeks, I'm still playing catch-up at the office."

"Again, I'm thinking...Rourke's fault," Sara Beth added dryly. "Good thing he had to make a business trip and give you a break. Where's he off to this time?"

"London. He leaves from New York tomorrow morning." He'd be gone for the week, returning the morning of the awards gala. She was to meet him in New York.

Sara Beth was wagging an invitation between her thumb and forefinger. "Well, I imagine when he gets back, he's going to prefer that your skin is intact."

Lisa managed a smile, but knew it was a miserable effort, particularly when Sara Beth dropped the invitation and reached over the stack of them to pluck the pen out of Lisa's hand.

"All right," she said, no-nonsense written all over her face. "You've been acting weird since I got here. Did you and Rourke have a fight?"

"No." She quickly shook her head and her hair slid over her shoulder. "Rourke's been...fine." Attentive. Passionate. Surprisingly good company even when they weren't in the bedroom.

"Then what's wrong?" Sara Beth nudged the neat stack of invitations and they slid sideways. "Surely you're not letting this stuff really get to you? I know she's your mother, but stressing out about getting these things in the mail a few days late isn't going to accomplish anything." Her lips twisted a little. "Whether they have two weeks' notice instead of three, everyone important enough to be invited is going to be there at Dr. G.'s party."

The invitations weren't Lisa's problem. She pressed her forehead to her hands. "I think I'm pregnant," she blurted.

And had to hold back the sob that wanted to follow on its heels.

She swallowed hard and finally looked up at Sara Beth.

She was watching Lisa with a crinkle between her eyebrows. "*Think?* Have you had a test? How late are you?"

"Well over two weeks, and no. I haven't done a test."

Sara Beth's eyebrows shot up. Not surprisingly. "It'd be pretty easy to run one at the institute," she pointed out.

"Yeah, if I wanted everyone to know my business." Lisa also could have done a test at home if she'd had any privacy in which to do so.

But until that morning when Rourke had flown back to New York, she hadn't *had* a private moment.

"Does Rourke know?" Sara Beth was still clearly trying to gauge the situation. And failing. But how could she not when she didn't know Rourke's real reason for marrying her in the first place?

"No." Her teeth worried the corner of her lip. "I don't want him to until I know for certain."

Sara Beth immediately stood up, and began pulling on the jacket she'd left tossed over the back of Lisa's sofa. "All right, then. Come on. You've got a drugstore nearby. Let's find out for certain."

Lisa didn't budge from her chair.

"Lis?" Sara Beth slowly sat back down. "What's going on? Don't you *want* to be pregnant?"

"The only reason Rourke married me was to *get* me pregnant." It was such a dizzying relief to actually say the words that she barely noticed the tears blurring her vision.

"I'm sure that's not true." Sara Beth's voice was gentle. Calm. "He's crazy about you. Everyone knows that. Even the reporter from that magazine knew that. You're probably just freaking out a little about getting pregnant so quickly. If you're even pregnant at all."

"He didn't invest in the institute because he is crazy about me," Lisa corrected. Her voice was thick. Her throat tight. "He invested in exchange for me giving him the child he wants. Period."

Even with the futile tears burning her eyes, she could see the shock settle over Sara Beth's face. "And you agreed to that?"

"How could I not? The institute would have gone under." Even now, she couldn't bring herself to tell Sara Beth the rest. That Rourke would have seen to it that no other investor would touch them. "Derek's embezzlement went too deep. Rourke knew how precarious things were."

"But nobody at the institute would have expected you to sacrifice yourself to save it!" Sara Beth pushed to her feet and paced the short distance between the dining room and the living room. "I *knew* something wasn't right," she muttered, pacing back again. "I should have listened to my instincts."

"It wouldn't have mattered what your instincts said. I knew what I was agreeing to and I'd…I'd do it again."

Lisa wiped her cheeks with the cuff of her sweater, only to realize the sweater wasn't even hers at all. It was Rourke's. She'd pulled it on that morning when she'd gotten out of bed. She hadn't taken it off since.

A fresh wave of tears burned past her lashes.

Sara Beth crouched down next to Lisa's seat. "Then why are you crying?"

"Isn't that what pregnant women do? Cry over nothing?"

"This doesn't feel like nothing to me." She hesitated. "So what is going to happen once you're pregnant?"

Lisa drew in a shuddering breath. "Once the baby's here, we…we can go our separate ways." That was what they'd agreed to.

"And the baby?"

"Joint custody," she admitted huskily. "If I want to be involved, he won't protest that."

More shock paled Sara Beth's cheeks. "You do, don't you?"

Lisa's arms crossed over her belly. A dim portion of her mind recognized the protectiveness in the gesture. "Yes." She wasn't sure when she'd realized it. But she knew, unquestionably, that she wouldn't be able to hand over her child. *Their* child.

"Oh, Lisa." Sara Beth sighed. "I hate knowing you've been going through this alone. I wish you'd have told me." She pushed back her thick hair as she rose and paced some more. "Actually, what I wish is that Ted had never set up that first meeting between you and Rourke."

"We would never have found another investor like Rourke."

"If I didn't know better, it would sound like you're defending him."

"He's a good man. We…each had something the other wanted. And he's been m-more than fair."

"Oh, my God." Sara Beth stopped next to Lisa's chair. Realization dawned in her eyes. "You're in love with him!"

"I'm…not." But her throat was closing up so tightly, all she could manage was a whisper.

"You are. You're in love with him, and you think once he finds out you're pregnant, that'll be the end of it. That's why you're so upset!"

She opened her mouth to deny it, but nothing emerged.

"Oh, honey." Sara Beth leaned over, wrapping her arms around Lisa in a comforting hug. "It'll be all right. Everything will be okay."

Hadn't Rourke told her that on their honeymoon?

Lisa's tears only came faster. "I don't see how."

Sara Beth looked teary herself when she straightened. She went into the kitchen and came back a moment later, handing Lisa a wad of napkins. "Wipe your eyes." Then with long familiarity, she went to the coat closet by the front door and retrieved Lisa's coat. "You can't hide from this. First thing we need to know is whether or not you are even pregnant. Maybe your period is late because you've been so stressed." She exhaled. "Heaven knows you've had reason to be. First the problems at the institute. Then Derek. Now this."

Lisa slowly took the coat and put it on. She scrubbed her cheeks with the napkins and left them balled-up on the table. "You're right." She hauled in a deep breath. Let it out. She wouldn't know anything until she at least knew that.

"And, you know—" Sara Beth tucked her arm through Lisa's once they were on the sidewalk outside

"—even if you are pregnant, who is to say that Rourke will still want you to go your own way? All right, so maybe you didn't go into the marriage with love in your heart, but look where you are now. You won't know unless you talk to him. You're going to New York next weekend for that award thing, right? His feelings could have deepened just as easily as yours."

"That's the romantic in you talking," Lisa said. Even though she'd become guilty of wishing that very thing.

"I just want you to be happy."

"And that's the friend in you talking." Lisa blinked hard, holding another spate of tears at bay. "I don't know what I'd do without you. You're the best friend I could ever have, and all this time, I've been hiding the truth from you. You'd never keep a secret like this from me."

Sara Beth's nose reddened. "Great," she mumbled. "You had to go and say something like that, didn't you."

"What?"

She stopped on the sidewalk and faced Lisa. "You know I love you, right?"

Bewildered, Lisa nodded. "Of course."

"And you know I'd never want to hurt you."

"I know. That's what I was just saying—"

Sara Beth caught Lisa's gloved hands in hers. "My timing stinks." She drew in a deep breath and let it out in a whoosh. "I'm not just your friend, Lisa. I'm…I'm your sister. Your half sister, I mean."

Lisa stared at Sara Beth blankly. A whining siren sounded in the distance. "What?"

"Dr. G. is my father."

Pinpointing, dawning horror closed in on her. She tugged her hands out of Sara Beth's. "Why would you say such a thing?"

Sara Beth looked tormented. "Because I didn't want that secret between us, either!"

"No. Why would you claim you're my father's daughter!"

"Because I am." Sara Beth lifted her gloved hands. "It's not like I planned it. Not even my *mother* planned it."

"You always said your mother used a sperm donor." It had always made sense. Sara Beth's mother, Grace, had practically been her father's first employee. She'd been the head nurse at the institute from the beginning and hadn't retired until Lisa's father had retired.

Grace had never married, but had had a child, thanks to the work of the institute. Lisa knew being the child of artificial insemination had never sat well with Sara Beth, but Lisa had always admired Grace O'Connell's independent style. She'd had a career. A home. A child. She'd lived her life to suit herself.

"Are you saying my *father* was the donor? God, Sara Beth. Hasn't the institute been through the wringer enough? Now you, of all people, are saying he would do something so unethical as switch his own sperm with a donor's?"

"He didn't have to switch anything. He and my mother had an affair. A brief one."

Her entire body tightened with denial. "I don't believe you."

Sara Beth looked as if she wanted to cry. "You've been my best friend our entire lives. Why would I lie about something like that?"

"I don't know." Lisa shook her head, backing away. "My father wouldn't—he *wouldn't* have done that. You're only a month older than I am, for God's sake. That would mean that—"

"I know how bad it sounds."

"Really?"

"I wasn't even planning to tell you," Sara Beth admitted. "To tell any of you. I told your mother I wouldn't and I meant—"

"My *mother!*" Lisa felt like she had the first time she and Sara Beth had ridden a roller coaster at the fair. Sick. And heading for the edge of a rail that would never contain them. "My mother knows?"

"Since I turned fourteen." Tears were on Sara Beth's cheeks now. "That's when your mother stopped liking me."

It made a horrible, awful kind of sense. Until she and Sara Beth had been young teens, Emily had been practically a second mother to Sara Beth. They'd even shared the same nanny when they'd been babies.

But then the day had come when, suddenly, Emily claimed that Lisa needed *new* friends. More suitable friends. Friends of their same class. She'd been hideous and Lisa had snuck out more than once to see Sara Beth. But not until she'd gone to college and had some real freedom had they been able to renew their friendship in full.

"And have *you* known since then?"

"No!" Sara Beth's hands lifted to her sides again. "I only found out earlier this year."

Lisa felt as if she was having an out-of-body experience, watching herself shake her head and back away from the girl who went back to diaper-days with her. She didn't know whether to laugh, or to cry.

How could her father have done such a thing?

"I can't deal with this right now."

"You don't have to deal with anything. Nothing has

changed, Lisa. I'm not chomping at the bit to be recognized as an Armstrong. I just…when you talked about secrets…I just wanted you to know. I love you—"

Lisa held up her hand. "Not now." She turned on her heel, running back up the short distance to her front steps.

"Lisa!"

She fumbled with the lock and darted inside, locking the door again behind her.

She heard the pound of feet on the steps, followed by the rap of Sara Beth's knuckles on the door.

"Lisa, come on. Please don't do this!"

It was the coward's way out and Lisa knew it. But just then, she felt incapable of anything else.

She left Sara Beth—her *sister*—knocking on the door and went upstairs. There, she closed herself in her bedroom and she didn't come out again until she was certain that Sara Beth had finally given up.

And gone away.

Rourke stared into the cut-crystal glass of Scotch he held, no closer to drinking it than he'd been when he'd poured the damn thing in the first place.

The New York view that he'd never before tired of was spread out in front of him. The sound system that was the best money could buy was silent. He had a stack of material tossed on the couch beside him that Cynthia had gathered for him, and which he needed to go over before he left for London in the morning, but even that held no interest.

All because of the woman who was his wife.

He sat forward, shoving the drink onto the coffee table, and pushed to his bare feet to pace the length of his living room. The floor here sure in hell wasn't cold like the floor at Lisa's. But after the two weeks he'd just spent there in Boston with her, he'd gotten used to that shocking contact every time he left the warmth of her bed.

Now, he had one of the biggest international deals of his life to prepare for, and all he could think about was getting back to that warmth.

He raked his fingers through his hair. Pressed the heels of his palms against his eyes.

It wasn't even just the sex. It was *her.*

But they had a deal. A deal of his own freaking making. And even if he had the guts to change the terms of the deal, why would she want to once she knew the whole truth about him and her sacred institute?

He muttered an oath, returned to the couch and snatched up the top file. But when the doorbell chimed a short while later, he was no more interested in the contents than he'd ever been.

He tossed it aside and went to the door. Cynthia was supposed to deliver one more report from his legal department, but he'd figured she wouldn't get it to him until morning. He yanked open the door.

It wasn't his wholly efficient and cantankerous assistant at all. It was his wife. As if he'd conjured her there by his thoughts, alone.

He frowned. She had circles under her eyes and her lips were practically colorless. "Lisa. What's wrong?"

"I didn't know where else to go."

The admission sent a jolt through him. He took her arms and pulled her inside. "You're not even wearing a coat." Just a familiar-looking ivory sweater that nearly drowned her to the knees of her narrow blue jeans.

She looked down at herself, as if surprised. "I…I

guess I forgot it on the plane." Then she chewed the inside of her cheek and warily looked around him. "Are... are you alone?"

His jaw tightened. She knew his body almost as well as he did; and he, hers. But she trusted him so little that she had to ask such a question? "It's nearly midnight. Who would I be with?"

Her lashes fell. "I don't know. I'm sorry." She shook her head and the strands of hair falling out of her messy knot clung to her cheek. "I found out today that my father had an affair," she said baldly.

He swallowed an oath, his frustration fizzling. "No wonder you look shell-shocked." He steered her from the foyer into the living room. "Sit." He shoved aside the mountain of paperwork on the couch. "I'll get you something hot to drink."

She was still sitting there, staring at the unadorned windows, when he returned. "Here." He closed her cold hands around the thick, white mug as he sat down on the coffee table in front of her. "Drink. It's coffee and probably too strong."

She lifted the mug. Took a ginger sip and winced. "Really strong."

"It's been sitting on the burner a while," he admitted. Ignored just as much as his Scotch had been. "Now, talk."

She drew in a deep, shuddering breath. "My father had an affair with Grace O'Connell. Sara Beth's mother. About twenty-nine years ago. Supposedly it ended almost as quickly as it began." She twisted the mug back and forth between her fingers. "He, um, he worked with her. She was the head nurse at the institute for years."

"How'd you find out about this now?"

"Sara Beth told me." Her jaw flexed. "Turns out that she's my sister and I accused her of lying to me."

"Obviously, she wasn't."

She shook her head. Looked upward and blinked hard. "I went to my parents. I didn't even need to see the guilt on my father's face. All I had to see was the iciness on my mother's." She looked at Rourke and the pain in her eyes made him ache. "Oh, God, I don't want to be like her."

He took the mug from her hands and set it aside. "Your mother isn't all bad." He closed his hands around hers, rubbing heat into them. "She raised you."

"Right. She raised Derek, too, and look how well *that* turned out."

His thumbs moved in circles against her wrists. He couldn't think about Derek. Not without thinking about his own secrets. "And Paul," he reminded her. "And Olivia."

"And she ostracized Sara Beth, who didn't do anything to deserve it. I don't know who to blame. My mother for driving him to another woman, or my father, for being so—" She shook her head. "I can't even come up with a word for it."

"Imperfect?" Rourke kept his voice mild. "Honey, don't forget that this all happened before you were born. What bothers you more? The fact that your best friend is not just a sister of your heart? Or the fact that she's proof that your father is more human than saint?"

"I don't know." She folded forward, pressing her forehead to her wrists.

His hands moved from hers to cradle her head, his fingers tunneling gently through her hair, loosening it from the band that wasn't doing a very good job. "It was a long time ago. And it has nothing to do with the way he was a father to you."

"And not a father to Sara Beth at all," she mumbled. "The only thing he did was ensure that when she retired, Grace was financially set."

"Did she want more than that?"

"She refused to take any sort of support from him. But he should have done better." She looked up. "Why don't you ever talk about *your* father?"

"The only thing that made Jack Devlin my father was his DNA." Rourke sat back. His voice was even. Entirely devoid of emotion. "He was a bastard and when he decided he wasn't interested in being a husband or a father, he locked us out of our own home and that was that. There's no point in talking about someone who, as far as I'm concerned, doesn't even exist."

"And your sisters?"

"Feel the same way."

"I'm sorry."

"Be sorry for my mother. She's the one who had to fight just to keep us all together."

"She did a tremendous job. Look at you." She didn't have to gesture to their palatial surroundings to make her point. It was evident in the man he was.

While she sat there, having denied her best friend and hiding the fact from her husband that she was very likely pregnant.

Maybe she was worse than her mother.

She stared at Rourke, the words that would probably have him routing out the manager of the nearest baby store to open it up for him, even if it was the middle of the night, jamming in her throat.

"Hey." He ran his thumb down her cheek. "It will work out."

That was what everyone seemed to keep saying. But he didn't know what she suspected.

"You've been friends with Sara Beth a lot longer than you've known she's your half sister," he went on. "You'll get past the shock. You'll talk. If the fights my own sisters have are any indication, you'll end up closer than ever when the dust is settled."

Her nose prickled. Her eyes burned. This man who'd manipulated her into marriage was way too good for her. "I'm…I mean I think I—" Her voice strangled to a halt.

"I think you just need a break." He pulled her to her feet, and she was too numb to resist. "Stay here for a few days if you need to. You'll have plenty of peace and quiet since I'll be leaving in the morning. You'll let the shock settle and you'll head back into it with everything you've got, just like you always do."

She looked up at him.

He was the same man whose intensity had been as captivating as it had been terrifying.

"Make love to me," she whispered.

His sharp gaze went even sharper and afraid that he'd see too much and what he'd see would be found wanting, she pressed herself against him. Slid her hands up into the thick, slippery black silk of his hair. "Right here." She brushed her lips over his earlobe. When the heels of her boots hit the floor again, she caught the way his lashes had lowered. The way his jaw was flexed. "Right now."

His hands closed around her waist. Slid up her spine. Down again. "Is this my sweater?"

"Yes."

A faint, low sound seemed to rumble around his chest.

And then his mouth was on hers and the taste of him filled her senses.

She was reeling when he finally lifted his head. His fingers twisted through hers and he led her through the penthouse until they reached his bedroom. And there, he undressed her slowly. Carefully. As if she were a precious package to be unwrapped.

And then when he was as bare as she, when there was nothing between them but her secret and he pressed her back onto the bed and his lips found hers again while his hands began playing her like a delicate instrument, she knew that whatever the future held, when it came to Rourke and her heart, she was utterly lost.

Chapter 13

"Do you remember the first time we danced?"

"How could I forget the Founder's Ball?" Lisa kept a pleasant smile on her face in honor of the photographer who stood to one side of the dance floor, capturing Rourke's image for posterity.

They were the first of the couples ceremoniously circling the dance floor in the Grand Ballroom of the Waldorf Astoria. Dinner had been served, speeches delivered, and Rourke—disarmingly deprecating over the honor—had received his philanthropic award.

The crystal globe signifying his worldwide efforts was now waiting at their empty table.

"It was the *only* time we danced," she reminded him.

Until now. And eight weeks of marriage to the man didn't make him any less disturbing to her senses.

If anything, he was more so, now that she knew for certain she was carrying his child.

While he'd been in London and she'd been essentially hiding out in his penthouse, she'd finally taken a home pregnancy test. Twice.

There was no question that she was pregnant.

"You looked very beautiful that night." His voice drew her thoughts out of darkness, the way it always seemed to. "As I recall, not thrilled that I'd crashed the party, though."

"And you were very objectionable that night." She managed a dulcet smile. "As I recall."

His lips twitched. His hand drifted dangerously low over the back of her black column dress. "Verbal sparring with you is almost as much fun as—"

"Don't even say it," she warned. "Not when your mother is dancing three yards away from us with Griffin Harper." Grif's wife, Nora, was sitting at one of the round crystal-laden banquet tables chatting with Rourke's sisters.

"As beautiful as you were that night—" he pressed his mouth close to her ear "—you're even more so tonight. But I can't wait to get you out this dress."

Anticipation dripped through her, measured equally by anxiety. That was what happened when you were afraid to tell your husband that his heart's desire had come true.

Her fingers trembled as they grazed over the fine black wool covering his shoulder. "We can't leave yet. You, um, you should dance with Nina and your sisters."

"That's nowhere near as much fun."

An unexpected smile hit her lips. "I hope not."

But almost as if he'd heard them, Griffin danced next to them. "Shall we change partners?"

Rourke gave her a look that had her nerve endings

dancing as he handed her off to the older man, and took his mother sedately across the dance floor.

"I think we could power the city for a few nights on the energy you two give off," Griffin commented. "It's obvious you're very happy together."

Lisa just smiled, not quite knowing how to respond to that. "This is quite an event you put on here."

"In this world, it seems we have to shell out money to bring even more in." He smiled ruefully. "Nora considers this quite a dog and pony show. Hates it more every year."

Lisa glanced toward his wife. "How is she feeling?"

His smile dimmed a little. "As well as we can expect. Fortunately, she still has more good days than bad."

Lisa could hardly bear it that this man was so in love with his wife, but was going to lose her in the end. "I'm glad to have this opportunity to see you both again."

Griffin chuckled. "Oh, my dear, as time passes, you'll probably get heartily tired of us popping in and out of your and Rourke's lives."

Her throat went tight. Her time in Rourke's life as his wife would be up all too soon.

She forced a smile and shook her head. "Nobody could get tired of either one of you."

Fortunately, the orchestra was concluding their song, and taking advantage of the break, Lisa excused herself, taking a quick break to the ladies' room where she managed, by dint of a little blush and gloss, to look much livelier than she felt. She adjusted one of the tiny, sparkling pins that held her mass of waves away from her face and brushed her hands down the front of her dress. Aside from the bodice fitting more snugly across her bust, there was no visible evidence of the changes going on inside her.

But she wasn't so confident that would be true once Rourke had her wearing nothing at all.

She returned to the ballroom where the orchestra was in full swing again, and Rourke was on the dance floor with Tricia. His sisters and their spouses were dancing, too, and she returned to her seat at their empty table.

She traced the golden imprint of Rourke's name on the base of the globe-shaped award.

Who was this man she'd married?

Generous philanthropist.

Powerful, corporate Midas.

Father of the baby growing inside her.

Man whom she'd impossibly fallen for.

"Excuse me, Mrs. Devlin?"

She looked up to see a young, petite blonde standing next to the table. "Yes?"

The girl smiled, looking vaguely familiar, and held out her hand. "I'm Victoria Welsh. I'm, well, I'm—"

"Ramona's sister," Lisa inserted. Of course, the resemblance was to her brother's fiancée. She was ridiculously grateful to have something else to focus on and she clasped the other woman's hand.

Victoria smiled faintly. "Yes. I'm afraid that fact still seems strange to me, even after all these months."

Lisa could well imagine. Victoria had been conceived using donor eggs through the institute. Ramona had been desperate to find a donor for her gravely ill mother, and it had forced her to use extraordinary tactics to find one when she'd learned her mother had once donated eggs to the institute. "I know how grateful Ramona is to you. And her mother, too." Not only had Ramona found Victoria, but she'd fallen in love with Paul. And Lisa knew her brother had never been happier.

Victoria waved a slender hand. "I'm just glad I was a suitable donor match for Katherine," she dismissed. "Finding a family I didn't even know I had is…quite remarkable. But I don't want to intrude on your evening. I just wanted to say hello. I know you're going to be Ramona's sister-in-law once she and Paul get married."

"Christmas Eve. You'll be there, won't you?" She knew that Ramona was hoping so.

"I'm planning on it." The younger woman tucked a lock of pretty blond hair behind her ear. She glanced toward one side. "I'd better get back to my date, though." She rolled her eyes a little. "An old friend, but if he gets bored, I'm afraid his hands will start wandering to one of the servers."

"Then you can do better," Lisa advised.

"Oh, we're not serious." Victoria's gaze went to the dance floor for a moment. "There just needs to be more men around like your husband." She smiled again. "Enjoy the rest of your evening and please tell Ramona that I said hello."

"I will." Lisa watched the girl gracefully weave through the tables until she reached a sulky-looking guy about her own age.

"Do you know Victoria Welsh?" Nora Harper slipped into the chair beside her. She looked brilliant in a royal-blue gown that set off her striking, silver hair. "The Welsh family have always been such good supporters of the foundation."

"I've just met her tonight."

"Ah. Well, she was always such a sweet child." Nora

gently squeezed Lisa's bare arm. "Have you been enjoying yourself?"

"It's a lovely event. And the setting—" She lifted her shoulders. "I can't imagine any location being more beautiful."

"It is quite grand." Nora watched the dancers circling around the floor. "Though, honestly, next year I'm going to insist that Griffin get a more lively orchestra. All we've heard tonight have been waltzes." She gave Lisa such a mischievous look that she couldn't help but smile. "Bo-ring."

"I think everyone here figures it's classic," she confided softly.

"How tasteful of you, dear." Nora patted her arm again. "Now go rescue your husband and take him out of here."

"But it's still early." Rourke was pretty much the guest of honor. It was a much better excuse than that she was afraid he would realize sooner rather than later what she hadn't told him since those little pregnancy test sticks had turned pink.

"Nonsense." Nora waved that off. "You're newly-weds. Anybody who expects you to hang around a stodgy awards dinner like this has just forgotten what it feels like to be young and in love."

Young and in love.

The phrase circled in Lisa's mind.

It might describe her, but she knew it didn't describe Rourke.

And how badly she wished that it did. If he loved her, they could have a future together. A real future. A real family instead of legal documents and visitation rights.

But she didn't argue with Nora. She knew full well

that Rourke was anxious to get out of there, and with Nora watching so benevolently, she didn't have any logical alternative.

So she wound her way through the dancers and patted Tricia on the shoulder, forcing a cheerfulness that she was eons from feeling. "Can I play fast and easy with traditional roles and cut in?"

Tricia grinned, quickly surrendering her brother. "Be my guest. Rourkey hasn't talked about anything but you, anyway." She winked and hurried off the dance floor.

"Couldn't stay away?" Rourke pulled her back into his arms.

It was more true than he knew. "I have permission from the hostess herself that you've been such a good boy, you can now be excused from the dinner table."

"Thank God. I've never hated traveling so much as I have this past week." His grin was decidedly unboyish as he immediately stopped dancing and herded her toward the nearest exit.

"What about your award?"

"My mother will grab it," he assured her. "And add it to the wall of shame at the house."

"I need my coat," she reminded him when it seemed as if he intended to forget that fact, too, in his rush to escape.

He veered the other way. Stopped at the coat check and gave the girl a tip along with the stub. Two minutes later, he was swinging her cashmere cape around her shoulders and they were on their way out into the chilly night air.

He didn't even bother to call for his driver, but hustled her into the first cab that came by. "Some people might consider your hastiness very unseemly," she pointed out.

"I don't have designs on some people," he returned.

She smiled faintly and rubbed her palm against his and felt the faint clink of her wedding ring against his. "It's been a perfect evening," she admitted softly. "I wish I didn't have to go back to Boston tomorrow." For that entire week, she'd hidden out in Rourke's penthouse, doing her work as best she could from the safe distance of knowing she didn't have to face Sara Beth, or anyone else.

"You still haven't talked with Sara Beth."

Lisa's throat tightened. "No."

"It's only going to get harder the longer you let it go."

"Anxious for me to go home?"

His hand tightened around hers. "No. As far as I'm concerned, you can just stay here."

There was an intensity in his voice that made her heart catch. "I've played coward long enough. I know that as well as you. And I can't let it keep getting in the way of work. I need to pull my own weight there."

"You don't *have* to work."

"The institute is who I am."

"Who you are is my wife." His thumb ran along her wrist. Pressed against the pulse that was fluttering uncontrollably. "Being the administrator there is what you do."

"It's my career." She was reminding herself just as much as him. "It's important to me."

"And you're important to me."

Her mouth went dry.

Even in the dim light of the cab, she could see the seriousness in his gaze. "Because of the agreement we have." It was a wonder he couldn't hear the ponderous thudding of her heart.

"Because of you."

She couldn't breathe. "Rourke—"

"Meter's still running, folks."

She blinked, realizing the cab had stopped in front of Rourke's building. Even Rourke had seemed oblivious to that fact.

He paid the driver and stepped out of the cab, holding her hand to help her out.

She had a dizzying flashback to the day of their wedding, when she'd stepped out of the limousine almost in this exact spot.

He'd kissed her, crushing her bouquet of flowers. The photograph that had caught them at that moment was still being splashed all over the news outlets, blasting their "fairy-tale" marriage.

And how true that fairy-tale term was.

Because fairy tales didn't come true.

"Lisa?" Rourke's hands closed over her shoulders. "You all right?"

She stared into his face. "I need to tell—"

"Lisa."

She jerked away from the hand that touched her from behind, sinking deeper against Rourke's chest even as she recognized the man who'd spoken. "Derek," she gasped.

He looked terrible.

Always thinner than the more athletically built Paul, he looked more like a walking skeleton than the brother she knew. His dark hair had unfamiliar strands of silver in it, there were sunken circles beneath his brown eyes, and his coat looked as if it was barely hanging on his frame.

"Armstrong. What the hell are you doing here?" Rourke was tucking her practically behind him.

But Derek wasn't so easily waylaid. He angled to the side, his eyes fastened on Lisa. "I've been watching the building all night waiting for you. I've been calling you for months."

Rourke shifted. Blocking Derek again. "And she hasn't called you back. Take the hint."

"Stay out of this, Devlin. This is between me and my sister."

"You mean my *wife*," Rourke reminded him and there was such loathing in his voice that it penetrated even Lisa's shock.

"That's right. Your wife." Derek suddenly focused on Rourke. "Is that why you don't want me to talk to Lisa so badly? I'm sure you're the one who's kept her from returning my calls. Or haven't you told her about our history?"

"The only thing I care about is you upsetting Lisa." Rourke's voice was flat. Deadly.

She avoided the arm he was using to shield her from Derek. "Rourke hasn't kept me from anything. What history?"

Derek shot her a glance. "I just needed to talk to you. Try to explain. Tell you I was sor—"

"*What* history!" Her voice rose. Even Louis, the doorman of Rourke's building, gave her an alarmed look from across the wide sidewalk. And she could see Tom, the intimidating night security guard, striding through the well-lit lobby toward the door.

Rourke's hands closed over her shoulders. "It's old news. It doesn't matter anymore."

"Right." Derek's face tightened. "When Taylor left you, you said there'd be a day I'd live to regret it."

"Taylor!" Her stomach clenching hard, Lisa looked from Rourke to Derek and back again. "What about your ex-wife?"

"Well?" Derek glared at Rourke. "Are you going to tell her or not?"

She twisted out from beneath Rourke's hands. "Tell me what?"

Rourke's jaw was practically white. "It has nothing to do with us—"

"Taylor had an affair with me," Derek inserted flatly. "We met when she was coming to the institute six years ago, trying to get pregnant with the kid *he* wanted."

Lisa's head felt light. Her stomach dipped woozily.

"Only it turned out that *she* wasn't the one with the problem," Derek added. His gaze was on Rourke again. "Did you want to get back at the institute for discovering the fact that you were shooting blanks all along, or did you just want to get back at me because Taylor decided she preferred my bed to yours?"

"She must not have preferred it for long," Rourke said curtly. "Judging by how quickly she moved on from it. She'd dumped you even before the ink on our divorce decree dried."

"Rourke's not infertile," Lisa inserted faintly.

Derek's lip curled, not listening to her any more than Rourke was. "But you never got over it, did you? You took the first chance that came along to get your revenge. You married my sister. You sank so much money into the institute we might as well take down the Armstrong part and put up Devlin in its place."

"And why did the institute need the money in the first place?" Rourke wasn't quite as tall as Derek, but he was far more powerfully built. And when he took a step toward Derek, her brother actually took a step back.

It didn't seem possible that they could come to blows but Rourke's hands were fisted and so were Derek's.

Lisa's mind was reeling, but she quickly wormed her way between them. "Stop it!"

"Stay out of the way." Derek's hand started to push her to one side.

"Don't touch her." With one arm, Rourke scooped her out of the way as he planted his other hand on Derek's chest. He shoved him back a solid two feet.

Derek caught himself from stumbling and advanced again. "You think I want to hurt her? She's my sister! I'm not the one using her to get back at me," he reminded him.

He finally looked at Lisa. "Yeah. I've made some mistakes. Big ones. But I'm finally getting help and facing my gambling and the drugs. I've been in rehab for the past two months. I'm trying to make things right again. While *he*—" he jerked his head toward Rourke "—is just using the situation for revenge.

"He warned me then that I'd live to regret crossing him. I never believed he'd wait all these years to prove it. But now he's got you shackled to him. Probably convincing you to stay away from the institute, even. Keep you busy so you wouldn't notice him taking it over right under our noses!"

"Stop." Lisa covered her ears, though it didn't stop the sounds of everything crumbling around her. Nausea rose in her throat and she struggled to stop it. "You're not part of the institute anymore, Derek. You gave up that right when you nearly ruined us!"

"Everything all right, Mr. Devlin?" The security guard, looking very uptight and very large, stopped next to them. His hand was on his radio, almost as if he wished it were a weapon. "If this guy's bothering you, I can—"

"It's fine, Tom." Rourke didn't take his eyes off Lisa's brother, not trusting him for a second. It was taking everything he possessed not to pound his fist into the other man's face and only the fact that the weasel *was* Lisa's brother was preventing him from doing just that. "Go back inside."

Tom gave Derek a hard glare, but he finally turned on his heel and returned to the building. He didn't go inside, however. Just stopped at the doorway next to Louis and folded his arms across his chest, clearly intending to bar Derek from the building, if the need arose.

"How'd you know I was in New York?" Lisa's face was pale and pinched.

"Ella told me." Derek made a face. "She said you'd been here for the past week."

"Paul knew."

"I wanted to see you first. Before I saw Paul."

Lisa swayed as if the words were a physical blow and Rourke tried to reach for her again, but she held him off just as surely as she was keeping away from her brother.

His gut tightened. He should have told her everything. He'd known it and now it was too late. She'd never believe him now. "Princess, don't let him get to you."

She fastened her glittering gaze on him. "Then tell me none of it is true." She made a visible effort to stop her lips from trembling. "Tell me he wasn't the one your wife cheated on you with. That you and Taylor were never involved at the institute before now."

He wished he could. And not because of Taylor, he knew. But because of the pain on Lisa's face.

Her lips twisted at his silence. "So. That's what it was all really about." A tear slid down her cheek, catching the light from the streetlamp as clearly as a diamond.

And the sight of it cut through him as surely as glass.

He took a step toward her. "No, that's not what this is about."

She gave him a disbelieving look. "You didn't find a whole lot of satisfaction knowing that it was *his* sister who was going to have to give you the child you wanted?" She waved at her brother. "The child your ex-wife didn't give you?" Her voice cracked.

"More like the child he *couldn't* give her," Derek corrected, cuttingly. "That's what they learned at the institute." He gave Rourke a goading look. "Taylor wanted me to get her pregnant, you know. As soon as the test results came back confirming that you couldn't cut it, she even suggested burying the results. Said she could pass the baby off as yours. Seeing as how the kid would probably be your only heir." His lips twisted. "All that money to inherit. It was the one thing about you that she really didn't want to give up."

Lisa's hand flashed out and she slapped her brother's face.

Derek slowly lifted a hand to the red mark she'd left on his cheek. He looked pained. "Lisa, I just wanted you to know the truth. I'm not trying to hurt you."

"No," she said thickly, "you've done enough of that, already, haven't you? And not just me. But Paul and… and everyone else at the institute. We would have had to close our doors if not for Rourke."

"Are you really going to paint him as some hero?"

Lisa laughed, but there was no humor in it. Only a deep dark pain that made Rourke ache inside, knowing that Derek wasn't the only reason it was there.

Rourke was responsible for plenty of it.

"Everybody has had secrets," she told them both. Or

neither one in particular. "But they always come out."
She looked at Derek. "If you're really trying to get better, then I...I wish you luck. But as far as what went on
with you and Taylor and the institute, obviously, someone was mistaken about Rourke."

She slanted her gaze to Rourke. More diamond-sharp
tears glittered on her lashes. "Otherwise, I wouldn't be
pregnant with your baby now, would I?"

Her words jerked through him. "You're pregnant?"

Her chin lifted. "Yes. So we can put an end to this
whole charade even sooner than I'd hoped."

His hands went out toward her, but she sidled out of
his reach, holding the folds of her cape closely, protectively, around her body.

"There was no mistake." Derek's voice reminded
Rourke that he was still there. "I saw the test results, myself. Dr. Adams was on staff then. He met with Rourke
and Taylor after hours. Kept everything nice and hush-hush and off the books so nobody would suspect that the
Midas-boy and his beautiful wife were having trouble
in the baby department. Rourke couldn't have gotten
anyone pregnant."

Rourke eyed the other man. He'd always wondered
how he'd feel, facing the man who'd been the final ruination of his marriage to Taylor, and knew the murderous anger inside him now had nothing to do with old
history. It had everything to do with the here and now.
With the fear of losing the woman he'd never expected
to love. "I'm going to give you twenty seconds to get
the bloody...hell...out...of...here."

"I'm not leaving until Lisa tells me to go."

Lisa looked straight at him. "Go."

Rourke could almost have felt a little sorry for the man if he weren't so close to wanting to kill him.

Derek's face fell. He nodded. "For what it's worth, Lis, I am sorry." Then he turned on his heel, holding his coat close around his skinny body, and disappeared around the corner of the building.

Lisa looked at Rourke. "You're the subject in Ted's study." There was no question in her voice. Only realization.

His hands curled at his sides. The truth. But it was too little. And way too late. "Yes."

She pressed her lips together. Her lashes swept down, hiding her eyes. Another gleaming tear was slowly creeping down her cheek. Her shoulders moved.

Then she suddenly lifted her head. Swiped her hand down her cheek. No longer was there an ocean of warmth in her eyes. No pain. No…anything.

Except ice.

"Then I guess you and Doctors Bonner and Demetrios all have reason to celebrate." She swept her cape more securely around her and looked over her shoulder toward the door. "Louis—" she raised her voice so the doorman could hear "—would you please hail a cab for me?"

"Yes, ma'am." Louis grabbed his whistle and headed toward the curb.

Rourke wanted to grab her. Keep her from going. But he feared that if he did, she would shatter. And he had nobody but himself to blame. "Where are you going?"

She didn't so much as look at him again. "Home."

Chapter 14

"All right." Lisa tucked her pen back into her portfolio and looked around the boardroom table at the members of institute's management team gathered there. "Thank you all for coming this morning. Let's all have a good week." She smiled as everyone began filing out of the meeting, though she felt nothing.

Had felt absolutely nothing since every hopeful dream she might have felt where her marriage was concerned had died an ugly death on the cold sidewalk outside of Rourke's beautiful apartment. She hadn't cared about the curious looks her formal gown had gotten when she'd managed to catch a late plane home to Boston. Hadn't been interested in the lights blinking on her message machine when she'd let herself into her chilly, dark town house.

When that morning had rolled around and she'd automatically prepared for work, arriving at the institute well before it opened, she hadn't even worried whether or not she might run into Sara Beth.

Her body was on autopilot. Anything but focusing on what needed to be done at the institute was cordoned off in another part of her brain.

And that was just the way Lisa wanted it.

"You going to sit in here all morning and stare at the walls?"

She blinked and looked toward the doorway. Sara Beth was standing there, wearing a pair of deep blue scrubs.

Lisa folded her portfolio with a snap and pushed out of her chair. She headed to the door, prepared to walk past Sara Beth, but Sara Beth stepped right in her path. "I'm not going to let you avoid me forever," she said bluntly.

"I'm not avoiding you."

Sara Beth's eyebrows shot up. "Could have fooled me." Her gaze was assessing. "You look terrible."

"Blame it on morning sickness."

Sara Beth's lips parted softly. "You *are* pregnant." She couldn't seem to help herself as she touched Lisa's arm. "Do I give you congratulations, or—"

"Congratulate your husband and Dr. Demetrios." Lisa stopped her before she could bring up Rourke. "Since they're the ones responsible for it. If either one of them had been present at our management meeting, I would have congratulated them myself."

Sara Beth's brows drew together. "What are you talking about?"

"Ted hasn't told you?" A tremble entered her voice and Lisa quickly plugged the trickle in the emotions she'd carefully dammed away. "About the study he and Chance have been working on?"

"You mean the sperm motility thing?"

"Rourke's been the study subject. If their success with him can be replicated, Bonner and Demetrios are going to make this institute famous all over again."

"Lisa." Sara Beth caught her arm as she slipped past her. "I swear to you. I didn't know Rourke was the one."

"That makes two of us." She started to turn away, only to stop. "About the stuff I said—"

"You were upset," Sara Beth said quickly. "And my timing couldn't have been worse."

"The timing shouldn't have mattered." She mentally shoved a fist into another trickle. "I know you were just trying to be honest. If anything, we all should be taking lessons from you in that regard."

"That's not true," Sara Beth dismissed. "What about Rourke? You've told him?"

"Yes." The trickle was in danger of becoming a deluge. She deliberately stepped away from Sara Beth, aiming blindly for the elevator down the hall. "I've got to get back to my office. I have a conference call in a few minutes." It was a bald lie. She wouldn't know what was on her calendar if she'd had it opened in front of her.

"What did he say?" Sara Beth trotted after her.

"There was nothing for him to say." Not even with Sara Beth, not even now, after all the secrets, the half-truths, could she bring herself to tell her what part she'd really played in Rourke's plan. She jabbed her finger viciously into the call button and the elevator doors immediately slid open. "He wanted an heir. He's getting one."

Sara Beth stepped into the elevator with her. "You didn't tell him you loved him."

Lisa looked up at the floor display above the door. The numbers wavered, like a wave of heat was shimmering in front of them. She blinked. The shimmer disappeared. "No point. I know exactly what Rourke wants." Her crisp voice cracked. "It is *not* me."

"Then he's a fool," Sara Beth said quietly. "What can I do?"

Another trickle broke through the dam. Lisa shored it up as best she could. "Just…be my friend."

Sara Beth nodded. Her eyes were moist but her gaze was steady. "Always."

Lisa smiled shakily. "Be my sister."

Sara Beth's nose turned pink. "Always." She reached out. Caught Lisa's hand and squeezed it.

A faint sob sneaked out of Lisa's throat. She coughed, trying—failing—to cover it.

Sara Beth laughed, just as brokenly. "What, um, whatever happened to the birthday invitations?"

The elevator reached the first floor and Lisa dashed her hand over her cheeks, stepping out. The waiting room beyond the receptionist's desk was already full of patients. "I dumped them back on my mother's desk to deal with."

Sara Beth looked surprised. "Well." A dimple flirted in her cheek. "Good for you."

"Yeah. Except it'll be all my fault if nobody shows up at the birthday party for Dad—" She broke off.

"It's okay," Sara Beth assured her.

Lisa exhaled. "Only because you are extraordinary."

"Stop." Sara Beth slid her finger beneath her lashes. "You'll make my mascara run and we've got a load of patients today. D'you, um, want to meet for lunch?"

It was such an ordinary thing. That meant so very much. Lisa nodded, unable to speak.

And Sara Beth seemed to know it. "I'll swing by your office then," she said.

Lisa nodded. She turned quickly to get back *to* her office before the dam could burst entirely and she'd start bawling in the corridor where anyone and their mother's brother could witness the flood.

But as she turned, the overhead lights seemed to tilt alarmingly. And all she could do was say "Sara Beth?" as the ground slid sideways and she went right along with it.

"She's coming around now."

Lisa groaned, pressing her hand against the throbbing pain at the back of her head. She opened her eyes and found herself surrounded. Paul. Chance. Sara Beth. Even Wilma, the institute's devoted receptionist, was hovering over her, looking worried. "What happened?" Her fingers gingerly felt around the knot on her head.

"You fainted," Sara Beth said.

"Nearly gave me a heart attack," Wilma added. "One minute you were standing there. The next we all heard your head cracking against the floor."

"Speaking of which," Paul said, "an ice pack would be good."

"I'll get it." Wilma hurried out of the room and Lisa realized they were all crowded into one of Chance's examining rooms.

She worked her arms behind her, trying to sit up, but Paul held her in place with a firm hand on her shoulder. "Just be still for a while longer." He flashed a penlight over one of her eyes. Then the other. "You hit your head pretty hard."

"I'm fine now." She stared at the ceiling lights over his head. No wavering. No nauseating shifting.

"Sara Beth told us you're pregnant." Her brother eyed Chance. "Dr. Demetrios is going to examine you. Just to be safe."

"All I did was get a little dizzy. And I know how busy Chance's schedule is without having to slide me in, too."

"I think he'll manage. Don't be a bad patient," Paul advised, his lips tilting. "Sets a bad example." He stepped out of the way. "Let me know what you find," he told Chance as he left.

Her brother was a fine doctor, but she was glad that he wasn't the one planning to examine her. She looked up at Sara Beth and Chance. "I really don't want to make a fuss."

"It's here or the hospital," Chance said. "Your choice." He smiled faintly when she made a face.

"Here you go, dear." Wilma hurried in with an instant ice pack that she was already shaking to activate. She handed it to Lisa and quickly exited again.

"Help her get into a gown," Chance advised, and he, too, left the small room.

"Come on." Sara Beth pulled a clean gown out of a cabinet and set it on the examining table next to Lisa's legs. She held the ice pack against the back of Lisa's head as she sat up and began undoing the buttons on her blouse.

"How long was I out?"

"Long enough to have everyone worried." Sara Beth took Lisa's blouse and bra when she slid them off and handed her the cotton gown. "You didn't even come to when I did a blood draw."

Lisa stared at her arm, noticing for the first time the little adhesive bandage holding a wad of cotton in the fold of her elbow. An exam maybe wasn't such a bad idea.

She slid gingerly off the table and toed off her pumps, then slid off her wide-legged pants. She realized that they were the pants she'd worn the day she'd met Rourke at Fare.

Her chest squeezed. She finished undressing and yanked the thin gown together, trying not to shiver in the room that, until that moment, had seemed overly warm.

"I need to get a chart started for you. I'll be right back." Sara Beth handed her the ice pack and let herself out of the examining room.

Lisa sat on the table, holding the pack against the back of her head, and looked down at the cotton crumpled across her belly. "Don't be scaring us like this," she whispered.

Then Sara Beth came back, asking about a hundred questions as she began filling out the medical chart. She took Lisa's blood pressure. Waved her out into the empty hall between examining rooms and made her stand on the scale. Then back into the room again. "I'll get Chance."

Sara Beth returned with the doctor within minutes and Lisa found herself answering a good portion of the questions that Sara Beth had already asked. By the time Chance finished examining her, she knew firsthand just how thorough the man was.

"Everything looks good," he said, when he took the chart from Sara Beth and began scribbling on it. "We'll schedule you for an ultrasound week after next. I think you're too early yet to have a good result. You'll start on prenatal vitamins immediately." He slanted a stern look at her. "And you'll beef up your diet. You're too thin." He tore off a page from his prescription pad and handed it to her. "I think our biggest concern is the conk on your head. So don't be alone for the next twenty-four hours. Dizziness. Vision problems. Nausea. Watch for them. And obviously call me immediately if you start spotting or cramping."

"I'll stay with you," Sara Beth offered even before Lisa could form a protest about the twenty-four-hour bit.

"Otherwise—" he grinned at her "—congratulations, Mom."

Lisa smile weakly. He was clearly aware that his and Ted's treatment of Rourke had led to her pregnancy. "Thanks." She folded the prescription into neat halves after he left. "I don't need help getting dressed, Sara Beth. This place is busting at the seams with patients. Paying ones."

"True enough. I'll just nip next door for a sec. If you get dizzy again, lie down." Sara Beth closed the file folder and took it with her.

Lisa slid off the table. The only thing plaguing her was the dull throb in her head but even that had begun to ease. She pushed the gown into the basket in the corner for just that purpose, and began dressing again. She was just buttoning up her blouse when she heard the door crack open. "I'm fine, Sara Beth," she said, without looking. "Go see your next patient."

"It's not Sara Beth."

She started so violently, the tiny pearl button she was

trying to slip through the hole pulled off right in her hand. She rounded on her heel to face Rourke.

He looked dreadful. As if he hadn't slept in days. His face was lined. His charcoal suit was wrinkled and his tie was hanging askew.

"What are you doing here?"

"Ted called me. Said you'd fainted."

She steeled herself against feeling anything. "Convenient that you were in town, then." Her voice was cool.

"I wasn't." His gaze was roving over her. "I was at my office." His lips twisted. "Not that I was doing anything productive there. What happened?"

She looked at the clock on the wall. If he'd only left since Ted had called him, he'd made the fastest commute from New York to Boston known to man. "I got dizzy." She turned her back on him to finish buttoning her blouse. It was probably ludicrous, considering the man knew her body even better than she did, but it still made her feel better. "Don't worry. Your investment is still secure."

"Don't." His voice was low. Rough. "Don't act like that's all this is to me. You know better."

The throbbing in her chest outdid the throbbing in her head by a mile. She couldn't do anything about the missing button just above the low band at the center of her bra, so she left the two above it open, as well. She shoved the silk shirttails into her pants and began fastening the wide belt. "I certainly know enough." She pushed her feet into her pumps and turned to face him, feeling more armored with her clothing intact. "Now, that is."

"You don't know that I fell in love with you."

She'd underestimated his ability to hurt her any more

than she was already hurting. And the blow of that shook her through to her soul.

She couldn't move forward to the door to escape the small room without brushing against him. So she did the only thing she could do. "You don't have to lie to me now, Rourke. You've got what you wanted. You've pulverized an Armstrong like you were pulverized and in less than eight months, you'll have the heir you'd feared you'd never have. All in a day's work for you. Well. I guess a few weeks more than a day. But still—" her lips twisted "—well done."

"I haven't got what I want. I haven't got you."

Her heart felt as if it was splintering. "What more do you want from us?" The ice in her voice was breaking into chunks. "Derek was right. You own more of the Armstrong Fertility Institute now than any of the Armstrongs do. What else is left for you to take?"

"I'm not trying to take anything. For the first time in a long time, I'm trying to give something!" His voice rose and he exhaled through his clenched teeth. He yanked an envelope out of his lapel pocket and tossed it on the end of the leather-covered examining table. "There. Take it. Do whatever the hell you want with it."

She stared at the envelope as if it was a snake. "What is it?"

"The prenup."

A snake, indeed. But she snatched up the envelope anyway. Pulled out the lengthy document that had outlined the terms of their agreement. She tossed it back on the table. "I'm sure you have copies."

"Is there nothing that you can let yourself trust me about?" His voice was tight. "That's the original. The only copy. You can tear it up. Walk away from me. Take half of everything I've ever worked for, but you're not going to do it without knowing the truth."

"Truth!" Her arms lifted. "I learned the truth on the sidewalk outside your building last night! I was the perfect tool for you, wasn't I? Dedicated-to-the-institute Lisa. Who'd do anything to keep her father's legacy alive, even though her father turns out to be as fallible as the rest of us. Who was too backward when it came to men to realize just how well she was being played. What an ideal setup it was for you, and you didn't even have to chase it down. *I* came to *you!*"

"I should have told you about Taylor and your brother. About everything. Including the treatment." His voice sounded like gravel. "But in the beginning, it didn't matter. And in the end, it mattered too much."

"Stop." She lifted her hand. "The day we got married, you said I'd at least have respect. So allow me that and stop…pretending…that you feel anything other than accomplishment." Her vision was wavering again, only this time it was due to tears. She flicked her finger against the wrinkled folds of the prenup. "As far as I'm concerned, everything in there still stands. You fund the institute in exchange for the child we'll share custody of." Blocking the door or not, she had to get out of there. She headed past him. "There's nothing else I want from you.

He shot out an arm, blocking her. "Too bad," he said unevenly. "Because you've got my heart. And believe me, princess, until you came along, I didn't know there was one left to give. Maybe we didn't start out the way we should have. But that doesn't lessen the way I feel now. I never meant to hurt you. Throw it back in my face if you have to, but I'm not letting you go until you at least believe in that."

He was hurting her now, by preventing her escape. And she couldn't even maintain the pretense that she wasn't utterly destroyed. "Please," she whispered. "Don't do this to me. I…can't bear any more."

"And I can't bear to let you walk away from me." His hands closed tightly around her shoulders. "Not again. And that has *nothing* to do with the baby we've made."

She closed her eyes. Looked away from him. "If I didn't look like her would you have ever even agreed to meet with me when Ted asked you to?"

"I've never mistaken you for Taylor." His voice dropped. "You weren't a substitute. You could never be a substitute for anyone. I wouldn't want you to be. You're entirely unique and the way I feel about you isn't in the same universe as what I felt for her. The only thing she took with her when I told her we were through was some of my pride. And I may have let that rule me for too long afterward, but I don't give a damn about my pride now."

She could feel his hands shaking as they moved from her shoulders to her face as he lifted it until she had to look at him.

His eyes were bloodshot. And they were wet.

"I don't have any pride that matters when it comes to you." His voice was as raw as his expression. "What I feel for you isn't about the baby. Or proving that I'm man enough to give you one. And it isn't about extracting some revenge that I don't even care about anymore. It's about you. And me. And the fact that when I'm with you, the only thing I care about is *staying* with you. Going to bed at night, knowing you'll still be mine when I wake up the next morning. Even when we're in different freaking cities. It's about sharing what's in your head and in your heart. It's about the fact that you've crawled inside here." He slapped his hand against his chest. "And I can't get you out." He exhaled roughly. "And I don't want to."

She stared at him, tears sliding silently down her face.

"Everything my mother raised me to believe that matters—children, family—is what brought us here. Whether I was right or wrong in the process. But right now, if I could take away the baby inside you just to prove that it is you that matters most of all, I would. But I can't. And I can't pretend I don't want our child more than I want my next breath. But it's because he or she is *ours*."

She sucked in a sob. "Rourke."

"All I can do is ask you to believe me. Believe *in* me. I love you. But if you can tell me right now that you don't love me, I'll let you go. Just as I promised the day we got married. But I won't be able to take back my heart." His jaw twisted to one side. "Because that is always going to be yours."

She stepped back from him. Saw the way the blood blanched from his haggard face.

Then she deliberately picked up the prenup and tore it in half. Then half again before she let the ruined squares flutter to the floor. "I love you, too." Her voice was raw. "And I don't want to go anywhere that would take me away from you."

He closed his eyes for a long moment.

Then he looked at her. Caught her left hand in his and slowly lifted it. He kissed the wedding rings she hadn't been able to make herself take off.

She bit her lip, her heart as open to him as the palm of her hand when he slowly turned it over to press his lips there.

Then he was pulling her to him, lifting her off her feet, his arms nearly crushing her ribs as his mouth found hers.

And there, in her husband's arms with his heart thundering against hers, she realized she'd been wrong.

Fairy tales *could* come true.

Sara Beth opened the door behind them, and smiled tremulously at the sight. Just as quietly, she closed the door once again. There was no need for her to worry about Lisa's next twenty-four hours after all.

Epilogue

"Happy birthday, Daddy." Ignoring the decidedly pinched look on her mother's face where she stood beside Gerald, Lisa leaned over her father's wheelchair and pressed a kiss to his lined cheek, very aware of the attention on them from the family members gathered in the drawing room behind her.

Among them were not only her original siblings, but her newfound one, as well. Lisa had insisted that Sara Beth and Ted join the family for the private dinner they were having before the rest of the guests arrived later that evening.

Sara Beth had reluctantly agreed, but only after insisting that Lisa confirm with both Paul and Olivia that they had no objection. Fortunately, her brother and sister had treated the news that Sara Beth was their sibling with more equanimity than Lisa had.

They'd immediately agreed that she and Ted should be there. And that evening, when he and Sara Beth had arrived at the Armstrong house, it was Olivia who'd beaten Lisa to the punch, giving Sara Beth a hug and pulling her into the study where Emily and Gerald had yet to join them. "Come and say hello to my sons. Your nephews."

Lisa smiled and leaned back against Rourke's shoulder, watching them. She felt the kiss he brushed across her temple, though his present debate with Jamison on some political point didn't hesitate for a moment. Then Paul and Ramona arrived. And he, too, headed immediately for Sara Beth. "I always did say you looked like that portrait of our grandmother," he greeted her and tugged her into his arms for a kiss. "Welcome to the family." He grinned a little crookedly. "For what it's worth."

"Thank you." Sara Beth's gaze found Lisa's. "It's worth quite a lot, actually."

"Drinks, anyone?" Jamison ambled to the bar.

"Fruit juice for Sara Beth and Lisa," Olivia inserted, her gaze twinkling. She joined her tall husband, looking up at him with nothing but delight in her expression. "No wine for the pregnant duo."

"Ramona? What about you?"

"Fruit juice will do for me, too."

Everyone stopped dead still, looking across at her. She laughed outright, particularly at Paul's stunned expression. "Don't worry," she assured them. "I'm just getting in practice. For *after* the wedding."

Paul let out an audible breath and everyone laughed.

Until they'd noticed Emily pushing Gerald's chair through the doorway.

And the fact that Derek was walking behind them.

Rourke had stiffened behind her, but he'd said nothing. Nor had Paul or Olivia.

And Lisa had finally taken the bull by the horns and walked over to her father. "Happy birthday, Daddy." She straightened and pressed a second kiss to her mother's cheek. "Mother. You look lovely tonight."

Emily couldn't hide the surprise that flitted across her face. "Thank you, dear. So do you. I hear from Paul that congratulations are in order." If she was hurt that Lisa hadn't told her about her pregnancy herself, she hid it well. "Are you feeling all right?"

"Never better," she assured her truthfully. Even with the nausea that had started plaguing her in the mornings, she had never felt better in her life. How could she not?

Rourke loved her. And she loved him.

"You can see that I've asked Sara Beth to join us."

Emily's lips pinched together again. "Clearly." Her chin lifted a little. "And you all can see that your father and I have asked Derek to be here." She drew him forward.

He looked only marginally better than he had when he'd shown up outside Rourke's apartment. Still too pale and much too thin. But his eyes were clear and steady and they met Lisa's head on. "Lisa."

Lisa felt Rourke come up beside her. His hand slipped protectively around her shoulder.

For a moment, Derek looked as if he wanted to turn around and leave. But he stood his ground. "Devlin."

"Derek."

Gerald cleared his throat, breaking the barely civil tension. "Before anyone says anything else, I have something to say." Waving off Emily's aid, he wheeled his chair into the center of the room. "Derek's told your mother and me everything." He closed his unsteady hands together. "About the embezzlement." He looked at Paul. "The real reason you told him to leave the institute." He looked at Lisa. "Which finally explains why your husband's money was suddenly fueling our coffers. And while that grieves me—us—deeply, what grieves me more is that none of you thought fit to come and tell me what was going on when it was going on. I had to find out about it when Derek's counselor at the rehab clinic he checked himself into called me."

"Daddy," Lisa said, "your health has been—"

"Bad." Gerald nodded. "Nobody knows that better than me. So you were trying to protect me." His gaze drifted to Sara Beth. "And Emily's tried to protect me. Protect her family."

"Gerald—"

"Enough, Emily. I've had enough. I'm not dead and in the grave yet and I'm going to have my say and then that'll be the end of it."

Emily blinked. Closed her delicately gaping mouth.

"The institute has weathered a lot this past year," Gerald said. "This *family* has weathered a lot. For a lot longer than just a year or two and Lord knows that I bear the responsibility for most of that." His gaze touched on Olivia and Jamison and their two new sons. Moved on to Sara Beth and Ted, whose arms were looped protectively around her. Then Paul and Ramona, and Lisa and Rourke, before settling on his wife again. "Nobody's perfect."

Derek's face flushed a little, but he didn't look down, or away.

"Least of all me," Gerald added. "But it's time to stop moaning over the past and *do better* for the future." He held out his hand toward Emily and she looked thoroughly unsettled as she moved forward to take it. "The fact of the matter is, both the institute and this family are still going on. The institute will be better than ever. And this family is going to *be* a family. All of us." There was steel in his voice. The kind of steel that Lisa hadn't heard in a very long time. "Are we agreed?" He looked at his wife. "Emily?"

She looked almost teary. "Yes, dear. Agreed."

He nodded. "All right, then." His voice went a little gruff and he cleared his throat. "Happy birthday to me. So let's eat before the staff and the rest of the city descends on us since I figure that's about how many people my wife has invited to celebrate the fact that I'm getting to be as old as Methuselah."

"Oh, Gerald." Cleary flustered, Emily took his chair and began wheeling him out of the room.

Derek's gaze ran over the rest of them. "For what it's worth, I am sorry." His voice was low.

Even across the room, Lisa could hear Paul exhale. Then he was drawing Ramona forward and he closed his hand over his twin's shoulder. "You heard Dad," he said gruffly. "Let's go eat."

Lisa watched them follow her parents. Olivia and her crew went behind and she was drawing Sara Beth along with her, wanting to know when the baby was due.

The last ones left in the drawing room, Lisa looked up at Rourke. "Can you stand to sit at the same table as Derek?"

"The only thing I care about is whether you can sit at the same table as your brother."

Just when she thought her heart couldn't pump out any more love for him than it already did, it leaked some more. "I can." She started to follow after the others, but Rourke reeled her back to him before she got more than an arm's distance.

"Your father *is* impressive," he murmured.

"He is." She smiled faintly. "Thank you."

A faint smile played around his lips. His gaze was as warm on her face as the hands linked behind her back that held her against his broad chest. "For what?"

"Loving me."

His lips grazed over hers. "I could no more stop that, than I could stop breathing."

"Good." She kissed him back. "But if you do…" She leaned up until her lips were inches from his ear. "Just remember, there's always a doctor around in this family who knows CPR. They'll keep you breathing one way or another."

He threw his head back and laughed. He pressed a hard, thorough kiss on her lips. "That's my girl."

She smiled at him, so deeply happy that it invaded her every cell.

Yes. She was his girl. And even when they were old and gray and their children had children of their own, she knew in her bones that was what she would always be.

And still smiling, fingers twining together, they went out and joined the rest of the family.

* * * * *

#2383 FORTUNE'S LITTLE HEARTBREAKER
The Fortunes of Texas: Cowboy Country • by Cindy Kirk

When British aristocrat Oliver Fortune Hayes gets custody of his young son, he's stunned. But little does he know that much more is in store! Oliver's world is rocked like a rodeo when beautiful cowgirl Shannon Singleton saddles up as his son's nanny. Can Fortune and the free spirit ride off into the sunset for a happily-ever-after?

#2384 HER BABY AND HER BEAU
The Camdens of Colorado • by Victoria Pade

Beau Camden and Kyla Gibson were hot and heavy years ago, but their passionate romance didn't end well. Now Kyla's back in town with a secret or two up her sleeve. Named as guardian to her cousin's infant girl, she has motherhood on her mind and isn't interested in reuniting with her ex. But the Camden hunk isn't going to take no for an answer when it comes to a happy ending with his former love!

#2385 THE DADDY WISH
Those Engaging Garretts! • by Brenda Harlen

Playboy CEO Nathan Garrett has no interest in making any permanent acquisitions in the marital department. He's happy living the single life! That is, until he shares one night of passion with his sexy secretary, Allison Caldwell, while they're stranded during a snowstorm. Now Nate is thinking a merger with the single mom and her adorable son might just be the deal of a lifetime...

#2386 THE FIREMAN'S READY-MADE FAMILY
The St. Johns of Stonerock • by Jules Bennett

Plagued by a tragic past, small-town fire chief Drake St. John is surprised when sparks fly with Marly Haskins. The beautiful single mom has only one priority—her daughter, Willow, whom she wants to protect from her ex. But where there's smoke, there's flame, and Drake and Marly can't resist their own true love.

#2387 MARRY ME, MACKENZIE! • by Joanna Sims

When bachelor businessman Dylan Axel opened his door for Mackenzie Brand, he had no idea that he'd find a whole new life on the other side. It turns out that their long-ago romance created a beautiful daughter, Hope, who's now sick. Can Dylan, Mackenzie and Hope each get a second chance to have life, love and the pursuit of a happy family?

#2388 HIS SMALL-TOWN SWEETHEART • by Amanda Berry

Down on her luck, Nicole Baxter is back home in Tawnee Valley to lick her wounds. She doesn't expect to come face-to-face with childhood friend Sam Ward, who's grown up into a drop-dead gorgeous man! When Sam puts his entire future at risk, it's up to Nicole to show him everything he wants is right there with her.

Newly promoted Nathan Garrett is eager to prove he's no longer the company playboy. His assistant, single mom Allison Caldwell, has no interest in helping him with that goal, despite the fiery attraction between them. But as Nate grows closer to Alli's little boy, she wonders whether he might be a family man after all…

Read on for a sneak preview of THE DADDY WISH, by award-winning author Brenda Harlen, the next book in the miniseries THOSE ENGAGING GARRETTS!

***

Allison sipped her wine. Dammit—her pulse was racing and her knees were weak, and there was no way she could sit here beside Nate Garrett, sharing a drink and conversation, and not think about the fact that her tongue had tangled with his.

"I think I'm going to call it a night."

"You haven't finished your wine," he pointed out.

"I'm not much of a drinker."

"Stay," he said.

She lifted her brows. "I don't take orders from you outside the office, Mr. Garrett."

"Sorry—your insistence on calling me 'Mr. Garrett' made me forget that we weren't at the office," he told her. "Please, will you keep me company for a little while?"

"I'm sure there are any number of other women here who will happily keep you company when I'm gone."

"I don't want anyone else's company," he told her.

"Mr. Garrett—"

"Nate."

She sighed. "Why?"

"Because it's my name."

"I meant, why do you want my company?"

"Because I like you," he said simply.

"You don't even know me."

His gaze skimmed down to her mouth, lingered, and she knew he was thinking about the kiss they'd shared. The kiss she hadn't been able to stop thinking about.

"So give me a chance to get to know you," he suggested.

"You'll have that chance when you're in the VP of Finance's office."

She frowned as the bartender, her friend Chelsea, slid a plate of pita bread and spinach dip onto the bar in front of her. "I didn't order this."

"But you want it," Chelsea said, and the wink that followed suggested she was referring to more than the appetizer.

"Actually, I want my bill. It's getting late and…" But her friend had already turned away.

Allison was tempted to walk out and leave Chelsea to pick up the tab, but the small salad she'd made for her own dinner was a distant memory, and she had no willpower when it came to three-cheese spinach dip.

She blew out a breath and picked up a grilled pita triangle. "The service here sucks."

"I've always found that the company of a beautiful woman makes up for many deficiencies."

***

Don't miss THE DADDY WISH by award-winning author Brenda Harlen, the next book in her new miniseries, **THOSE ENGAGING GARRETTS!** *Available February 2015, wherever Harlequin® Special Edition books and ebooks are sold.* www.Harlequin.com

⊕ HARLEQUIN®

A *Romance* FOR EVERY MOOD™

JUST CAN'T GET ENOUGH?

Join our social communities
and talk to us online.

You will have access to the latest
news on upcoming titles and special
promotions, but most importantly,
you can talk to other fans about your
favorite Harlequin reads.

Harlequin.com/Community

Facebook.com/HarlequinBooks

Twitter.com/HarlequinBooks

Pinterest.com/HarlequinBooks